HOUSE
OF
SHIFTING
TIDES

OLIVIA WILDENSTEIN

HOUSE OF SHIFTING TIDES

BOOK 4 OF *THE KINGDOM OF CROWS SERIES*

Copyright © 2024 by WildStone Publishing

For information contact:
OLIVIA WILDENSTEIN
http://oliviawildenstein.com

Cover design by *Olivia Wildenstein*
3D feather on cover by *@miriamschwardt_designs*
Art underneath the hardcover by *@jjflorentina*
Art underneath the softcover by *@elizianna.the.one*
Zendaya and Cathal portraits by *@falloutbryan*
Map art by *@chaimscartography*
Chapter headers by *@mageonduty*
Editing by *Rachel Theus Cass*

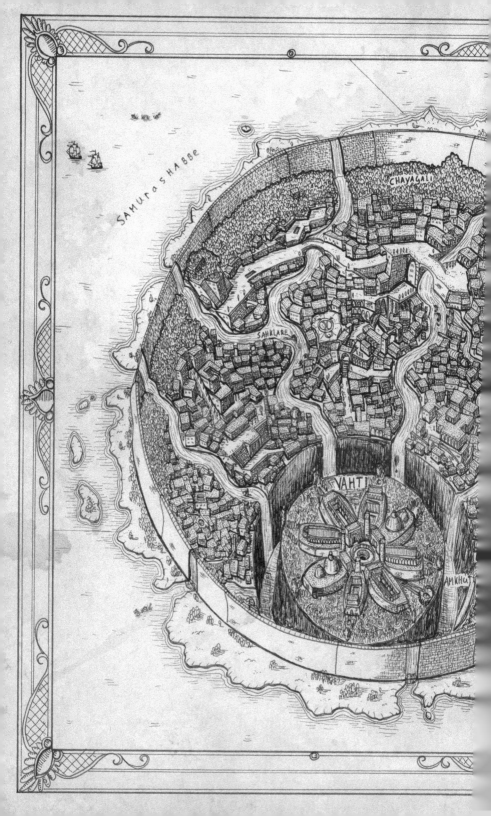

MAHANANDA

VAHTI

N

Queendom of Shabbe

Dare to swim against the current.

Prologue
Cathal

The pink ramparts of Shabbe and the placid waters of its climbing rivers shimmer gold in the light of a new dawn. Though the rising sun's radiance fans across my sweat-glossed brow, it doesn't breach my mood.

I cross my arms and glare at the moat that loops around the palace gardens, my trepidation rising like the limpid waters that Priya's coven—or Akwale, as they prefer to be called—is coaxing upward. Thank Mórrígan I'm immortal, for my poor heart would've stopped ticking long ago. It's a wonder it hasn't, between my daughter's misadventures and the fate that awaits my—

I swallow and replace the word titillating my tongue with the name of the woman the Cauldron birthed from serpent scales a fortnight ago: Zendaya.

Lorcan steps up to me, the contours of his body firm, unlike mine, which bleed smoke. "Priya has conferred with the Cauldron, brother. There's no risk of Daya remaining in scales."

Kanti, my daughter's cousin and a prominent member of the Akwale, glances up at us from where she kneels at the moat's edge, luring the waterline higher. "If it makes you feel any better, she might not even be able to shift."

No, it does not fucking make me feel better. If anything, it tautens my skin and tenses my muscles, for if the Cauldron stripped

Daya of her ability to shift, then why did it bring her back so physically altered? Why did it leave an ivory bead between her eyebrows and paint her eyes lid-to-lid black?

"She'll shift," whispers Behati, the queen's advisor and seer, who also happens to be Kanti's grandmother.

I look away from Zendaya just in time to see the veil of clairvoyance clear from Behati's pink eyes.

"You saw her shift, Taytah?" Kanti pushes her long black hair behind an ear that bears more piercings than Lazarus's.

"Yes," Behati says. "The Mahananda has just shown me."

The knot of my arms tightens in front of my stiff chest. "What else did the Cauldron show you?"

"That is all I foresaw, Cathal. Daya in her Serpent form."

"Did you see her shifting *back* into skin?" I press.

"I only saw her transform into scales."

As long as she desires to shift back, Lorcan says through our people's mind link, **I'm certain she'll return.**

"As long as she *desires*?" I snarl at my oldest friend and king. "What if she doesn't care to remain two-legged, Lore?" My muscles punch against the cage of black fabric that was stitched to measure but which, at the moment, feels maladjusted and shrunken. "What if she longs to return to the ocean for good?"

I've changed my mind. I suddenly wish for Behati's vision to be erroneous. For Daya not to shift, for what if she loses herself to the ocean and chooses scales over flesh? I crush my lids closed to bury the selfish thought. How dare I worry that she might not shift back? My self-absorption is repugnant. If I could no longer sprout wings and take to the sky, who would I be?

Fingers wrap around my arm. I startle until I notice the hand belongs to my daughter. She places her sweet cheek against my twitching bicep.

"Is everything all right?" I ask her when I notice how wildly her violet eyes shimmer.

"I just wanted to stand beside you."

Perhaps it's the truth, or perhaps her empathy springs from the same marrow-deep fear that gnaws on my soul.

I stare over at the pink-haired woman whose forehead rests in her grandmother's palms. "What is Priya showing your..." I swallow down the word *mother*, replacing it with a pronoun that won't sadden Fallon: "...her?"

"What might happen to her body."

"What *will* happen," Kanti says, before gesturing to Behati. "Taytah had a vision of her shifting."

Fallon blinks at her fellow Shabbin, then at me, before finally locking eyes with Lorcan. "She truly is a new breed of shifter." Wonder brightens my daughter's pitch.

If only some of it could breach my heart.

The briny moat has risen so high, it now spills over the lip of the sunstone cliffs and froths around Daya's bare feet. I squint, scrutinizing her deep gold skin for bright pink scales, but none appear. I loathe the relief that floods my veins, loathe it with every beat of my bestial heart.

As the sun climbs higher, the swoop of dwellings that blanket the hollowed land begins to shimmer as though crafted from gold instead of sunstone. Shabbe is awakening, and the Shabbins along with it. I spy many trickling down to the moat's razor-sharp cliffs, gazes pinned to the recessed vale, to the white-haired queen and pink-haired princess. I spy some contemplating the water's surface, which glistens a mere dozen feet away for once.

"It seems that word of the princess's dip has spread," Kanti murmurs.

My jaw feels like granite. "They better not be thinking of jumping in."

"The fine for swimming in the Amkhuti would drain their savings." Kanti's pink eyes scan the distant shoreline. "Besides, who truly wants to dive in with a wild creature?"

I snap my attention back to the tall Shabbin female. "*Wild creature?*"

"Yes, Cathal." Kanti narrows her eyes on me. "*Wild*. For all we know, the serpent version of Zendaya will be a ruthless carnivore."

"Like us Crows?" My brusque tone must reach Zendaya, for her gaze slides over me, then over Kanti who doesn't even bother looking her way, much less smiling at her.

Ever since the wards crumbled and the Cauldron brought Daya back, Kanti, who's of Priya's bloodline, is no longer next in line for the throne.

"In her human form, she doesn't eat meat, so I doubt she'll have a taste for it in scales." Fallon's tone sparks with antipathy.

"You're probably right," Kanti concedes. "I wonder if she'll be larger than she was the day Cathal plunged her into the Mahananda."

I shudder at the reminder of how we got here.

"Do you think she'll be able to communicate with fish?" Kanti asks.

"I can't communicate with pigeons," Fallon snipes, "so I doubt my mother will speak Minnow."

Kanti snorts as though Fallon had cracked a joke. "Oh, you know what I mean, chacha."

Fallon scowls, loathing when Kanti calls her 'cousin,' for it reminds my daughter that the same blood flows through their veins.

"Technically," Kanti continues, evidently not done giving her opinion, "your mother was born a serpent and you were born human, so maybe I'm not entirely off the mark."

Could Kanti be onto something? Even though Zendaya's shown herself an avid listener, she's yet to utter an intelligible word. Or even a sound, for that matter.

Where most believe she'll never be capable of talking, Fallon and I are convinced it's a matter of time before she proves the world wrong. Then again, I still believe that I'll wake up to the sound of Zendaya's voice in my mind.

My nostrils flare, cycling a ragged exhale against Fallon's dark-auburn locks. I've become delusional. The bond I shared with

Zendaya is gone, and forever at that, according to Priya, who conferred with the Cauldron on my behalf.

Gone, like my brother Cian.

Like his mate Bronwen.

Like the Regio dynasty.

Like the wards around the queendom.

I'm tempted to kneel beside the source of all magic and barter a piece of my soul for another chance at being Zendaya's mate, but I'd be wasting my breath for the Cauldron only listens to its guardian.

The belt on Daya's twilight-blue robe falls like a pitched snake at her feet. Although it makes no sound, I feel as though it smacks the earth like an anchor chain. She parts her robe, letting it drift down her shoulders, her back, her ass, her legs. Lorcan glances away, but everyone else, men and women alike, stare. I want to gouge out their eyes with my iron talons. I want to choke her perfect hourglass figure in my smoke.

I do neither, for her body isn't mine to shield or possess.

Her body isn't mine, period.

I grit my teeth. Even though the woman inching toward the water is different than the one I fell in love with two decades past, when she's near, my heart beats fiercely and my skin burns. How I long to shape her waist like I did the day she teetered out of the Cauldron. How I long to feel the probing scrape of her fingertips against my beard.

"Breathe, Dádhi," Fallon instructs as she trails her mother's progress.

I haul in a breath, hold it until my lungs ache, and gasp it out only when Zendaya jumps. I move away from Fallon to shift and take to the skies. My heart misses a beat. Two. Three. Four.

Another Crow circles the liquid trench—Fallon. Her violet eyes are trained on the moat, on the serpent undulating through its limpid waters, pink scales refracting the rising sun. I soar as fast as Daya swims, dread coalescing beneath my feathers that she will dart sideways, toward one of the rising falls.

Would it be strong enough to lift her giant body into the rivers that flow upward, toward the ocean? I'm guessing it's a possibility, considering Priya has stationed sorceresses at every junction. Sorceresses who dribble blood into the water. I vaguely remember the Shabbin Queen mentioning nets during supper last night. Is that what they're doing? Casting a spell to keep the female serpent caged in the moat?

I flick my attention to the white-haired monarch, who kneels at the water's edge and wriggles her fingers. Daya swims up to her, her giant white tusk carving through the surf. I spy her forked black tongue emerging from her maw and wrapping around her grandmother's fingers.

The words *shift back* stick to my iron beak, tacky like the humid air.

Priya tries to seize her granddaughter's equine-shaped head. Her movements must be too abrupt for Daya's liking because the latter lunges back, then sinks so deep, her color dims.

I jolt as Fallon shifts in mid-air, her fingers swiping against the sides of her neck a second before joining in front of her. Even though I sense she must've painted gills on either side of her neck, I drop lower, ready to dive in after her if the creature that my former mate has turned into decides to...to hurt our...*my* daughter.

Calm down. Lorcan's voice blisters my temples.

I send him a scathing look.

Fallon's reminding Daya of her human form. Daya's calm. She listens.

The circles I fly tighten until I'm all but spinning on myself like a top, dizzy with panic. *Come on, Princess. Come on.*

Like a tree riven by lightning, Daya's pink tail splits and retracts into legs, and then the water around her body shimmers and foams. When its radiance dulls, two women tread water.

My daughter.

And my...my nothing.

Chapter 1
Zendaya

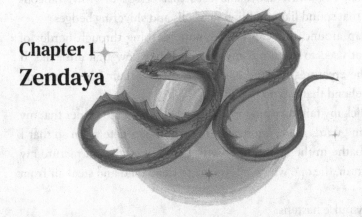

I peer up through a cluster of fish that glow like stars and see *him*.

He is always there. I believe it's because he worries I might find a way to leap up into the Sahklare—the rivers that flow through the queendom—and escape into the ocean beyond the great walls of my home. He forgets I've neither the ability to make the waterline rise, nor to sprout wings, so I cannot escape the Vahti—or Vale, as I've heard the Crows call it.

How I long to wander, though. If only I had the words to ask the queen to show me the land over which she rules. Perhaps the Crow with three names could give me a tour on his back. The thought brings my swim to an abrupt halt. That male would never accept to be ridden. I suppose I could ask Fallon or her friend, Aoife, or possibly Aodhan, the only three Crows whose lips curve at the sight of me when every other shifter's lips flatten.

Especially the Crow pacing over the stars overhead. The corners of his mouth never rise. Not for me. Not for anyone. Not even for his daughter. He wears his anger like I wear the ocean's salt, in a thin, coarse layer that forever envelops my flesh and seasons the air.

If only I could read the reason for his menacing mood off his palms. Unlike Pink-eyes, though, Crows—save for Fallon—cannot communicate with their hands, only with their mouths. More often than not, the Crow above me uses that orifice to growl raucous words that sound like tumbling seashells and shivering hedges.

I lap around the Vahti once more, dashing through hordes of fish that used to scatter at my approach but now trail after me. If only the creatures on land could also surpass their fear of me and comprehend that I'm no predator.

I flick my tail, thrusting my body toward the vine ladder that my Shabbin guard, Asha, knotted to the trunk of a date palm so that I could bathe in the Amkhuti at will. I close my lids and picture my other form, the one which allows me to tread land and steal air from the sky.

My pulse hastens.

My scales tighten.

My tusk twinges.

My bones grind.

Seven heartbeats later, I shrink into a creature made of skin instead of scales, of limbs instead of fins. One heartbeat faster than yesterday. I am improving. Perhaps someday, I will be able to shift as fast as Fallon. I roll onto my back and float atop the starlit waters of the Amkhuti, my waist-long hair, that is fanned out like seaweed, tangling around my smooth arms. My toes poke out from the placid surf, the same hue as my locks, thanks to the coat of polish that one of the palace attendants applied before she plucked every hair off my body, leaving me with only the bundle atop my head and above my eyes. When she'd smoothed the warm wax over my skin, I'd frowned. When she'd removed it, I'd hissed and snarled.

If Fallon hadn't pressed her palms to my forehead to show me that it was a Shabbin custom, I would've stormed out of the humid stone room. But I hadn't. I'd borne the discomfort, so desperate was I to belong.

Fallon may claim I'm a shapeshifter like her and her people, but I am nothing like them. Not only am I not part of a flock, but the shape I take is also different. I've neither feathered arms to carry me skyward nor metal protuberance with which to pinch. I have a tail I can snap to glide through water, an ivory horn I can wield like those blades Two-legs carry, and a forked black tongue which can heal flesh wounds.

I'm a creature that inspires fear in almost all. In a corner of my mind, I believe that once I learn to string together all the sounds Two-legs produce...once I'm able to comprehend their meaning, I will be gazed at with kinder eyes. Then again, my Crow sentry can produce all those sounds, yet he still causes pulses to hasten. Even his king—Fallon's mate—is less feared. Perhaps because Lorcan Ríhbiadh's tone is more dulcet, and his demeanor, less forbidding.

A screech rents the night, making my skin pebble, not with scales, but with those same bumps Two-legs develop upon beholding me. I hinge at the waist, sinking back into the water, then pitch my head backward to glimpse what's got the Crow with three names so agitated. Though he's black like the heavens, I don't miss his trajectory toward the cliff opposite the palace, nor do I miss how a Two-legs scrambles away from the stone sill.

I shake my head, the bumps on my skin receding. What an odd specimen Dádhi Cathal Báeinach is—always watching me, yet abhorring when anyone else does.

As I carve through the liquid expanse toward my ladder, he wheels over the sprawling moat, wingspan as wide as my serpent body is long, gaze pummeling the bloom-spangled foliage for more intruders. Not even my guards are out at this late hour. Most Two-legs sleep when the stars come out and wake when the stars extinguish.

I find I much prefer to drift from dream to dream when the sun is at its apex. At first, I wondered if it was a shifter trait, but soon discovered it was a *me and my Crow sentry* trait. We seem to be the only two souls voluntarily awake from sundown to sunup. Though it could be that his wakefulness isn't deliberate. That he has no choice since the Two-legs who guard me cannot trail me when I'm in scales. Not to mention that my guards have homes and families they're eager to return to when off-duty. From what I've gathered, Dádhi Cathal Báeinach has no female, and his home is across

9

Samurashabbe, in a land some call Luce, others, *Rahnach Bi'adh*—the Sky Kingdom.

By the time I've clambered up the vine ladder, the cool, shimmering droplets on my skin have dried into a veil of salt, toughening the beads of duskier flesh on my chest. I've yet to understand their use, or why they vary in size, or why they harden when the air is brisk and soften like butter in the heat.

The first time I observed this phenomenon, I'd worried they would melt like wax and had fingered them so many times that Dádhi Cathal had growled at the guards in attendance, which had made a lovely sound spill from Asha's lips. She'd later explained that it was called laughter and that it's produced when someone feels joyous. Obviously, my winged guard, who now stands on two legs beside me, scarcely feels jubilant, for I've never heard him produce this bright melody.

Although clothing reappears on my body once I shift out of my Serpent form, I dislike the sensation of wet cloth, so I swim in the nude.

Severe gaze pinned to the palace sentries, Dádhi Cathal holds out the purple fabric I cast off before tonight's swim. *"Dréasich,"* he grumbles.

I wish he'd speak in the tongue Fallon and Asha are teaching me, especially since he's fluent in it. I've heard him carry on entire conversations with Behati and Asha in Shabbin.

As I relieve him of the dress, I behold his fingers. They aren't tipped in iron when he's in skin, but they're just as alarming—long enough to circle my neck, thick enough to shell it whole. A shiver scurries up my spine. Has he ever used those fingers to harm another? Would he ever use them to harm me?

Something tickles my arm after I've fed it through the sheer sleeve—a land serpent as slender as my pinkie. My lips curve as I herd the animal onto my palm and caress its scaly throat before setting it on a wide, heart-shaped leaf. What did Fallon call these miniature serpents again? *Che*-something. *Chehpah? Chepassee?*

"Chepahsslee!" The word trips off my tongue in a hiss that

makes the Crow swing around to face me. My cheeks blister like the pads of my fingers had the day I touched candlelight.

His eyebrows, barely distinguishable amongst the black stripes he wears, taper as he asks me—in Shabbin—whether I spoke.

I'm so stunned that he's used my homeland's tongue that I freeze. He reiterates his question. I keep myself from nodding, worried he'll make me repeat myself. Until I work out how to eradicate my hissing, I intend to keep practicing words in the privacy of my chambers.

I scrutinize the star blooms that dapple the hedges of the palace gardens, my inhalations so brisk that my lungs cramp around the deep, dusky fragrance that lifts off the Crow's neck.

"Daya?" The male makes the fragment of my name sound so brutal that my fingers tremble as I belt my robe with a braided strand of violet silk.

Pretending like I didn't hear him call out my name, I sidestep him and follow the serpentine walkways toward my wing of the palace.

Dádhi Cathal fractures into smoke and reappears on my path. My breath catches when I almost bump into him, and I clap my chest.

"*Chepahlee.*" There's no hiss when he pronounces the word.

I tilt my head.

He dips his chin before creating another sound: "*Deark.*" When I frown, he adds, "In Crow, *chepahlee* is *deark.*"

Durrk. I slot the single syllable away to rehearse later.

He rolls his lips, pinkening the flesh framed by bushy black hair. The day the Mahananda turned my scales to skin, I'd touched his jaw. I do it again tonight, but with a new intent. That of understanding what it's called.

"*Dahadee.*" His harsh intonation makes my nerves skip and my hand lower. "*Dahadee. Fruhlag.*"

That must be the name of the hair that grows on his face. I do not have a word for it in my mind's tongue. Because the language

11

inside my head is that of a serpent, and serpents do not have hair on their bodies? Then again, I have the word for *hair*...

I touch my own jaw—smooth. Will it stay this way, or will *dahadee* sprout there someday?

The Crow's nostrils flare with a chuff and a single corner of his mouth tucks upward. Is that a lip spasm or is the forever-austere male smiling?

Dádhi Cathal shakes his head, which sends his tousled black locks sailing in all directions. "*Mahala nahen dahadee.*"

I startle that he's read my mind.

He points to me. "*Mahala.*" Female. He points to himself. "*Parush.*" Male.

I smile because I learned the distinction when I stared a little too long at what hung between the legs of Fallon's golden-haired friend, Phoebus, the day he joined us in the balmy stone chamber where I was divested of body hair. I'm sad the Faerie left Shabbe, but I also understand that he wanted to join his mate back home.

I rake my gaze down the Crow's chest, imagining that, like Phoebus, he must have an extra limb there as well. What did Fallon's friend call it again? The skin around my retracted tusk pleats as I try to recollect the term. When I can't, I tentatively poke the Crow *there*.

The male goes so still that I peek up at his face. His skin, usually as pale as the moon, has deepened to the hue of the corals that tile the Amkhuti's walls. I slide my fingers farther down the limb I don't possess, my confusion increasing when I feel it move.

"*Príona,*" he rasps.

I frown some more. That cannot be the thing's appellation since 'Príona' is the name he calls me. I tap on the hardening limb, then tilt my head.

The Crow with three names stares and stares, throat dipping, stunted limb throbbing. Smoke gathers around his skin, thickens, until he bursts and reappears farther down the path.

Too far to reach.

My throat constricts like the curved bones around my heart. I must've done something wrong. Why else would he have added so much distance between us?

I curl my fingers into my palms and slice my eyes in the direction of the Mahananda, ruing it for having tossed me into the realm of Two-legs with no knowledge of their ways and words. Yes, I'm learning both, but it is hard, and most of the time, I feel so out of my element. I may resemble them, but I'm not *like* them.

Would I feel more kinship with serpents? Would my mind attach to theirs like Crows in beast form? Perhaps I should find a way to climb into the Sahklare, which I hear are full of sea serpents.

My sodden hair suddenly lifts. I think the wind must've picked up but soon realize it isn't the weather that whips my pink locks; it's a churning of dark wings. Two Crows land around Dádhi Cathal Báeinach and immediately shift into skin—Aodhan and Reid. Both males are a comely gathering of burnished skin and chiseled curvatures, nothing like the stark angles and harsh bleakness of the Crow who guards me.

When Aodhan spots me, his mouth crooks. I start to smile but halt when an impenetrable wall of smoke pounds between us before reshaping into my Crow sentry's familiar physique.

Dádhi Cathal commands them to talk, and as they do, the newcomers' mien turns grave, causing chills to scurry along my spine. Although they speak in their tongue, I grasp a few words: *Rahnach Bi'adh* and *Mórrgat*.

Did something befall their king?

Did something befall his kingdom?

Chapter 2
Zendaya

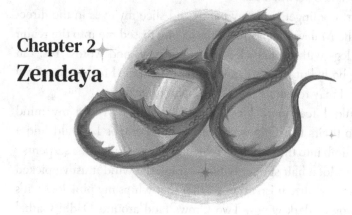

When the silvery light of a new dawn finally slashes the horizon, I stride across my bedchamber and wrench open the heavy door.

Abrax must've just arrived, for my guard is still tying the wide carmine sash that all royal guards wear around their cream-colored tunics and pants. "*Rajka*." He blinks at my salt-crusted hair that has set in stiff waves.

I should've probably bathed after Dádhi Cathal escorted me back into my bedchamber and urged me to rest, but I'd been too distracted by the Crows' tense expressions.

Abrax asks whether I need anything. *Yes.* I need to learn why Reid and Aodhan flocked to Shabbe in the middle of the night.

I hurry past my guard in the direction of the Kasha—the wing of the palace where the queen holds court. I squint past the tall wooden doors that are chiseled like sea fans to find the queen and Behati seated in their usual spots on the circular carmine divan.

Fallon's there as well, but she does not sit. She stands between her father and Lorcan, her shoulders squared beneath a silk dressing gown that gleams gold like her mate's eyes. Her fingers cut the air while her lips move over a flow of words that do not reach my ears because of the sigils painted into the walls to keep sound from escaping the Kasha.

14

I nod to the doors, but the two female guards stationed outside do not let me pass. Luckily, Abrax has followed me. He translates my desire to enter with a command that the sorceresses shielding the queen don't heed.

I'm so desperate that I consider letting my voice squeak past my teeth, but I'm saved from having to do so by Abrax, who hardens his pitch. It's the first time he uses a tone that isn't as placid as the Mahananda's surface. Though both guard's eyebrows arch at his outburst, neither relents.

I cross my arms and tap my foot against the buffed sunstone. If I have to stand outside the Kasha until the meeting adjourns, then so be it. Fortunately, Behati spots me through the lattice doors and alerts the queen, who turns and crooks her finger, signaling to let me pass. As her guards open the doors, she chides them for keeping me out.

She pats the cushion beside her. *"Haneh, emMoti."* Come, my Pearl. She calls me that because my retracted tusk reminds her of the iridescent beads that sprout inside oysters.

Like Fallon, Priya still wears a nightgown. Unlike the Crow Queen, the Shabbin one tamed her hair into pinned swirls.

I kneel at her side while Dádhi Cathal mutters something under his breath in Crow, leveling me with his lightning-bright stare. I truly must've imagined the soft look in his eyes earlier, because there is *nothing* gentle about him now.

Louder, he addresses the Shabbin Queen—still in Crow. I circle her wrists and lift them to my forehead, entreating her with my stare to show me what troubles everyone so. Dádhi Cathal shakes his head. Priya quietly but sharply tells him that I should see. Fallon agrees. Behati doesn't give her opinion.

Dádhi Cathal glances at Lorcan, probably for support, but the Crow King's eyes are glazed, harboring the same sheen as the giant gold platter heaped with plump fruit. It's possible he's communicating with his shifters. I hear he's capable of this in both skin and feathers, whereas his people can only mind-speak when in their beast form.

When the queen sighs, I pivot my head back toward her, the three syllables for *please—krehiya*—warming my tongue. I rein them in behind my teeth, flattening my palms over her blistered ones, choosing a silent entreaty instead of a hissed one.

I draw in a breath when a twilit forest develops on the back of my lids, one that mustn't be in Shabbe, for the trees that line the queendom's ramparts have thin trunks and broad, glossy leaves. The ones in the queen's vision have fat trunks impaled with slender branches dappled in thumb-sized, papery leaves.

I slither through the forest like a serpent, stopping only once I reach a clearing strewn with three black boulders. The queen glides me closer to these dark mounds, close enough for me to realize that they are, in fact, effigies of giant birds.

I wonder why she shows me these statues. Do Crows not appreciate replicas of themselves? She must feel my brow furrow, for she directs my stare toward striped brown feathers that protrude from a splayed wing. Before I can comprehend why feathers have been glued to stone, the landscape of her mind changes and I catch her hand folded around a dagger tipped in black stone. I see her stabbing it through Lorcan's heart and his skin hardening to iron.

She yanks her palms off my forehead, her gaze wide with what resembles fear, while mine is narrowed with a frown, one that grows when Fallon points to herself and says: *"batara azish."* I know the meaning of *azish* for it's been used many times to describe my condition—*curse*—but I'm unfamiliar with the term *batara*.

As I sit back on my heels, my temples buzz as though a bee were trapped behind them. What link exists between the forest statues and Lorcan's stabbing? And why does the queen's hand tremble as she reaches for her glass of steaming date tea?

When her gaze flicks to Behati's, the buzzing grows so insistent that I knead my temples. Were those visions? Did she not intend to show me the one of her stabbing Lorcan? Was it even her? The Two-legs holding the dagger had long white hair. Behati's is also white, though hers is streaked through with gold.

The seer directs words to Fallon in Crow. She usually always speaks to her in Shabbin. Has she switched languages to thwart me, or is it simply for her audience's benefit?

Smoke slithers around Lorcan like vines as he growls something at the Shabbin Queen that must concern Fallon since he uses the Crow term for mate. Fallon sidles in front of him and brackets his cheeks between her palms. His complexion, usually moon-pale, currently resembles the berries clustered in the platter before him.

Lightning cracks and thunder grumbles over the window that stretches almost the full length of the Kasha's ceiling. Fallon once told me that her mate can control the sky. Is the incoming cloud front Lorcan's doing?

Out loud and in Shabbin—for my sake, I imagine—she asks why he and Dádhi don't trust the Mahananda. My frown deepens, for what does the Mahananda have to do with the bird statues and Lorcan's stabbing?

Dádhi Cathal Báeinach folds his thick arms and slits his dark gaze. *What?* I want to ask. *What did I do wrong now?*

I hear Fallon murmur the name she sometimes calls me to Lorcan—Mádhi. I'm not sure what it means, only that it sounds vaguely similar to how she refers to her father. Since I'm not a mother, I suppose the likeness is coincidental.

"*EmAzish,*" Lorcan murmurs. *My curse.* And then he says something else that starts with -*em* but finishes with a word I'm unfamiliar with.

His curse? What is his curse?

Fallon shakes her head and murmurs that it's hers, that she's the "*batara azish.*"

I blow out my cheeks, my frustration mounting. What does *batara* mean?

As the queen takes a sip of her tea, her eyes whiten like Behati's. Except, in the Shabbin monarch's case, it happens when she convenes with the Mahananda. A moment later, she proclaims, "*Mahananda keteh ab.*" *The Mahananda says now.*

Lorcan closes his eyes and shakes his head, repeating the word "no" in both Shabbin and Crow.

The queen sets down her glass of tea. "*Ab va kada.*" Now or never.

Lorcan's jaw turns bladed. "*Kada.*" Never.

Never what?

A meaningful look passes between the queens that makes Priya climb to her feet. As she strides toward Lorcan, she asks everyone to depart, save for the Crow King. Does she believe he'll change his mind if we're gone? And what of the dagger? Is she planning on hurting him? I reassure myself that she'd never harm her descendant's mate, for it would hurt her beloved Fallon.

For some reason, this is when I comprehend the second part of her vision. The stabbing had been an explanation of the forest statues since, when the dagger had breached the Crow King's skin, it had hardened his flesh like theirs.

"Daya?" Behati holds out her arm to me.

I stand, then pad over to where she sits, take her forearm, and boost her up. Once she's stable, I reach for her cane, but she shakes her head and curls her callused fingers around my elbow.

All right...no cane.

Behati's body might be brittle, but her mind's alarmingly firm. There's no changing it once she's decided something. And apparently, today, she's decided I will be her crutch instead of the gnarled branch carved to resemble a coiled serpent. I suppose that if Kanti had been present, Behati would've taken her arm.

Fallon catches up to us, her features blurring and writhing behind the gossamer veil of smoke that envelops her. I wonder if it's her mate's smoke or her own beast pushing against her flesh, desirous to emerge. She says something to her father in Crow that has the umber rings surrounding his pupils shrinking and his scowl darkening as though his smudged stripes had penetrated into the pale canvas beneath.

He shoves open the door just as Fallon pricks her finger on the shell she wears around her neck and sketches a motif in blood. Though my stance is solid, Behati teeters and grabs ahold of the wall on our way out. I try to ease her away but she resists. I soon understand why when I catch her finger traipsing over the door frame, leaving behind knots of blood that quickly absorb into the stone.

She doesn't meet my stare as she tucks her bleeding hand into the pocket of her wide-sleeved carmine robe. I start to ease her forward when she halts once more to grumble something that includes Cathal's name and a nod at the cane she left behind.

What are you up to, Behati?

As Cathal goes to fetch her abandoned cane, Fallon steps out of the Kasha, drumming her fingers on her thigh, speckling the gold with vermilion droplets. Did she, too, just bloodcast? When she catches me observing her, her shoulders turn needle-straight and she gives the murky sky beyond the honeysuckle-laden trellis her full attention.

Behati tugs me forward, crooking her finger toward one of the female guards, who hinges to accommodate the seer's shorter stature. Behati whispers something about gathering the Akwale that makes the guard spin on her heel and rush away. Why does Behati request the presence of the strongest sorceresses?

My skin begins to prickle, not with the need to shift, but to understand what—

A tremor ripples through the air behind me. Brow puckered, I twist around. And then I gasp, because Cathal's fist is sailing toward my face.

Chapter 3
Cathal

My fist connects with the ward that Behati must've conjured into existence to keep me locked inside the Kasha. From the way my daughter gnaws on her bottom lip, I sense she must've aided the seer.

I get confirmation of this when she murmurs, "Sorry, Dádhi."

I roar at her to remove her magic. When she doesn't, I smash Behati's cane into the invisible wall, reducing the knobby wood to splinters that I cast aside before pummeling the air with my fists. When no fissure forms, I disintegrate into smoke and rush at the barrier.

A smirk tugs at Zendaya's lips. I bare my teeth. Not at her. At Behati. But since Daya stands so near the seer, her delight stumbles off her pretty mouth and a good dose of fear soaks into her.

Remembering that Lorcan and Priya are locked in with me, I whirl. Though I see Lore break into five shadowy plumes, I don't spot the Witch Queen. I soon understand why when a body shimmers into existence beside Zendaya.

After recalling her invisibility sigil, Priya lowers her palm from her forehead. "The Mahananda is always right and always just, Cathal. No need to act like an uncivilized beast."

Are her words supposed to calm me? To reassure us that planting an obsidian dagger into my daughter's chest and feeding her to the Cauldron holds zero risk? What if the Cauldron doesn't release Fallon? Or what if it does, but altered?

"I'm the curse-breaker, Dádhi." Fallon's teeth-bitten lip glows as red as the tip of her seashell necklace.

She already broke one curse—Meriam's. Who's to say, besides two old crones with pink eyes and a magical basin, that my daughter is also *our people's* curse-breaker?

Daya untangles her arm from the seer's and reaches for Fallon's wrists. I hold still as she rests Fallon's palms on her forehead.

What does she want our daughter to show her? The reason why she painted a ward? When Daya rears back, eyes so big they devour more of her face, my eyebrows pitch low. Didn't her grandmother show her Behati's vision when she entered the room?

The Serpent Princess joggles Fallon's wrists in an attempt to draw her backward, toward where I stand, trapped and quaking with fury, praying that Lorcan's found a way out. My prayers are reduced to dust when the air churns beside me and five dark streaks bang into one.

I understand from his reddened stare and the purpling sky that the ward encapsulates every wall, window, and ceiling.

"What of the mind link?" I ask him.

Blocked.

Fuck.

Zendaya heaves Fallon back once more, this time, managing to make her stumble. Lorcan snaps his hands up to catch his mate, but all he catches is a palmful of air. I, on the other hand, catch an arm—Daya's. Before she can snatch it away, I yank her inside the Kasha and gather her against my chest.

"Fallon," I roar. "Get inside! NOW!"

My daughter doesn't indulge me. No, she abuses the word "sorry" and her bottom lip some more. She is *not* sorry. If she were, she would rethink this self-sacrificial insanity.

Daya writhes. In case her plan is to return out there, I tighten my grip on her biceps. She begins to shake like the sky over Shabbe. I imagine with irritation until I spot her fingers lifting to her scar

21

and rubbing her neck manically. Perhaps she *is* frustrated, but mixed into her resentment is a weighty dose of panic. One that makes her pulse go so wild that it tramps past her silken sleeves and absorbs into my palms.

As Lorcan's storm erupts into a deluge of raindrops, Fallon flattens one palm against the wall between them and murmurs, "Trust the Cauldron." And then she repeats it in Shabbin, probably to quell Zendaya's fear.

Trust the Cauldron to what? Keep her alive? Return her in one piece? Return her—period?

Why must my daughter have inherited my stubborn streak and taken it to the next level?

Why is she allowing Priya to inflict bodily harm on her just because the Cauldron showed Behati that was the way to go?

"It returned Mádhi." Fallon's wispy reminder snakes through the invisible divide between two rolls of thunder.

I stare past Fallon's head at the Cauldron. Yes, it returned her mother, but it didn't return her intact. It stole her memories. Stole our bond.

Before I blemish Zendaya's skin with twin bruises, I relax my grip but don't release her. I physically and emotionally cannot.

To placate me, Fallon adds, "That was Meriam's doing, Dádhi, not the Cauldron's."

"We do not know that, ínon!" I growl.

Daya twists around and cranes her neck. Our eyes collide. I expect belligerence but find apprehension, and it kinks my heart. Does she fear me, or is the mention of Meriam's name to blame for her perplexing pallor?

"Sumaca." The slap of sandals directs my attention off Zendaya and onto the gold box one of Priya's guards is proffering. "Your weapon." As Priya draws a sigil on the miniature trunk, the female says, "The Akwale is assembled and waiting."

Does she expect Lorcan to have mobilized a winged army? She must know Behati and Fallon's ward is mind link proof.

"Trust the Cauldron, Dádhi," Fallon repeats *again*, fostering a smile that doesn't extend to her eyes.

"It isn't the fucking Cauldron I have trust issues with," I growl in Shabbin against the top of Daya's head. "It's your great-grandmother and her seer."

Daya goes stock-still and then she glowers up at me. What was I expecting? Both she and Fallon hold Priya on a pedestal. Even Lorcan thinks the woman's inherently good. The only thing the queen is good at is controlling all those around her.

When the obsidian dagger is extracted from the box, Zendaya sucks in a breath. For long seconds, she gawps at the weapon, then at Fallon, and finally, at Lorcan. The slant of her dark eyebrows is so vertiginous that it cuts furrows around her retracted tusk. It's the same expression that apprehended her face earlier.

"What did Priya show you when you walked in?" I murmur between barely separated teeth.

I wait a beat. Two.

Daya's lips remain sealed.

I repeat my question, using a more urgent tone. "What the fuck did she show you?"

She flinches.

I gentle my tone. "What happens after she stabs Fallon with obsidian?"

Her frown digs deeper.

My frustration escalates because I realize she mustn't understand what I'm asking. I try not to hold it against her. It's not her fault.

When her lips finally part, I think I was too rash in my judgment, but then she murmurs in that odd raucous hiss of hers, "Lorcan."

23

Chapter 4
Zendaya

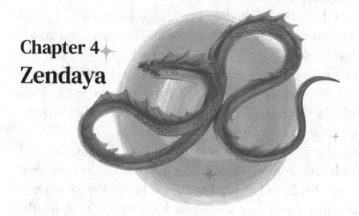

The Crow's grip on my arms is starting to anger me. More so than having staggered into the Kasha after Fallon showed me her intent of heading into the Mahananda to break her people's curse. To think I could've been out there with her instead of in here with two seething males, all of us helpless to stop her.

I reach for Cathal's fingers and peel them off one of my arms. I'm almost surprised when they loosen and fall away.

As I reach for his other hand, Fallon gasps. My hand freezes against his as she utters a string of excited words. She speaks so rapidly that the only ones I decipher are names: *Mahananda, Bronwen, Alyona,* and *Glace.*

The Shabbin Queen's expression turns guarded as her blood penetrates the lid of the golden box and makes it click. She doesn't hinge it open as she asks Fallon why she's interested in Princess Alyona's fate.

Of course... Alyona is one of the princesses of Glace. Behati told me about her when she showed me a drawing full of lines and letters enclosed in rectangles called a family tree. Apparently, every family has one. I long to see Fallon's, since she calls Priya, "ImTay-tah," which means "mother of my grandmother." I was hoping to understand who this grandmother was, since neither Ceres Rossi nor Cathal's deceased mother are related to Priya.

I shake away the tangent my mind has taken and concentrate on Fallon's mouth, catching the tail-end of her reply...something about how *knowing would appease Dádhi and Lore.*

I glance at Lorcan, then at the sulking giant at my back. I'm about to hiss at him to let go, when Behati uses the word *"kill"* in Shabbin and brackets it with both Fallon and Alyona's names. I forget all about Cathal's unyielding grip then.

Fallon cocks an eyebrow, then asks Behati something about hair color.

The seer's forehead grooves beneath the golden-white strands that drape across it. *"Kahala."* Black.

Fallon smiles at Lorcan. Again, I feel like I'm grasping at water. Why does she seem glad to learn that she kills Alyona of Glace? Because it proves she'll reemerge from the Mahananda if she goes inside to discuss the Crows' curse? And who has black hair? Alyona?

Behati blinks the shroud of magic away, murmuring something about how, in fact, the girl's features *do* differ from Fallon's, while Cathal mutters something in Shabbin—I imagine for my sake—about their personalities evidently being one and the same.

Priya glances toward the Mahananda where the members of the Akwale are painting sigils on the drenched sunstone. Though the clouds are still menacing, and the sky as gray as iron, Lorcan's storm has eased.

Fallon had said that *knowing would reassure Dádhi and Lore.* Clearly, it has. Or, at least, it's reassured Lorcan. Cathal remains tense, his pulse so loud that it rumbles from his rigid fingers into my captive arm.

When metal groans, my mind jumps to the conclusion that the ward has collapsed, but I'm wrong. The sound emanates from the box that the queen has flicked open. As she reaches inside, I hear her tell Lorcan that if his daughter—*he has a daughter?*—is destined to kill the Princess of Glace, then breaking his curse is all the more important for his race to survive King Vladimir's wrath.

My lungs seize around a breath, and not because the pieces of their conversation are falling into place, but because the Shabbin Queen now holds the weapon I saw her plant inside Lorcan's chest. Is that what she's about to do? Is that why Fallon trapped her mate inside the Kasha? So he would calm and allow the Mahananda's keeper to transform him into a statue? How does cursing the Crow King break his curse?

The buzzing from earlier returns, this time pressing against my eardrums instead of my temples. Though it creates a din, I somehow hear the queen explain that the Mahananda never takes, merely transforms: a Two-legs into a Crow, a Serpent into a Two-legs.

As Fallon backs up from the invisible ward, Lorcan murmurs words in a tone that chills me to the bone. I don't know what he's saying, but it sounds like a plea. Is he begging her to convince the queen not to stab him with the dagger? Is he asking her not to go barter with the Mahananda?

I might not understand his whisper, but I understand his disquiet, for the Crows have *one* mate, unlike the Shabbins, who have multiple, sometimes at once. I learned this when I dropped by Priya's bedchamber and found her lounging on her floor pillows with two males and one female, all of them disrobed.

After pressing a kiss to all three and wishing them a pleasant slumber, she'd turned to me and suggested a walk through the palace gardens. It was two nights after I'd shifted for the very first time. I remember sliding my gaze over the Sahklare, aglow with phosphorescent algae, and wondering if my kind mated for life like Crows, before remembering that I was the first of my kind. That I didn't *have* a kind. That I was the only Serpent shifter.

Unless there were others out there, waiting for me beyond the pink ramparts...

I startle out of my contemplations when I see the queen follow Fallon toward the Mahananda. And then I scream.

Chapter 5
Zendaya

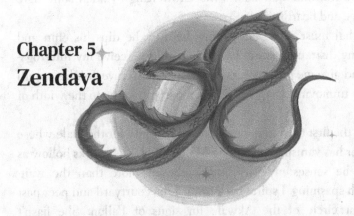

Shock ripples through me as the Shabbin Queen buries the black stone dagger inside Fallon's chest.

The brutality of the act cinches my lungs, and I think I'll never be able to draw breath again, but I'm wrong, for a second horrified cry escapes me as Fallon turns to stone and sinks. I slap the ward, claw at it, desperate to find a breach so I can race over and dive into the Mahananda to retrieve her.

If only my blood carried Shabbin magic, but all it does is stain. The only part of me that possesses any power is my tongue. Useless, since it cannot carry me through wards. Or can it? I lick the transparent barrier. Though it captures the attention of Kanti, who grimaces as she stands, hand-in-bleeding-hand, with the rest of the Akwale, it fails to soften the wall.

I freeze as Cathal's earlier question tumbles back into me. He'd asked what would happen to Fallon *after* she was stabbed, not *if*. *After*. I thought he'd mistaken the two words. But he hadn't. He'd *known* the queen was going to stab Fallon.

I spin around, riffling through my mind for the words to ask *how* and whether it had been Fallon's choice to take Lorcan's place. However deep I dig, though, I cannot produce any intelligible sounds; they've all deserted me.

Dádhi Cathal and Lorcan stand so still that I suddenly worry

27

they, too, have morphed to stone, but then Cathal's throat bobs around a murmur that makes the Crow King's golden stare flare with rage and heartbreak.

Cathal must sense me gaping, because he dips his chin and meets my distraught stare. I wish he could perceive my interrogations and give me the answers I so desperately crave, but his mouth remains unmoving. Only his pupils move, retracting to the width of a seed.

For the first time in my existence, I feel pity for the male whose daughter has vanished inside the Mahananda. His cheeks hollow as though he senses my pity and loathes it more than the wait. Stomach spasming, I spiral back toward the courtyard and peer past the tight circle of the Akwale for signs of Fallon. She hasn't emerged.

Where worry rucks the queen's face, the members of her Akwale—those whose faces I can see—seem unconcerned. Kanti is downright grinning, lips curled around teeth that shine white in the gray light. Can she see to the bottom? Is the Mahananda transforming Fallon from stone back into skin? Is Fallon still stone?

What if...what if—

I shut my eyes and give my head a harsh shake. How dare I so much as contemplate this?

Warmth seeps into my cheeks as though the sun were blistering them, but there's no sun. Only hot coils of shame. I roll my fingers and retreat into the farthest, darkest corner of the Kasha, so that the two males I'm trapped with cannot spot how, for a fragile moment, I wished to curse Fallon with scales.

The wait is so endless that I sidle down one of the stone walls and gather my knees against my trembling chest. I don't know how long I sit there, hunched in the shadows, watching shards of candle-light dance on the sunstone floor, but it feels endless. Like Lorcan's earlier storm hasn't just beat the sun back beneath the ramparts of Shabbe but extinguished it forever.

For the first time since my birth, I loathe the darkness.

FALLON DOES NOT GET SCALES. I SHOULD FEEL RELIEF; I DON'T.

When she returns from her dip in the Mahananda, her eyes are bright, her cheeks even brighter. She exudes happiness. She is the only one who does, though. Priya seems to have aged a century, Cathal is as grim as he was when she left, and Lorcan...he is as taciturn as I am guilt-ridden.

His lips don't even bend when Fallon skips through the ward, clutching the dagger between her palms. She presents it to him. He doesn't take it.

She turns toward her father and urges him to seize it...to *try it*. Lips flat, jaw hard, he relieves her of the blade and rolls it between his palms, as though to test its weight, before strangling the hilt with his huge fingers and propelling the blade into his muscled thigh.

I suck in a breath.

I don't expel it.

Even though I'm still crouched in the shadows, the fragrance of his blood reaches me, wrapping itself around me until my tongue tingles with the need to lap and seal his wounded flesh. I resist the urge. He is Crow. He will heal on his own. He does not need me.

Yet I picture myself kneeling in front of him and licking at his torn flesh. Would he grimace like Fallon's friend, Sybille, the day I'd healed the scrape she'd gotten on her palm while climbing out of the Amkhuti?

Priya scans the obscure Kasha, presumably for me. Sure enough, when she spots my form, she takes off in my direction, asking Lorcan something about his fallen Crows. Did they awaken? *Awaken?*

He nods, and then he does something I never imagined him capable of: he walks right past Fallon and asks her not to follow him, before shifting into five crows and taking to the steel-colored sky. The pink flush of delight in Fallon's cheeks recedes as she watches her mate leave. Cathal drapes his arm around her curled shoulders and gathers her into his chest. His lips move over a whisper, probably a reassurance that her mate will return.

Are Fallon and Lorcan still mates? He spoke aloud to her. Does that mean—

The Shabbin Queen's shadow drapes over me. With a sigh, she murmurs an apology for leaving me in the dark. Does she mean in the shadows of the Kasha, or by not explaining what was about to happen? She tells me that Fallon is safe. Unharmed. That she broke the Crows' obsidian curse. Then she crouches before me and lays her scarred palms on my knees. "EmMoti, *kaeneh shileh*."

I frown because I do not know what she's asking me *not to do*. "*Shileh?*" I croak.

The sound of my voice makes her lids flutter. Her eyes begin to shine and then her mouth begins to curve. She reaches over and touches my cheek. And then she holds her fingertip in front of my eyes. It glistens with moisture. "*Shil*."

I palm my cheeks that are as wet as when I surface from my swims. Where is this water coming from? Did my skin absorb the Amkhuti? I lick the moisture...taste salt. Why is seawater dribbling from my eyes?

Priya must read my alarm because she offers me a gentle smile. And then she takes my fingers and brings them to her cheek. I frown until I catch a bead of moisture sliding out of the corner of her eye. "*Shil*."

I blink, because she isn't Serpent, yet the ocean also flows down her cheeks.

She places a kiss inside my palm, then releases my wrist to glide her hands on either side of my head. My mind fills with images of wet lashes. *Everyone*, I hear her whisper, *shileh*.

She must mean all land creatures, for if serpents shed water from their eyes, I'd have a word for it, and I don't. She takes my hand once more, this time to steer me back toward the others. Fallon's crimson-veined eyes and wet cheeks draw another sigh from Priya, who assures her that the male will return. The queen presses a kiss to my forehead, then to Fallon's, before retreating to her chambers, flanked by her guards.

Fallon's lips wobble. It hurts me to see her like this. "*Soliya, Mádhi.*" Sorry, Maji.

Why is she apologizing to me? Before I can ask, she races out of the Kasha.

Concern over the Lucin monarchs' mating link takes precedence over her apology. I turn toward Cathal and tap my forehead, pointing between the blur of gold that's his daughter and the gloomy sky. His eyebrows sink toward his crooked nose. I should use words, but it's suddenly so quiet that I worry my voice will reach farther than just his ears.

"*Foroshock,*" he suddenly says.

Foroshock? What does that mean? He must be speaking in his tongue again.

I push a lock of hair off my face, trying to wrangle it behind my ear, but the strand refuses to cooperate. "*Nahen behiboleh Crow.*" *No speak Crow.*

He dips his chin, pinning me with a look that makes heat tiptoe up my neck and into my cheeks.

"*Krehiya,*" I add, feeling like adding the word *please* will soften his irritation.

For a couple heartbeats, he just glares, and then his mouth curls and laughter leaps out.

How dare he laugh at my diction, especially considering his accent. I might not be entirely comfortable with the Shabbin tongue, but I can tell he doesn't speak it like Pink-eyes.

I plant my hands on my hips and narrow my eyes, and then in my best Shabbin, I tell him not to laugh at me. He sobers instantly and mutters that he wasn't. Then why did he make that sound after I spoke?

He rubs his hand through his snarled midnight locks, then across the growth on his jaw. He repeats what he's just said, swapping the word *not* for one that sounds similar but that is stronger,

31

especially in his mouth—*never*. And then he admits that he was speaking in Shabbin.

I feel like even more of a fool.

He nods to the sky and repeats his earlier word, breaking it into syllables: "*For roshock.*"

I frown and repeat his words out loud. It takes them rolling off my own tongue to make sense of them: "*Phar rosha.*" *Still mates*.

My cheeks must match my hair because the skin over them feels lit by twin flames. I palm one, my thumb bumping into the thin scar that dips from my left eye like a *shil*.

Dádhi Cathal's mouth moves again. So focused am I on the blaze of my cheeks that I'm not quick enough to snatch and iron out the syllables that spool off his tongue. I don't ask him to repeat himself since I've learned that most Two-legs find this practice exasperating. Fallon and Asha are the exception. Both will repeat words without me ever needing to ask. Aoife, too, come to think of it, but she speaks almost exclusively in Crow. I've decided not to try and learn another foreign tongue until I can express my Serpent thoughts in Shabbin.

I moisten my lips with the tip of my tongue. "Fallon *phar* Crow?" *Fallon still Crow?*

"*Phar* Crow," he replies, enunciating the first word even though it still sounds like he's attached an 'o' to the end of it.

I know he's not mispronouncing it for my sake, but is it wrong of me to appreciate that he does? That I'm not the only Two-legs maiming the Shabbin tongue? He mentions that he will go check on her and asks me if I want to accompany him. And I do, but Fallon's his daughter. I'm certain she'd much prefer to see him alone.

As I decline his invitation, I glance at his maimed thigh. The scent of his blood has changed. Instead of wet metal, it now smells... *not good*. I almost suggest taking a look at it, but I don't care to remind him that beneath my smooth Two-legs' flesh, lurks a creature better suited for the deep.

Smoothing away my grimace, I stride toward my wing of the palace. Abrax falls into step beside me and sighs. When I cock an eyebrow at him, he tells me something that makes my footfalls falter and my heart stop beating.

I halt and twist around. The Crow hasn't moved from the threshold of the Kasha.

As I stare at him and he stares back, my heart remains suspended like the clouds over Shabbe, like the smoke around his limbs.

Now that their curse is broken, he's leaving.

They're *all* leaving.

I don't realize I'm rubbing the skin over my heart until Abrax asks if something's wrong. *Yes,* I think. *I will be even more alone now.*

Chapter 6
Zendaya

I consider resting but cannot lie still, so after Abrax drops me off, I sneak out of my private gardens and dive into the Amkhuti without any palace sentry being the wiser. The instant my body meets water, I morph, and then I swim hard and fast. When my muscles ache and my energy wanes, I just float, barely flicking my tail. The clouds start to thin, the air grows lighter, the world brighter.

Do clement skies mean Lorcan has calmed? Has he forgiven Fallon? He must have if they are all leaving tonight. Unless she's not going? What am I thinking? Of course she will leave. Mates cannot live without one another. I must drift off while mulling this over, because suddenly, my body bangs against rock.

I startle awake. Though there's no pain, my surprise is so great that I wink out of my Serpent form and into my Two-legs' one. I whisper Dádhi Cathal's favorite word: "*Focá.*" I'm not entirely certain what it means, but since he uses it when something goes wrong, it seems appropriate. Not only is the sun a burst of faded gold, but I also coasted all the way across the channel that separates the palace from the rest of Shabbe. How didn't I notice the current snatching my body? Though a tad distressed, curiosity tempers my alarm.

I paddle toward one of the liquid curtains that link the Amkhuti to every river flowing through Shabbe and stick my palm in the wall of glistening droplets. The pressure is strong, but is it strong enough to carry my body up the steep cliff wall? Naturally, I test this out. No sooner have I penetrated the liquid screen that I begin to rise. My marveling is cut short by a shrill squawk.

I lurch sideways, flopping back into the Amkhuti. My body sinks, but my heart...it feels like it's scaling up my throat. Iron slices into the water, followed by an enormous feathered body. I squeak and kick my feet to get out of the creature's way, but apparently, I *am* his way, since the giant bird swims after me, using his wings like I use my limbs.

I twist around, recognizing Dádhi Cathal by the force of his glower. I don't think he's ever stared at me with such absolute fury. Because I left my quarters without warning anyone or because I just discovered how to venture out of my gilded cage?

My lungs squeeze and a trickle of bubbles sneaks out of my mouth. Though I can breathe underwater in this form, too, I swim back to the surface. I mustn't go fast enough to the Crow's liking, however, for he swoops beneath me, forcing my legs apart until I straddle his back.

I just have time to clutch the feathers at his neck before he carves out of the water and into the sky, toward the Vahti, which sits like a frosted cake on a golden platter. The air is sweet but so cold at this altitude that I shiver, the dusky caps on my chest tightening into points that could surely whittle sunstone.

In mere heartbeats, we're landing in my private garden. Dádhi Cathal crouches and I slide off. As I wring my hair, he shifts back into skin and growls at me in Crow. Actually, not in Crow; in Shabbin. He's asking if I've lost my mind.

I frown, because minds are inside heads, and since mine is attached to my shoulders, his question makes no sense.

But then he says something that makes a lot of sense. "I will kill Abrax and Asha."

I snap my rope of hair behind my shoulders, then stalk up to the Crow and hiss, "If harm them, I kill you."

35

That knocks his lips shut. It also knocks his eyebrows low. So low that the black arcs of hair tangle with the swoop of his thick lashes.

I poke him in the chest with a finger—it feels like poking a wall —and warn him that I'm serious, then toss my hands in the air and bellow, "Look me. I safe!"

My exclamation gives me pause. In which language are we arguing? It's the first time the syllables pop so naturally off my tongue that I cannot tell.

I stretch my lips over more words, speaking slower this time— not for the Crow's sake, but for my mind's. "Glad you leave tonight." *Shabbin.* Definitely Shabbin.

It's as though anger has made all the words I've learned layer themselves over their Serpent equivalents.

I'm still reeling from this phenomenon when Cathal's mouth slits into a crooked smile that demolishes my wonder.

I fold my arms. "Why you smile?"

"Because, *Príona*"—he takes a step into my body, the leather cuirass he wears over his long-sleeved black top punching into my little beads—"I'm not going anywhere." The corner of his mouth that hadn't yet lifted flips upward.

"But Abrax say all Crows—"

"Except me."

"But you second to King."

"You hid your hand well, Daya."

Though both my hands are buried beneath my elbows, I don't understand what their position has to do with our conversation.

"Barely one full moon cycle, and you're fluent in Shabbin. Is that how long it will take you to master Crow?"

I still don't grasp the connection between my hands and my understanding, but I choose to focus on a more pressing matter. "Why you no leave?"

"Because I do not trust Asha and Abrax. Or you, for that matter."

My arms tighten. "You no trust to *what*?"

36

"I don't trust them to keep you safe, and I don't trust you not to find a way into the ocean."

"I belong to ocean," I remind him.

"No, you belong to—" He stops talking so suddenly that I peer around the tall shrubs aglow with star blooms and phosphorescent moths, assuming that we have company.

We don't.

I cant my head. "Where I belong, Dádhi Cathal?"

He blinks. Then blinks again. And then he grimaces. "Dádhi?"

"Isn't that name?"

His lids squeeze so hard that his lambent gaze becomes a striation on his kohl-striped face, like those iridescent veins in sunstone. "It's not a name anyone but Fallon should be using."

"Why?"

"Because it means Father in Crow."

Oh.

I suddenly see how that is inappropriate, but it does beg the question: "What she call me sound same."

Like those marauding barracudas that taunt the smaller fish, his lips part and then shut, part again before shutting again.

"What mean Mádhi in Crow?"

The spike in his throat jostles. I noticed only males have it. I heard they were called after a fruit that doesn't grow in Shabbe. I've yet to understand why males store fruit in their necks and not females.

"So?"

"It means"—he rolls his neck, making it crack—*"favorite older female."*

I can feel my brow crinkle. "I old?"

"You're, um..." He hooks a finger in his shirt collar and tugs. "Older than my daughter."

"How old me?"

"Your serpent was born a few moons before Fallon."

"So I almost same age as daughter..."

"You're—you're—I suppose that yes, you are." Is it me, or is his jaw crimson?

"Why you red?"

"I'm not red," he grumbles, snatching his hand away from his shirt and smacking his leather pants. He winces as his fingers connect with his thigh, springing that ripe, stomach-churning scent into the air between us.

"No heal?"

His eyebrows slant, so I gesture to his leg.

"Want me try?"

His chin lowers. "Try what?"

"Heal you." I tap my lips. "With magic tongue."

Although it seems impossible, his flush intensifies. "I—" He clears his throat. "No. I'm a Crow. My body will repair itself."

"But I repair fast." I begin to kneel when he fractures into smoke and reappears beside the farthest hedge.

"Get dressed." His tone is as cold as his stare. "You're late for the farewell supper."

I cock an eyebrow as I straighten. "You odd male, Dádhi Cathal."

He grumbles something about how I shouldn't call him Dádhi because he's not my father.

I glance at him over my shoulder as I head to my bedchamber. "But you say I same age as Fallon, so possible."

"No. It's *not* possible." His skin now resembles a berry. "You're *not* my daughter," he all but snarls.

His reaction strikes me as disproportionate. "I sorry I no understand word."

He cuts his gaze to my shimmering hedge. "Supper will start in thirty minutes." Even though his tone is flat, the throbbing vein at the base of his neck betrays his jagged mood.

With a sigh, I climb up my balcony's stone stairs, my hair still dripping seawater into the runnel of my spine, and I think about what he confessed before he got angry: that he isn't leaving. Surely another Crow can relieve him of his loathed guarding duties. Perhaps the one named Aodhan who doesn't hate me on sight.

As my bath fills, I practice the question I will ask the queen tonight, then practice it some more as I massage nut oil into my skin and hair. I speak it aloud one final time as I slip into the backless pink sheath that feels like water against my skin.

I drag my fingers through the steam filming my mirror and articulate the title she's asked me to call her: "Taytah." *Mother of my mother.* I suppose it's appropriate since she's the Mahananda's keeper and I'm its daughter, though it admittedly feels a little odd to have a special word for her when she insists everyone else—save for Fallon—call her Priya or Sumaca.

I start over: "Taytah, I no desire Cathal; I desire other Crow—Aodhan." I've noticed that if I add volume to my pitch, it abates my hissing, but powering my words means making them ring louder.

Am I ready for Shabbe to hear my odd voice? *No.* But am I ready to be rid of the male who doesn't trust me? *Yes.*

Chapter 7
Zendaya

The queen sits at one end of a long banquet table, Lorcan at the other. Relief fills me when I glimpse Fallon at his side. Even though the tendons in the male's neck are strained and Fallon's eyes shimmer beneath her black stripes, the mated pair must've reconciled if they're sharing a meal.

I twist a greeting around my tongue, but a snatched glance around the crowded table has me gulping it back. Every member of the Akwale has been invited to dine, as well as every Crow from Lorcan's Siorkahd.

A chorus of "Good evening, Rajka" pronounced in thick Crow accents echoes off the tall sky-bloom hedges and glittery flagstones that hem in the garden dining area. I'm tempted to reply with words, but my breastbone grows hot and I smoosh my lips. I do, though, dip my head while folding myself into the seat beside Priya's.

Just as one of the Shabbin attendants tucks my chair close to the stone table, Cathal makes his appearance and drops into the last empty seat, which he scrapes in himself. The conversation, which hushed when I arrived, resumes.

The Shabbin Queen leans forward and slides her elbows onto the table. Her split sapphire sleeves, bound around her wrists by jeweled gold cuffs, billow open around her sun-kissed arms. "You were saying, Lorcan? The Crows in the forest...they still bleed?"

Fascinated once more by my flawless comprehension, I almost miss the Sky King's reply.

"That's correct. They awakened on their own, but their wounds won't seal."

"Fallon's did," the Shabbin monarch replies, her pink eyes tangling with Fallon's violet.

"Fallon was in the Cauldron, Sumaca." The reminder's spoken by the black-skinned, white-haired female who's part of Lorcan's inner circle.

I vaguely remember her attending my "rebirth," but do not recall her name. The single detail that did stick with me is that she mothered Phoebus's lover and grandmothered Reid, a male who comes often to Shabbe.

Kanti, who loves little more than discussing people, says he travels here to visit Fallon's Faerie mother, Agrippina Rossi, who—still according to Kanti—has a broken brain. I'm unsure what this means, besides the fact that Kanti, who I've heard discuss *my* reptilian brain with the Akwale, seems to have a fascination with the insides of heads.

"The Crows back in Luce..." Imogen—Aoife's older sister and one of the few people whose company Cathal enjoys—breaks off a piece of fried, phosphorescent algae and nibbles on its corners. "Their wounds are festering." Though her coloring is the same as her sister's, her features are sharper—bladed.

"Have your injured Crows tried serpent healing?" Behati asks.

"The serpents won't approach them." Lorcan flexes his jaw. "You know Crows and serpents have never been..." When he catches me sitting up straighter, straining to hear his next words, he says, "We're hoping that Fallon will be able to weave relations between our two species."

"Fallon and *me*," Kanti says. "Have you forgotten that I'll be joining you in Luce?"

"How could we forget?" Fallon grimaces. "You've reminded us

hourly since Behati foresaw how instrumental you'll be at seducing one of our many enemies."

"Have you foreseen which enemy, Behati?" Lorcan leans forward. "I have so many..."

"The Mahananda hasn't given me a name or shown me a face. It's only shown me that Kanti must head to Tarespagia."

Two-legs' politics is so tedious, everyone vying for power and control. Why can't the world above the ocean be as simple as the one beneath, where minnows do not aspire to become barracudas, and barracudas do not desire to duel me?

"Cathal, your wound? Has it improved?" Aza's query makes the Crow's dark stare lift from his bare plate and settle on the strikingly beautiful Shabbin with hair the same sapphire-black as Crow feathers.

"It hasn't worsened," he mutters to the youngest member of the Akwale.

Priya snaps her fingers. "Call for my healer."

Two guards whirl and disappear behind a hedge.

"There are plenty of serpents in the Sahklare." Aza's expression is alight with satisfaction, as though she's singlehandedly solved the Crows' tribulations. "You could go for a dip with your daughter while you wait."

Cathal mutters something in Crow that makes the black-haired beauty narrow her eyes. "It's not a trick. We do not trick people. The Mahananda does not trick."

"If you believe it's a trick, then perhaps Zendaya could lick your wound better?" Kanti smiles at me. "After all, you trust her and she does so love lapping blood, amongst *other things*."

I frown, because one, Cathal does not trust me, and two, I'm no fan of the taste of blood. Also, what else have I lapped? Is she referring to the ward?

Cathal growls something in Crow that makes Kanti's expression pinch.

"Careful, Crow"—Kanti squares her shoulders—"or I may reconsider playing diplomat between your king and his enemy."

Cathal's eyes twitch as though it's taking every last shred of his strength to repress his reply. Or perhaps they twitch because Lorcan is asking him, through the mind link, not to anger his future ally. "I'll swim with the serpents."

The idea of someone else's tongue on his skin hardens my insides, so I push out of my chair and circle the table toward Cathal. When I start to lower myself to my knees, he melts into smoke and reappears behind Imogen's chair.

Kanti drapes one arm around the back of her chair. "Huh. She really does understand what we say."

"She understands *everything*," Fallon snaps.

"Pardon me for doubting it. She's always so quiet." Kanti wriggles a hand. "Anyway, let's see if it works."

"No!" Cathal says.

Kanti frowns. "Why not? Saves you from getting wet."

"Because this could hurt her!" Cathal bellows. "Daya's not just a serpent; she's a shifter."

Is it truly my health he worries about, or is repugnance what keeps him from letting me try?

The female healer I met the day after my rebirth as a Two-legs arrives in the company of a silver-haired male twice her size, and with ears so broad and pointy, they skim the top of his head. Though their appearance doesn't entirely smother the ambient tension, it seems to lower its volume. I suppose that if a Shabbin crystal leads to Cathal's full recovery, all will be forgiven.

But what if neither crystal nor serpent can mend obsidian injuries? What will happen to the relations between sorceresses and Crows?

"Soorya, one of our guests needs healing from a dagger wound." The queen nods to Cathal.

"Right away, Sumaca." Soorya's pink eyes roam over the shifter in a way that makes me want to step between them.

I realize she's probably seeking the wound in need of mending, but I find her smile too bright, and her stare, too intrigued. When she looked me over that first day, her expression was as bland as the tapioca pudding Kanti eats every morning.

"Which part of your body needs healing, Cathal?" When he points to his thigh, her slightly hooked nose wrinkles. "What did you stab yourself on?"

"Obsidian."

The giant Faerie shadowing Soorya blinks. "Obsidian? But I thought—I thought you were rid of your curse!"

"You and us all, Lazarus." Erwin drags a freckled hand through his red locks. I recall his name because, his hair, like mine is a flamboyant color not worn by many. "Seems like obsidian remains toxic to our kind."

Soorya's layered necklace clinks as she hooks one of the six chains, then runs her fingers over the gold baubles dangling from each link until she feels out the appropriate medicinal crystal. According to Behati, they hum to her.

"*Kavari*," she says, twisting the ball until the bottom half comes loose. I imagine it's a land substance, for I don't have an equivalent in Serpent. She props it in front of Lazarus, who leans over and takes a long whiff. "It counteracts toxins." She rubs the tip of her index finger against the salve until her skin is as green as a lizard's. "Your wound, Cathal."

The Crow grows out his talons and swipes them through the leather cloaking his thigh. When Soorya kneels in front of him and pinches the flap, I grit my teeth and hiss because the veins orbiting around his puckered flesh are black.

"Great Mórrígan, how are you even walking, brother?" Lorcan exclaims.

Soorya traces the extent of the infection with her gaze before tracing it with her healing salve. I will the darkness in Cathal's veins to seep out as she collects more salve and spreads it over his flesh.

Lazarus crouches beside her. "How about *turga?*"

"*Turga* clots vessels. If anything, we need his wound to bleed." Soorya bites down on her upper lip. "May I try to slice you open with my blood, Cathal?"

My nails aren't talons, yet they score the skin of my palm just the same. I do not want this female to butcher my sentry's thigh with her magic. I do not want her to harm him further.

"If you're trying to widen the cut, Soorya, I've tried, but the skin doesn't tear." Cathal's complexion is as pearlescent as the inside of an oyster shell. "Not even with obsidian."

He's used the dagger on himself a *second* time? How foolish is this male? I might not have been part of the Two-legged world for long, but it strikes me as absurd to employ the cause of the issue in the hopes that it'll have an adverse effect.

The Shabbin healer swipes her thumb over a serrated link in her chain, then draws a line down the blackened skin with blood; it doesn't penetrate. Tongue tucked in the corner of her mouth, she widens the gap in the leather sheathing his thigh and paints a noose around the black veins.

"The blood's not penetrating," Fallon murmurs, coming to stand beside me. "Put some on his wound."

He hisses as Soorya presses her cut to his, which makes my teeth grind and my feet itch to squeeze in between them.

Soorya studies the circle of blood. "The blackness hasn't receded."

"Maybe it takes time?" Fallon proposes.

We wait, and wait. It feels like an entire day has come and gone before anyone speaks again.

"Perhaps *your* blood will work on him, Your Majesty?" Lazarus suggests.

Fallon grabs a napkin from the table, saturates it with water, then wipes down her father's skin. And then she pricks her finger on her neck ornament and circles the wound. Her blood, like Soorya's, sits atop Cathal's skin like wet sand. Mouth twisted, she touches his cut. Another hiss drops from his mouth.

She cranes her neck, tipping her face toward his. Though I can only see the back of her head, I've no trouble picturing how tormented she must feel. My abdomen hardens until it's become as tight as the fingers I've balled at my sides, fingers that grow infinitesimally tighter when Soorya glances over her shoulder at Priya. Although they don't exchange words, the apprehension sizzling between the two females bites my spine like an icy current.

"A trip to the Sahklare it'll be," Kanti chirrups, as though alluding to an exciting jaunt instead of a last resort.

"Can you fly, Dádhi?" Fallon asks.

"I'm not infirm," he grumbles. "Besides, it's my leg. My wings are fine."

I think of the Crow from the vision the queen showed me before Fallon went inside the Mahananda—the one with the arrow protruding from its wing. Can *it* still fly?

As father and daughter shift, I take a step toward them, desirous to accompany them in case...in case my fellow serpents prove unkind or uncooperative.

"No, emMoti," the queen's voice is low but resonant.

I'm about to beg her to allow me to join them when a gust of air streaks across my cheek and kicks up the ends of my hair. By the time I've spun back, Fallon and Cathal have departed.

Without me.

I grind the ivory inside my mouth, wishing I had wings instead of fins.

"Good evening, Zendaya." The mammoth Faerie, who accompanied Soorya, is staring down at me with a kindly smile.

Although it doesn't completely blow away my annoyance, it does appease it.

"I hear you've mastered shifting from beast to human."

I tilt my head, unsure how to answer since it isn't a question.

His amber gaze roams over my face, lingering on my retracted tusk. "A serpent shifter." He shakes his head, still smiling. "In my long years, I've never seen anything quite as surprising as you. The Cauldron's magic is truly astounding." He speaks of the Mahananda with stars in his eyes.

It may have split my scales, but it doesn't only produce miracles. Though, admittedly, if the serpents manage to heal Cathal, I may admire it once more.

"I'm curious." Lazarus tucks a long, silver strand behind his pointed ear that shines with a dozen golden hoops embellished with Shabbin crystals. "Can you communicate with them?" At my frown, he adds, "The serpents."

A slender hand winds through mine. I know it's Priya's before I even spot the blood-coated ring gracing her index finger. She says something to Lazarus in his tongue before switching to Shabbin. "Will you be returning to Luce with Lorcan and Fallon, Lazarus?"

"I was hoping you'd allow me to stay in Shabbe, Sumaca. I do not have anyone to return to in Luce."

"Ah, yes. Forgive me for forgetting about your loss. You're welcome to stay for as long as you wish. I hear you and Soorya are getting along swimmingly."

Swimmingly? Since I've never crossed paths with a Two-legs in the Amkhuti, besides Fallon and her friends, I assume Lazarus must've bonded with Soorya in the Sahklare.

"Your royal healer is a most wonderful teacher."

Soorya sidles close to Lazarus, threading one of her brown arms around his. "Only because you are a wonderful student."

How can they jest at a time like this? I look up at the sky, hoping to spot beating wings, but Cathal and Fallon don't magically appear. Food does, though. Well, not magically. The vibrant dishes must've been deposited while Soorya melted crystals between her fingers.

"Enjoy your dinner, Sumaca." Soorya nods before retreating with Lazarus beyond the hedges.

The queen guides me back to my seat. As she regains her place at the head of the table, she reaches for the spoon tucked into the wide-brimmed terracotta bowl brimming with flame-broiled beans and warm grain and serves herself. When I make no move to ladle any on my plate, too flustered to eat, she reaches over and serves me. I push my food around, creating shapes...letters. I suddenly wonder if my reading will have improved now that my oral comprehension has clicked into place.

"Everything all right, emMoti?" Priya rubs her thumb over the diamond tusks that protrude from her gold ring, a jeweled rendition of the Shabbin crest and of the crown glimmering amidst her white strands—two serpents coiled around a circlet that symbolizes the Mahananda.

Though many stares warm my cheeks, I decide to voice what I practiced earlier. Just as my lips part, Behati releases her fork, and its clatter snatches everyone's attention.

"What is it, Taytah?" Kanti covers Behati's hand with her own. "Was it a vision of me again? Did you see who—"

"Kanti, quiet," the queen snaps. "We do not interrupt visions."

Kanti herds her hand onto her lap, chastened by the queen's reproof.

Several minutes slip by before Behati's eyes clear of their white veil. Nevertheless, her silence endures. I've come to learn that there exists many types of silences in the world of Two-legs, some that are soothing and others that are loud. The one that drapes over the palace gardens rings louder than any scream.

Behati combs aside her pale bangs. "The Mahananda has changed its terms."

Chapter 8
Zendaya

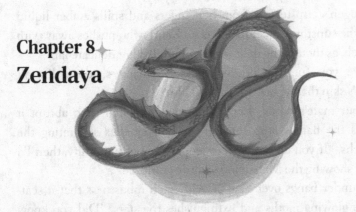

P riya reaches for her wine glass and takes a slow swallow. "Do share the Mahananda's new terms, Behati."

"Do they concern my seduction mission?" Kanti asks.

I don't miss Imogen's eye roll. Even Erwin seems to have trouble keeping his eyeballs level.

"The Mahananda's decided that the Crows' immunity to obsidian will be merit-based."

"Excuse me?" Lorcan squeezes the handle of his knife with such vigor that he manages to warp the metal. "Merit-based?"

A smirk tugs at Kanti's lips. "Does this restore your faith in the Mahananda, sisters?" Though she directs her question to all her fellow Akwale members, she singles out one in particular with her gaze—Malka.

"There was nothing to restore, Kanti." Though Malka's brown cheeks don't deepen in color, her voice seems uncharacteristically strained. Not to mention that her pink eyes flick to Priya, as though to check whether her lover believes her. "I trust the Mahananda with all my heart."

The Shabbin Queen seems too preoccupied to challenge her bedmate. "Tell us more, Behati."

"What I've gleaned from the vision is that Crows will not turn to stone immediately—or to iron, in your case, Mórrgaht. The change will happen gradually after an injury."

Imogen's cup teeters from her fingers and spills amber liquid across the sunstone tabletop and onto Kanti, who pushes away with a screech, as though the date wine had broiled her delicate lap.

"Are you fucking kidding me?" So many shadows lift off Lorcan's skin that he becomes a steel blur.

"Your mate's cured, Lore." The queen's pitch is so abrupt it disturbs the flames atop the long row of candles separating the monarchs. "If you do not wish to jeopardize her immunity, then I'd suggest showing the Mahananda a little gratitude."

Thunder bangs over Shabbe with such robustness that it scatters the glowing moths and extinguishes the stars. "Did you know this was a possibility before you incited her to step into the Cauldron, Priya?" The Sky King remains all-shadow.

The queen slits her eyes. "No one forced Fallon inside."

Lorcan's smoke funnels back underneath his skin and then he presses away from the table. I think he's about to stand, but he merely readjusts his posture. "If the *Mahananda*"—for once, he uses the Shabbin term for it instead of the other non-Shabbins favor— "doesn't make mistakes, then could your seer have *misinterpreted* the vision?"

Behati glowers at the Crow King but doesn't speak. Perhaps she senses that defending herself would only make her seem guilty.

Aza scoffs. "Our seer has never once deceived you, Ríhbiadh, for if she had, she'd have lost her gift."

He grips his bent knee with one hand and the armrest of his chair with the other. "I've learned there's always a first time for everything."

The queen shoves back her chair so violently that the grind of its feet rivals Lorcan's thunder. "You're mated to my flesh and blood, yet dare question my intent?"

The sky flares with zigzags of lightning.

"Behati's, actually," Lorcan says with false calm.

My ribs clench as the monarchs keep glowering at one another, the rift between them widening. Unease lends every being in attendance glass-sharp edges that fray the tenuous relations between the shifters and the Shabbins. For several heartbeats, I feel as though I'm teetering on the brink of a war.

On what side of the battlefield would I end up? Beside the queen, or with the other creatures shaped by the Mahananda? But more importantly, did Behati deliberately betray Lorcan? Is that why I saw the queen stab Lorcan's chest in her vision?

I yearn for Fallon and her father to return to restore the peace.

"How long will the Cauldron be out of sorts, Sumaca?" Erwin scrutinizes the trail of wine that's yet to be sopped up by the attendants. It only strikes me then that most have scattered. Because of the tension, or did someone command them to leave?

The guards are still here, forming a loose circle around us. I catch Abrax's stare, see his hand poised on the pommel of the sword belted at his waist, smell the fresh blood pooling off Asha's fingertip. I'm not sure when she arrived, or why she's on duty at the same time as Abrax, but her presence is comforting.

"Because you believe it will welcome you after the king questioned its keepers?" Priya shakes her head a great many times, dislodging strands from her intricate, braided updo. "Show yourselves out of my queendom." And then she turns and hastens away.

My distress grows because I've never seen the queen rush anywhere. I almost go after her, but Malka is already out of her seat, fisting her long white gown to avoid tripping over it. The rest of the Akwale—save for Kanti and Behati—stand and glower at the Crows.

Kanti coils a lock of her straight black hair around her finger. "Must I still travel with them, Taytah?"

Behati disregards Kanti's interrogation. "I saw snow fall on the obsidian bodies of your injured, Mórrgaht."

"Because the Cauldron abandons us?" Imogen asks. "Or because it will stay sealed until the winter months?"

"I cannot tell." Behati reaches for her cane, this one made of gold and embedded with pink rubies.

While I wonder what snow is, the black-skinned female Crow sighs. "So our injured have a month. Two, at best."

"Kanti?" Behati stands, leaning heavily on her cane. Once her granddaughter has risen, she takes ahold of her arm. "Which one of you will fly my child out of Shabbe?"

The Crows exchange glances.

Finally, a pale-faced male with black eyes and no hair sighs. "I'll take her."

"Contain your excitement." Kanti wrinkles her nose. "On second thought, I'll sail there."

"No. You'll go with Naoise so he can help you get sorted and settled. And so he can introduce you to the Tarespagian governor," Lorcan replies, just as Fallon and Cathal finally reappear.

"What's going on?" The swim has wiped away every last fleck of black powder on her face.

On her father's, too. Where her complexion is pink, Cathal's is waxen.

"We were discussing travel arrangements for your cousin." Lorcan nods to Cathal's thigh. "Did it help?"

"The serpents wouldn't approach." Fallon's shoulders are hunched, unlike Cathal's that are as rigid as a pillar.

"So, only the Cauldron can heal us?" Reid's grandmother murmurs, while Erwin says, "*If* it deems us worthy of being healed, Iona."

My insides feel cold, as though I've gulped down one of those cubes of hardened water the attendants use to keep the fruit from spoiling.

"What if it doesn't deem us worthy?" Iona murmurs. "Does that mean we've lost our immortality?"

The air grows quiet and stiff. Unbreathable.

"So we're just supposed to sit back and watch Dádhi transform into obsidian?" Fallon's cheeks glimmer with—*what had Priya called them again?*—*shil*.

"What if he saws off the infected limb?" ever-practical Kanti suggests.

"I'm not fucking sawing off any of my limbs!"

Kanti rolls her large pink eyes. "Don't bite my head off, Crow; it was merely a suggestion."

"And a sound one." Behati raises her chin. "One which you should take under consideration, Cathal."

"Does the Cauldron have thoughts on amputation, Behati?" Imogen asks.

"Not that I've foreseen, but once Priya calms, I'll ask her to confer with the Mahananda."

"I should never have gone through with it." Fallon wets her trembling lips. "I made everything worse." Her body flickers behind thickening smoke. I think it's hers until her mate materializes at her side and cloaks her white-knuckled fist with his hand.

"Like Priya, I trust the Mahananda had its reasons," Behati says, lumbering toward the pathway on Kanti's arm, cane clicking.

"Yes. To keep the Crows weak and under Shabbe's thumb," Lorcan murmurs just loud enough for us all to hear.

Behati's pink eyes tighten on him. "Before you motivate the Mahananda to lock itself up for another five centuries, Mórrgaht, take a second to turn over what it's done and its reasoning. Imagine if it had made your kind immune to obsidian. Your species would've become infallible. And even though you've proven yourself a noble leader, not all Crows are beyond reproach." Her rickety voice cuts across the moist air. "The same way not all Shabbins are saintly. Beneath our magic, we all remain animated and consumed by our desires."

"I'm immensely grateful that it's made my mate immune." Lorcan lifts Fallon's hand to his lips. "Truly, I am," he repeats, staring over Behati's shoulder, in the direction of the courtyard. "But I wish we'd been told of the consequences. I wish we could've discussed it with our people and given them the choice of whether to preserve our curse as it was or warp it." His eyes now rest on Cathal, who hasn't uttered a single word since his earlier outburst.

"What about my blood?" Fallon asks suddenly.

"It didn't penetrate your father's skin earlier," Behati reminds her.

"What if he ingests it?"

"I'm not drinking your blood, ínon." Cathal's face is tense and pale, as though the mere thought is turning his stomach.

"Perhaps it could help you."

Behati's lashes sweep low before rising anew. "A few drops may slow the progression."

The answer invigorates Fallon and makes her reach for the mollusk dwelling she wears around her neck. After pricking her finger, she drips blood into Lorcan's wine goblet and tenders it to her father. "Drink."

"No." A drop of seawater glides down the side of Cathal's face —or is it perspiration?

"Please, Dádhi."

"No." I suppose the male, who already trusts almost no one, isn't about to trust the seer who set all of this in motion.

"We'll test it on the others, Behach Éan." Lorcan kisses Fallon's temple before murmuring, "Come. Let's go home."

More *shils* brim over Fallon's lash line. Is she imagining the large male gone from this world forever? Though he and I have our differences, the possibility makes my fingers rise to my neck and trace my palpitating scar.

His love for his daughter and devotion to his king will make him worthy in the Mahananda's eyes...right?

Chapter 9
Zendaya

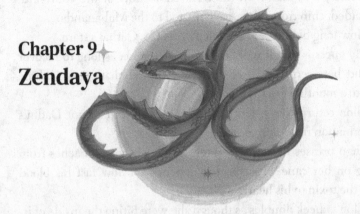

I hug Fallon tightly, my heart aching that she's leaving me behind.

"I'll come back any chance I get," she says, before proceeding to prove this to me with images that she pours into my mind.

I see us swimming together—in the Amkhuti. I see us lounging around my garden and sharing meals around the table we've just vacated. Although it should ease the ache behind my ribs, it doesn't, because I don't want to only see Fallon in Shabbe. I want to see her in Luce.

I suddenly remember how the waterrise plucked my body from the moat. How far could I swim before someone notices my absence and forces me back to the Vahti? Could I reach the ramparts? Could the waterrise there lift me over the isle's fortified walls without anyone being the wiser?

The prospect buoys my trodden spirits. Even if I don't reach the ramparts, I'd meet other serpents. What if I could converse with them? Maybe they could help me find my way out of Shabbe... What if they hate me and gore me with their tusks?

"As soon as the Mahananda speaks to Priya, I will send word to you," Behati says, hand wrapped snugly around the pommel of her cane.

Fallon's palms slip off my forehead as she twists toward her quiet father, who stands in the trellised shadow of the courtyard, arms folded, chin tipped low, gaze riveted to the Mahananda.

"How long before...?" Her voice drifts like Cathal's stare.

"My guess is that it will take the Mahananda as long to recover as it did between Zendaya's and your dip," Behati says. "Three weeks to a month. Perhaps longer."

Fallon returns her attention to the seer. "No, I meant Dádhi's transformation from skin to stone."

Behati presses herself straighter, as though her arm aches from leaning on her cane. "I suspect it depends on how fast his blood carries the toxin to his heart."

Fallon's cheek dimples as though she were biting the inside of it.

"I understand you feel duped by what's happened," the seer says, "but the Mahananda's intent wasn't to harm."

The corner of Fallon's eye twitches. "He'd have been unstoppable without his curse."

Behati inhales slowly, exhales even slower. "The Crows are our allies and emissaries, Fallon."

"Except you can travel freely now, so what need do you have for emissaries?"

"We still need allies. Even though our ramparts are strong, you'll find that the world's thirst to possess the Mahananda is stronger." Behati cants her head, sending the river of white and gold flowing over hunched shoulders. "You don't believe me, do you?"

"I believe everyone wants to own the source of all magic. What I have my reservations about is the second thing. Sending me in his stead."

"How can I dispel your doubts, child?"

"Blood-bind Lorcan and me."

I frown.

"I'd need to ask Priya, but—"

A resounding, "No," slips from Lorcan's tense lips.

Fallon swings her gaze his way. "Why not?"

"The Cauldron may interpret having access to your magic as greed and refuse to break my curse."

"It's not greed if I give it to you willingly, Lore."

He must refuse once more through their mind link, because Fallon works her pointy jaw from side to side.

"How about I swear to bind you and Lorcan in Shabbin matrimony once his curse is broken? Would that restore your faith in the Shabbins?" Behati suggests.

Fallon's lips part, and I think she's about to say, "Yes," but a sideways glance at her mate quiets her. "Lore says no bargains, but thank you, Behati." She gives the seer a smile that unravels some of the tension between the sorceresses and the Crows. "Let me go say goodbye to my father."

Goodbye? After everything that came to pass, I imagined Cathal might've changed his mind about staying. Then again, if he's going to turn to obsidian, it's probably best he remain in close proximity to the Mahananda.

Behati stares after Fallon. "Do not turn her against Priya, Mórrgaht. She is of her blood."

"So was Meriam. Sorry. So *is* Meriam."

I've heard that name susurrated parsimoniously around the Vahti. It's forever accompanied by a beat of weighted silence and a quick press of lips, as though it isn't a name but a curse. Sure enough, that's exactly what happens to Behati whose lips thin and pupils retract.

"A shame we cannot drain her," Kanti chirrups from right over my shoulder.

I jump, not having realized she'd crept so close, and shimmy away. When shadows churn beside me, I startle again, settling when they take the shape of my Crow guard.

"Geez"—Kanti blows air through lips slicked with a fresh coat of pink—"it wasn't a threat, Mórrgaht."

Did he speak into her mind? Fallon mentioned he could pour words inside the heads of non-Crows. Well, except into mine.

"I'm well aware of the reason the traitress must be kept alive," Kanti continues.

This is the most information I've gathered on this Meriam: she's a traitress of Priya's bloodline.

Cathal fists his fingers, then stretches them, eliciting cracks. "In case you ever forget the reason, I'll be glad to remind you."

"Now *that* sounded like a threat," Kanti whines. "But are we sure the spell endures? You know, since she doesn't have blood magic?"

Meriam's of Priya's bloodline but doesn't have magic? How's that possible?

"It's not a risk we're willing to take." Lorcan's timbre is so dark and cold it thrusts a chill up my spine.

"Priya gave you an oath that no harm would befall Meriam, Mórrgaht." Behati's reminder seems to ease the Sky King's tension. "Are you ready?" he asks Kanti.

She flourishes a hand toward two giant trunks filled with her belongings. "All packed." She leans over to kiss Behati's cheeks. "You'll have to send word of how tomorrow goes." Her eyes flick to me. "Daya's first swim with—"

"Kanti." Behati's eyes widen, a warning for her to hush.

The tempo of my heart peaks anew. My first swim with *what?* With *who?*

"Oops." Kanti shrugs and mentions how I surely have no clue what she's going on about. She's right, nevertheless, it irks me. "Off to conquer an enemy heart." She flings me a smile that glows as bright as the moon moths fluttering around the Vahti. "Farewell, scaly one."

I will not miss her.

"Shall we depart, Lore? I'm simply dying to set my eyes upon your kingdom!"

"Mórrgaht," he says. "Not only am I your elder, but for the foreseeable future, I'll also be your ruler."

Her white smile loses much of its vigor. "You'll still be my elder once I'm queen. Will you demand I call you by your title then,

Mórrgaht?" She rolls the 'R's in his name, snapping them out disdainfully.

Queen? Queen of what?

Lorcan's golden eyes flick toward Behati. "I wasn't aware Priya was planning on abdicating."

"Every good monarch needs to allow the next generation to rise at some point," Behati says.

"And Priya's thinking of naming Kanti as her successor?" One of Lorcan's eyes spasms as though the news unsettles him.

I imagine it's because it would mean the male Kanti's destined to seduce would rule alongside her. I might not understand every intricacy about reigning, but I do understand that having an enemy guarding the Mahananda cannot possibly please the Crow King. I suddenly worry that sending her to Luce is a terrible idea. Especially since she knows what obsidian can do to Crows.

"She knows Shabbe and its people better than any other blood relative of Priya's," Behati says, her gaze drifting over a wing of the palace I've yet to explore before settling over me.

Kanti raises her chin, pride wafting off her sun-kissed skin like fragranced oil.

Lorcan frowns. "Correct me if I'm wrong, Behati, but I thought the incumbent queen could only volunteer a successor. Isn't it ultimately the Cauldron's choice?"

"That's correct."

What a frightening, fascinating entity, this Mahananda…

After Kanti and the Crows depart, I mull over everything I learned tonight. Because of this, I forget to corner Cathal. As I reach my bedchamber door, I glance over my shoulder, but no large, brooding male stands in the courtyard. I lift my gaze to the sky—full of constellations but empty of birds. It's possible Cathal's injury drove him to retire in the guest wing. How empty it must feel tonight. I could ask Asha to lead me to him, but I suppose it can wait a day.

I try to sleep but my mind crackles with so many things that I toss the sheets off my legs and open the doors to my garden, and then I plod down the stone steps, through the lush palms and low brush toward the tall hedge that keeps my quarters secluded from the rest of the royal gardens.

I haven't lain all five fingers on the hedge before smoke billows before me, thickening into the shape of a male.

"Going somewhere, Príona?"

Chapter 10
Zendaya

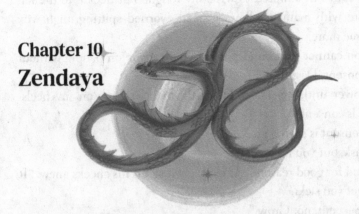

I'm about to tell Cathal I was going for a swim when an idea sparks. "I look for mollusk dwelling. I drop it here."

"A mollusk dwelling?"

"Seashell." I twist my finger in the air to mimic a spiral. "Like Fallon's."

"And you lost it in these hedges?"

"I not know where." I fleetingly eye the torn leather at his thigh, before moving my gaze to the ground beneath my sandaled feet.

I realize that I probably have one shot at tonguing his wound. Would one lick suffice to heal the extent of the damage or would it only seal the infection beneath his skin? What if I make it worse?

When I look back up, I find his stare fastened to my face. "Find shell, Crow?"

"Crow?"

"Shell. Focus." I snap my fingers in front of his face. "See it?" I point to the grainy mixture of pink sand and umber earth.

The second Cathal's gaze flicks off me, I drop into a crouch and wedge the tip of my tongue against his wound. The muscle in his thigh tautens before turning into air. When Cathal reappears at a distance from me, he growls something in Crow. I might not understand the words but his sentiment is clear—he's furious.

I stay low but tip my head high. Unlike Shabbin and Lucin

blood, Cathal's tastes like licking a dirty knife dragged through rotted fruit. I'm tempted to wipe my tongue but decide to drench the taste with many swallows instead, worried spitting might vex him some more.

"You cannot go around putting your tongue on people without their consent, Daya!"

I lower until my knees hit earth, then sit back on my heels. "What is consent?"

"Consent is saying *yes*."

"I ask, but you no want try."

"And for good reason!" At least, color stains his cheeks anew. "It could get you sick."

"I Serpent, not Crow."

"For all we know, obsidian is toxic to *all* shifters."

I frown, taking inventory of my body. "I feel same."

"I didn't feel sick at the beginning either. I *still* don't feel sick," he adds, but his insistence makes me wonder if he speaks the truth.

"I'll fetch something to rinse your mouth."

"Rinse?"

"In case my blood is toxic to you."

"I swallow already. I no die."

The ball in his throat sharpens. "Go back to your chambers and wait for me there." Smoke seeps from his skin, but he stays in his Two-legs' form long enough to add, "I mean it, Daya. In your room. Now."

I hate how his command makes me feel like I've done something wicked. When he morphs into his bird, I climb to my feet and tread back to my living area. My eyes sting, not with shame, but with annoyance. Now that I think of it, I shouldn't have tried to heal him. After all, if he turns to stone, then he wouldn't be able to shadow me everywhere.

I fling my terrace door shut and bolt it. Even though physically it cannot keep him out, perhaps it'll give him pause and make him leave.

Sure enough, he raps a fist against the glass. "Open up."

I cross my arms. "No."

His head rears back.

"I no want drink."

He vanishes.

I almost think he's gone, but of course, he's not.

"Take one sip, and I leave."

I cross my arms. "I say no. You still come inside. Against consent."

"It's not the same."

"You right. Not the same. I try heal you. You try drunk me."

"For Mórrígan's sake, I'm not trying to get you drunk," he grouses. "I'm trying to cleanse your stomach of any toxin."

"My stomach fine."

"It'll be finer once you take a swig of this."

"I no like this liquor."

He scoffs. "You *adore* this liquor."

"No," I lie.

"Then why do you drink a glass of it every night at supper?"

"Because polite."

"Oh, come the fuck on, Daya, each time you take a sip you fucking rattle."

I suck in a breath. Do I? I know I did it once, because it drew the queen's stare, but I try so hard to keep my Serpent reactions from bleeding over my Two-legged ones. "Take off pants and I take drink."

He chokes on air. "Wh-what?"

"You show wound; I drink."

"You can see it just fine through the rip."

"No. Rip too small. Take pants off."

"No," he grits out.

"Why?"

"Because..."

"Because *what*?"

He drags a hand through his hair. "Fine, don't drink."

"You prefer I die than show me legs?" I'm not certain why his reaction tilts the corners of my lips, but it does. "You shy, Dádhi Crow?"

His nostrils flare. "I told you. Don't call me that."

"Show me legs, and I stop call you Dádhi *and* Crow."

His eye twitches. "Actually, if I show you my legs, you will solemnly swear to never approach a waterrise again, Zendaya of Shabbe."

I frown.

"If you find our deal agreeable, then say, *If I approach a waterrise, Cathal Báeinach, I will owe you.*"

My retracted tusk sinks deeper into my forehead's furrows. "Why you suddenly happy?"

"Because I enjoy reaching agreements." His gaze remains steady on mine as he waits...and waits. "Fine. Don't take my deal. Fallon left me a vial of her blood that should last me until she returns."

"Blood *maybe* slow, but blood no heal."

"As long as it slows the infection long enough so that I am able to stand at her side the day of her nuptials—"

"Nuptials...?"

"Her wedding." At my frown, he explains, "Even though Lore and Fallon are mates, for her to be considered a queen by the humans and the Fae of our kingdom, they will exchange vows in front of all."

"When?"

"They were waiting until"—his tongue wets his lower lip—"until the curse was broken."

"But curse no broken."

"Yes. I'm aware. But Luce needs its king, and its king needs his queen."

"When marry?"

"Soon."

"In Luce?"

"Yes." Cathal must read my overwhelming desire to witness this exchange of vows because he attaches it to his deal. He tells me that he will let me see his legs and take me to Luce for the nuptials if I swear never to approach the waterrises.

Even though I realize that his reasons for me not to go close to them is to keep me from venturing out of the Vahti, I say, "Not just show. You will consent I lick."

His throat dips twice before he rasps, "All right." He scrapes his palm across his flushed jaw. "All right." He repeats the deal with my addendum.

This time, I speak the promise he's asked of me. When the words *I swear* slip off my tongue, I hiss and grab the front of my dress, dragging down the pink silk, because it feels like a bee's just stung me. Although there's no bump, a dot glows on the swell of my right breast.

I touch it, then scrape it with my nail. It doesn't go away. "What this?"

When Cathal doesn't answer, I look up at him, find his eyes shut so tight that the skin around them is rucked.

"Cathal, why dot?"

He cracks his knuckles, then his neck. "It's the mark of a bargain."

"Bargain?"

"When two people with magical blood strike a deal, the deal inscribes itself into our skin. The bargainer gets a dot atop their heart; the bargainee gets a band around their bicep. If you try to approach a waterrise now, the dot will burn to remind you of the promise you made me."

My hands drift to my sides. "You fool me?"

"No." His lids lift. "I assumed Fallon had explained how bargains worked to you." He jams a hand through his hair, then says some more things that I don't quite grasp since his words are running together, but I sense he's genuinely apologetic, so I sigh and tug on my dress's cord, settling it back on my shoulder to hide the glowing reminder that the world still has many secrets from me.

"Daya, do not strike bargains with anyone, except for me, all right?"

"I learn lesson. No say I *swear* again."

"I'm sorry. I—"

"It fine. You promise to take me to nuptials, so I see world soon." I smile. When he doesn't smile back, mine collapses. "You say swear, so you—"

"Yes, Príona. I will carry you outside these walls. Those are the terms of our agreement." He seems as thrilled to uphold his end of the bargain as Fallon was to have Kanti tag along with them to Luce. "I appreciate you trying to help, but everyone said serpent healing is useless."

"They not know since no serpent lick. Besides, I special Serpent."

His face softens a little. "You are."

"Pants, Cathal."

"Not tonight, Príona."

"But you say—"

"I said I'd let you. I didn't say when."

I bite down so hard the ivory in my mouth clicks. "Why wait?"

"Because you need to rest before tomorrow." Under his breath, he adds, "And so do I."

"Why?"

"Because tomorrow, you swim with the serpents."

Chapter 11
Zendaya

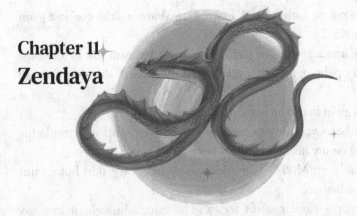

My blood rushes like the minnows swarming beneath the surface of the Amkhuti as the queen signals for Behati to transform one of the waterrises into a waterfall. The silent air suddenly fills with the crush of water and I startle.

"Shh, abi djhara." The queen strokes the base of my spine. "You'll be swimming with no more than *one* other serpent. And I'll be inside the water with you at all times."

A crow-shaped shadow swathes me. It steals the warmth of the afternoon sun but fills my veins with comfort. Before shifting, Cathal warned both the queen and me that he wouldn't hesitate to snatch me from the moat if the serpent gave any sign of aggression.

I pray to the Mahananda that my scaled companion will prove kind. And that he or she be small. My prayers must not land for the yellow body that flops from the Sahklare into the Amkhuti is colossal, with a tusk as long as my leg. It sinks out of sight before goring the surface as the animal ribbons toward us with great flexes of its body.

The queen smiles at the advancing serpent as though glad to see him. Or is it a her? How does one tell? Does something dangle from his abdomen like male Two-legs'? "Well, hello, Sun Warrior."

I imagine that's the creature's name. Does the queen have names for every serpent?

"Do not be intimidated, Daya. Sun Warrior's the gentlest giant in my realm."

My stomach feels as hard as the rock beneath my bare toes. I press my palm against it, eyes riveted to the tusk shearing through foam.

"I'll go in first. You dive in as soon as you feel ready."

I've been yearning to meet others, so why am I contemplating whirling on my heel and bolting back to my bedchamber?

"Ready, emMoti?" The queen sheds her flowy skirt but retains the fitted bodice.

I wear a similar outfit today. The queen brought it into my chambers when she came to wake me only to find me up and pacing. Though I'd flopped across my bed at some point between Cathal's departure and Priya's arrival, my mind had been so abuzz that I hadn't even attempted to sleep.

The queen takes my face between her hands, the callused tips of her fingers resting lightly on my skin. "Everything will be fine."

"What if Sun Warrior try eat me?" I ask.

The queen's eyes begin to glitter. I realize it's with *shils* when one spills over her lashes and trundles down her cheek. "How well you speak…" Her voice shimmies with the same emotion that wets her cheeks. "Who else has heard your voice?"

"My Crow sentry."

"Your Crow sentry?"

I roll my eyes skyward.

She sighs. "Though, admittedly, the male does guard you like a feral creature, he isn't your guard, Daya."

I frown. "You not choose he?"

"No. The only people I've appointed to watch over you are Asha and Abrax."

"Then why he always with me?"

The queen releases my face and turns toward the Amkhuti.

"How about that swim? Look how eager Sun Warrior is to meet you."

Lid-to-lid black orbs roll over me. Though I've caught glimpses of myself in the air bubbles trapped beneath the Amkhuti's stone shelves, until now, I hadn't realized just how beastlike I truly am. Save for my coloring, do I resemble this creature in every way? Is my tusk as massive, my eyes as bulbous, my nostrils that slitted? Do my scales shine like his? Is my dorsal fin as sheer and ruffled? I cannot decide if I find the serpent hideous or beautiful.

He whips the surface with his tail, plucking me out of my contemplation. Do I ever flick my tail? Besides when I swim? Does it mean something?

I'm about to ask the queen when I catch her striping her neck with blood in order to breathe underwater. And then she's diving, hands extended in front of her head, spine arced. I rush to the edge, almost toppling right over. I'm aware the queen's immortal, but hitting the water from so high up always stings my feet. Won't it fracture her fingers or fissure her skull?

She slides in like a needle through silk and sinks out of sight.

I wait for the serpent to dive after her, but he waits. And waits. When the queen still hasn't surfaced, I jump. The instant my body hits water, I shift. And then I hunt the clear depths for her white hair. Although I sense the other serpent swimming parallel to me, I don't pay him any mind, wholly centered on Shabbe's ruler. I find her kneeling on the pale sand, one arm outstretched, fingers waving like the green sea fan beside her. I nuzzle her forehead on the hunt for an injury. When I don't scent broken flesh, my pulse begins to quiet.

Something hits my body. Hard.

I recoil, whirling my face toward the yellow serpent, whose nostrils flare. And not in a *pleasure to make your acquaintance* way but in a *back up* way. The queen flutters her feet and rises between us. She clutches Sun Warrior's head. I assume it's to prevent him from goring me with his tusk until his eyes glaze and I realize she's pouring pictures into his mind. As I watch them, I suddenly think of all the words lodged inside my head, the ones I assumed were Serpent because they didn't belong to any other tongues. How do I shape them underwater?

I part my lips and try to push some out, but all that does is send a rush of brine down my throat. How do serpents communicate? Do they press their heads against one another? Why didn't I think to ask the queen before diving in?

A strident bleating jerks my body and tautens the already tight coils of my body. It takes Sun Warrior reproducing the sound a second time for me to realize it came from him. Why is he... screeching?

The queen smiles at me expectantly. Is she waiting for me to replicate the sound? I roll my lips a few times before managing a weak wheeze that creates more bubbles than sound. Priya claps while the serpent cants his big head, clearly not impressed by my communication skills.

Suddenly a terrible smell permeates the water. Sun Warrior swivels his head, then hissing, backs away in a haze of foam. Once the bubbles clear, I spot the intruder.

The queen's gaze cuts to my Crow sentry. *Not my sentry*, I remind myself.

Although she cannot use words beneath the water, her snappy hand gesture conveys her irritation. She points to the surface. Cathal follows her command, but I soon realize, it's only to take a breath. The second he's filled his lungs, he kicks back down toward us.

Sun Warrior's stopped retreating and dangles like a vine between sky and sand. His slitted nostrils flaring like mine. This must've been why the other serpents wouldn't approach last night... because the water somehow amplifies the noxious scent.

Although my stomach clenches, I edge closer to Cathal, to the black ooze that lifts from the flap in the leather. The odor, like wilted blooms dusted in cold ash, grows so pungent, so sour, that my head jerks, and I sink.

I'm suddenly furious with myself for retreating. I'm stronger than this. Stronger than a regular serpent. I dart back up, shooting straight for the injured Crow, but I'm bounced off course by a hard jab to the abdomen. I blink, trying to grasp what's happened when I feel something lace snugly around my body and yank.

Something covered in yellow scales.

Sun Warrior releases another bleat, this one so shrill it vibrates the water and stabs my eardrums, as he drags me away from Crow and Queen.

Chapter 12
Zendaya

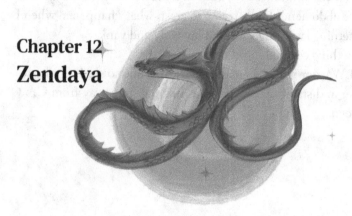

S un Warrior swims so fast that the ocean froths and whitens. By the time I've gotten over my surprise at being violently bundled and carted away, the queen and Cathal are mere dots bobbing on the surface.

I try to wriggle out of Sun Warrior's grasp, but his body is far more muscled than mine. I hiss. He doesn't let go. I try to growl my discontent, but none of the sounds scrolling through my head spool out. Whatever language I think in mustn't be Serpent speech since I cannot, for the life of me, craft intelligible sound in this form.

I resort to nipping at his scales with my teeth. Although stunted, they're sharp and more numerous in this form than when I am Two-legs. Sun Warrior freezes, his spherical eyes rolling over the blood puffing off his scales like grains of burnt sand. As he swipes his forked, black tongue against my bitemark, healing the puncture wounds instantly, he sends me a scathing look.

I narrow my gaze right back on him, demanding, without words, what came over him. The only answer I get in response is a low hiss. As brusquely as he wrapped himself around me, he releases me, pitching me far and deep.

I watch him swim away before heading toward the queen and Cathal. I'm tempted to lash the Crow's thigh with my tongue, but remember our talk about consent. I will wait for him to be ready.

Besides, considering how my stomach lurches as I drift nearer, I suspect I'll need to be in my other form, the one where my senses aren't as heightened.

Right before I crest the surface, I hear Priya mutter, "My child's no longer your mate, Cathal."

The word *mate* stills both my thoughts and ascent. Cathal has a mate, or rather, *had* one, and she is Priya's child? Who is her child, and why is she no longer Cathal's mate? I linger just beneath their fluttering feet in the hopes I'll hear more on the subject, but the next thing out of the queen's mouth is a threat to banish the Crow from Shabbe if he ever intercedes with my lessons again.

I will my body to shift, and it does, right before I crest the surface. I can't even rejoice that I'm getting better at swapping forms, too agitated am I over the animosity that ripples around me.

When my head pops out, my caregivers both turn. Where Cathal doesn't even attempt to mask his anger, Priya curls her lips into a smile that is clearly just for show, for it hides all her teeth.

"Already done?" she asks.

I nod.

"How was it? Were you able to communicate?"

I shake my head.

"Maybe next time."

I doubt it since he speaks in resonances instead of syllables.

"Would you like me to remove him from the Amkhuti or would you like for him to stay so you can meet up later?"

Cathal mutters something in Crow that is as incomprehensible to me as Serpent bleating. The queen slices her gaze toward him, comprehending him just fine.

"Cathal, understand birds that no shift?" My question redirects the queen's stare.

"No. I do not. Lore can transfer images into their minds through thought, but we possess no common tongue, so why Priya imagines you'll share one with an animal baffles me."

"I was hoping Daya would find comfort in her fellow creature's company."

"Shifters are her fellow creatures," he growls. "Not animals."

"You may share the power to shift forms, but Daya isn't one of you."

"How Crow made?" I suddenly ask.

"They mate the same way humans do," Priya huffs. "In bare flesh."

I frown.

"She asked how they were *made*, Sumaca," Cathal grumbles, "not how they fucked."

The queen blinks, but then recovers and says, "Technically, it's one and the same, is it not? The original Crows were created by the Mahananda, but new Crows can only be made through coupling."

The slant of my brows deepens.

Cathal's chin dips but his lips stay above the waterline. "I take it you haven't discussed the birds and the bees yet."

Birds couple with bees? *Shifter*-sized birds?

The queen takes a deep breath. "Let's get out of the water. We'll talk in my chambers when we're dry." When she reaches the stone wall, instead of grabbing ahold of my ladder, she draws a sigil that slants the rock and makes it reshape itself. "Come before my staircase washes away, emMoti."

I glance at Cathal, wondering whether he will attend this talk I am to have with the queen. Before I can ask, he shifts into his Crow and takes to the sky, then hovers, shadowing my body until I'm back on dry land. Why does he act like my guard when he isn't?

I end up asking the queen after I've changed into dry clothing and joined her in her wing of the palace.

"Because he's stubborn and stuck in a past that no longer exists." Her answer does nothing to quell my confusion.

I take her wrists and raise her palms to my forehead. "Explain with picture."

The servants in attendance inhale sharply and gawk, evidently surprised I can talk.

The queen's palms don't settle. They hover. "That story will be for another day. What I will show you today is how babes are made."

"Babes?"

"New Crows. And new humans."

When her fingers land, I get flashes of a male and a female rubbing the front of their bodies together, followed by the image of the female's body rounding and reshaping itself like the cliff earlier. The last image that illuminates my lids is a miniature Two-legs screeching in the crook of the female's arms.

As the queen lowers her hands, she says, "Coupling is like growing flowers, Daya. The male plants his seed inside the female's soil, and nine moons later, a small version of them sprouts from the female's body."

"What job have bees?"

A vertical groove forms above her nose. "Bees? They pollenate and make honey."

"Honey is babe?"

The groove deepens. "I'm sorry but I'm not sure I follow."

"Cathal speak birds and bees."

The queen stares at me stunned, but then she breaks out into great peals of laughter. "Birds and bees is an expression, emMoti."

"*Expression?*"

"An expression is an idiomatic..." She stops talking. "Simply put, it's a phrase used by way of another."

Forget confused...I'm lost.

"For example, in Shabbe, we'll say *the serpent is in your river* when we want to convey that it's someone else's turn, or *as thick as serpents*, which means to be very close and share many secrets."

I doubt I will ever be able to use that one.

"*Straddle the ward* is another. It means to avoid taking sides. Though truth be told, that expression irks many because Shabbe was imprisoned for five hundred years. Best not to use it, actually."

"Imprisoned?"

"One of our people betrayed us."

"Meriam?"

Her pink stare widens. "Where did you hear that name?"

"Kanti," I say, even though I didn't hear it from her. At least, not at first.

"That girl..."

"Meriam family?" I point to the queen.

"No." Her response is so abrupt that it makes me wonder if I misheard Lorcan last night. "Let's not talk of her anymore. It spoils my mood. What other questions do you have for me?"

"How serpent make babies, Taytah?"

She blinks at me, then murmurs, "*Taytah.*" She presses her palm against her chest. "I don't think you understand what it means to me to hear you call me that."

"Why? It's name of mother of mother, no?"

Her long lashes sweep low. "It is."

I point to me. "Mahananda is mother of me." I point to her. "You mother of it."

A beat of hesitation echoes before she says, "Yes." She folds her legs beneath her on the cushion. "So serpent babies... The male's reproductive organ emerges from a hollow at the base of his abdomen and penetrates the hollow at the base of the female's abdomen."

"Hollow?"

"A hole."

I look down at myself even though I'm not in scales. "Do I have *hollow*?"

"I must admit, I didn't look, Daya. I imagine you do, though."

I make a note to inspect myself during my next shift.

"However, I imagine you will couple in your human form like Crows?"

"Human?"

She nods to my body.

Ah...so this is what this two-legged form is called—*human.*

"I could be wrong since you're the same size as real serpents, whereas Crows are so much larger than the birds the Mahananda

76

shaped them after. It's possible you *could* reproduce with a serpent."

I suddenly picture Sun Warrior trying to rub his body against mine. I don't like the image. I want to pluck it from my mind and pitch it beyond Shabbe's fortified walls.

"Since we're on the subject, you failed to answer my question earlier. What do you want me to do with Sun Warrior? Should I let him stay in the Amkhuti or send him back into the Sahklare?"

I roll the seafoam silk of my dress between my fingers. "He no like me."

The queen props her elbow on the low cushion at her back. "That's not true, emMoti. He didn't appreciate Cathal's intrusion, but that's because serpents are sensitive beings who can feel when someone dislikes them, and that Crow likes neither humans nor animals. The only people he tolerates are his fellow Crows."

Does that mean he dislikes me? "Taytah, who is child?"

One of her servants slips a cup of date wine inside her hand. "Anyone below the age of puberty."

Again, she's lost me. Though I want to know about this puberty, I decide to rephrase my question so as not to veer off course. I point to her stomach. "*You* child."

She coughs out her swallow of wine, which dribbles down her chin. Though the attendant who handed her the cup produces a piece of cloth from his pocket, Priya uses the back of her hand to wipe her face. "*My* child?"

I nod.

She stares at the shivering fronds swaying against her tall, arched windows. "My child is dead."

"But—" I tilt my head. "But Shabbin live always, no?"

"No. We're not immortal. We're merely harder to kill than others."

How incredibly heartbreaking. No wonder Cathal's mood is pitiful. "Your child was Crow?"

The queen purses her lips. "No."

So Cathal Báeinach once loved a being who wasn't a Crow... I suddenly wonder if that's the reason he stays in Shabbe. Because this land reminds him of her. Though that's even more tragic.

I may still not understand why he's so determined to guard me, but at least, now I understand why he's forever discontent. My hands have left my skirt to settle on my neck, on the strip of fabric that buttons around it and holds the rest of my dress up thanks to thin chains made of pearls and cyan gems.

I knead the skin that my aching heart makes flutter. "That so sad, Taytah."

She shrugs. "Such is life."

Behati bustles in then and settles on another cushion on the queen's floor. We discuss my swim—*again*—then Sun Warrior's presence in the Amkhuti—*again*.

I wrinkle my nose when Behati says it would be good for me to keep him close so he can teach me the way of serpents. "I no want Sun Warrior as mate," I say, sitting up.

Behati's pink eyes go as wide as the supper plates that servants are setting on the table.

"Yes. Zendaya speaks," Priya muses.

Behati pales, becoming almost as insipid as the queen's locks. "Since when?"

"I only heard her today, but perhaps my granddaughter's spoken before?"

"I no want baby with Sun Warrior." It seems more important to drive this point in than to explain when and to whom I first spoke.

The queen's lips curve gently. "You do not have to couple with any being you do not desire. One's partner needs to be one's choice."

I'm greatly reassured.

"May I speak with you in private, Priya?" Behati asks.

"Once I'm done speaking with Zendaya."

Though I'm grateful Priya chooses me over her advisor, I get to my feet. I've taken up enough of her time. Besides, she's given me much to think about.

After bending my forehead to receive her kiss, I depart for my rooms, Asha's sandals slapping the stone right beside me.

"I cannot believe I had to learn you could speak at the same time as the queen's entourage." With a pout, Asha adds, "I thought I was special."

"You special. Plus, you know before Abrax."

"That is true. Oh, how I'll rub it in his face." Her grin is so wide, it glows brighter than the moon moth that's landed on her shoulder.

"Rub what in face?" At her frown, I deduce it must be an expression. "What mean?"

"Ah. It means to tell him—*repeatedly*—that I knew it before he did."

"He no like that."

"Nope. He will certainly not like that."

Her delight lures a smile to my lips. "You a little wicked."

"*Very* wicked, but wicked *nice*. Unless someone tries to hurt you. Then you can bet your royal ass I will be wicked mean."

Bet my royal ass? My ass is royal? But more importantly...or rather, as importantly, people gamble their backsides? At what? Those card and pawn games so many play?

I graze the back of her hand. "Thank you, Asha, for being friend to me."

Her lower lip overtakes her upper lip and then she's blinking a little hurriedly.

"Why *shileh*?"

"I'm getting tearful because I'm touched."

Tearful. Huh. So Serpents do have a word for wet eyes since my mind translated the word.

I roll the word around my tongue. *Tearful.* Fearful means *full of fear*. Meaningful means *full of meaning*. Does tearful mean *full of tears*? Could *shil*'s translation be tears?

"Daya," she says as I pass the door one of the guards has propped open for me, "if you feel like going for a swim, can you please come get me or Abrax? We'd prefer to avoid another lecture from Cathal."

"He no harm you, right?"

"Sticks and stones, Rajka."

"He hit you!" Gone is my good humor.

She blinks, then shakes her head, sending her thick black braid swinging like a chain. "No. It's an expression. *Sticks and stone may break my bones, but words will never hurt me.*"

The breath I blow out the corner of my mouth sounds like a small growl. I really hate expressions. Why must people replace adequate words with inadequate ones?

She must think I'm not reassured, because she adds, "Big Bird didn't hurt me. Promise."

"All right."

"But I appreciate that you'd care. Now off to bed. Your undereye circles have undereye circles."

I trace my lash line as I finally enter my bedchamber, which flickers with candlelight, then raise my gaze to the silver squares tiling the ceiling to check my appearance. All I see is starlight, the intended effect of the domed mirrors—or so explained Asha. It had been Queen Mara's idea. After gluing them to the ceiling over her bed, she'd had them added everywhere in the Vahti.

Since I'm looking up, and the mirrors reflect only flames, I fail to spot that there's a person in my path and bump right into them.

Cathal's arm snaps up and out, snaring my waist to keep me from stumbling backwards. "Had a pleasant conversation, Príona?"

Chapter 13
Zendaya

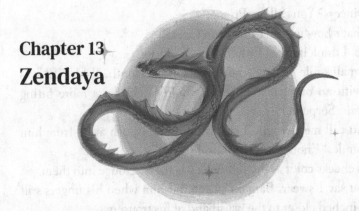

My palms remain flush with the leather gloving Cathal's chest. I wonder if he'll go back to wearing armor now that obsidian can still harm him. Then again, he's already harmed. "Why here, Cathal?"

"I was waiting for you."

"Why?"

"To check how you were faring."

My gaze locks on his thigh. "How you faring?"

"You didn't answer my question."

"I not hurt."

"I was talking emotionally, not physically, Daya. How do you feel after having met another serpent?"

I shrug. "I feel *not* serpent."

His jaw tightens, flexes, like the line of his shoulders. Like all the lines on his body. Unlike serpents that are all curves, the Crow before me is all edges. "So you're not champing at the bit to rendezvous with Mister Yellow again?"

I have no clue what *champing at the bit* means. What I do have a clue about is who Mister Yellow could be. "No. I no want see Mister Yellow." My lips twitch at the name Cathal gives Sun Warrior. "Call me Mister Pink now?"

He snorts. "No *Miss* Pink in your future. I'll stick to calling you Princess."

"Princess? You call me Príona."

"That's how we say Princess in Crow."

"Ah. I think it mean Fish."

A small smile titillates the corners of his mouth. "Fish? If I was going with an original moniker, I would've chosen a more fitting one: *Sífair*. Serpent."

"You call me Serpent, I call you Crow." I push away from him with a smile. "Enough chat. Take off pants."

His cheeks color as though Asha has rubbed rouge into them.

"You say I swear. Bargain," I remind him when his fingers still haven't inched closer to the waistband of his trousers.

"You must be exhausted from your swim."

"I no tired." I add a headshake in case he isn't convinced.

"Daya, I've—I don't—" He grimaces, then mutters words I don't understand. I think he must be in pain because his hands tremble as they finally grip the cord that secures his trousers over his hips and fusses with the knot.

As he upholds his end of the bargain, I pray to my mother, the Mahananda, that I will be able to help, because I'd like to have a useful power.

Cathal's throat jostles as he finally pushes down his pants. The crimson flush on his face doesn't extend to his thighs, which are moon-white beneath the sprinkling of black hair. Manifestly, the Crows do not wax. Is that why he didn't want to show me his legs?

In case that was his concern, I say, "I no have wax in room, Cathal, so no need afraid."

He blinks. "Wax?"

I gesture to his legs, then drag my long skirt up to display my hairless shins. "You scared wax, no?"

His eyes grow infinitesimally larger.

I tilt my head. "Reason you red. You scared...no?"

His mouth curves with a full-blown smile that transforms into a rough, marvelous boom. Although his laughter has neither color nor temperature, it feels golden and warm like sunshine dripping through water...like a drizzle of syrup.

He rubs at his mouth as though to force his lips to flatten. "I do not fear an impromptu waxing session, Príona."

"Then what you fear?"

"I...I..." He sighs. "I just...I'm not used to pulling my pants down in front of people."

"I am not people, Cathal."

He swallows, and his lashes sweep low.

"I am healer." I bite my lip. Let it go. "Maybe."

The extra limb between his legs bounces as I kneel, and then it juts out and to the side as though demanding I pay it some attention, so I do. And my heart misses a beat because... "Did poison dagger go inside there?"

"What?" he croaks.

"There." I skim my finger over the puffed, purple tip. "Little leg is swollen." My fingertip comes back wet with something transparent and sticky. "And ooze." I carry my finger to my nose, then dart my tongue over the spot of wetness. It does not taste bad like his blood. It tastes like the ocean.

He asks Mórrígan for strength. Is the pain so great that he has trouble standing?

"If you weak, you need sit or you fall."

"I do not feel weak." He chafes the growth on his jaw. "And to set your mind at ease, I did not stab myself in the cock."

"*Cock?*"

He grumbles in Crow, then addresses Mórrígan once more. "That is the word for my 'little leg.' Didn't Priya teach you about this yet?"

"Cock," I repeat, moving my head back a little because his cock is growing very long, like my horn. Is he about to shift into his other form? I sweep my gaze over his legs, but neither smoke nor feathers obscure his skin. "Why get bigger?"

"Because it's sensitive," he mumbles.

"So it swell? Like when I bump head?"

"When did you bump your head?"

"No important this, Cathal. What important is—"

One of his hand settles on the back of my head, then combs through the thick mass of pink. His touch sends a shiver down my spine...many shivers. Although I rattle, it's Cathal's breathing that seems to intensify. Because his fingers are distracting, I seize his wrist and carry it away from my head.

"It gone. It was small lump." I jut my chin toward his cock. "*You* have big lump."

"It's not a—I didn't run into anything." The muscles along his stomach clench. "I can't believe I'm about to offer to have this conversation with you." He purses his lips, which deepens the hollows beneath his cheekbones. "It's probably retribution for being a block of stone when Fallon needed to learn about how bodies worked."

I sit back on my heels, head tilted sideways.

"I need a drink. Or ten." He pulls his pants back up and then walks toward the tufted chair, his strides so long and rushed they make every flame on the way shiver.

I stand and follow at a slower pace, the bare soles of my feet whispering over the heated stone. "After you drink and talk, I heal. We bargain."

I take a seat on the sofa cushions across from him and tuck my legs underneath me. The date wine he brought to my chambers last night is already tipped to his lips. The ball in his throat bobs many times before he lowers the bottle and plants his elbows on his wide knees. "All right." He rolls the slender glass neck between his palms. "So..."

"So?"

"So males have cocks, and females do not."

"I know."

"The same way females have breasts and males do not."

"Phoebus has little beads on breasts too."

Cathal coughs, then rakes his throat. Is it possible he swallowed an insect? "Those are called nipples."

I touch mine, and their points sharpen. "Why males flat under *nipples?*"

"Because it's the females who store the milk for babes."

I glance down at my breasts. "I have milk in body?"

"Not yet. But if you ever grow a babe, then yes, chances are you will produce milk."

"Sybille grow babe. Mattia plant seed inside."

His gaze flips off the neck of the bottle. "You know about the male seed?"

I nod enthusiastically. "Taytah show me that female and male rub front together until seed come out."

Even though a table rests between us, I see his pupils dilating, the black chewing through the brown but not spilling over. "Did she show you exactly where the seed came from?"

"From male."

"I meant, from—*focá.*" One of his hands slicks back his hair while the other tilts the bottle to his mouth for another drink. Once he's swallowed and swiped his tongue over his lips a few times, he says, "What oozed from my cock"—he grimaces, his gaze going to the forever-filled water carafe—"that is a male's seed. That is what we plant inside a female's womb to grow a babe." Another pass of his fingers through his hair. Another gulp of wine.

"I lick it from finger."

"I know." His lids slam shut. "I'm so sorry. I should've—I should've explained things before. I thought...I assumed—"

My pulse picks up speed. "I grow babe now?"

He hangs his head low, then rubs his nape as though it aches. "No. You only grow a babe if the seed enters another cavity in your body."

"Which cavity?"

"A hole located between your legs."

I untuck my legs from beneath me and grip my dress's hem to lift it when Cathal lets out a strangled, "Please, Daya, this is hard enough as it is. Don't—" He swallows. "Please inspect your body after I'm gone, all right?" His eyes are bright, but not with mirth; they're bright with pain.

I wonder why, but decide not to ask. He's already answered so many of my questions. "Thank you for talk."

He goes back to rolling the bottle. "You're welcome."

I stand and go toward him. "I promise I no touch cock this time."

When I reach him, he cranes his neck and stares at me, his expression a mixture of so many emotions that I cannot pinpoint one in particular.

"I look only at wound." I unscrew the bottle from his fingers and set it down beside the water carafe. "Pants."

Reluctantly, he stands, towering over me, and pushes his trousers back down. His cock has shrunk again, but the second I kneel, it starts to expand. I assume it's because he's cold since my *nipples* grow stiff when the air is brisk. I become convinced that's the reason when he shells it with his fingers and pins it to his abdomen.

I study the wound. It's deep and black, as though the stone left a layer of dust that's climbing into his veins. "Pain?"

He swallows.

"Cathal?"

He shakes his head.

"You consent I touch leg?"

The tendons in his neck strain. "Yes."

I lightly grip the outer edge of his thigh, making sure not to touch the infected skin. The muscle is so hard and jagged, it feels like a ledge. As I bring my head closer, my stomach spasms because the smell... It is terrible.

You are better than those serpents, Daya. You can do this.

I curl my tongue and jam it into the oozing wound. The dreadful savor makes my throat clench with the need to retch, but I sense doing so will make Cathal cancel our bargain, so I pool more saliva onto my tongue and into the wound.

"*Focá.*" His thigh trembles like the surface of the Amkhuti after I dive into it.

I lift my head and look up into his face. "What?"

"Burns."

I stare at the wound, at the trickle of deep crimson that oozes down his pale skin and mattes the black hair. Did my saliva make him bleed? I swipe it with my fingertips and rub. The texture is grainy, as though sand has mixed with his blood.

"I make ooze more."

"Yes, but I think... Do it again, Daya."

What is it he thinks? That it's helping?

I spear my tongue back inside the narrow crevasse. This time, I cannot swallow. I reach for the small bowl beside the fruit basket, the one filled with water and a citrus wedge. I spit. Cathal's grainy blood stains the water black.

His mouth twists. Before he can change his mind, I penetrate the wound with my tongue again, and...is it me or has it become shallower? I spit, lick, fill the gap with my tongue, then wipe the trickle of spit and blood. My heart begins to beat faster when I note that the web surrounding his wound has receded. I think it's working but don't dare share my impression with Cathal, for it would be cruel to give him hope if I'm wrong.

I lick and spit until my tongue barely pokes past the surface of his skin and his blood becomes silky and sweet. The muscle in his thigh remains hard, but the tremors have quieted. I flatten my tongue over his skin once more, heart lancing in my jaw when the puckered flesh smooths like the buffed sunstone beneath my knees.

Could I have managed to break the Crows' new curse?

Chapter 14
Zendaya

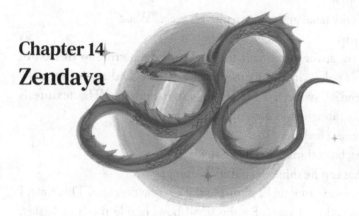

I seize the hem of my dress and ball it to wipe down Cathal's leg. The wound has sealed, and the only hints of black on his thigh are the dark hairs peppering it. "How feel, Cathal?"

When he remains quiet, I crane my head to look up at him. His eyes are incandescent in the candlelit darkness, shinier than the wax stalks burning down to stumps, and glitterier than the ceiling with its myriad of mirrors.

"Cathal, how you—"

The hand not warming his cock cups my jaw. "How do *you* feel?" He thumbs my chin, probably to clear it of any lingering unsightly smudge.

"I not one sick; you—"

He releases himself and hikes up his pants, the leather whispering over his healed skin, then drops into a crouch in front of me, his fingers still cocooning my face. "Does your head feel light? Do your lips tingle?"

My lips buzz. My head, too. And my stomach churns.

"No," I lie. When the skin around my tusk begins to tingle, I realize that my body is about to betray me. "I need swim." The room spins. My forehead now burns. The Serpent within is overpowering my Human. "Cathal—"

Arms scoop me up and carry me to my garden, then lay me

gently down on the gritty soil. And then I'm floating. The brisk air makes my long hair flog my overheated cheeks. Is it the obsidian that's clouding the careful control I have over my body, or is it Crow blood?

The instant liquid gloves my fiery skin, the pressure in my veins releases and my tusk shoots out. The transformation is so fierce and fast that my vision goes black and I sink, hitting the sandy bottom of the Amkhuti with a heavy thump.

The chill of the deep coats my scales and caresses my fins. It strokes the sensitive flesh around my tusk and sweeps down the length of my nose. Murmured words land against my buzzing ears like whispered promises spoken in the middle of a deafening storm.

I try to make sense of them, but they echo and skip without penetrating, echo and skip, echo and...

"EmMoti?" A callused hand smooths across my cheek. "Wake up." It must be the queen, since she's the only person who calls me that. Her voice thins before growing thick and raucous with a growl that includes Cathal's name.

She must speak in Crow, because I cannot grasp what she says to him or about him. Is he even still there?

There...

Where am I?

Her palms sweep faster down my cheeks, her desire for me to awaken, urgent. "Wake up, emMoti. Wake up."

I try, but my lids are heavy.

Too heavy.

I INHALE. GAG. MY THROAT CLOSES AROUND A SWALLOW OF liquid salt. I shove up onto my forearms so fast that my fingers sink into wet sand. I cough, desperate to ease the burn.

A hand grips my hair and spins it into a rope. "Deep breath, Príona."

I inhale through my nose, then clear my throat and spit out a glob that foams against the damp, pink sand. There are no beaches in the Vahti, which means...which means I must've swam out of Shabbe.

I crane my neck. Before me looms a shimmering sunstone wall. It reaches so high it melts into the cloudless blue. Are those the ramparts? Did Cathal carry me out of—

Why is there another wall behind us?

I push into sitting, my gaze skipping over the curved beach, surrounded by curved walls.

"Priya drained the Amkhuti because she didn't trust me to fly you out of it." Shadows squirm across the jagged edges of Cathal's face, not all of them created by the white sheet snapping over us.

I trail the sheet to four wooden posts planted inside the sand, then squint because...where are all the fish? Where is Sun Warrior?

Cathal must read my anguish because he says something about the Akwale herding the animals into the Sahklare.

The queen drained the moat. What an extreme measure to reach me.

"You've been asleep for days, Daya," Cathal says, releasing my hair but remaining in a low crouch.

I turn toward him, taking in his purple-rimmed eyes. "Days?"

He nods, sliding his tongue over his lips that are pale with salt and peeling skin. I reach up and touch them. Cathal stiffens but doesn't move. Though his lips aren't ample like mine, they feel gritty and taut.

"Need water." My voice is no more than a thin croak.

"I've got some right here." He reaches around him for a jug and offers it to me.

Though I need some, too, I push the jug toward him. "You."

His lashes flutter.

"Drink," I command.

He does, but his sip is reluctant, as though I were forcing him to ingest something rank. Which reminds me... I drop my attention to his leather-clad thigh. The trousers are either new or have been hemmed seeing that there's no more tear in them.

"How infection?"

He presses the jug into my hands, but keeps his palm on the bottom of it. "Small sips," he instructs, right before murmuring, "Gone." And then, because I sit there in shock, he lifts the jug and proceeds to feed me the sweet water.

My throat burns, and I cough.

"Sips, Príona."

My next mouthful is tiny.

He splashes water into his palms, then rubs it across my brow, but my skin is caked in so much sand that his attempt at cleaning it is surely pointless. Still, I appreciate his little act of kindness.

"Zendaya!" the queen's voice makes me twist. She traipses down stairs of her blood's making, Behati on her arm. Once she reaches the bottom and Behati is stable on her cane, the queen lets go of the seer and streaks toward me.

My Crow's jaw flexes. "I told them heartbreak was keeping you from shifting back." At my frown, he adds, "Fallon's departure. I didn't want to tell them that you broke our new curse because... because, Mórrígan forgive me, but I'm not entirely certain whether I trust they didn't inflict it upon us in the first place."

I stare at him.

"I won't keep you from telling them, but possibly...wait? I'd like us to discuss this with Lore and Fallon. Would you mind waiting?"

I shake my head.

He mouths a silent *thank you* as he straightens, the top of his head brushing against the canopy.

The lilac silk gloving the queen's body coils around her legs like windblown petals. "I want you to promise me to never again stay in scales for so long. I thought...I thought you'd ventured up one of the waterrises to follow Fallon until Cathal explained you were moping down here."

I push my sandy ropes of hair over my shoulder, working hard on keeping my gaze from straying to the Crow, who's backed up to allow the Shabbin Queen through.

"I understand your heart hurts that Fallon's left, but she said she'd return soon, emMoti."

Cathal crosses his arms. "I believe a trip to Luce would settle her, Sumaca."

Without taking her eyes off mine, she says, "No."

A startled breath leaps out of me, eliciting a renewed bout of coughing. She didn't even pause to consider the suggestion.

"She isn't ready," Priya says.

"I'll keep her safe, if that's what concerns you." Cathal's posture is as rigid as the post next to which he stands.

"She's not yours to keep safe," the queen growls, her pink gaze roving over his thigh. "For Mahananda's sake, Cathal, she's not yours anymore!"

Anymore? Did I once belong to the Crow? And if so, in what way, since he insisted, a great many times, that I wasn't his daughter? Most importantly, though, why does no one believe I can keep myself safe? How wicked is the world beyond the Amkhuti?

I push myself to stand, done being kept down by all of them. "*I* keep *me* safe."

Cathal tilts his chin a little higher, as though proud how my impudent remark widens the women's stares.

"Fallon nuptials." I slip a finger under the ocean-hardened silk around my neck and dust off the sand digging into my skin. "I go."

"Fallon's nuptials? How did you hear of them? Let me guess..." Considering she looks straight at Cathal, Priya must have no trouble guessing. "Abi djhara, the vows Fallon will speak in front of the Lucins are only for show."

I'm not certain what she means by that, but I remain steadfast. "I go, Taytah. Cathal take me." I'm about to add that it's part of our bargain, but decide not to divulge this in case it cancels the bargain.

The queen draws her gaze down his thigh. "Not in his state."

"Thanks to Fallon's blood, my state has improved. I thank you for your concern, though." I frown because the queen didn't sound concerned.

Lips pinched so hard their corners tremble, she extends her hand to help me up. "If anyone takes Daya to the lands where serpents are still slaughtered, it will be me."

Though I still hold her hand, I teeter from how fast I spin my head toward Cathal.

"Did your Crow *companion* fail to mention how serpents are treated outside of Shabbe, Zendaya?" Behati sounds almost smug about her question.

Before I can ask Cathal if this is true, the queen brackets my head and pours images of gored scales, quartered flesh, and ripped tusks stacked in wooden chests. Water—tears bleed from my eyes and down my cheeks, carving into the salt and sand, eroding my desire to step out of this fortress of sunstone and blood magic.

I clasp Priya's wrists and tug. And then I step back and back, away from her and everyone, wincing when my foot sinks onto a jagged coral. "Why Lorcan no stop slaughter?" I squint as black rivulets of my blood flow through the coral's yellow folds.

"He has," Cathal grits out. "Anyone who so much as harms a serpent with a weapon or magic is immediately punished. Anyone who kills them meets immediate death at our talons."

"What happens if the Lucins go after Zendaya, Cathal?" the queen asks him.

"I'd kill them."

"Of course you would." Behati pops the bottom of her cane out of the sand and props it against a coral. "Crows so love beheading Faeries."

He narrows his gaze on the Shabbin advisor, which leads me to think that *beheading* must be something truly evil. "So what's your plan, Sumaca? Imprisoning Daya like you've imprisoned your daughter?"

My heart lurches, because...*what*? Priya imprisoned her daughter...Cathal's mate? Why? And when? I thought her daughter was dead? Did she die in prison?

The queen's shoulders sharpen as she twirls to face Cathal and growls something at him in Crow. The only word I make out is a name: Meriam.

The name that causes everyone to either hush or scowl. "Meriam is daughter, Taytah?"

Silence stretches and stretches in the chasm of Priya's making, reverberating against every beached coral and ruffled stone shelf.

The queen hisses at Cathal in Crow. So much blood has risen into her cheeks that even her irises appear crimson.

"I think it's time, Priya." Behati keeps her voice soft, as though she senses that speaking any louder will make her monarch rage. "Especially if we *are* taking her out of Shabbe."

"I've changed my mind about the trip. She stays here." The queen takes off toward the steps still jutting from the sandstone wall.

Cathal's arms fold a little more snugly over the black top that clings to his broad chest like sand clings to mine. "I'm afraid that's not going to be possible for I struck a bargain with Daya the other day."

She swings around. "You did *what*?"

"She figured out how the waterrises operated, so I bargained for her to never approach one in exchange for which I'd fly her out of Luce for Fallon's nuptials."

The queen's full lips are a pale slash on her tanned face.

Cathal fixes her with his penetrating stare. "You know as well as anyone that one cannot renege on a bargain."

Though I follow their discussion, a part of me remains stuck to the question Priya failed to answer. I repeat it, because I want an answer. I *need* one.

"Yes." It's Cathal who replies. Not Priya. Priya's too busy glowering at him.

Meriam is Cathal's mate.

Meriam, who isn't dead.

94

No wonder the Crow stayed in Shabbe if his mate is here. And no wonder he loathes the queen if she imprisoned her. The only thing I do still wonder is why he spends so much time with m—

Oh.

The answer drips over me like the coolest water—it pebbles my skin and chills my spine. Not even the sunlight baking the land manages to reach me. I clutch my elbows and glare hard at the male who pretends to care, even though all he truly cares about is securing a stay in the queendom to remain near his imprisoned mate.

"You trick me again, Crow." I shake my head. And then I turn and stalk past a confounded Priya, leaving black footprints in my wake, ones Cathal Báeinach better not follow.

But he does, for when I storm into my bedchamber, there the male is.

Chapter 15
Zendaya

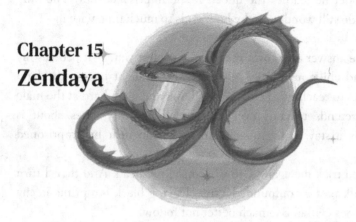

"**G**et out," I snarl.

"Not until you tell me why you're so livid."

"I no want talk to you. I want bathe." I streak into my bathroom and slam the door.

Nevertheless, the Crow swirls underneath the door.

After spinning the faucet, I whirl on him and smack his chest with both palms. "I heal you. Go home." I try to shove him away, but his boots remain firmly planted on the stone.

"Like I said, Príona, I'm not leaving until you enlighten me about this mood you're in, of which I seem to be the cause."

I grip his shirt, sad I cannot shift into a bird for I would love to sprout talons and shred the fabric like he shredded my trust. "You use me, Crow!"

His thick black eyebrows dip over his craggy nose. "*You* offered to heal me, Daya."

"I no talk about infection. I talk about stay in Shabbe."

His frown deepens.

"You *not* my sentry. Queen *no* employ you! She say to me this."

He dips his chin. "This is what angers you? That I appointed myself as your guard?"

"No, Cathal. What anger me is—is..." I side-eye the steam rising from the golden tub. It must engulf my lids, because they burn.

96

"Is what, Daya?"

"Is you hide true reason why you stay!"

"How exactly was I supposed to tell you when Priya refuses that we speak about your past?"

"*My* past?"

He cants his head. "Daya, what reason do you think I have for staying in Shabbe?"

"Your mate."

His neck snaps straight. "I don't have a mate. Not anymore."

This time, I'm the one who frowns. "Fallon say Crows mate forever."

"That's usually the case...yes."

"But you and Meriam not mate anymore?"

His head rears back. "Meriam?"

"I hear Taytah say child is mate."

"Oh, Daya." His lids slip shut.

"What, *oh, Daya?*" Did I misunderstand something? Is he trying to fool me again?

He lowers his face, burying his lips and nose into my hair as though his head were too heavy for his shoulders and he has to rest it on mine.

I don't push him away. Merely repeat, "What, *oh, Daya?*"

"Meriam was never my mate, Príona."

"But Taytah say—"

"Her daughter was."

I roll my head, dislodging his in order to look at him. "Meriam have daughter?"

His wary eyes open and lock on mine. "Yes."

"Where?" I swallow, my throat as parched as the Amkhuti. "Where is daughter?"

"Dead. Meriam slayed her."

I blink hard. "That why prison?"

"No. She did other bad things."

"She kill mate, Cathal. What worse?"

He tips me the saddest, most forlorn smile.

"I sorry I shout."

"You had every right to shout at me. I deceived you by keeping quiet about my reasons for remaining in Shabbe."

I release his shirt and ball my fingers at my sides. "You stay to kill Meriam?"

He runs his thumb up my cheekbone, lingering at its apex where Crows wear an inked feather. "Take your bath."

I frown and am about to tell him that my bath can wait, that I'd prefer to discuss his intentions, but the male fades to smoke and withdraws beneath my door. Why is he always there when I don't want him to be, yet leaves when I want him to stay?

I sigh as I knead the skin over my heart to ease the harsh beats beneath, but instead, the press of my fingers seems to make my heart leaven with more pain.

Pain for Cathal and his impossible loss, and pain for Priya who had to imprison her own daughter.

Neither steeping in warm water, nor scrubbing scented oil into my skin manages to dislodge any of it. When I emerge from my bathing chamber, I expect—*hope*—to set eyes on the Crow, but his face isn't the one I see.

Chapter 16
Zendaya

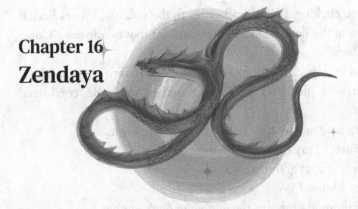

Behati must hear the door opening because she turns away from the spectacle of the monkeys swinging from branch to branch in my garden. "Are you feeling better, Zendaya?"

I shrug. My body does, but my heart...my heart hurts, and I don't understand why. "Why here, Behati?"

"Because Priya refuses to be." Her pink gaze shines darkly amidst the sweeps of white-gold. "Cathal's right. Now that you understand everything, it's only a matter of time until you learn all of it. Especially since you'll be traveling to Luce tomorrow."

"I go?"

"Yes."

"Taytah go?" My hair bleeds water into my white silk sleeping gown.

"Naturally."

"She still mad?"

"Yes and no. She's not angry with you, though."

"Only with Cathal?"

Behati presses her lips together. I'm taking that as a yes.

"You go Luce also?"

Her mouth curves, which makes the outer corners of her eyes crinkle like crushed parchment. "Someone has to stay to guard the Mahananda."

I wonder if the Mahananda, like me, ever feels annoyed that no one believes it can take care of itself.

Cane clicking, Behati walks over to the sofa and lowers herself onto one of the floor cushions, then pats the spot beside her. "Come close, Daya."

I don't especially want to sit, but I *do* want to hear about Meriam, so I plod over and take a seat on the wide, coral-hued cushion.

For a long moment, all Behati does is stare at me.

"I listen," I say to remind her to speak.

"Priya is your grandmother."

"Yes. I know."

"Grandmother means the mother of one's mother."

"I know, too."

"I thought..." Her lashes flutter in surprise. "I thought you weren't aware that Meriam was your mother. Did Cathal tell you?"

My heart holds so still that I think it's stopped beating. "Meriam? No. *Mahananda* mother me." Silence. "No?"

Behati inhales a breath that makes her narrow ribs dig into her crimson robe. "Yes and...no."

"What mean *yes and no*?"

"It means that the Mahananda had a hand in making you, but so did Meriam."

"Mahananda make me *with* Meriam?"

"Yes."

"Mahananda is father?" My question comes out as an exclamation.

"Not exactly. You had a father, but he no longer lives."

My eyebrows draw so close on my forehead that they jostle the root of my tusk. "I lost, Behati."

"I imagined as much. Your past is quite...thorny."

It must be another expression, because the past isn't flora or fauna.

"What I meant by that is that your past is a complicated thing to grasp, like a stalk full of thorns."

"Stalk full of thorns make bleed. My past make bleed?"

"In a way, yes." The curve of her lips holds such melancholy that it dims the air. "Your past made many hearts bleed, most of all Priya's. It filled her with such pain that she contemplated slumbering in the Mahananda."

I frown. "I no see bed when I went; only darkness." It had enveloped me like the ocean, swathing me in complete and utter tranquility.

A small laugh traipses from Behati's lips. "*Slumbering in the Mahananda* is the expression we use when we are ready to return our magic to the Mahananda. It's one of the only ways we, Shabbin women, can end our lives."

Oh. I make a note to stay wide awake if I'm ever submerged in the Mahananda again. "Why Taytah so sad?"

"For you to understand this, I'd need to start at the beginning. Well, at your beginning. Five centuries ago, Meriam had a baby with a Shabbin male. That baby was you. When you were very young—around four or five—your mother fell in love with a Lucin, a Faerie named Costa Regio, who was Lorcan's general."

I've heard the name Regio. Like Meriam's, turbulent silence ensues its mention.

"Costa betrayed Lore and, aided by Meriam, managed to subdue him by staking him with obsidian. You may now have an understanding of what obsidian does to regular Crows, but to their king, it transforms him to iron and knocks down *all* his people. In other words, if Lore is immobilized, so are all his shifters. This sparked the first Great War in Luce—the Magnabellum—after which Costa crowned himself king."

I feel like asking for a quill to squiggle all these names and events down, but obviously I do not...for I cannot. I stare at my hands, which are as useless as the blood inside them, and fold my fingers over one another in my lap.

"For years, we thought he'd made Meriam his queen, but then the serpents started arriving on our shores, carrying banished Lucins, who explained Meriam had disappeared."

"Disappear? Where?"

"No one knew at the time."

I imagine they have the answer now, and although I'd like to learn it, something else feels more essential: "Why you not go Luce and save Lorcan?"

"Because your mother had erected wards around Shabbe that kept us locked in. For five hundred years."

My mind feels as snarled as the tresses atop my head before my bath. If she left when I was four and this is five centuries later, then... "Why I no remember?"

"Because, when the Mahananda brought you back as a Serpent shifter"—Behati runs her finger along the seam of the velvet cushion against which she reclines—"it erased your memory."

"Why?"

She stares straight ahead at the prickly fruit with curved leaves that lords over the rest of the fruit like a juice-filled king. "We don't question the Mahananda, Daya."

Perhaps, we should. I wonder if I could ask it for my memories back. Do I even want them? "What about dead sister?"

"Hmm." Behati returns her attention to me. "Dead sister? *Who's* sister?"

"My."

Behati's thin eyebrows writhe beneath the stroke of hair. "You're Meriam's only daughter."

The pulsing beneath my ribs quiets again. If I'm Meriam's only daughter, then that means...

That means...

"How far did you get in Daya's history?" Cathal leans against one of the pillars holding up my ceiling, arms folded beneath a fresh shirt, his hair slicked back from a bath of his own, black stripes fresh and dark against his pale skin.

"I cannot tell her everything at once, Cathal," Behati says. "It would overwhelm her."

The Crow didn't stay behind to avenge his mate; he stayed because I *am* his mate.

Chapter 17
Zendaya

I am Cathal Báeinach's mate.

I have a mate.

Does that mean that Fallon is *ours*, or did he have her with that other female she refers to as Mamma?

My fingers pace the scar around my neck, back and forth, back and forth. Cathal said Meriam killed her daughter. If my mother killed me, then how—

The Mahananda! That's what Behati meant when she said it had brought me back. She meant it had resurrected me.

The scars that blemish my skin and scales must be remnants of Meriam's attack. How brutal was my death?

I spring my hand off the paler band of flesh and onto the cushion beneath me as I try to recover from the blow of Behati's words. I feel drained and laid bare like the Amkhuti, unrecognizable yet composed of the same bones, a trench instead of a river, a wasteland instead of a thriving milieu.

Heat bursts through my chest at the sudden realization of all I've lost. It claws up my ribs and grips my heart before moving farther upward to throttle my throat. I want to rage and scream. I want to run through the courtyard to the Mahananda's edge and demand why it had to steal my past when it breathed human life into my scales.

But I don't.

I just sit there, motionless, my lungs barely filling, my heart barely beating, strangled by shock and horror and—and devastation.

I had a daughter.

I had a mate.

I had a life.

The heat seeps into my face, into my cheeks, into my eyes before collapsing out of me, draining me some more.

"What exactly did you tell her, Behati?" Cathal's voice booms against my buzzing eardrums like waves crushing stone, and then smoke sweeps up my trembling arms, becoming more solid as it strokes and enfolds.

"I only told her what Meriam did to Shabbe and to her as a child."

"Daya, look at me."

I can't. Not yet.

"What else did you fucking tell her, Behati?"

"Great Mahananda, you have no manners."

"For fuck's sake—"

"The last thing I told her was that she didn't have a dead sister. I don't know why she'd even ask me that. Did *you* tell her she had a sister?"

"Leave," Cathal growls.

"Pardon me?" Behati wheezes.

"Please. Please leave us."

The cushion beneath me shifts. "Zendaya, would you like me to stay? Because I will if you don't want to be left alone with Cathal."

I've neither enough air to breathe out an answer nor enough energy to shake my head.

"Zendaya?"

"She and Fallon are my only reasons for existing, so if you think I'm going to harm her, then—"

"I do not stay because I fear you will harm her, Cathal. I stay because I worry you'll take advantage of her."

The silence that ensues is so terrible that it makes my lids snap up. Although Cathal's hands are on my body, his incendiary gaze is on Behati.

"Planning on draining me of blood, Crow?"

"Leave," he says. "If you ever imply that I might take advantage of Daya, so help me Mórrígan—"

"Mara," Behati snaps. "Not Mórrígan. And I'll leave only if Zendaya wants me gone, otherwise—"

"Go, Behati." My voice is as thin as a sea fan. "I no want anyone get hurt."

Cathal's next breath is abrupt.

"I don't fear him, Zendaya." She tries to reach for my hand but retracts her fingers when she encounters smoke.

"Thank you for truth, Behati, but you go now. I deal with... mate."

Her lips purse while Cathal's part around a sigh. It's almost as though the word has tugged at some thread keeping them stitched shut.

Behati stands, smoothing her robes. "Walk me to the door of your chambers?"

I look up, and then nod. My legs prickle as I stand. Cathal must sense it because his grip on my arms tightens.

"Alone," Behati says.

"Is this some trick?" Cathal glares at my grandmother's advisor.

My flesh and blood grandmother...

"No. We Shabbins don't trick people. Unlike the Faeries. Unlike the *non*-Shabbins."

The accusation—*unlike you*—glimmers in the air between them. I suppose Cathal does merit this, for he did trick me, but didn't they all in some way?

"It's my only condition for leaving her here alone with you."

"Is all right, Cathal." I shrug his hands off my arms.

Though his reluctance to let me go is whittled into every line and hollow of his face, when I walk Behati to the door, he stays put.

Right before she reaches for the handle, she slashes her finger on the back of her pearl earring. "I'll be happy to answer any questions you might have. I fathom you have many."

Since I imagine this isn't what she stole me away from Cathal to say, I remain quiet as she paints a sigil on my door—the one to slip through walls.

Sure enough, before pressing her palm to it, she leans over to kiss me on both cheeks, except she doesn't do it to wish me farewell but to disguise a whisper. "That male isn't your mate. Not anymore." She moves her mouth to my other cheek, brushes her lips against it, and adds, "I had a vision." And then she presses her palms to my forehead. The scene plays out in devastating detail.

For long seconds after she leaves, I stare at the door, at the bloodied drips of the cross circled in more blood.

I didn't think anything could stun me more than learning I had a life before this one, but I was evidently mistaken, for her last confession has rooted my feet to the stone and the air to my lungs. I close my eyes to gather my bearings, but all that does is drive her vision back to the forefront of my skull.

"What did that woman say to you, Príona?" Cathal's voice strokes over my forehead.

I startle and winch my neck. Anger exudes from his stare like smoke from his pores. In silence, he watches me and I watch him back. It's become so quiet that I can hear my white nightgown move over my pounding chest as though it were crafted from rows of pearls instead of silk and lace.

I sense his shadows wanting to devour the distance between our bodies, the same way I sense him restraining them.

"What did she show you?" he grits out. "Why have you lost all color in your cheeks?"

His anger used to scare me, but not anymore. Not now that I understand its source. Mates are sacred to Crows, and he lost his.

"In past, we mind-speak?" I twirl my finger to indicate him and me.

"Yes."

"Is it?"

He frowns. "Is it what?"

"What make mates? Mind link only? No mark on skin? Or..." I shrug. "Or other?"

"The mind link is the most obvious sign."

"What else?"

He takes a step toward me, but I hold up my palm to keep him at bay.

"Mates cannot live without one another, Daya. When my sister-in-law was killed, my brother—" His voice breaks, but then he repairs it with a deep inhalation. "My brother asked Lorcan to end his life."

"When Meriam kill me, you ask die?"

"I—I..."

I wait, not even certain why I want to know this. What does it matter anymore?

"I didn't know she'd...I didn't know what..." He balls his fingers as though he wants to strike some invisible wall. "I *felt* you were still alive, Daya. And there was Fallon to consider. My brother didn't have a child to live for."

That's fair. My mother may have picked her lover over her child, but she also ended my Shabbin life. Cathal doesn't strike me as the sort of man who'd ever inflict harm on his daughter. Speaking of which. "Is Fallon...*our*?"

"Yes."

I want to weep again. I don't. "Why she no say?"

"She tried, at the beginning. But then, once we realized you didn't remember your life...us...we decided to wait."

"For what?"

He hangs his head and palms the back of it, mussing his—for once—tamed locks. "For you to understand our tongue, our customs, the way the world worked. We were afraid that telling you too soon would confuse and frighten you."

It still does. I am confused and I am frightened because I'm not sure what to do. How to act. What is expected of me now? Does

Fallon even want a mother? She's all grown up. Not to mention that I don't even know what being a mother entails. I imagine it's loving your child and not killing her.

I have a child.

Yet something keeps niggling me. "What Mamma mean?"

"It's the Lucin way of saying Amma or Mádhi in Crow. Why?"

"Fallon call Agrippina Mamma."

"Ah. Yes."

"Yes...?" I prompt, when he still doesn't shed light as to why Fallon would call someone, who didn't give birth to her, Mamma.

"Agrippina and Ceres raised Fallon."

Because I couldn't. Because my mother ended my life.

I didn't get to raise my child because of Meriam. Cathal didn't either.

I swallow, suddenly mad, but not at Meriam. Mad at myself for not realizing who Fallon was. My hands land on that place on my body that the queen showed me rounding when a female grows a babe. I feel hollow, like a shell that's lost its dweller.

"I'm so sorry." Cathal's fingers sink deeper into his black locks.

I, too, am sorry. Sorry that Meriam stole so many years of his life. "Maybe, if ask kindly, Mahananda give me back memories."

His face lifts, his gaze filling with surprise, but also hope. "You'd want them back?"

"I forgot daughter and Taytah. I forgot"—*you*—"Meriam." Her name tastes foul upon my tongue, but speaking his will only feed the flames crackling between us. Besides, do I really want to recall my life with this man when I am destined for—

"If the Cauldron doesn't give you back your memories, Príona, I'd be glad to fill in all the gaps. I'd be glad to tell you about *us*."

"No."

"No?" he repeats.

"No tell me, Cathal." If he reminds me of all the ways he loved me and I loved him back, because I imagine we must've loved each other a great deal if I bore a child, I might not leave for Luce in the morning. I might stray from the new path the Mahananda has traced for me.

A fissure forms along my heart, a hairline fracture that cracks farther apart when I catch Cathal's eyelashes batting as wildly as his wings when he's in his other form.

"You are free, Cathal," I tell him to unshackle him from his past and from me.

Chapter 18
Zendaya

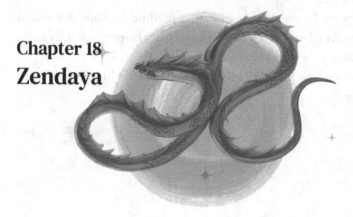

Aship bobs on the Amkhuti which the queen and the Akwale have filled once more. And not just halfway, but to the very brim. The limpid water that abuts the stone is smooth like a mirror, casting the illusion that one could step onto it without falling through.

As the guards load trunks onto the vessel, I stand on the rocky cliff turned shore beside my grandmother whose face looks carved out of the same sunstone as her land this morning. Although the skin around her eyes isn't rimmed with fatigue, the shadows are there, crowding her expression, reddening her irises, ruffling the skin around her lids and mouth.

I try to locate a shred of excitement for this trip that I've longed to take since I learned there was a world beyond Shabbe's walls, but the emotion filling me isn't warm and light; it's cold and heavy and sits atop my chest like a boulder.

I don't think I've taken a proper breath since I woke up drenched and gasping for breath, clutching at my chest, convinced a sword protruded from my scales. Not only was I not in Serpent form, but also no weapon had sliced through my white gown. What stuck the silk to my skin wasn't blood, but perspiration.

Though my heart had raced for some time after rousing, I'd

flopped back onto my pillow, the words *not real* clinging to my trembling lips. The scene had been a product of my imagination. A—*what had Fallon called it?*—night terror. One made of the images my grandmother and Behati had shown me the day before.

A shudder races up my spine and clacks the ivory inside my mouth as I picture the slaughtered serpents again. Another shiver follows suit when I picture the mate I'm about to meet. And yet another tremor racks my body when I recall the aggrieved shock and fierce hurt that warped Cathal's features when I asked him to keep our past in the past.

I curl my fingers until my nails bite crescents into my skin. I suddenly don't want to leave the safety of Shabbe's walls. I don't want to meet a stranger. I take a step back. "No go."

The queen pivots her stare off the large auburn ship that bears the Shabbin crest of two golden serpents, complete with tusks created in mother-of-pearl.

I shake my head, which shakes my body. Or maybe my body hasn't stopped shaking since I awakened. "I no ready."

The queen's black eyebrows lower. "What changed?"

"No want die." I say, even though that's only one reason. Granted, a good one.

"EmMoti, no one will harm you." She catches one of my fists and forces my fingers to open to wind hers through. Once she succeeds, she squeezes our palms together.

"But you say Faeries hate serpents. I Serpent, Taytah."

"No one knows this but us."

I blink in surprise, but then realize this isn't the truth. "Many Crow know."

"Lorcan has sworn his people to secrecy."

I try to step back. Her grip around my fingers tightens. Here I thought she'd been offering me comfort, when actually, she's holding on so I cannot race back into the palace. "Why you want me go now?"

"Because that is your destiny."

My skin coats in tiny bumps. Did Behati tell her about the vision, or did the Mahananda inform her?

"Although I would've preferred for the Mahananda to let you steer your heart, I'm not surprised it has found you a mate, for you are a shifter, and that is the way of shifters."

I've stopped shaking, but not because my shock has lessened. The tremors have stopped because the cold has spread and hardened me like ice.

"I know how alone you've felt, Daya. Perhaps that is why the Mahananda chose your mate."

"I no alone. I have Fallon and you, Taytah." *I also have Cathal.* Well...I had him. I very much doubt he'll want to remain my friend after the way we parted.

Maybe if the Mahananda found him a new mate also... The thought is a fiery burst against the ice, one that keeps burning long after it's thawed me. What is this emotion? Why does it make my jaw clench and my heart ache?

"Fallon has Lore, and I have Shabbe," Priya is saying. "You need someone who's wholly yours."

I squint at the sky with its blistering midday sun. This must be why I feel like I'm gloved in flames. Because I'm not used to being out during the day. A violent splash carries my attention back to the Amkhuti and to the scales whitening the glassy surface with foam. I spy yellow ones, but also blue and purple and orange.

Although no water droplets sprinkle my skin, the fire ravaging me snuffs out, leaving behind trenches of cold ash. Though the serpents' show is mesmerizing, it is also—and especially—painful, for it thrusts my loneliness deep.

As deep as the dream sword plunged through my chest.

My skin prickles with the need to slip into scales, but I force my Serpent away, sensing that if I jumped in, I'd spook the others. Until I learn their tongue and their ways, I will stay an outcast. But what if I can't learn their tongue and ways?

Cathal said shifters cannot communicate with the species they were molded from. Until I have a babe, I will be alone. This must be why the Mahananda picked a mate for me: to aid me in creating a small version of myself.

Fallon's face swims before my eyes. To think that she was mine before becoming Lorcan's. If only she could've been mine *after* the Mahananda turned me into a shifter. Perhaps then, she could've taken my shape instead of her father's.

As though Cathal sensed my thoughts, he appears, not in skin but in feathers. Admittedly, it could be someone else, someone tasked to escort us to Lorcan's realm. Though why would a vessel filled with seafaring, bloodcasters require an escort?

Shabbin females, according to what I've cobbled together, are the most feared people in the realm, because they hold the most power. Crows come second. Faeries next. Then humans. Where does a lone female with a magical tongue end up on this pyramid of power? With her fellow shifters, or somewhere between human and Faerie?

The Crow glides over the ship, casting it in full shadow since his wingspan is as broad as the vessel is long.

"We are ready to embark, Sumaca." Abrax's voice tears my gaze off the sky.

I wondered where he was when I didn't see him amongst my guards this morning. He must've been getting ready for the voyage. Though the male's eyes aren't colored by blood magic, he has a sword which, according to Asha, he's terribly good at wielding. I imagine she's watched him train, or maybe even trained with him. I hear some female guards study swordfight since sigils take concentration and time to draw. Unless she knows how Abrax fights because she's watched him fight off an enemy? Do the Shabbins have enemies within their walls? Besides my mother, that is.

I look over my shoulder at the palace with its eight wings shaped like flower petals. Is the female who made me before unmaking me imprisoned in one of them? "Where keep Meriam, Taytah?"

"Somewhere she cannot reach you, emMoti."

"But here, in Shabbe?"

"Yes."

This time, when the queen leads me closer to the smooth wood that glows amber as though lit from within, I offer no resistance. The world beyond the sandstone walls may scare me, but suddenly, the idea of being trapped on an isle with a murderess frightens me far more.

Chapter 19
Zendaya

Abrax comes to stand beside me at the helm. He watches me watch the queendom. Everyone aboard the ship watches me. The same way the Shabbins crowding the shores of the Sahklare watch. Except, they cannot see the real me, for the queen gave me another's face—a female with eyes as pink as her own, skin the hue of toasted seeds, and hair the color of molten cocoa.

As she painted the transformation sigil on my forehead, Priya explained that she or Asha would refresh it as soon as it faded, so I need not be alarmed once we crossed into Lucin waters. No one would know I was amongst the procession attending Fallon's nuptials.

When I asked her why I needed a disguise since no one knew about me, she'd answered: "So you can reveal yourself when you feel ready."

Her reply had lengthened my breaths. That is, until the vessel ground to a halt and bumped into an embankment. Once I realized we'd stopped to pick up two new travelers—Ceres and Agrippina Rossi—the pressure in my lungs eased, however the one around my heart tightened. I was grateful to these women for having reared and loved Fallon, but dear Mahananda, how I ached with envy.

"So, what do you think of your queendom, Rajka?" Ceres asks, coming to stand beside me. Did she figure out who I was on her own, or did someone divulge my identity?

"Please refrain from using her title, Shrima Rossi," Asha murmurs.

"Forgive me," Ceres murmurs, her accent thick like Cathal's, but melodic, unlike his.

I smile to show her that she's forgiven, then say, "Great beauty, Shabbe."

"I think so as well."

"Fallon say Luce great beauty, too."

Ceres's emerald stare acquires both shadow and shine. "Yes. I suppose it is quite beautiful if you overlook its people."

I frown, not certain I understand what she means by this. When she doesn't elaborate, I say, "You home for good?"

"No." Ceres casts a look at her daughter, who sits on a chair that Abrax helped carry aboard and that Asha affixed to the deck with her blood. "Not until..."

"Until...?"

"Until Agrippina's ready to leave Shabbe."

Here I'd imagined she'd want nothing more than to leave now that the girl she and her mother raised had moved back to Luce. "Agrippina love here so much?"

Ceres's knuckles whiten around the railing as though she fears the ship's angle may send her toppling over. "Yes," she finally says. "We are both happy here."

"Yet you mate live in Luce."

Her black eyebrows spring up. "My mate?"

"General Rossi is mate, no?"

"Ah. Justus and I haven't been *mates* for a while now." She turns to look at her daughter.

I do as well. Abrax stands beside the redheaded female, pointing out birds and telling her their names. Apparently she's a great fan of birds. Or was, back before she took a knife to her ears to protest her lineage. I shudder at the idea of carving through one's own flesh.

Ceres watches me stroke my throat, something I do often, I realize. I wonder why I reach for my scar. Do I hope to coax a memory from my injured flesh, or does it offer me solace to know that I healed...that I survived?

"You no love old mate?" I ask.

"It's complicated." She pushes a lock of black hair behind her long ears.

To think I mistook her for Fallon's true grandmother. To think I mistook Agrippina for her mother. These two women look nothing like my daughter. Then again, both are here, sailing back to Luce to be at her side during the ceremony.

When my chest burns hot with that ugly feeling, I refocus on the wide, crystalline river that bursts with not only serpents and fish, but also with curious Shabbins out for a swim and tiny boats brimming with fresh produce.

Little by little, the heat swamping my chest climbs into my eyes and spills over. "Thank you," I croak, knuckling away a tear.

Ceres frowns. "For what, Rajka?"

"For raise Fallon. For love her." I knuckle away another tear, then heave a deep breath and concentrate on the land and its people.

"She was easy to love." With an easy smile, Ceres adds, "Not as easy to raise."

I laugh.

"Anytime you want stories, come to me and I will fill your ears with your daughter's penchant for misadventure."

With a grin, I say, "I ready to hear all."

So Ceres begins to recount Fallon's childhood while I watch the landscape tighten into slimmer dwellings and slighter gardens the farther up we sail. By the time we reach the tiniest abodes, I feel like I've salvaged some of the years of which I was robbed.

"The Queen!" a diminutive Shabbin yells, rushing to the embankment and diving in. Dozens more follow. Where many kick their legs and thrust their arms, a few grab onto tusks in order to keep up with our brisk cruising speed.

Ceres interrupts her storytelling when my grandmother approaches and opens one of the four trunks that were hefted aboard. The sun catches on a mound of gold coins stamped with the Shabbin crest.

"Have a blessed journey, Sumaca!" one of the swimmers yells as their body is dragged parallel to our vessel by a serpent as large as Sun Warrior.

The queen thanks the small Two-legs with a majestic smile and a sprinkle of gold coins that makes them release the tusk and dive to pocket them.

Another glistening face pops out in the foamy wake of our ship. A small female with pink eyes and a coin tucked inside each hand. She displays her loot with great pride.

"What wrong with mouth?" I ask.

Ceres frowns.

But Asha comprehends my question. "Children lose their teeth before regrowing adult-sized ones."

Of course. *Children.* That is why they're so small.

Asha puffs out a laugh when a juvenile serpent bumps his tusk —more of a nub, really—into one of the little girl's hands, making her coin slip.

The child scowls at the serpent, then mutters an, "Oh, no you don't," before plunging after it to retrieve her prize.

"That's something you won't see in Luce," Ceres says. "No one swims there."

"Why?" I ask.

"Because they fear..." Asha must give her a look, because Ceres purses her lips. Even though she ends up saying, "Because they aren't taught," I know the reason the Lucins do not swim.

They fear serpents.

They kill them.

Like my mood, the air darkens. I think it's because of the Crow's shadows but soon find out the darkness isn't of any giant bird's making. No, what casts us in shade are the queendom's walls.

The trunk, now empty of coins, is clapped shut and carried

away. No new one is brought out. Probably because no Shabbin splashes in the water here. A glance around reveals that not a single dwelling dots the tangle of trees and shrubs.

"Welcome to the Chayagali, where only the wildest prowl." Asha gestures to the eerie hoop of vegetation that races around the whole queendom.

According to my daily lessons with Behati, the Shadow Forest is the only part of the isle that never gets sunlight. As the vessel glides deeper into the darkness, lambent eyes peer at us from the obscurity and branches crack, trodden on by furred land beasts. Though they fight amongst themselves, they don't attack Pink-eyes. They do, however, occasionally attack serpents.

Little bumps rise over my skin. Though magic cloaks me, does it cloak my true nature, or can the beasts sense me like I can sense them? Movement on the shore of the Sahklare snares my attention. A beast in fur the same shade as the abounding shrubs, and with eyes full-black like mine, shoulders its way to the cliff overlooking the river and sniffs the air with its flat nose.

"The tendu better not try and jump aboard," Abrax mutters, reaching for his short sword.

I was so engrossed by the shifting landscape that I didn't even realize he'd swapped places with Ceres.

"Have no fear, Abrax," Asha singsongs. "Pink-eyes are near."

Tendus are the rulers of the Chayagali, and serpents' only predators in Shabbe. They're fearsome creatures with a single mortal flaw—sunlight. The faintest ray will singe their hide and boil their blood, so they never venture out from the shadows they rule.

The creature's eyes lock on mine, and it crouches with a low growl, its bladed shoulders digging into its fur. I spring my fingers off the railing. If only the Akwale could steer the boat away from the shore, but the river here is so narrow, and our ship so wide, that we'd bump into the opposite embankment.

"*Periculo*," Agrippina suddenly says, proceeding to repeat the word over and over. "*Periculo. Periculo.*"

"What mean *periculo*?" I croak.

"Danger. But it won't attack. Not with the queen aboard," Asha says while Agrippina repeats that single word.

Over and over and over. With each reiteration, my heart clamors louder.

She's right. There is danger. I can sense the tendu's malicious intent the same way it can surely sense my fear. It licks its wide mouth, flattening the fur around it. It isn't my fear it scents; it's the Serpent squirming beneath my skin.

The tendu leaps.

I stumble backward and bang into Asha.

The creature squeals. What I take to be a battle cry turns out to be a howl of pain, for only half of its body lands on the deck. Something severed it in half. I soon realize what that something is when iron talons dripping blood materialize out of thin air. The Crow accompanying us swoops low, squawking a warning to the rest of the predators lurking in the shadows that the same fate awaits them if they try to board our ship.

"We should get you inside the hull." Asha plucks my clammy hand and starts to tug me toward the front of the vessel where the Akwale are adding blood to the sigil that seals our ship to the flowing waterway when a bolt of smoke pounds into the deck.

"*Corvo*," Agrippina gasps.

Ceres nods. "*Si, mi cuori. Corvo.*"

"*Accipe me a Luce. Accipe me a Luce.*"

Ceres shakes her head, then replies something with a nod in my direction, but it doesn't seem to quiet Agrippina, who keeps repeating the same four words.

"What she say?" I murmur as Cathal growls something at Priya in Crow.

"That the Crow takes her to Luce. I think she believes Cathal is here for her."

My lips flatten. Why would she think this? Because he's Fallon's father and he considers herself Fallon's mother? The Crow isn't here for her. He's here for me. I know it even before I become the object of his scorching glower.

The male is furious. Because of yesterday? Because of the tendu? Because of something else that has nothing to do with me? Has his infection returned? I drop my stare to his thigh and try to concentrate on his scent when he snaps, "Help Zendaya climb onto my back. She'll be flying the rest of the way."

I blink as he shifts and crouches like the tendu. *I'm going to fly?* My heartbeats quicken and remain elevated as I peer over his shifting body toward my grandmother, waiting for her assent. It's slow to come, but she nods. Because she senses more tendu attacks?

"You land back on board before we reach Tarecuori so I have time to refresh her sigil. Understood?"

The Crow nods as Asha and Abrax help me scale his massive form.

"Hold on to his neck," Abrax instructs me, which makes me think he must've already ridden a Crow.

I do as I'm told.

Cathal stands and steps gingerly toward the railing, his talons clicking against the wood. And then he jumps off the stern of the ship. For a heartbeat, we're in freefall, but then his wings fan out and we soar. My fingers tremble, but not with fear this time, with exhilaration. He rises slowly, as though to give me time to drink in the beauty spilling around us—a pink jewel veined with liquid silver and vibrant greens with a shimmering heart, no larger than a dot, that holds more power than the world it hatched.

If only the Mahananda had given me—

I press the ungracious thought away before it's fully-formed. The Mahananda gave me the power to shift from scales to skin. How dare I complain.

Cathal whirls away from the land of my birth and rebirth and flies up the length of the waterrise. The angle of his climb is so vertiginous that I flatten my torso against his spine and strangle him with both my arms and thighs. I must hurt him for he rights his body.

"Sorry," I murmur.

I squint past his plumage at the ship that bobs like a tree nut down the sinuous shadows. How long will it take it to reach the top? And once they do reach it, will the ocean be right there? I find out the answer to my second interrogation before the boat penetrates the waterrise: the ocean isn't right there. The ocean is *far* below. Not as far down as Shabbe, but still...

Even though the sun is hot on my skin, a shiver courses down my spine. Cathal does one more loop of the sky above Shabbe before cresting the shimmering pink walls. My lungs slacken around a gasp as I lay my eyes on the world beyond—a bolt of sapphire capped with golden foam that stretches and bleeds into sky on one end and land on the other.

Luce.

A land I've traveled to in the past but of which I've no recollection. A land where I awakened a dormant king and gave birth to a violet-eyed child. A land where I met my first mate and will now meet my second.

Instead of smooth beats, the pounding in my chest is erratic and causes me to tremble. Cathal must feel it for he twists his face toward me. I swallow and try to smile, but it won't hold.

Why do I feel so...so...restless? Why do my lids burn and my heart ache? Because I've lost my grip on the past, or because I fear the future? The pink sand, that rings the sunstone walls like a stroke of paint, blurs. I blink back my tears before Cathal can see them carve down my cheeks.

A wave claps the ramparts and swallows the sand, then remains there, lapping at the stone as it darkens, blackens. I frown until something shimmers out of the blemish: the ship. Is the channel always there or did the Akwale make it appear? And if it is the latter, how do serpents come and go? If I ask, will I be told?

Cathal shoots forward with such speed that Luce comes into sharper focus, a rolling land of green and gray. My Crow sentry—*not my sentry*—hasn't, to my knowledge, gone home since I stepped out of the Mahananda. How eager he must be to return to his friends and sleep in his rock chamber in the clouds.

"Cathal?"

He slows and rolls his head.

"Put me on boat."

Though he has no eyebrows, I can sense them slant.

"So you can home." I nod to the rising gray rock which Fallon explained houses Lorcan's castle.

I tighten my grip around Cathal's neck, expecting he will dip now, but instead, he beats his great wings, sending us careening forward, straight for the tower of rock and clouds.

Did the wind distort my words or did Cathal Báeinach decide to squeeze in a visit of his home? I glance over my shoulder, and although I cannot see Taytah Priya, I can feel her glower cutting through the growing distance between us and them.

When we swoop over jagged rock, I stop looking back and begin to look ahead. Might as well, since I'm at Cathal's mercy and will be going wherever it is that he goes. Perhaps Lorcan instructed him to bring me to the Sky Kingdom before the nuptials?

I soon find out that the Crow King had no hand in Cathal's decision.

Chapter 20
Zendaya

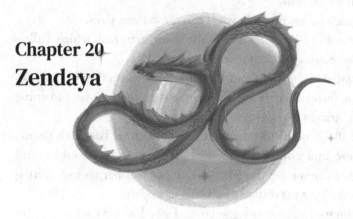

After plunging into a notch in the rock, we soar down a hallway wide enough to accommodate Crows in their beast form. Torches grip the walls, splashing an amber glow over the gray. Below us, Crows traipse in human form, toting baskets filled with produce and soaps and cloth as though they've just come from a market or are heading to one.

A small Crow jabs a finger our way, and then he's racing underneath us, repeating Cathal's name and the word Shabbin. Cathal slows and swoops low, allowing the child to catch up. And the juvenile does, which earns him a brush of Cathal's wingtip. Like the little girl in the Sahklare, the boy smiles, revealing a mouth full of missing teeth.

I relax my hold on Cathal's neck and straighten, and then I curve my lips. The small Crow blinks, then pushes a lock of black hair off a face still bare of feather tattoo and gapes at me. I assume it's my temporary pink eyes that are giving the child pause, but a glance at the braid that's slipped over my shoulder reveals it's the sight of my uncommon hair color.

Did my grandmother's magic wane already?

When more Crows begin to gather and gape, I sink my fingers into the feathers of Cathal's neck. Cathal must sense my anxiety for he rises and increases his speed, leaving the crowd behind. We fly for long minutes before he drops again. This time, his talons click against stone.

He morphs into smoke before I can climb down, then winks into skin and encloses me in his arms. For a long moment, he doesn't speak, just stares, and I stare back. So distracted by the tendu's attack, I hadn't paid attention to the Crow's appearance. He looks ravaged by fatigue. His hair pokes out in black tangles that halo a face as pale as the child's, but smudged with purple. What holds my attention isn't so much his pallor, but the crimson veining the whites of his eyes.

"Is infection back?"

With a frown, he sets me on my feet. "No. Why?"

"Eyes very red."

His throat moves over a swallow as sharp as the serrated peaks of Monteluce. Without replying, he turns and shoves open a large wooden door, then nods to the room beyond. I slip ahead of him, squinting into the obscurity. It is a cavern with many armchairs set around a metal table that appears wrought from the same metal as Crow talons. It shines darkly in the faint light cutting into the room through slits in the walls. I pad closer, my lids lifting at the sight spilling before me—rolling rock covered in trees like none I've ever seen before. Their leaves are fiery—a medley of gold and orange sprinkled through with green.

The air stirs as Cathal comes to stand beside me. "Autumn has come early."

I glance up at him, at the sunrays carving into the darkness of his face, making his features starker instead of brighter.

He gestures toward the trees. "I can tell by the color of the forest." At my frown, he explains, "When the weather grows cold, the trees here change hue before losing their leaves. They'll remain bare throughout winter, then sprout new leaves during spring. It's called seasons. You do not have them in Shabbe." He turns fully toward me now, his gaze stroking over my face, as if hoping to locate a shred of memory. "When you arrived in Luce, the first time we met—"

Though I suddenly want to hear all about it, I shut him down with an abrupt, "No talk of past," for I know it will hurt us both. Especially him. I don't add this out loud, sensing the male might take offence at being found weak in any way. "Where Fallon and Lore?"

"It was winter when we met. There was snow everywhere. When you noticed it, your eyes grew fucking huge because it was the first time you had ever seen some." And then he stalks past me and throws open a set of wooden doors.

I wedge my lips together, because I want to know more about this *snow* and why my eyes widened, but if I dip a single toe into my past, it'll create ripples, and those ripples are bound to have consequences.

I follow him past the doors, repeating, "Where Fallon and—"

The male's tossed off his shirt. His skin, although shades paler than mine, is riddled with the same puckered flesh as mine—scars.

I touch the one around my neck. "What doing?"

"I'm getting a change of clothes."

I stare around me, suddenly understanding where it is we are. "You cave this?"

He snorts as he drops down onto the large bed to remove his boots. He tosses them aside before standing and pushing down his pants in one fell swoop. No color stains his cheekbones this time.

I find my hand floating to the doorframe as he pivots toward his armoire, the muscles beneath his skin roiling and clenching as he moves. Even though I'm uncertain how it's possible, he seems so much broader without his leathers.

He turns and catches me staring.

Since he's stared his fill of me every time I've swam in the Amkhuti, it feels fair to study his front, which is just as muscled as his rear. The only remotely soft spot on this male's body is the cock that hangs between his legs, but even that begins to harden as I stare.

"It's *our* cave, Daya. The one you picked for us to live in as a family. You and me and"—there's a hitch in his breathing—"our child."

My heart emits a beat that is so bladed it gores me.

"You loved the snow so much that you wanted to live in the north." He throws on a black shirt that clings to his skin like my swallow clings to my throat. "With *me*."

I roll my lips, pushing down the lump that's making it difficult to breathe. He needs to stop living in the past. For both our sakes.

I turn toward the living area. "Where Fallon?"

"She's already in Isolacuori."

I faintly remember Phoebus telling me that this was where the kings of old had made their home in Luce. "So why we here?"

"Because"—leather whispers up legs, boots clunk—"like I said, I needed a change of clothes"—metal grinds and clicks—"and my armor."

"Why no leave me on boat?"

"Your safety is my number one priority, Príona." His voice is so near that I whirl back around.

"I safe with Taytah and Akwale."

"Didn't look it when that tendu tried to maul you."

"I pink eyes on the boat." I almost jab my finger into them to drive my point in. "Tendu no harm Pink-eyes."

He dips his face low. "They should've known better than to trust that the spell was enough to disguise your scent." His nostrils flare. "I could smell you from the skies, Sífair."

I swallow, my saliva gliding right through this time. "How I smell?"

"Like the ocean. *Mach mo moannan.*" *Mok mo meanan.*

I know the last word, but what does *mok mo* mean? I purse my lips, wishing I understood his language so he could stop using it to confuse me. He tilts his face, waiting for me to ask for a translation... daring me.

I don't take his bait. We've been gone long enough. "You done dress?"

He nods.

"So we go." I start toward the door.

Cathal doesn't follow. He just stands there, arms crossed over an iron breastplate. "You and I aren't going anywhere until you share with me what it was that Behati told you before leaving your chambers."

I cast my eyes on the leather armchairs. "No."

"Then I guess we'll miss our daughter's nuptials."

I glower at him. "You no want to know. Trust me."

"If I didn't want to know, I wouldn't be asking, now, would I?"

My jaw grinds from how hard I now clench it. "Just vision."

"Of?"

"Of me. No concern you, Crow."

He cracks his knuckles. "Yet I feel concerned, so do tell me more, Sífair."

"Cathal, please. Go."

"The instant you tell me, I'll take you to Isolacuori."

Since I don't feel the prick of a bargain, I suspect this isn't one.

The stubborn Crow continues to push. "If it doesn't concern me, then I really don't see why you're so reticent about—"

"Behati see new mate!" I feel winded shouting the words. "You happy now, Crow?"

I can tell from the nerve jumping in his jaw that he's anything but pleased. Well, too bad for him. Perhaps it'll teach him not to pry into someone else's business.

"I tell you. We go. *Now.*" I march toward the door. "Do I need drag you or you come?" I perch my palms on my hips. When he makes no move to follow, I huff a "*Fine*" and retrace my steps, clasp his wrist and yank.

Futile. Unless he chooses to move, he won't.

"Please, Cathal."

"So impatient to meet your new mate?" His voice is as cold as his stare.

"No. I impatient see Fallon! I impatient heal wounded Crows! I impatient get sigil before everyone see pink hair!"

Icy umber meets blazing black. "Who?"

"Who *what*?" I snap.

"Who is to be your new *mate*?" He bites out the word as though it now tastes foul.

"I not know him."

"But, perhaps, I do? Who?"

"Why you want know?"

"Call it morbid fascination."

I don't understand what that means, but I say, "I meet him on beach tonight. He no hair."

"Did he have a feather? Stripes?"

I dig into my memory. "No. Face bare."

His lips curl.

"Why you smile?"

He walks toward the door and opens it.

"Cathal Báeinach, why you smile?"

"Because your mate is not one of my brothers."

My eyebrows glance against one another. I hadn't even considered the Mahananda mating me to another Crow.

"Come, *mo Sífair*."

The word serpent, I understand, but not *mo*. That's twice that he's used it. "What mean *mo*?"

The impossible, mercurial male grins wider, so wide that it makes my heart hold still before bumping like a tossed pebble. He flings open his cave's door and waits. It's only as I step past him that he murmurs, "My."

He shifts before I can remind him that I'm *not* his. I suppose he'll only understand this once he sees me with my new mate. I suddenly picture how this will go and the expression that'll score his face. It's best if he never lays eyes on the male, for Cathal might decide to also lay a talon on him, and since the male the Mahananda chose for me won't be a shifter, a talon would hurt him.

My breath suddenly seizes, and not because we hurtle out of the Sky Castle, but because I finally grasp the cause of Cathal's dusky smile. Had my mate been a shifter, nothing could've harmed him, neither the Crow I ride, nor a weapon made of obsidian, thanks to my healing tongue.

If my mate is human...

Oh, Great and Powerful Mahananda...

What will Cathal Báeinach do to him?

Chapter 21
Zendaya

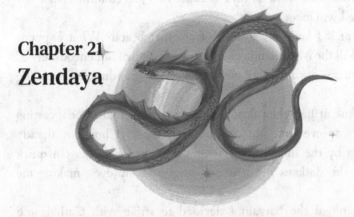

I'm still running through the terms of the bargain I've concocted inside my mind when Cathal flaps his wings and pivots. Instead of heading toward a patch of water crawling with boats and Crows, we arrow toward a lone ship that bobs just off a beach of black sand. Even without its blood-red flag, I would've known it was Priya's vessel from the number of frolicking serp—

Black sand.

I snap my gaze off the undulating scaled bodies and onto the beach.

That was the color of the sand in Behati's vision.

I'm still scrutinizing it when Cathal lands. I dismount from the Crow to the sound of Priya's frustrated diatribe, entirely aimed at Cathal, and walk on gummy legs toward the stern of the ship.

"Are you all right, Rajka?" Abrax asks, coming to stand beside me.

"Black sand," I murmur.

"Yes. Not exactly inviting, is it?"

Not a single soul wanders on the beach, yet I can smell burning wood and baking bread, which leads me to think there must be dwellings inside the neighboring forest. "All beach in Luce black?"

"No. Only this one." Abrax says something about the rock being volcanic, then proceeds to explain what it means, but I cannot concentrate on a word he says, because he's just confirmed that *this* is where I will meet *him*.

What if I keep my distance from that beach? What happens then? Will the Mahananda change the location of our encounter?

Someone grazes my elbow—Asha. "Your grandmother is calling you."

I blink at her, then float back to where Cathal stands, casting shadows on everyone but my grandmother. Her finger is already bleeding by the time I come within arm's reach of her. In quick strokes, she darkens my hair and brightens my eyes, making me other.

I think of the bargain I decided to strike with Cathal, and consider striking it then and there. But the male is so proud, that if I ask him in front of an audience, odds are that he will scoff, and it'll fan his desire to keep me from the human I'm not entirely certain I *want* to meet in the first place.

Great Mahananda, what *do* I even want?

I want to see Fallon. I want that. "Nuptials when?"

"Now. We're just waiting for our escort. Ah, here is Justus Rossi now." The queen turns toward a cloud of gleaming vessels crafted from wood as black as the sand on the fateful beach. "Generali!" she calls out in greeting.

"Sumaca. Welcome." Lorcan's Fae general bows deep, the sun burnishing the long orange and silver braid that rests against his Crow-black uniform.

The soldiers, too, wear black. They all gape at our ship filled with Pink-eyes. Though the Shabbins have ventured out of the queendom since the wards have come down, they apparently remain an arresting sight. I suppose it'll take centuries to repair the damage that my mother reaped.

"May I lend you some air-Fae, Sumaca?" Rossi asks. "Though there's no hurry, it'll make your trip to Isolacuori swifter."

After Priya nods, one of the ships sidles up to ours, which allows two men and one woman to hop aboard—all of them have gray irises like Sybille.

Fallon once explained that magic colors Faerie eyes like blood-magic colors Shabbin eyes. Gray irises master wind; red, fire; blue, water; and green, nature.

Rossi yells orders in Lucin to the soldiers, and then we're off, clipping the waves at a speed that makes me cling to the mast for fear of being blown away. The wind is loud and cool, the air, rife with sun and salt and gyrating Crows. For a heartbeat, my lids close and my worries melt with the thrill and heat of the journey.

But then Cathal's muttering makes them open anew. He's glaring at the dense throng of vessels bobbing on the stretch of limpid water that separates a tiny atoll of white marble and gold from a rainbow city built around thin waterways. Isolacuori and Tarecuori. The latter is where my daughter grew up. Where she swam and befriended a serpent she named Minimus—*me*. Where she laughed and ran amok with Phoebus and Sybille. Where she worked inside a tavern called *Bottom of the Jug*, owned by Sybille's family.

As I watch the splendor of Lorcan's kingdom, sorrow curdles my heart for all the bygone years. "Fallon know?"

"Know what, Príona?"

I meet his gaze that is still enflamed by exhaustion and anger. "That I know she *ours*."

A muscle jumps beside Cathal's temple. "No. I thought you might want to tell her."

I nod. "Thank you."

The air-Fae must snuff out their magic for the sails shrivel and our ship slows.

"Cathal, I bargain for you."

He turns toward me, his expression wavering between amusement and doubt. "I'm listening."

"Shabbins have many mate."

"No."

133

I gasp. "I no say bargain."

"You're going to bargain with me to let you run into the arms of your new mate in exchange for which you'll string me along. Am I correct?"

I release the mast and fold my arms. "I Shabbin."

"You're a shifter."

"Not Crow."

He turns more fully toward me, eclipsing everything and everyone. "Perhaps, but I'm a Crow, and Crows have *one* mate, Daya. And they don't share."

"I no choose this new male."

"But you can. You can choose him, or you can choose me." Cathal, in that moment, resembles the craggy peaks of his mountain home, where few can thrive—least of all a serpent. "You cannot have us both." He searches the face that isn't mine for an answer that will be mine.

"What if Mahananda pick new mate for you, Cathal. What you do?"

His rough hand cups my cheek with the utmost tenderness. "Zendaya of Shabbe, you are and will always be my one and only."

My chest heats. At first, I think it's because I must've struck another bargain, but when the heat spreads, I realize it doesn't stem from magic but from how powerfully my heart beats for Cathal.

I am a breath away from promising him that I will never venture toward the black beach when the air churns with smoke right beside us. Smoke that turns into the most beautiful girl in the world, wearing a gown made of violet stones that shimmer like the trapped bubbles in the Amkhuti.

Fallon glowers at the hand resting on my cheek. "What the fuck, Dádhi?"

My breath skips, and I take a step back, making his arm fall. Was she not informed I'd come? Was I not supposed to be here?

Cathal sighs, then in Crow, he murmurs something that widens Fallon's mouth and softens her stare. When I catch the word *Mádhi*,

I realize the reason for Fallon's outburst: she thought her father was touching some stranger's face.

She says something in Crow that makes the tough male crack a grin as lopsided as his nose. Cathal reminds me of my beloved moat —full of stone shelves, each one hiding a world of color and life amidst the shadow of another. He also *feels* like the Amkhuti—like a haven, a place in which I can exist without fear and explore without haste.

"I so happy see you, Fallon." I reach out to take her hands. "Miss you so much."

Fallon gulps in a shaky breath. "I knew you'd learn to speak Shabbin fast, Daya."

The sound of my given name on her lips shrivels my joy. "Mádhi. No Daya."

"I..." She licks her lips. "All right." She glances up at her father, but his eyes remain fastened to my face. I know what she's seeking— whether I understand what that word means.

"Behati say history to me. I know I make you"—I meet Cathal's eyes—"with mate."

His chest lifts with a long, slow breath.

I know what I want. I want him. I want Fallon. I want my old life, not a new one.

I choose you. You and Fallon. I choose never to visit that black beach.

As I stare at him, his face dims and becomes another's, as though my conscience isn't pleased with my decision. I squeeze my eyes shut to chase away the image of my intended mate, but it clings to my lids like the Shabbin children had held on to their gold coins.

Go away.

Behati's vision unspools in greater detail until I think I could pick the male out in a crowd: his nose is long, his lips almost as full as my own, his jaw, smooth, and his shorn hair...his shorn hair shines an odd shade of emerald.

"I feel like I've missed so much," Fallon murmurs.

Though I take her in my arms and focus on her, *he* keeps haunting me.

Go away, I repeat in my thoughts, clasping my lids as tightly as I clasp my daughter. This time, his image fades but the odd hue of his hair lingers. I decide it must be a trick of the moonlight, because as far as I've heard and seen, no one has hair the color of leaves.

Chapter 22
Zendaya

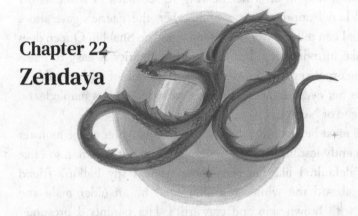

"The Glacin galleon just pulled in. It's time," Fallon says. "Will you both come stand by my side?"

"Yes." The answer rushes from my lips at the same time as Cathal says, "We better not, sweetheart."

"But no one will know who she is since she *is* concealed."

"They'll wonder—like you did—why I'm standing beside a stranger."

"They'll assume you fell for a Shabbin during our month-long stay."

"I would never." Cathal balls his fingers, which makes the leather he's wrapped around his forearms creak.

Fallon rolls her eyes. "I know this, but the Fae don't understand much about our customs, Dádhi."

"I will not risk it."

As Fallon's smile slips, I say, "Cathal, you go. I stay on ship with Taytah."

"I—" He stares at our daughter, then at me, then back at our daughter. "I—"

"Important to Fallon. Go." I squeeze her hand once more. "I hear Taytah call me."

I don't. I imagine they both know I lie since their hearing is as sharp as my sense of smell. I sidestep the beast with the sad eyes and our beautiful, grown-up child to join my grandmother. She's chatting with a woman on a neighboring vessel that's as white as my tusk. When I approach my grandmother, the Faerie's gaze slides over me. I can tell she wonders who I am. The Shabbin Queen does not make introductions, but the Faerie's identity is easy to guess from the ornate crown she wears, a composition of cut emeralds as green as her eyes arranged around a crest depicting a maple leaf—the Queen of Nebba.

She must be Eponine, the sympathetic daughter of the monster who recently lost his life. Fallon despised him but likes her, so I like her by default. I like her even more when I spy Fallon's friend Sybille aboard the white ship, bracketed by an older male and female with brown skin and gray irises. Her parents, I presume? And the woman with the halo of dark curls standing in Eponine's shadow must be Sybille's sister, the one Eponine chose as her foreign advisor. Her features and stare are as sharp as Eponine's ears, a stark contrast to her younger sibling, who's all curves and laughter.

I'm trying to recall her name when my gaze clocks a mammoth vessel pulling in beside us, flanked by a myriad of other ships. All of them fly pale blue flags adorned with the Glacin crest—a white snowflake. Its sight steals my breath for it represents what past-me had apparently adored: snow.

Asha arches her eyebrows and snorts. "Did the northerners' invitation mention a war instead of a wedding?"

"They come fight?" I murmur.

The queen clasps my hand. "No, emMoti. King Vladimir merely enjoys having an entourage."

"*And* the largest ship," Asha says. "Probably to compensate for what rests between his legs."

I squint to make out what *rests between his legs* but spot only something resting on his shoulder—a slumbering white-furred beast.

Wait...does legs mean shoulders? Did I confuse the words?

As I contemplate this, I study the monarch whose hair is the same white as my grandmother's, the same shade as the male standing right behind him. I imagine it's his son, just like I imagine the two young females framing him must be his daughters. I'm struck by how much the girls resemble one another. It's as though they are one and the same.

Music suddenly rises from the ocean. Well, not *from* the ocean, but from little boats garlanded in roses in full bloom where males in great regalia are stroking instruments made of wood and strings. The melody is lovely, delicate, like a warm, lulling breeze that dances through leaves and flutters petals.

It casts a deep tranquility over Lorcan's land. One that is only disturbed by the swivel of heads as everyone looks between the sky and a large wooden raft shaded by an arbor festooned with black ribbons and crimson roses in full bloom. Next to one of the four slender pillars stands Cathal and a woman with silver-black hair wearing Crow stripes—Arin.

When I'd first met her at my "rebirth," I assumed she was Phoebus's mother from how affectionate they were, but then Fallon had explained that Arin was *Lorcan's* mother, and that she and Phoebus had bonded when he'd moved into the Sky Castle.

A deep voice suddenly rolls over the string music, matching the subtle notes, before strengthening and overpowering them. Though I don't grasp the words, their unctuous beauty coaxes little bumps over my skin and carries Arin's hand to her lashes.

Two more people join Arin and Cathal on the floating platform —Justus Rossi and...and Ceres.

I turn toward Priya. "Why Ceres and no you, Taytah?"

"Because I'd rather watch over them from here with you, emMoti." She squeezes my fingers, drawing them to her lips for a kiss.

The gesture catches Sybille's sister's eye, who seems to be the only one not waiting with bated breath for the arrival of the Lucin King and his mate. I can feel her giving me another long once-over. Will she figure out who I am or will she assume I'm one of the Shabbin Queen's lovers? I realize I don't much care, for I like Sybille and she loves her sister. I've nothing to fear from them.

My thoughts evaporate when five streaks of darkness strike the platform and knit into the shape of Lorcan Ríhbiadh. Like Cathal, he wears leather and iron. Like all the other monarchs, he wears a crown, though his is so thin and simple, it gets lost in his wind-tossed black locks. He extends his hand toward the sky. A Crow sweeps low before becoming smoke and finally flesh.

Fallon's appearance causes another wave of goosebumps to dash across my skin. It also causes the water to churn and foam around the platform. I think an air-Fae must be blowing on the bobbing platform, which agitates my heart, but soon realize the commotion isn't Faerie-made.

Dozens of serpents rise and slap the water around Fallon, all of them seeking her attention, which she gives them in spades. While she crouches to stroke their tusks and the skin around them, Lorcan speaks words in Lucin to his people. I don't even attempt to glean what he's saying, my skin tightening and tightening.

"Taytah," I whisper.

"What is it, emMoti?"

"I need—"

"What do you need?"

My fingers jerk out of hers. "I need—I need shift."

"Right now? You cannot repress..."

I shake my head, my vision crackling at the edges, my bones aching. If I don't dive into the water, I will shift right here on the deck and everyone will see what Priya took such care to hide.

Her warning about Faeries slaughtering serpents brightens my mind. What if one of them tries to kill me? What if the Nebban queen grows vines and trusses me up in them? Could she squeeze the air from my lungs? Could she kill me?

My ears buzz. My jaw clenches. A blaze pricks my forehead.

"Asha, dive with her," Priya murmurs.

Asha removes her weapon's belt and tosses it at Abrax.

"And do not let her wander."

"I won't leave her side, Sumaca," Asha promises, already

painting the stripes along her neck that will help her breathe underwater.

"I'm sorry," I murmur, my lips tingling as hard as the rest of me.

Asha grins. "I was getting too hot, anyway."

She jumps in before me, which garners quite a lot of attention.

"What if...?" I side-eye the serpents around the wedding platform, but the more I stare at them, the more my desire to shift becomes pressing.

The queen brackets my cheeks. "Every serpent in the ocean is your friend, emMoti. You are safe."

I blink away the heat creeping under my lashes.

"You—are—safe," she repeats, and then she kisses my forehead that tingles so hard, I push away from her before I spear her mouth and jump in after Asha.

The instant my skin connects with the ocean's salt, my scales pop free. For a moment, I'm overwhelmed by bliss, as though my human flesh had been compressing all of my organs, but then I catch sight of the whirlwind of serpents ringing the wooden platform upon which my daughter stands. I snap into movement and muscle past them. Although they hiss and bleat, I shove them aside, using both my tusk and body, which are significantly larger than theirs.

And then I spring my face out of the water. It is only once my gaze meets Fallon's that I calm. She blinks at me, then glances over her shoulder at the Shabbin ship as though to ascertain that I'm missing from it. At Priya's nod, her face spins back toward me. Cathal's, too. Where Fallon smiles, he scowls and pops his fingers into fists.

Fallon presses her lips to the slit that is my ear in this form and murmurs, "Mádhi, I will always love you most."

I gobble down her words, hissing when a blue serpent attempts to steal Fallon's attention.

She kisses my nose before standing. I stare as Justus hands Lorcan a golden crown that isn't the same as his. Though simple, it's composed of sticks of gold that stick up like my tusk. The king speaks a few words before slipping the crown into Fallon's braided hair. And then he molds her waist with his palms and slants his mouth over hers.

The music slows, coming to a standstill before picking up in both volume and speed when Fallon and Lorcan break apart under a thunder of smacking palms that has me twisting around and around.

It's all so loud, so pungent, so much. My crazed gaze snares Cathal's a second before I topple back, and my place is usurped by another serpent craving Fallon's attention.

A rattling tail slaps me across the face, and I blink. Sink. Something grazes my scales. I whirl to find Asha's pink eyes steady on my rounded ones. She tries to press her palms to my forehead, but I don't want her thoughts.

My thoughts are already too much.

Too much.

I roll away, head spinning, heart galloping. The water beneath me is so murky that I think night has fallen, but a glance above reveals a glimmering cyan striated with foam and—

Something large and dark carves into the water. I think it's a sinking ship, but then I spy feathers, a metal beak, and black eyes that shrink into brown ones. Bubbles snake out of Cathal's nose as he flutters his feet and windmills his arms to reach me, but the deeper he dives, the deeper I drop, until my body hits something so sharp it tears a shriek from my mouth.

I crane my neck and wring my body until I've managed to unhook myself from whatever coral impaled me. I jerk around, then recoil when I meet a giant, vacant stare. Arms band around me, clasp me from behind, and then a hand snares my tusk, pink eyes replacing the colorless ones.

Asha sets one palm on my forehead, then slowly unwraps her other hand from my tusk. As she smooths it across my forehead, my gaze snicks on the giant's eyes again. They belong to a bloodless face that's topped with a crown made of sticks like Fallon's, only these are as tall as Cathal and pure white, save for a black smear on top of one.

Suddenly the giant's face fades and I see my human self walking in the palace's Shabbin gardens, pink hair bouncing against my hot nape, sunshine glinting against my retracted tusk. Hands clasp mine, squeeze. And then Fallon's face materializes before mine and she says, "Shift, Zendaya."

I blink. I don't want her to call me by my name. I want her to call me Mádhi. I want to be her mother.

"Shift," she repeats. And then another voice, a deep raucous one, garbles the very same word.

My throat clenches as I wrench my face from Asha's and twirl. Two tiny bubbles pop from Cathal's lips. And then his eyes roll and his strength wanes, the knot of his arms slipping.

Air. He needs air. I coil my aching tail around his large body and grip him. And then I shoot upward, swimming fast in spite of the weight I carry. Asha swims beside me, propelling herself using her arms.

When I reach the surface, I sweep my tail and bowl Cathal's body upward. Asha snares him around the torso. The ocean suddenly flickers, darkens, and my body shudders. When light fans across the obscurity, I find that my tail has split.

I give a hard kick. Pain flares down my leg. I hook the pink fabric of my gown and pluck it from my skin, finding a deep gouge weeping black blood. I squint at the ocean floor, toward that spot of white, but get distracted by the long, indigo slit and the scaled bodies undulating over it.

A few serpents look up. Their nostrils flare. A juvenile darts toward me but halts, scrutinizes me, then curls in on itself like a millipede, before dashing toward the underwater trench. I'm still staring after it when two rough palms seize my cheeks and hinge my neck back.

Cathal nods to the surface, to the only place where we can coexist. I use my arms to avoid jostling my legs, but stretching my arms shortens my breaths and stokes the fire engulfing my upper thigh. The second we break the surface, I gulp in the warm, bright air as though my lungs had been stripped of it since I dove off my grandmother's ship.

Cathal's thumbs arc across my cheekbones. "Shh."

Asha murmurs a word which the Shabbins use when something not good happens. One glance upward reveals the reason for her word. We've emerged right beside the Glacin galleon, and everyone aboard is peering down at us.

At me.

Chapter 23
Cathal

King Vladimir stands at the railing of his galleon, his silver eyes stroking over Daya's features in a way that shakes her body with shudders. "Now, what have you fished out of the deep, Cathal Báeinach?" he asks in Glacin.

"Is that a mermaid?" one of his twins shrills.

"Mermaids only exist in those terrible books you read, Izolda," her sister quips.

Though I realize I cannot shield Daya entirely, one of my hands slips into her pink braid and presses her face into the crook of my neck, while the other curls around her waist.

"They're great books," Izolda mutters just as Daya releases a small whimper.

I faze the Glacins out and murmur in Shabbin, "What is it?"

"Nothing." Though she clenches her teeth, I catch a second whimper.

Evidently, it's not nothing.

"Would you like us to toss you a buoy?" As Vladimir caresses the dead fox ornament draped over his shoulder, his ivory bangles clink together.

That must be the reason for Zendaya's whimper: because she recognizes his bracelets' provenance. I want to rip them off his arms.

145

"Can you fly her back to our ship, Cathal?" Asha asks, not bothering to answer the Glacin King.

I will fly her out of Filiaserpens, but not onto any vessel. I cannot risk her jumping into the ocean again. I don't think my heart or lungs could take another fevered swim.

"Príona, get on my back and hold on to my neck," I whisper into her ear.

Once she does, I allow my body to swell. With a snap of my wings, I soar off the ocean's surface and past the gawping crowd.

Lore, please tell my daughter that I'm sorry for leaving.

Is everything all right?

It is now. Oh, and inform Priya that I'm bringing Daya home.

Which home?

Mine.

He snorts. *Cannot wait for that conversation.*

Daya is my mate.

Lorcan's silent, but it's a wrought silence. One that feels loaded with warnings not to get reattached. It's too late for that. Our minds may no longer be linked, but Zendaya's become the axis along which spins my entire world.

The metallic tinge of fear that washed over me when I realized the pink serpent was Daya... When her head vanished beneath the surface... When...

I beat my wings, hastening to outrun my fear, but it adheres to me like the woman on my back. When I feel her cheek press into my nape and her body relax against mine, my nerves stop crackling. Which isn't to say I calm—because I don't. As we crest over swamp, forest, and hill, tension bites at my marrow and nips at my muscles.

It's only once I swoop through the northern hatch of the Sky Kingdom hours later that a sense of ease washes through me. My journey down the hallway is slow and steady, my transformation, on the other hand, is short and abrupt. The second I am flesh, I whirl

146

and snatch Zendaya's body before her feet can even graze the ground.

I thought she was sleeping but find her lashes lifted. I carry her over the threshold. I should probably set her down, but since she doesn't ask this of me yet, I transport her all the way to my bed. My relief winks out of existence when I notice the black stain on her dress. I crouch and grow out my talons to shred the dried fabric and get a clear picture of what I'm contending with. My gums ache when I spot a deep cut on her upper thigh.

If only I could lick her wound clo— I raise my hand to her mouth, hoping that the Sky Kingdom's walls won't block her healing ability. After all, it doesn't block Shabbin crystals. "Spit."

"What?"

"So you can heal yourself with that extraordinary saliva, *mo Sifair*."

Her cheeks pinken. I hope it's because of my new nickname, and not because she's embarrassed to spit.

"My tongue heal, Cathal. Not water in mouth."

"Let's try it anyway."

As she props herself up onto one forearm, her cheeks hollow and she spits. I carefully drip the transparent salve into her cut.

I wait with bated breath for the skin to seal, but Zendaya's saliva merely pools in the wound before dribbling out, carrying along a streak of her black blood.

"I tell you. Tongue. And I no can reach in this form." She sticks out her tongue and hinges at the waist to demonstrate.

"But in your serpent form you could..."

"Yes."

"Do you need water to shift?"

She shrugs. "I need ocean, I think. I no turn Serpent in bath." She must sense my reticence to carry her back out of the castle and into the sea, because she grazes my cheek. "No hurt. I heal fast."

"Give me a second." I stand, throw off my armor and vambraces. "Don't move."

She stares up at me with those unfathomable eyes, made larger and blacker by the thick rim of her lashes. I wait for her nod before turning into smoke and streaking toward the healing quarters, which Arin stocks with salves that she pulps and brews herself, thanks to her flourishing herb garden.

I gather gauze, a safety pin, and a bottle labeled: "Staunches bleeding."

I tuck everything inside my trousers' waistband, then shift and return to my injured mate.

Who is *not* in my bed.

I'm about to storm the castle to locate her when I hear the water running in my bathing chamber. I step inside to find her standing naked in my shower with her face tipped up and her eyes closed. I pull my healing paraphernalia from my waistband and lay it out on the dark stone sink top.

Zendaya must sense my presence because she glances over her shoulder at me and sighs. "No work."

"What"—I swallow—"doesn't work?" I clear my throat that's grown husky at the sight of her glistening, tanned flesh. It isn't the first time I've laid eyes on her naked form, but it's the first time she stands naked in a space that is mine, knowing full well how fucking attracted I am to her.

"Shift to Serpent." She spins the dial on the wall. I'm surprised she even knew how it worked considering they don't have showers in her homeland, though they do have pipes and levers.

I rub the back of my neck and attempt to keep my gaze leveled on her face as she takes a towel and pats her skin dry, avoiding her gash.

"What you bring?" She is now rubbing the towel over her hair while the rest of her...the rest of her is bare.

"What?" I blink at her.

A small smile plays on her lips as she nods to my sink top.

"Ointment to stop the bleeding and a bandage to wrap around your thigh." My heart begins to racket as I picture wrapping the dressing and, holy fuck...I should probably suggest she do it herself.

My leather breeches are suddenly so tight that I half expect to burst through the laces.

She's hurt, you fucking creep, I chide my cock that keeps swelling.

I close my eyes, nostrils flaring as I try to calm down before I put my hands on her body and play doctor.

"Cathal?" Her bright voice agitates my blood some more.

When I feel her hand on my jaw, I snap my lids up.

She flinches and lowers her arm. I want to snatch her wrist and carry her palm back to my cheek. I want her to touch me again. Instead, I snatch the bottle of ointment and unscrew the lid, and then I sprinkle the elixir onto my fingers and carefully slather the wound. Her hiss catches on my earlobe.

"Bearable?"

Teeth denting her bottom lip, she nods. Arin's ointment works like a charm. Although it doesn't magically seal Zendaya's wound, the black essence that runs through her veins no longer dribbles out.

My hand shakes as I set the bottle back down and seize the gauze. "I—um...I..."

She tilts her head.

"I'm going to wrap this around your, uh, leg."

She nods.

I step to the side before crouching, because unlike when she crouched before me, I've not an ounce of innocence. If I crouch in front of her mound, or in front of her ass...Mórrígan have mercy on my soul.

Keeping my gaze locked on the gash and the bruised skin ringing it, I unroll the gauze and begin to wrap it. Too low. I tug the strip up until it shelters the wound, then loop it once more, a little more snugly this time. As I pass the roll between her legs, my knuckle grazes her slit which causes a shallow breath to leave her lips and a ragged one to leave mine.

"I'm sorry. I didn't mean to—" I glower at her wound. "Touch you there."

Her throat clenches. "Like Fallon say, fair and square now."

149

"Let's not talk about our daughter right now."

"Why?"

"Because, Daya"—I tuck the safety pin through the gauze—"I'm having very unfatherly thoughts at the moment."

"Like what?"

I tip my head back to meet her stare. "Like how I'd like to touch you *everywhere*."

Her throat dips. "I have question."

I sit back on my heels, spinning the gauze bobbin between my fingers to keep them at bay.

"Do I look like old Zendaya?"

"Identical."

"Except hair, eyes, and forehead." She pokes at the pearl.

"Yes. And scars. You got those when you became a serpent."

"So, skin was more pretty before?"

"No. Your skin is fucking beautiful now." As I stand, I smooth my fingers over the bandage, then allow them to drift higher, over the marked indent of her waist and the flared ladder of her ribs, before skimming them toward her spine. How I long to feel it bend like it would when she'd ride my dick. My balls tighten and my cock...it weeps for this new version of my mate. "Any lingering pain?"

When she shakes her head, I chuck the gauze aside, then wash my hands with soap that I end up scrubbing over my ugly face.

"Taytah angry that everyone see me?" she asks, winding the towel around herself.

"They would've eventually seen you, Daya. Besides, you've nothing to fear from any of them, for if they so much as caused your heart to beat out of rhythm, I'd kill them. And Lorcan would sanctify the killing since no one threatens a Crow's mate."

Her silence irks me. Is she thinking of that human the Cauldron foresaw her with? The mere thought of him has my innards cramping.

I will her to shatter the quiet. In her past life, she was so vocal and vibrant. Full of confidence and laughter. Mórrígan, how she could laugh. It would roll over the old stones of this castle and illuminate the dimmest hearts, especially mine. Always mine.

"Is Fallon angry I ruin nuptials?"

"You didn't ruin anything. Besides, like your grandmother said, the ceremony was all for show."

"Do Crows no marry?"

"We do."

"Before, we...marry?"

"No. We were in the middle of a war. Marriage wasn't exactly on our minds. Besides, we were mates with a child on the way." After toweling my face dry, I grab the block of charcoal and baste my fingers before painting fresh stripes. "We didn't need to prove we were together by exchanging vows in front of a crowd. In our case, the only thing marriage would've changed was my status, since you were slated to inherit the Shabbin throne."

She watches my blackened fingers drag from the shattered bridge of my nose to my throbbing temples. "Kanti want crown."

"She may want it, but it's still yours by birthright."

"Do you want crown, Cathal?"

Slowly, I turn and lean back. "I've never cared about crowns. The only thing I've ever given a damn about is my family."

I don't clarify who my family consists of, worried she may feel pressured to feel a certain way toward me since I still consider her my mate.

"Where you go?"

I frown. "I'm not going anywhere."

"Then why draw on face?" She flutters her fingers in the direction of my cheekbones.

I smile. "Because I'm a creature of habit."

"What is habit?"

"It's doing the same thing over and over."

"What habit else you have?"

"My life has always been so centered on fighting and keeping the Sky Kingdom safe that I never really developed other habits."

"You no read books like Phoebus?"

"Occasionally."

She tucks her tongue into the corner of her pillowy lips, making my attention taper there. "What do when no fighting or staring at me?"

I choke on a swallow, then cough.

She smiles. "You pink again, Cathal Báeinach."

I cross my arms.

"Why color change?"

"Because you make my heart beat erratically, which tosses the blood in my veins, causing it to converge in my face"—I nod to my crotch—"and lower."

She frowns.

I readjust myself.

Her eyes jump to mine. "I make cock pink?"

"You make my cock hard."

Her forehead scrunches. "I no understand. I thought cock hard when male is cold."

I balk but then laugh. "The opposite happens when a man's cold, actually. It retracts."

"Like tusk!" She says this excitedly, as though the parallel enchants her.

I smile gently. "How did you come to the conclusion of temperature?"

"When I cold, nipples get hard."

And now I'm staring at her breasts and those pretty beads presently digging into her towel. Fuck. She must be freezing. I push away from the sink, walk into my room, and bang open the door of my closet, coming up with a long-sleeved shirt.

When I turn, she's standing on the other side of the bed. "Until I find you more appropriate apparel"—I tread toward her—"here."

"Thank you." She unwinds the towel, exposing her perfect body to my depraved eyes before garbing herself with my shirt, and Great Mórrígan, I didn't think she could look sexier than she does naked or in her Shabbin gowns, but the way my shirt clings to her curves...

I refuse to believe that she isn't my mate. The pull I feel toward her is far too great.

She sits on the edge of the bed and wrings her hair. "I like room."

"Good, because it's yours."

She peeks at me over her shoulder.

"If you want it to be..." I add, praying she does.

"I want little Serpent." She strokes her flat abdomen. "I need seed to make babe. You have seed."

My heart misses a beat. Is she saying— "You want me for my seed?"

She blinks at my brash timbre. "Why this make mad?"

My throat contracts around a pissed-off swallow. "Because here I was, foolishly hoping you still felt something for *me*."

She keeps studying me, and it feels like she's plucking me feather by feather, laying me bare. Finally, she asks, "You no want babe, Cathal, or you no want babe with me?"

I stab my hair. "I'm a Crow, Daya. Odds are, any child of mine will be a Crow. Like Fallon."

She stares down at the hem of my black shirt that hits her mid-thigh.

"Didn't consider that, did you?" I say gruffly.

She flinches.

"I'm guessing you don't want my seed now."

I will her lips to part and tell me that it doesn't matter. That she still wants me and my Crow seed. But she doesn't. Because it does fucking matter.

"I need to fly," I mutter.

Her onyx stare rises back to my face. I don't expect her to ask me to stay. I don't expect her to tell me that it isn't only my seed that she wants. I've no expectations yet I'm disappointed all the same when she doesn't call me back or ask how long I'll be gone.

If only my brother were still alive. I would've filled his ears with my pathetic anguish, but my brother can no longer give me advice, and my best friend is too busy convincing a bunch of idiot Faeries that he's the righteous ruler of this land. My annoyance is mine alone to carry and sort through.

I stalk out of the apartment, the wooden door groaning as I slam it shut in my wake. I don't shift immediately, preferring to pummel the stone with my boots. It's only once I've reached the hatch that I allow my blood to turn me into a beast.

Perhaps that's the reason the Cauldron didn't mate us in this lifetime... Because her intended is capable of giving her a baby Serpent.

I soar over the Sky Kingdom until stars prick the heavens and clarity pricks my mind. I may always belong to her, but in this lifetime, she doesn't belong to me. When I step back into the apartment, a dress I've borrowed from my daughter's closet slung over my forearm, an indigo veil has fallen over Luce and steeped my chambers in shadows.

My heart expels a pained beat as I take in the spillover of pink strands on the padded leather arm of the club chair Zendaya dragged toward the window. Was she watching for me? I shake my head at the selfish thought. The only reason anyone ever looks out is because they find their surroundings lacking.

Though my throat feels wadded with wool, I call out her name to warn her of my return. She doesn't stir so I set the dress down on the sofa and round the chair. Her cheek is pressed to the leather, her mouth parted around slow, rhythmic breaths, her lashes fanned out over her bronzed skin. Save for that pale dot in the middle of her forehead, with her eyes closed, she's the doppelganger of the woman Meriam robbed me of. How cruel. Why couldn't the Cauldron have given Daya another face?

With a sigh, I scoop her up and lay her on my bed, and then I stretch out beside her.

Tomorrow, I'll set her free.

Chapter 24
Zendaya

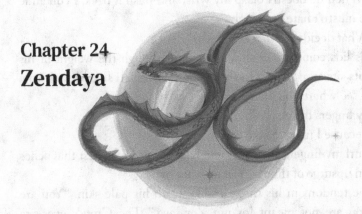

Cathal is sprawled out beside me. I don't know what his return means, the same way I don't know how I climbed inside his bed. Did I sleepwalk or did he carry me? If it was the latter, does that mean he doesn't loathe me for desiring his seed?

I tuck my hands between my cheek and pillow and watch him like he's watched me since I stepped out of the Mahananda. He must sense my attention because his lashes snap up and he pivots his head toward me. A tussled strand collapses into his eyes. I reach out and smooth it back. He goes so still that even his chest no longer skips with breaths.

Unlike mine. "Why you leave, Crow?"

His lashes drop, shielding his still reddened stare. "I went to collect a dress from Fallon's closet since yours is ruined."

"You leave to get dress?"

"No." His eyes shut completely. He must squeeze them for the skin around their outer edge grooves. "I left because I needed space to think."

I wait for him to elaborate, to tell me what he thought about. When silence stretches between us, I begin to worry he doesn't speak them because he intuits they will make me sad. The wayward strand falls again. Again I press it back, threading my fingers through the rumpled mass, which elicits a low rumble from the male. When he doesn't clasp my wrist and push it back, I conclude that he mustn't hate my touch.

"What decide, Cathal Báeinach?"

His lids come up in slow motion, as though the weight of his thoughts sits atop them. "In the vision that Behati shared with you, do you see where you meet him?"

My fingers freeze. "Why?"

"Because I need to take you there."

I curl my fingers and tow them back toward my chest that aches from an upsurge of thuds. "You no want me?"

The tendons in his throat roil beneath his pale skin. "You are not—you are not meant for me, Zendaya." The Crow's eyes are glossy in the leavening dawn. I might not be meant for him, but he evidently wishes I were. Instead of keeping me away, the fissure of heartbreak makes me shuffle nearer, lay my head on his shoulder and drape an arm over his chest.

For a long moment, he stays motionless, but then he curls his own arm around my waist and tucks me close.

"This isn't helping, Daya," he murmurs into my hair, but he doesn't push me away.

"If this about babe, I change mind. I no—"

"You deserve to have another child. One like you."

"Fallon enough." I shrug. "Beside, she same as old-me. Magic in blood."

"But she also took after me." His gentle voice warms my forehead. "We may manage to produce another child together, but what sort of monster would we create? A Serpent with feathers? A Crow with scales? If the Cauldron foresaw you with another male, then that—" His lips flatten, disappearing into the coarse hair bordering them. "Then that is who you need to lay with." A deep shudder rolls through him and into me.

I crane my neck to stare up into his face, but his eyes are shut once more, and he's pinching the bridge of his nose, croaking a, "Focá."

I lift the hand I have on his chest and cup his cheek, and then I'm pivoting his face, driving my fingers through his hair to snare the back of his head and carry it lower, closer to mine. "Cathal, consent I kiss?"

His lids come up so fast I feel the rush of air from his lashes.

"Yes?"

"Príona...it's a terrible idea."

"Why?"

"Because how the fuck am I supposed to let you go if I get a taste of you?"

I hope a taste will be enough, for I'm terribly fond of the vigor of his arms and the heat of his eyes. I love his fragrance and his scratchy timbre. I like how deeply possessive he is of me, how attentive, how considerate, how gentle.

Even though my bandaged thigh smarts, I climb atop him. His stare is wild, his breathing chaotic. Only his hands on my waist are steady.

"Daya..." he rasps.

I take his bristly jaw between my palms and lean over, and then I slant my mouth over his like I've seen embracing couples do. His lips are as hard as bone. His exhale, scorching like a flame.

Though my heart pounds, I find the act a little underwhelming and suddenly wonder why so many do it. Sure, the connection is intimate, but it's hardly worth moaning over. I start to pull away when one of his hands all but claps the back of my head, and then his lips are moving against mine, and his tongue...it sweeps and plunders. Like a fishing lure, it hooks my rushing exhales, dragging them out of me in the form of an infinite gasp. One which transforms into a moan, and oh, Sweet Mahananda, I finally understand everyone's fondness for kissing.

It's...it's a coming together of so much more than lips and tongues; it's a merging of breaths and heartbeats. One that sweeps through the body like a wave, stirring everything in its wake. It's a current that envelops and tows toward the deep. That could drown souls if one were to give in too often and too long.

I want often. I want long. I want to drown against Cathal's mouth. I think he wants that, too. But I'm wrong, because he flips me onto my back, then pulls away as though I'd bitten him. In case I did, I hunt his lips for a trickle of blood. Though flushed and pulsating, there are no crimson slicks.

"Never." He growls, palms flat against my pillow, knees flush with the side of my knees. I think he's about to warn me that this can never happen again, but then he says, "You can never fucking leave me now. Not for your true mate. Not for the ocean. I won't survive losing you again." He brings one of his hands to my face. His knuckles shake as he skates them across my cheek, across my forehead, across that pale bead that marks me as other. "Swear it, Zendaya of Shabbe. Swear you'll be mine, always."

"New bargain, Cathal of the Sky Kingdom?"

"Just a vow. Just for me. Not a bargain."

"Like marriage vow?"

His throat clenches and I hear him swallow. "Not today. But perhaps you'll do me the honor someday?"

His desire for me dispatches the beats of my heart into every corner of my being and ferries a smile to my mouth that glosses his eyes with new emotion. I raise my arms and curl them around his neck. "I be yours as long as I exist, Cathal of the Sky Kingdom."

His breath clips past his trembling lips. "You will exist forever. *Forever*."

I'm not certain how he will go about convincing the Mahananda to make me immortal, but I like the dream of this always he promises, so I reword my vow. "I always be yours, Crow."

Though no magical dot singes my heart, my skin blazes all the same. I once heard Phoebus say that it burned for his lover. I hadn't understood what he meant, but I do now. Cathal has ignited my body and warmed my heart to the point of melting. If he pressed his chest to mine, I'm not entirely convinced our bodies wouldn't weld together.

"But only if kiss me again."

"Always," he murmurs, his voice trembling like his big body.

"Always, mo mila Sifair." He must sense my devouring curiosity for the new word, because in Shabbin, he says, "Always, my sweet Serpent."

He aligns our lips, but before he can press them to mine once more, he jerks back with a low snarl.

Chapter 25
Zendaya

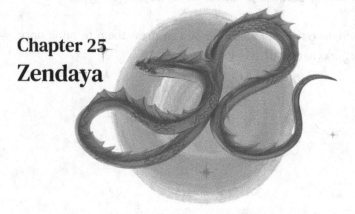

My heart has missed every beat since Cathal rumbled and vaulted out of bed. I prop myself up and scrutinize every last inch of him as he stalks into his living room. He doesn't seem injured or worried, which is somewhat reassuring. What he does seem is furious.

"What wrong?" I ask, as he pounds back toward me holding a sheath of stone-gray satin, the same hue as his bedchamber. *Our* bedchamber. "Lorcan and Fallon want to meet with us now."

My frown grows because, although their timing is inopportune, their company isn't. "And why this make mad?"

"Because I didn't exactly feel like getting out of bed," he mutters, the hollows of his cheeks as high in color as the harsh bones forever casting them in shadow.

I smile. "Soon as meeting over, we come straight back. Deal?"

A small smile jumps onto his lips before jumping off. Does he doubt I'll still want to, or is he worried Priya will cart me off to Shabbe?

I climb to my knees and seize his shoulders. "Cathal, where you go, I go. And where I go, you go." I cant my head. "Yes?"

He expels a harsh, "Yes," on an even harsher exhale.

"Even to Shabbe? In case Taytah send me—"

"Even to Shabbe." He presses his mouth against mine as though to seal his promise. And then we are kissing again, and my head feels light, light, light, as though it's filled with air bubbles. "You need to get dressed," he murmurs against my lips.

I nod and pull off the shirt he lent me. His eyes flare, the brown burning a fiery red around his shrunken pupils.

"Actually, fuck them."

My brow rumples. "What mean *fuck them?*"

"It means that they can wait." His palms shape my waist before gliding over my ribs and up to my breasts, which he cups in his rough hands. He leans forward, his face angled toward one of my very sharp nipples but halts his approach with a new snarl and a snap of his neck. "Oh, how I will cockblock him. Just he wait. Just he fucking wait."

I've no clue what Cathal is going on about, but he's even more livid than before. He pecks my lips, then tosses the gray satin over my head and helps guide my arms through the sleeves that stop mid-forearm, unlike the hem, that breaks past my ankles. The material is soft but stiffer than I'm used to, and grows even more so when he laces a wide strip of black leather around my navel. A glance into his bathing chamber mirror widens my eyes, because I discover I resemble a seasoned warrior instead of a delicate princess.

"Fuck, you're beautiful," he murmurs, coming to stand behind me, and my heart gambols at his compliment.

He tucks my hair to the side to kiss my neck, then must realize the strands are in dire need of brushing, because he seizes a wooden comb and runs it through the waist-long mess. Once he sets aside the comb, I recline against him and burrow my face into his corded neck. A deep pull of his scent—warm musk and wild moss—has my nerves quieting. I wonder if the fragrance of my skin is as alluring. What if I smell like a beached shell, or worse, like a dead fish—briny with a side of seaweed rot?

"What?" he murmurs.

I blink out of my musings.

He strokes the bridge of my nose, smoothing out the rumples. "What's with the grimace?"

I twist my lips.

He slides a knuckle beneath my chin to tip my head up. "Tell me."

"How I smell to you?"

He snorts. When he notices that his snort doesn't ease my qualms, he spins me. "You smell like my mate. Intoxicating. All-consuming." Cathal drags his nose over my forehead then through the part in my hair, his jaw hair tangling with my pink strands. "You smell like my home." His nostrils suddenly flare so wide they waft air. He mutters that word again: "Cockblocker."

Before I can enquire as to what it means, he plucks my hand and pulls me out of our little cocoon of privacy.

"Once I shift, get on my back."

I'm guessing the distance to Lorcan's chambers must be quite great if we must fly there. Crow-Cathal crouches and extends a wing, which he nods to, apparently urging me to use the appendage as a ladder. My climb is hesitant. Though he doesn't flinch, each time my bare feet squash feathers, I do. Stepping on his wing *must* hurt, no? Once settled astride him, I loop my arms around his neck and lean forward.

He jumps into the air, then soars down the hallway before surging through the same hatch we used to enter the castle. I imagined we'd remain indoors but open air must be more agreeable for the shifter's impressive wingspan.

I feel his shoulders roll against my thighs, see his wings tilt, and then he's snapping them, soaring so fast, that I lean forward even more. The male is evidently impatient to get the meeting over with. So am I...

I'm very much looking forward to picking up where we left off. And sit astride Cathal in flesh. Just the thought of it has my pulse quickening, pounding hard against my wide leather belt. Especially when my mind begins to turn over the images my grandmother had shared about the rubbing of naked bodies.

But then my imaginings come to a hasty halt, because the rubbing of two bodies results in babes, and Cathal doesn't want any more. Does that mean we can never explore each other, or are there methods to prevent reproduction? I nibble on my lip, deciding to ask Asha later.

Not for the first time, I wish I could've been reborn with a complete understanding of our world. Since my frustration won't help me figure out how my human body works, I press the emotion away and focus on the land that stumbles out on either side of the castle. Sure enough, the vistas rid me of any and all worries, for they are spectacular. On one side, a raging river carves down a gilded, amber forest; on the other sprawls a luxuriant jungle that melts into dunes of honeyed sand.

I suddenly envy Lore for having such varied landscapes. Shabbe may be lush, but it's all pink stone, green foliage, and aquamarine water. I'm glad Kanti wants the isle, for I much prefer to stay here. The thought of Behati's grandchild has me squinting around Luce. Where is it that she was sent again? Beyond the desert or on one of the land tiles near where Fallon was crowned queen? I wonder if she's met the enemy she was destined to seduce. And then I stop wondering because Cathal is diving through another hatch.

Like the last time he landed, he morphs into flesh before my feet can touch the ground and catches me around the waist. For a moment, he just holds me with both his arms and eyes, but then he sets me down and brushes a feather-light kiss to my lips that renders me breathless.

He steals my fingers and clasps them tight as we traipse down a short hallway toward an enormous wooden door that's already propped open. The instant we step over the threshold and into the vast stone chamber, everyone seated around the wooden table turns toward us, everyone being Lorcan's Siorkahd, our daughter, her grandfather, and my grandmother.

Cathal's fingers tighten as though he's suddenly worried someone may try to wrench us apart. In truth, Taytah, who sits between Justus and Fallon, does seem inclined to do so, what with her tapered stare and pursed lips. Everyone else either seems glad to see us or disinterested by our hand-holding.

"You look well, Zendaya." Lorcan gifts me a rare smile that doesn't quite reach his tired eyes.

I'm guessing the coronation was followed by a party and, perhaps, even some diplomatic talks considering all four monarchs were together. From what I've gleaned, it was the first time in several centuries.

"Has Nebba and Glace departed?" Cathal slides a chair out for me to sit in, his fingers still firm around mine.

Does the male truly worry he'll lose me if he lets go? If we'd been at ocean level, I suppose his fear could've been warranted, but so far above the clouds, the only way out of Lorcan's castle is up, and neither Taytah nor I have wings.

"Eponine has, but Vlad and his entourage are currently lodging in Isolacuori, waiting for us to return to smooth over the finer details of our alliance. They've reiterated their hope that we'll arrange a marriage between the next generation."

Cathal's gaze soars toward Fallon. "What next generation?"

"Relax, Dádhi. There is no next generation yet." She pats her belly, and I realize they're discussing babes, which makes me sit up straighter. "You'd totally be the first to know." She offers him a smile which he's too tense to reciprocate, while my palm drifts to my hollow abdomen.

What if Cathal's wrong in assuming we'd create a monster?

What if Cathal's right, and we do?

Perhaps Behati can foresee or my grandmother can ask the Mahananda?

"Vladimir enquired about a possible *melihap* between Shabbe and Glace." The Shabbin Queen rests her elbows on the table.

Fallon gapes at her, before gasping out a, "What?" while I lean toward Cathal to murmur, "*Melihap?*" hoping he'll define it for me.

The male's so entirely focused on my grandmother that I don't think he's even heard me, but *she* must have, for she explains, "A *melihap* is a coming together of two nations after a period of hostility. A union of sorts."

Cathal growls something in Crow.

"I'm far too old to take a husband." Her pink gaze settles over me, which deepens my frown.

"No." Cathal's timbre is as glacial as his stare. His fingers finally stop strangling mine, but it's only because he's become more shadow than flesh.

"I wasn't contemplating sending Daya to Glace. Not when she's about to meet her mate. I was actually considering offering up Kanti. Since we Shabbins aren't monogamous, a marriage wouldn't prevent her from seducing your enemy, Lore. Unless Konstantin is *the* enemy, in which case—"

"I'm sorry, but what did you say, imTaytah?" My daughter sounds alarmed.

"That monogamy isn't—"

"The part before that," Fallon interrupts. "The part about my mother."

"Oh, didn't your father tell you? Behati foresaw Zendaya meeting her mate in Luce. It's one of the reasons I allowed her to make the trip, since I know how precious true mates are to shifters."

Fallon's complexion whitens while Cathal's purples.

"Isn't it wonderful?" Priya's voice skips around the deathly quiet chamber.

It's not wonderful and I'm not happy she's bringing it up. "I choose Cathal, Taytah."

She sighs. "Though you are Shabbin, abi djhara"—she pushes away from the table and stands—"I'm afraid you'll have to give up polygamy, since shifter mates do not share. Isn't that right, Lore?"

Lorcan doesn't answer. He doesn't even seem to register Priya's question, so focused is he on Cathal.

"Anyway, thanks for keeping my granddaughter safe, Cathal. Shall we?"

"Shall we what?" I ask.

"Head to breakfast in Isolacuori with the Glacins before sailing home. Vladimir's simply dying to make your acquaintance, emMoti."

My tongue feels swollen with heartbeats. I do not want to meet the Glacins, the same way I do not want to go home. This time, it's *my* grip that tightens around Cathal's.

He shoves his chair back and stands, then helps me up. "We're done here."

Lorcan must speak to him through their mind link, because Cathal's shoulders jerk and he turns his glower onto his king. Aloud, he says, "Let Zendaya go. We will join them in a moment."

Cathal's nostrils flare.

"Just to Isolacuori for breakfast. Fallon and Imogen will accompany them. The rest of Priya's guards are already on site."

My daughter bounces out of her seat and rounds the table toward me, her complexion still wan. She speaks softly to her father, who finally relinquishes my hand to her.

Chapter 26
Zendaya

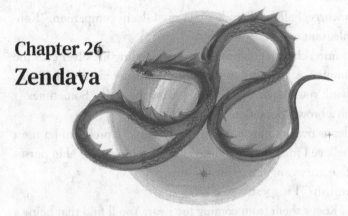

Although Lorcan said they'd join us soon after we left, breakfast comes and goes and they still haven't floated down from Monteluce.

Fallon suggests a walk through the estate gardens. We all stand and trail after Vladimir and Priya, shadowed by guards from all nations. The Glacins wear pale blue; the Lucins, black; the Shabbins, red and white.

"Where Lore and Cathal?" I whisper to Fallon.

She pats my hand. "They should be here shortly, Mádhi." Suddenly she perks up. "Look! It's Syb and Pheebs." Her two friends are bobbing down one of the crystal-clear canals of Isolacuori in a boat that is as slender as it is shiny. She starts to wave at them excitedly but then stops and peers around. "Goddess, I'm terrible at this whole stately queen-thing," she mumbles in Shabbin, which earns her a soft snort from the Prince of Glace, who masters my mother tongue better than I do.

"Give it time, Your Highness," he says. "Soon you'll be just as arrogant and jaded as the rest of us."

Fallon laughs and kisses my cheek, promising she'll be right back. Then she starts toward the golden bridge that my grandmother and Vladimir are crossing, but stops and whirls. I can tell she's concerned about leaving me alone with Konstantin, even though *alone* is a stretch considering Asha and Abrax are but a stride away.

"No worry, Fallon." I smile up at my Glacin companion. "Konstantin pleasant male."

A stunned chortle escapes the Faerie, lending his silver eyes the same glimmer as the cut stones running up the shell of his ears. "Why thank you, Rajka. I try." With a wink, he adds, "Sometimes."

I arch a brow. "Sometimes?"

He leans over to murmur conspiratorially, "I prefer to let most people believe I'm...how do you say it in Shabbin again?" He purses his lips that are as angular as his jawline.

"Churlish?" I suggest.

"Yes. Keeps them from coming too near. You'll find that being a royal is more of a burden than an advantage."

The male may be young but he seems wise beyond his years. To think Kanti is around the same age yet acts like Konstantin's decades younger twin sisters. I don't think the three of them—yes... Kanti was there when we arrived—have stopped gossiping or giggling since our two families sat down in the flower-covered stone veranda, around a table overflowing with Lucin delicacies.

Not even when an uncomfortable silence settled between father and son following the discussion of the railway system that links all sides of Glace. Though Fallon had translated the conversation, she'd left out the query that Konstantin uttered, which had led to the cold front.

I'm tempted to ask him about it, but considering how it had spiked his mood, I decide to reserve my question for Fallon. "Excited for nuptials, Konstantin?"

His eyebrows, that are as black as his hair is white, quirk. "They were quite exciting. Though admittedly, the serpents—and I mean the animals, not you—seemed the most excited of the bunch, didn't they?"

I frown. Why would the serpents be excited about his marriage to Kanti? "Kanti tell serpents?"

This time, Konstantin is the one to frown. "What?"

It strikes me that we mustn't be speaking of the same nuptials. "I talk of *you* and Kanti." I point to him to make sure he understands.

A choking sound reverberates up his throat. "I'm sorry." He wheezes, pounding a fist against his chest to ease his sudden bout of coughing. "Me and Kanti?"

"Apparently King of Glace want Shabbin mate for son. You not hear?"

"No." Konstantin's silver eyes taper on his father's white plait that swings like a clock's pendulum across the back of his sky-blue jacket.

I don't understand how he hasn't peeled the fabric off his shoulders, what with the stifling Lucin heat. "Good for peace."

One of Konstantin's eyes twitches. "Treaties of non-invasion are good for peace. Nuptials are overrated."

"You no want mate?"

That does away with his residual cough. "I'd prefer not to get tied down." Under his breath, he adds, "Especially to someone of my father's choosing."

"Do you have lover?"

He turns his stare toward me. "I'm not lonely, if that's what you're wondering."

"No. I wonder if you already have lover you want marry."

"No." With a sigh, he adds, "The longer I can avoid it, the better. What about you, Rajka? Any...*mates?*"

A hand winds around my waist and tugs me against a body that feels wrought from metal. "Yes. *Me.*"

I glance up at my possessive Crow just as Phoebus, Sybille, and Fallon trundle over to us.

Phoebus has his palm pressed to his chest and says something that makes Sybille and Fallon snort. "Zendaya of Shabbe, you look..." His eyes skim my body.

He says something in Lucin that has Fallon rolling her eyes. "Yes, it's one of my dresses. As for reforming Crow fashion, have at it, Pheebs." Mirth brims in her eyes. "Can't wait to see the new uniforms you'll cook up for the Siorkahd."

Phoebus grins, and I can tell he's already designing new suits for my mate's people.

Sybille asks for a translation, since she isn't as fluent in Shabbin as Phoebus. After hearing all of it, she laughs, head tossed back, palms splayed on her belly. I stare at her babe-filled abdomen, my chest clenching. My daughter must pick up on my envy, because the shimmer has snuffed out of her violet irises. She's staring between me, Sybille's stomach, and her father, who still holds me tight.

Too tight.

The dress also feels suddenly too tight. I glance at the nearest canal, desperate to jump into it. I press away from Cathal, then start walking, reaching around my back to tear off the wide band of leather.

"Daya?" Cathal calls out to me.

"I hot. I need swim." I don't turn around as I say it.

"Here?"

"Let her, Dádhi. There are never any serpents in these waters."

I finally get the belt off and drop it onto the trimmed grass that is as soft as velvet underfoot. I start to gather my skirts to get my dress off when Cathal's smoke congeals in front of me.

With gentle hands, he clasps my wrists. "Please don't take the dress off."

I frown until I catch him glowering at the people around us. I release the stiff gray satin and traipse right to the water's edge. It is as clear as air, with not a single fish or coral blighting the bone-white basin. I dive in feetfirst. My dress balloons around me. I try to sink but there's too much fabric, so I shift, my scales soaring from within and wrapping around me.

My gills must flare from how deeply I exhale, but then an odd prickle seizes them. I attempt to siphon in a breath, but no cool air cycles through my Serpent lungs. I flick my tail to steal a breath farther down the canal, but if anything, the prickling worsens.

What's inside this water?

My tusk breaks the surface and then my head. I try to sneak oxygen from the sky but something must be wrong with my gills, because they don't flutter.

What's happening to me?

I sink back under and try to breathe, but the burn spreads like melting wax. I visualize my other shape, but for some reason—possibly, my rising panic—I cannot melt into flesh. In some distant recess of my brain, I hear my grandmother's warning about the Lucins' hatred of serpents, and I realize that someone must've poisoned my food or this water to tamper with my magic.

I should never have come to Luce. I should've listened to her and to Cathal and stayed in Shabbe.

I crest the surface of the Isolacuorin canal once more, searching for Cathal in the sea of Two-legs. Through my dotty vision, I see him. He's crouched by the water's edge, half-smoke, half-male. His lips move, but my roaring pulse chews up his words. I shoot nearer but misgauge the distance and bang against the stone embankment. Cathal must grab me by the tusk because my head is suddenly out of the water and on his lap.

He speaks again, but again I don't hear him. The dots in front of my eyes become smudges. The smudges, a veil. I shake my head and blink, but no amount of headshaking or blinking manages to disperse the obscurity closing in on me.

I don't want to die. Not again. I want to live.

I want this so fiercely that I muscle more of my clunky body out of the water and onto the land, praying to the Mahananda that exposure to air will bring about my shift, but I dangle haplessly, half in, half out.

My head must slip from Cathal's palms, because he's suddenly gone. Or am I the one who's gone?

Chapter 27
Zendaya

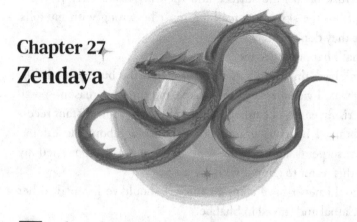

I *refuse* to be gone.

I crack my lids open. Amidst the ashen veil shines twin spots of pink. The spots become brighter, clearer, until I recognize Taytah's eyes.

She strokes my cheek, my neck. My starved brain wonders if it's a dream, but then I feel the faintest trickle of air carve through my scales. Priya doesn't caress; she paints. I'm not sure what sigil she's used, but delicious, sweet oxygen suddenly streaks through my gills and fills my giant body, which lies entirely flopped and coiled on the emerald embankment.

"Shift," my grandmother whispers.

This time, when I call upon my other form, my scales split and my body shrinks. My lips come apart around a gasp that is so violent, it scorches my lungs. And yet I lap at the air, drinking it in tremendous drafts until my head spins from my immoderation.

"Easy, emMoti. Easy." Priya is still drawing on my neck.

My skin tautens, tingles. She must be healing me. My lids bloat with tears.

A soft cloth swooshes over my neck and chest. I turn my head to find Fallon mopping down my skin. The whites of her eyes are as red as garnets, which makes her irises appear luminescent like the algae in the Sahklare. The thought of it makes me ache for my homeland.

She gives me a watery smile that trips right off her lips and murmurs that she's sorry. I imagine for my predicament, for she's not at fault. Could this be my mother's doing? Could she have broken out of her prison and gotten past Behati and the members of the Akwale who stayed behind to guard her and the Mahananda?

I croak out Meriam's name, which makes Fallon's eyebrows wing up. Didn't she consider that this could be my mother's doing?

"No, emMoti. It's not Meriam's fault. Not this time." Priya rinses her hands in a bowl that Abrax has just set beside her.

Though he straightens, my guard doesn't move away. His soft-brown eyes shimmer with the same concern that warps Asha's face, as well as Aoife's, Sybille's, and Phoebus's. I squint into the bright sun, searching for my mate amongst the Two-legs ringing me, but he isn't there. A few Crows are treading the sky above us. Could he be amongst them?

"Lore and Dádhi flew to Nebba," Fallon says, guessing who I seek. The deep furrow that grooves my forehead leads her to add, "To have a word with Eponine since the toxin that poisoned you is produced—*was* produced there."

Phoebus snorts, repeating, "*Have a word.*" Clearly, he doesn't believe our mates' plan is to speak.

I rub my aching neck as Fallon expounds on the subject of this toxin. She tells me that the reason I couldn't breathe is because the Regios filled the Isolacuorin canals with it to keep serpents out.

"I'm sure it's no longer being manufactured," she says, her gaze flitting to the queen, who keeps rinsing her hands even though they're no longer coated in my blood. "You don't think Eponine lied to me yesterday, do you, imTaytah?"

My grandmother finally looks up from the basin and its soiled contents. "If she did, she better prepare for war."

My pulse strikes my neck and the fingers I still have wrapped around it.

"Did she swear an oath that she was no longer producing it, or merely uttered a vapid promise?" my grandmother asks.

Fallon twists her lips. I'm guessing there was no oath swearing.

Sybille says something that includes her sister's name, and then she addresses Aoife. After a rapid exchange in Lucin, the shifter grows out her feathers and crouches. Phoebus helps Sybille climb, muttering something that makes her swipe the back of his blond head.

As she and Aoife take off, he chortles, then ambles back toward us. The second his gaze touches my neck, though, his mirth wanes, and he grimaces. A glance at my filthy frock has my own lips coiling.

Asha crouches beside me. "You didn't suffer when we swam yesterday, did you?"

I shake my head.

"Then the substance must be contained inside these canals."

"How long have they been poisoning the water?" The queen's lips barely flex as she speaks.

"I don't know, imTaytah, but Eponine mentioned—the first time we spoke about it—that at the rate they were dumping it, Mareluce would be salt-free by Yuletide."

The queen goes so quiet that I can hear the Glacins' murmuring even though they stand at a distance from our little party.

"But they've stopped dumping it for at least a month, so—"

"You do not know that, child!" Priya exclaims. "You and Lore have been in Shabbe. You weren't here."

Fallon stands, her expression tightening. "We might not have been *here*, but our people were. Justus was! Luce wasn't *unattended*, imTaytah."

My pulse harshens as the two females I love the most glower at one another. "No fight. Please. I alive." With the help of Asha, I stand, shearing off Fallon's line of sight to her great-grandmother. "Please."

"Let's go." Priya winds her arm through mine. "And, Fallon,

send news with the serpents as soon as you have some." Her tone is so brittle, it scrapes through the air and chafes my wet skin.

She begins to tug me along but I plant my bare feet into the grass. "Where going?"

"Back home."

"Wait, Taytah. Cathal."

She whirls on me. "We are not waiting on that man."

"But—"

She slashes a finger across my mouth, silencing me with a spell. "His home is inhospitable to you, Zendaya." In a lower voice, she adds, "That's twice now, by the way. I'm keeping count."

My eyebrows dip.

"Twice that you almost perished because you couldn't manage to shift back. Twice that he was present when it happened. Have you considered that perhaps, *he's* the reason your magic keeps faltering?"

I try to pry my lips apart to tell her that the two incidents are entirely unrelated, but she's sealed them like the toxin in the canal sealed my gills.

When we reach the golden quay where bobs our ship, I hear her murmur to the sorceress nearest her, "Lock Shabbe off until an antidote is found. Land *and* air. Make the wards porous to animals." Her eyes cut to mine. "*True* animals."

I suck in a breath and shake my head, desperately trying to shape the word, "No," but her blood stifles my scream. I crane my neck, hunting the sky for a Crow, but no winged beast soars over us.

I look over my shoulder for Fallon, but between the dense vegetation and the throng of Shabbins and foreign soldiers on our heels, I cannot spot her. I spot Abrax, though, just off to my right. I flick my gaze toward the sky repeatedly. If he grasps my imploration to send word to Cathal of the queen's intent, he doesn't act on it. Merely transfers his gaze to the ship I'm forced to board.

I understand that my grandmother is trying to shield me. I genuinely do, and I *am* grateful. What I don't understand is why she's so adamant to separate me from Cathal. She cannot actually believe that he's the source of what's befallen me, can she? I mean, yes, the first time I failed to shift back into skin, it was because of his obsidian-laced blood, but he didn't force me to ingest it.

By the time Priya removes her silencing spell, we're halfway back to the pink isle, sailing so briskly that my dress and hair have dried, unlike my anger. I seethe. Especially since my grandmother has bound my backside to the deck's bench to prevent me from diving into the ocean.

She carries a cup of water to my lips.

I turn my head, refusing her offering. "What about mate?"

"The Crow will be fine." I'm about to tell her that's not the mate I'm referring to, when she adds, "Especially since you've healed him."

She's rendered me speechless, and not with her blood this time.

"You seem surprised." She cants her head, drawing the cup down to her hip. "Not only am I the queen, but I'm also the Mahananda's confidant. I know *everything* that transpires within my walls, emMoti. *Everything.*"

I tilt my chin higher, narrowing my eyes. "Then you aware *I* choose heal him. He no force me."

"Yes. I'm aware. The same way I'm well aware that he and Lorcan are planning on using you to heal the others. Why do you think they sent us to Isolacuori ahead of them? To iron out the details of how best to go about it."

"Cathal never force me."

"If it had endangered your life, he wouldn't, but since it merely weakens you—"

"No, Taytah." I shake my head with such vehemence that it jostles my long locks. "You wrong."

"Oh, Daya. You still have so much to learn about our world."

In that moment, I dislike my grandmother. I dislike how she belittles me and vilifies Cathal. How she dismissed Fallon. "Mahananda will be mad at you, Taytah."

"For keeping you away from your Crow lover? I doubt it since it has another mate in store for you."

Gaze fastened to the sky, I say, "A mate you keep me away from."

"Only until an antidote is found."

"He round-ears. If no find antidote soon, maybe he die."

Her pupils shrink as she stares toward the faraway Lucin shore. "If you're bound to meet, then you will meet. Be it next month or next year or next decade."

I blanch because I know what a decade is.

"Once a cure is found, I'll crumble the wards, but until then, I'll not risk your life or the serp..." Her voice dies out as clouds streak over the sun, smothering its light.

Not clouds.

Crows.

Chapter 28
Cathal

Zendaya's beautiful face tilts toward the sky. Toward me.

The anger, which had rushed over me when Fallon's voice resonated through our people's mind link, crackles through my bones, making my wings feel crafted from pure iron.

I will not lose her again.

The Shabbin Queen stares up as well, her white hair snapping behind her like those flags which are brandished when one surrenders. Except, in Priya's case, she's just declared war. As her sorceresses bloody the deck with sigils, I dive toward Daya. My claws knock against something solid...something that repels me. Priya's warded the ship!

I screech with a fury that must skip over the ocean because Lorcan's voice lights up my mind.

Cathal?

I dive again. Again, I hit a translucent wall. I roar.

I will speak with Priya. I will get her to see reason. Come home.

Not without Daya, I growl.

He must understand it's nonnegotiable because he doesn't reiterate his command to turn back.

Fallon, can you penetrate your grandmother's wards? I ask without tearing my gaze off the ship and the pink-haired woman whose hands lay flat against the bench beneath her. Is she trying to stand or keep her body steady?

Can't get past them, Dádhi, Fallon says.

Then we sink the ship! Since everyone aboard is Shabbin, they'll manage to swim. ***Lore, we need a storm.***

Daya wriggles on the bench. Though I cannot hear her, I see her mouth round around shouts. She *is* trying to get up! She *is* trying to get to me!

What I wouldn't do for you, brother, Lore murmurs as a thunderous peal resonates through the darkening sky.

Those sigils they painted are for speed! Fallon exclaims.

Sure enough, the boat is surging toward the ramparts at impossible velocity, one that even I, however fast I beat my wings, cannot match. ***Waves, Lore! We need waves,*** I yell.

I'm hoping that if salt water connects with Zendaya's skin, she'll be able to shift and rid herself of whatever spell her grandmother cast to keep her from diving overboard.

Even though our king's still in Nebba with Justus, he manages to stir the ocean into a frenzy. Foam webs the ashen-sapphire swells, sending Priya's small ship rocking, and everyone—save for Zendaya—skidding across the deck.

On a scale of one to ten, how high are the chances that the Cauldron will seal itself off from our people? Fallon asks.

This fight is between your great-grandmother and me. It has nothing to do with the Cauldron.

In other words, we may have a chance it'll allow Lore to dip a toe in once it recovers?

I cannot think of this now, though as Lorcan's general, I should. I pledged to put our people first, but I cannot think of our people. Not when my mate is being stolen from me.

As I soar faster, the sky flares with lighting that catches on her forehead. Though she's still in flesh, her tusk is lengthening, and her skin, coloring. A wave claps the hull of the boat and closes over the deck. When it recedes, my mate is fully shifted and slithering away from the blasted bench.

Abrax throws himself on her. Asha, as well, but however hard they clasp her, her slick body glides out of their arms and plunges past the railing into the ocean. Her grandmother shrieks. Asha jumps in after Daya.

Lore, Daya broke free, I tell him as my fellow Crows catch up to me. *Stop the storm so I can track her.*

A handful of minutes later, my friend clears the sky and settles the ocean. Priya's boat has stopped barreling toward Shabbe and is turning at such a sharp angle that its mast brushes the flat surf.

A moment later, Asha's head pops out. "I don't see her, Sumaca!"

I don't either. Alarm judders my daughter's voice.

Priya raises her incendiary gaze to mine, her hair so wet, it lies matted to the oval frame of her face. "I will *never* allow Lorcan inside the Mahananda. Not as long as I am queen. *Never.*"

I vow, in that moment, to put Zendaya on the throne.

Priya trembles from the force of her anger. "You've damned your people, Cathal, and you did all of this for a woman who isn't even your mate."

She is my mate! Our minds might not be bonded anymore, but our hearts and souls are. I felt it when we kissed. I feel it every time Zendaya's hand brushes across my skin.

Behati lied. I'm certain of it. The same way I'm certain the pink serpent carving through the ocean belongs with me.

Fallon must read my temptation to gore Priya because she flies right into my face. *Operation* **Keep Shabbin Queen Talon-Free** *starts now.*

I glower at my daughter.

Seriously. She flaps her wing in my face. *Find Mother.*

I afford Priya and her little ship one more scathing look before giving the ocean my full attention. My certainty that I will sense my mate begins to wane when after an hour, no Crow or Shabbin has caught even a glimpse of pink. And then dread sets in.

What if she rests at the bottom of the ocean because her gills wouldn't lift?

What if another serpent attacked her?

When the first star pricks the horizon, my dread turns to terror. If only Priya could drain the entire ocean like she drained the Amkhuti. I wonder if she's considering it. I wonder if she could. I'm tempted to swallow my pride and land on her ship to ask when a guttural shout rends the air.

I turn sharply, then swoop low. I expect to come across Zendaya but find only two fishermen brawling over Cauldron only knows what.

A fresh layer of fretfulness coalesces behind my breastbone as I beat my wings and rise, hunting the darkening ocean for my mate's pink body.

Chapter 29
Zendaya

I think for certain that the boy's dead the moment his body splashes the water.

I think the long piece of wood tipped in sharp metal that protrudes from his chest must've ended his mortal existence, but then his fingers spasm around the stalk and bubbles leak from his flaring nostrils. There's still life in him!

He tugs on the rusted spear. Though the thing moves, it's so long that he remains skewered upon it. His green eyes find mine in the dark, wide with desperation. I bite the wood and pull until I've disconnected it from his abdomen. He gasps, but the sound is consumed by the churning of water above as the fishing vessel clips away at great speed.

My blood boils with the desire to avenge the boy who threw himself in front of a spear destined for me. Though the glimpse I got of the murderer was distorted by water, I heard him speak and glimpsed yellow hair bound in a short tail.

I'll hunt the monster and make him pay, but first...first, I lap at his victim's gaping wound, hoping that my tongue will have the power to seal his flesh. The human's hand falls against my cheek and strokes, before drifting away. When his body gives a hard jerk, I glance at his face. His skin is as white as the moon gilding his listless body.

It's only then that I recall that humans can't breathe underwater. *An idiot, Zendaya. That is what you are. How could you forget such an important fact about humans?*

I coil around him and lug his limp form to the surface. His chest doesn't move. Neither do his lips. Both remain motionless, unlike my heart, which slams against every one of my bones, dumping adrenaline into my veins.

I tow the boy toward land, hoping that a Crow will spot my bright scales, snatch us both out, and carry us to the nearest town so a Lucin healer can succeed where I failed. Or Fallon! Perhaps my daughter knows a sigil that can drain his lungs and restart his heart?

I think of my grandmother as I swim. If anyone can resuscitate the male, it'll be her. But what if she turns saving his life into a bargain to trap me inside Shabbe without Cathal? Without Fallon? I can't risk calling upon her, so instead, I search the sky for my mate. For my daughter. For any Crow. When I catch the gleam of talons, I shift, loop my arm around the lifeless human, and yell.

A wavelet slaps me in the face before closing over my head and pressing me under. I kick my legs hard, reawakening the ache in my thigh. Something crashes over my head. I think it must be another wave, but it's a Crow. Its talons snag my dress and then it's lifting me. The fisherman's body is slipping, slipping.

"Wait!" I cry out. "The boy!"

My ride must call for reinforcement, because a second Crow swoops right underneath us and hovers until I've released the body of my protector onto its back. And then, skimming the surface of the ocean like a skipping stone, it takes off toward the beach and gently deposits the body there before morphing into skin—Fallon.

"Take me to Fallon," I yell, rolling my face toward the Crow's, recognizing him. "Please, Cathal."

Though I sense my mate wants to whisk me toward Monteluce, he indulges me. Six heartbeats later, I'm kneeling beside my daughter, who is inspecting the wan, lanky body. "I try heal him, but he drown."

Fallon frowns, pressing two fingers into his neck. "Well you revived him, Mádhi. He has a pulse."

I blink. "He do?"

She nods.

"Who is this man, Daya?" Cathal stands over us, a deep scowl marring his tenebrous face.

"He fisherman I follow to find Luce. He save me from yellow-hair human who try stab me."

Cathal's eyes skim the horizon, his attention locking on something in the distance. "Imogen, bring me the blond captain of that boat." He juts his chin. "Alive." As she flies off, he mutters, "Your grandmother's on her way. Unless you want to see me eviscerated, we should leave soon."

I glance toward the ocean, toward her red sails that are bloated even though there's not a single drop of wind.

"Don't you want to deal with the *annos dòfain* first, Dádhi?"

Cathal snorts. "Yes. But as soon as that's done, we leave. If..." His eyes go to mine. "If that is what you want, Daya?"

"Yes." My answer smooths all the fine lines crinkling his face.

"I'll wait here until imTaytah docks." Fallon straightens and dusts the sand off her sodden dress.

Black sand.

I swing my gaze back to the male lying on the beach, my chest tightening, my breaths shortening.

I palm his bony jaw, twisting it toward the moon.

The hooked nose. The wide lips set in a face that doesn't bear a single wrinkle. The cropped hair that is...that is...I can't tell its hue in such faint light.

He stirs. I release him so fast that his cheek smacks the sand. I rock back, then scuttle away. I think Cathal is calling my name but I can't hear him over my rushing pulse.

The boy's lids open, and I gasp because...because...

I lick my lips. How is this possible?

Cathal clasps my biceps and rights me before twirling me into his body, and then he scrapes his palms over my arms, ribs, cheeks.

"The Queen of Luce and her father are standing beside me. And...is that...holy *castagnoli*, that's the Princess of Shabbe." The unfamiliar voice must belong to the Serpent boy. "This must be the afterlife."

Fallon gasps, "Dádhi!"

Cathal tears his gaze off mine. I know the instant he sees what Fallon saw, what I saw, because his chest grows eerily still and his hands freeze on my body. I close my stinging eyes as Fallon asks the man a question in Lucin.

"Enzo, M-Maezza," he replies.

A tear slips down my cheek, chased by a second and a third.

"My head. My head!" At his howl, I pry my eyes open and spin. He's swiping at his black-smeared forehead.

Cathal stands rigidly at my back, his armor cold against my spine.

The fisherman grits his teeth, stifling another gritty howl before rubbing his forehead once more. This time, I realize it isn't sand— it's blood. And amidst the black, blooms an ivory dot.

Although my heart still thunders, I hear Fallon murmur, "I think Mádhi did more than heal him."

Cathal doesn't speak. I don't either.

The boy holds his hands in front of his face. "What is all this black goo?"

"Blood," I reply.

His lid-to-lid black eyes snap to my lid-to-lid black ones. "D-Dhoon?"

I frown. "Yes. Blood."

His forehead furrows as he looks at Fallon and asks her something in Lucin that includes the word for blood in Shabbin.

"A Serpent..." he breathes. "I've transformed into a freaking almighty Serpent!" It is only then that I realize that his lips didn't move over *any* of those words.

He turns his awestruck expression toward me just as a wave froths around his body and completes his shift.

185

Chapter 30
Zendaya

"I'm sorry," I whisper to Cathal as he stares at the coiled green monster on the black sand.

"You *made* a serpent, Mádhi." The wonder in Fallon's tone feels like iron talons to the heart.

I tremulously tuck my wet hair behind my ears, refusing to let Behati's vision seep into my thoughts. The Serpent isn't my mate; the Crow, devoured by gloom, who stands before me is.

"Can you hear him?" The bones in Cathal's face sharpen as he continues to scrutinize the boy. "Inside your mind"—his pitch is so grave it weighs on my heart—"can you hear him?"

I want to lie. I want to shake my head and pretend like I can't. Instead, I reach up and cradle his jaw to force his gaze to mine. "Look me. Please look me."

His eyes twitch.

I'm a Serpent. A freaking Serpent! Son of a biscuit eater. The boy sounds so horribly joyful.

How can he be jubilant? He'll now be hunted and reviled.

I was a human. The lowest of the lows. You just gave me magic, Princess. Magic!

I don't realize I've covered my ears until Cathal pinches my wrists between his large fingers and carries them away from my face. I steal my wrists from his grip and lace my arms around his

186

torso, wishing there wasn't so much cloth and metal separating our bodies. "I choose you, Cathal Báeinach."

With a sigh, he props his chin atop my head and winds his arms around my waist to hold me. Not tightly enough. Not long enough. I burrow my wet cheek against his armor.

What are my odds of surviving Daddy Crow?

I spin around and hiss. *Never call him that.*

Sorry. I didn't mean—I won't. Sorry. A body thumps beside his, sending him recoiling toward the water.

I trail Imogen's boots to the yellow hair that's no longer bound in a tail. The captain sputters as he rises onto all fours, and then he blanches as his gaze trawls our loose circle of shifters.

Imogen asks something in Crow. When she gestures toward the Serpent, I imagine it has to do with his presence on the beach. Fallon must explain who he is, because the whites of her eyes expand.

"Is this the male who tried to gore you, Zendaya?" Cathal asks, his voice so dry it strips my blazing lids of moisture.

"Yes."

"Would your..." His throat bobs. "Would your mate mind if I severed his head?"

My heart shrivels. I suddenly hate the captain as much as my mother, for he's the reason I'm about to lose my mate. If he hadn't driven a spear through the boy's chest...

My lips tingle from Cathal's hot breaths. "*You* are mate. Not he."

The Crow's gaze finally rolls to mine. For several seconds, we stare at one another. *Into* one another. And then his lids sink, and he gives his head a small shake. "Ask him, Príona."

I don't want to ask the new Serpent anything.

Cathal turns toward my fellow shifter and reiterates his question in Lucin.

Tell him to go for it. Sami's a massive faehole.

"What is his answer?" Cathal asks.

187

"I decide! Not boy." I squeeze my scorched eyes shut. "Kill Yellow-hair."

The air shifts and then I catch the wet snap of flesh.

Remind me to never cross your husband.

I propel my fists into my eyes. *What have I done? What have I done?*

No one will miss the guy, Princess. Not his wife, who he beats up on the regular, or his customers, who he swindles of coin every chance he gets.

I whirl and lock eyes with the scaly shifter's. "I no talk about dead man! I talk about *you*." I fling an arm in his direction.

He falls quiet. Everyone does. The world's immobility is so profound that I hear water lap against wood a moment before my grandmother's voice grinds up the silence.

"Cathal Báeinach!" His name vibrates with a fury that pales in comparison to the one striking my heart. "I have half a mind to plunge an obsidian dagger into your..." Her voice fades as her attention locks on the Serpent, on the shimmer that envelops his scales before returning him to his other shape.

Though the moonlight is scarce, and his hair cropped close to his scalp, I don't miss its emerald hue as he scrambles to his feet to sketch an awkward bow. "Maezza," he all but gasps.

The queen's pink eyes linger on his dark ones. "How?"

"Mádhi turned him," Fallon says, twining her fingers through mine. She gives my palm a squeeze. "Serpents can be made, imTaytah."

"Blessed Mahananda." My grandmother blinks those heavy-lidded eyes of hers that are aglow with absolute wonder.

This is not wondrous. This is disastrous.

Ouch. My new mate rubs his nape.

I scowl at him. *Quiet.*

He presses his thick lips together, chastened.

"I'm sorry about—about the storm," Cathal murmurs.

The queen's chin tilts up. "I've no doubt you are." Her smugness incenses me.

I must roll my fingers too tightly to Fallon's liking because she murmurs, "I won't let her take you away if you don't want to go to Shabbe."

"That isn't what's troubling your mother, now is it, Zendaya?" Priya asks.

Fallon frowns. "It isn't?"

My teeth chatter too hard to explain.

"I don't understand." She turns toward me. "You dreamed about there being another Serpent shifter, and now there is one. And there could be more. You could have an entire den if..."

The sob that notches my throat quiets her.

Please don't cry, Princess. If you don't want me to exist, I'm sure Fallon's father will be only too glad to give me the same fate as Sami's. He wrinkles his hooked nose and looks down at boots that are so scuffed I can see a hint of toe. *Just ask him to do it quickly.* He kicks a shell.

I'm not going to ask him to kill you, I murmur.

He blinks as though my mercy genuinely surprises him. *Thank you.*

"I won't take you by force to Shabbe this time, emMoti, but I urge you and..." The queen switches to Lucin to ask the male a question to which he replies: *Enzo.*

I surmise this is his name. *Enzo.* Enzo the Shifter.

"I urge you and Enzo to head to Shabbe with us. Especially *now.*"

Now that I've made a shifter.

I *made* a shifter.

If it wasn't for the mind link, I would, like Fallon, find this most extraordinary.

Mind link, Enzo murmurs in wonder. *That's why I can talk without moving my mouth. What language are we speaking? It's not Shabbin, is it?*

I grimace.

Sorry. My mind is just... Enzo kicks another shell. *Sorry.*

189

Stop! Stop apologizing! I growl.

His eyes grow as wide as the stupid wound I healed. That'll teach me to keep my tongue off foreign bodies. The second the thought enters my mind, I turn toward Cathal. When our eyes collide, my lungs tighten.

Ask me to stay, I think, but unlike Enzo, Cathal cannot penetrate my mind—only my heart—so he doesn't hear my silent entreaty.

I realize *I* could ask to stay, but what if he refuses and turns his back on me? Or worse, what if he seeks a mate of his own?

Ask me to stay, I beg.

"You should go with your grandmother." His words are a blade that flay me open from collarbone to navel. "She's the only one who can truly keep you and your—" His jaw flexes. "You and the kid safe."

I blink back the wetness pooling behind my lids.

"I won't seal off Shabbe," Priya says. "Not unless the toxin spreads. If it does, though, wards will go up, but in the meantime, you may come and go as you please."

It doesn't matter whether she puts up wards or not. Cathal will not visit.

Fallon gives my fingers another squeeze, forcing a smile. "We'll come every day. Right, Dádhi?"

He stares at the mirror-smooth ocean that unspools toward my birthplace. "I'll go inform the Siorkahd of this new development. Imogen, dispose of the deceased, and please fucking remind everyone that they will incur the same fate if they so much as look sideways at a serpent. Evidently they didn't think we were serious when we passed the edict."

Without so much as a backward glance or a goodbye, Cathal dissolves into smoke before morphing into his winged form. I press my palm against my chest that feels hollow, as though he left with not merely a piece of my heart but the entire thing.

I'm going to Shabbe! Enzo's exclamation clangs against my eardrums.

I stare at his excited face, at his cheeks that are high in color, at his mouth that is round with wonder, at his gangly limbs he's yet to grow into. Why in the world would the Mahananda match me with a juvenile?

Was this how Fallon...or rather Lorcan viewed his match when they first met? Like an unappealing child?

I don't think Enzo hears my deliberations, entranced as he is by the queen growing a gang plank from the bow of the ship so we can climb aboard.

"You made a Serpent. I can still hardly believe it," Fallon murmurs as Enzo walks up the plank toward my awaiting grandmother. "I'll come for breakfast." My daughter drops a kiss on both my cheeks. "I love you."

"I love you, too, Fallon. So much." I turn my gaze toward the starlit heavens, hunting its infinite depths for the male who, once upon a time, would never have left me.

"I think Dádhi's a little bit in shock." Of course, she guesses who I seek. "But you know him...a restorative stroll through the clouds, and he'll be right as rain."

Though I've never heard the expression, I twig its meaning. I give her a sad smile and hesitate to tell her that nothing will ever be *right as rain* again, but I cannot get my throat to move around more than a distressed swallow.

I stroke her cheek that is perched as high as her father's, even though it's curved like mine. Cathal and I might not share a mind link, but we share something even more precious. We share *her*.

I give her one last hug before finally turning toward my grandmother and the life the Mahananda has in store for me.

Chapter 31
Zendaya

S uns and moons rise and fall, and although Fallon keeps her promise of visiting, her father doesn't come once. She tells me that he's busy in Nebba, ferreting out every last stock of serpent poison. It's been five weeks. Either he truly is going door to door, or he's using his hunt as an excuse to avoid *my* door.

Thankfully, I've got a new Serpent and an insatiably curious Asha to keep me distracted. Upon our return to Shabbe, my female guard stole into the healer's library and borrowed a book about poisons. After reading it cover to cover, she suggested that Enzo and I start ingesting a minuscule amount of serpent toxin daily in order to build a natural resistance. I thought her idea was brilliant; my grandmother did not. She went so far as to threaten to dismiss Asha if my guard ever suggested harming her granddaughter again.

I reassured Asha that she would never be dismissed. And then, after explaining Asha's theory, I asked Fallon to procure us some serpent poison. Reluctantly, she had.

I now possess a palm-sized vial filled with shimmering lavender flakes. It seems incredible that something so innocuous-looking— pretty, even—could create so much damage. Once a day, after break- fast, since I still prefer to slumber during the hottest hours, I ingest a single flake. Always under either Asha's or my daughter's watch.

The first time, it had prickled my airway before settling on my lungs like a damp cloth. Fallon had paled and bloodied her finger, ready to flay my throat open like Taytah had done, except in human form, it wasn't my throat that ached, but my lungs.

I'd kept her trembling finger at bay, since I could still manage faint wheezes. By the time the sun dipped beneath the horizon, the pressure on my lungs had eased. My daughter said *never again*, but I did it again. And again. A week into my makeshift treatment, I even upped my dose to two flakes because one no longer affected my lungs. It seemed like the book Asha had read had been telling the truth: I *was* developing a resistance to the toxin.

Asha suggested starting Enzo on the same regimen, but hurting the sweet creature felt wicked. *Yes...he was sweet.* Unfortunately. How I'd wished he were awful.

Anyway, I'd told her that if I managed to swim in freshwater, we'd begin dosing him as well, but until we tested the result, I'd spare him the unpleasant side-effects. I was now at five flakes per day. I still couldn't shift inside my bathtub. When I suggested a trip to Isolacuori, my poor daughter turned as green as Enzo's hair, so I let it go.

For now.

I'd eventually need to test my immunity, but I wouldn't risk doing so without a Shabbin present, preferably my daughter, because she was of royal bloodline, so her magic was superior to Asha's.

What I wouldn't give to show the Fae back in Luce what I've become. Enzo's voice carries my mind off my contemplations and onto his sprawled form. He rests beside me on my patio sofa, absorbing the nascent rays of sunshine. ***How high the bumbler has risen.***

I take his hand in mine and give it a squeeze. His fingers are long and bony, like the rest of him, in spite of all the rich food Asha feeds him. "Never call yourself a bumbler in my presence again, for it makes me angry, and the world does not want an angry Serpent unleashed upon them."

His black eyes roll up toward me, buffed with emotion. I don't think a day goes by when the boy doesn't get all *in his feels,* as Asha calls it. He has an incredibly big heart and strives to fit everyone he meets—be they legged or winged or finned—inside. Many times I've been tempted to urge him to seal it off, but who am I to give him advice about hearts when mine has been bleeding since the fateful day I made him?

"As soon as Taytah allows us to journey to Luce, we will show all those bullies."

"What will we show them?" Asha asks, plopping herself down beside Enzo and shoving a bowl of fried cheese puffs doused in date syrup onto his lap. "Cook made extra for his favorite Serpent." She waggles her eyebrows at me. "Sorry, Day."

Day. To think that nickname was born from Enzo's clumsy speech. Leaving out the last letter was easier on his human tongue, so I suggested he forgo it always. Over time, Asha adopted the new moniker.

Her teasing raises the corners of my lips, but the sight of not one but three Crows flying overhead have them plummeting. Enzo's hand tumbles from mine as I jump to my feet and rush across my chambers.

When I burst out my front door, I come to an abrupt halt. The Crows are already in skin and funneling into the Kasha. Cathal isn't amongst them. Smothering my disappointment, I cut across the courtyard, circumventing the still-resting Mahananda, and enter the Kasha.

When my grandmother sees me, she pats the divan next to hers. "To what do we owe the pleasure of your visit, Lorcan?"

"I've come to ask for your aid, Priya. Seven more of my people have now been infected with obsidian."

As I sit cross-legged on the crimson velour, the queen says, "The Mahananda isn't ready. I would've sent word if it had been."

"They didn't come for the Mahananda, Taytah; they came for me."

Both Erwin and Lorcan blink, probably stunned by my diction that has become as fluid as the Serpent tongue Enzo and I have been teaching Asha and Fallon. Try as they might, our language is more hiss and clucks than syllables, which makes learning it a true feat. Even my grandmother's trying, and although she masters *all* languages, there are many sounds she's incapable of reproducing.

Sure enough, Lorcan says, "How well you speak now, Zendaya."

"All thanks to my tutors."

"Yes, I've heard. I've also heard you're teaching your tutors Serpent." He smiles. "It's been rather *entertaining* to hear Fallon practice."

I cannot help but bristle. "My language may be different than all the others in the realm, but it's not any less intricate."

Lorcan's pupils shrink. "I did not mean to slight you, Daya. I find it entertaining because my mate is desperately trying to transcribe the sounds into syllables in order to create not only an alphabet, but also a dictionary. She's gone through at least six trees worth of pressed pulp and forty pots of ink."

Oh. "So that's the reason her fingers are forever black?"

"Yes."

"When I asked her about the stains, she told me she's been penning a novel with Phoebus."

A grimace reshapes Lorcan's face. "Because she meant to surprise you with it. And now I've just ruined the surprise. Will you please act exceedingly shocked the day she gifts it to you?"

I rub my chest that's suddenly full of scattered heartbeats. "Of course." *Oh, Fallon, you sweet girl.* "So tell me who needs healing, and how long ago has it been since they were infected?"

"Liora," Erwin says, his big arm wrapped around a female Crow not much larger than his limb. Liora stands at half his height and appears to be half his age. "My mate," he adds.

I assume the match is recent. Though I'm glad for him, I cannot help the jealous twinge that seizes my wrecked heart. I will it away...will all thoughts of Cathal away.

"She was hit with an arrow yesterday when we were ambushed by that colony of jungle zealots," Erwin explains.

I'm not certain whom he means, but I suppose it doesn't matter. I stand and pad closer to the girl whose hair is the same color of cooked carrot as Erwin's. If he hadn't said mates, I would've assumed she was his daughter. "Where did they get you, Liora?"

She blinks up at Erwin who replies, "In her shoulder. Forgive my mate. She doesn't speak Shabbin, Princess."

"They got Erwin in the back of the knee," Lorcan adds, arms crossed in front of his armor.

Erwin's face snaps toward his king, and in Crow, he says something about how his injury isn't important, only Liora's and only because of the baby. Yes, I understand. Now that my oral Shabbin comprehension is impeccable, Fallon has started teaching me her paternal tongue. My grasp of it is rudimentary, but if spoken slowly, I understand. Unlike ordinary-serpent speak which I cannot figure out for the life of me.

My gaze skims the female's abdomen. "I'll perform the healing inside the Amkhuti so I can shift immediately afterward."

My grandmother hasn't spoken a word, but I don't need her to utter any to know what she is thinking: she doesn't approve. If she had, she'd have let me heal the first Crows that were harmed. She hasn't, and now they're all stone.

"Perhaps your mate can take care of both healings, Daya?" Lorcan suggests.

Although I've grown quite fond of Enzo, the word *mate* feels ill-suited. He's my Serpent, the same way the two striped warriors are Lorcan's Crows. Every day, I grow further convinced that our connection has nothing amorous about it, but the only way to prove this would be to make another Serpent, which would require taking a human life.

Though people die in Shabbe, it doesn't happen often, and by the time I hear of it, it's too late. I've come to the conclusion that the person must be on the brink of death for my magic to absorb into their blood. I've asked Taytah to find me a sickly volunteer. Though she promises she will, she's yet to deliver a dying body at my feet.

"I like Lorcan's suggestion. Enzo will heal them both. We have lodgings. You and your mate are welcome to stay in Shabbe while Enzo recovers between lickings."

Lickings? It's the first time I've heard anyone refer to my healing method as a licking. I'm not fond of the term, however fitting it is. "That won't be necessary, for I'll be healing Erwin today."

My argument with the queen makes the big redheaded Crow wince and his mate cower.

"It's either Enzo, or they both wait for the Mahananda to unseal and—"

In Serpent, I hiss a single word. One I know she'll understand. "Stop." And then in Shabbin, I say, "My body. My tongue, Sumaca."

She scowls, detesting when I call her *Your Highness*, which is exactly why I do it. I do love the woman dearly, but she's stuck in her ways and often forgets that I'm not some dullard incapable of educated judgement.

"You slept for three nights in scales after you healed Cathal. Three nights!" As though she senses the reminder won't be enough to dissuade me—*she's right*—she traipses over and claps my forehead with her palms to pour the images of my listless form coiled at the bottom of the Amkhuti. "What if it takes you longer this time? What if you don't shift back?" Her tone is bright with worry.

"Ask the Mahananda. Actually, ask it how it will affect Enzo."

She huffs.

"Please, Taytah."

She twists her ring around her finger with another huff. I think she's about to object when her eyes whiten. A moment later, she mutters, "The Mahananda says you and Enzo won't perish."

I smile. "See." I gesture for Erwin and his mate to follow me, then call out to my shifter.

I'm right outside, Day.

Sure enough, he and Asha loiter beneath the honeysuckle-wrapped arbor. ***We've got Crows to heal.***

Enzo trots after me, his linen robe flapping open around the skintight trunks he wears to swim. ***Crows need healing? I thought they were invulnerable.***

Only my daughter. The others remain susceptible to obsidian.

He blinks. Though I've gotten used to the sight, I can't help but sometimes wish our eyes held a stroke of white and color. Granted our lurid hair does compensate for our reptilian orbs.

How do we heal them? he asks.

"What's happening?" Asha asks, falling into step beside us.

"Erwin and his mate have been infected with obsidian. I was just about to explain to Enzo how we will have to lave the wounds until the stone detritus oozes out. It'll smell horrid, Enzo, so it's best to do it in skin. Also, we'll need to shift immediately after. Lastly, it may make us unconscious for a few days."

Enzo nods. Anyone else may have questioned if it was a sound idea, or if we risked more than forced respite, but not my selfless shifter.

"We'll do it inside the Amkhuti." As we move down the path we take daily, I think of Cathal. I think of how I'd kneeled before him and licked his thigh. Of how his cock had hardened and leaked for me. Is it leaking for another?

The thought makes my ribs clench and my stomach fold in on itself like those paper serpents Asha folds while Enzo and I swim. She's crafted so many that Enzo has begun to thread them into garlands to decorate the walls of his chamber.

When we reach the Amkhuti, Enzo divests himself of his robe and dives in headfirst. I sometimes think the boy was already part-Serpent and that I simply activated that side of him.

He treads the water while I instruct Erwin and his mate to rid themselves of their clothes and armor before walking them through the process. Erwin translates it all for Liora. I commit each new word I hear to memory, trying to elucidate what it stands for.

Droplets splash my skin as our two patients dive into the moat. I'm about to duck beneath the surface to inspect the wounds when I catch sight of the Shabbin Queen standing beside Lorcan on the embankment's edge, deep in conversation with the male. I try to parse out what they're saying but their voices are too hushed.

I refocus on Erwin and his mate. After observing Liora's wound, I dive to get a look at Erwin's knee. It's swollen and black, which makes me wonder how he even manages to walk. When I surface, I ask Asha to magick some palm fronds into sturdy floats for the two Crows so they avoid unnecessary movement.

As she does so, I hear Erwin mutter to Liora something about Cathal staking them with obsidian if he catches wind of their visit.

I purse my lips, trying to stifle a retort, but it soars out regardless, "Just because Cathal doesn't care to see me doesn't give him a right to dictate who does *care*."

Erwin's pale lashes flutter.

"Sorry for eavesdropping," I add.

Once he recovers from his shock, he licks his thin, pink lips and in Shabbin, he says, "What I meant was that he'd run us through with more obsidian for causing you harm. That's why Lorcan hasn't come to you for the others. Cathal has forbidden us from importuning you, and considering his mood since...since you left, we've tried to respect his wishes."

I stare at the redheaded Siorkahd member for a long moment, tempted to ask him for news about my former mate. Yes, Fallon reports on Cathal's Nebban dealings, but not on his private ones. I'm guessing she doesn't share those out of respect for all parties involved.

"If my mate hadn't been pregnant, and we weren't worried about how the curse will affect the baby, I wouldn't have come."

"I require no explanation, Erwin. Enzo and I are glad to help. And if this goes well, you can send the others."

His face scrunches up. "I'm afraid that won't be possible."

"Why not?"

"Because as you may have heard, the first three to be injured are blocks of obsidian, and the two others are days' away from the same fate." He shudders.

Just as Asha tosses in the fronds, I say, "I could come to them."

Sure, I'd have to convince my grandmother to let me leave Shabbe, but it could be done. Plus, that way, I could visit Isolacuori. The more I turn over this plan, the more I grow determined to put it into action.

"Cathal would never allow it," Erwin says, as he hands one of the buoyant branches to his mate.

"Why would he need to be told?"

"He'd find out. The only reason he hasn't flocked over here is because he isn't aware that Liora and I were injured."

I roll my gaze toward the dawn-filled immensity, wishing he'd learn of it. Cathal might not want to see me, but I would very much like to lay eyes on him. If only to make sure he's well. "Ready?"

Erwin nods, reaching for his mate's hand. "Thank you for doing this. I owe you, Zendaya of Shabbe."

I suck in a breath when something stings my bicep. I pop my arm out of the water to find a glowing band circling my skin.

When I look back at Erwin, his expression holds no inkling of surprise. "It's the least I can do to show my gratitude."

I nod my thanks and sink. As I lap at his noxious blood to draw out the toxins, I decide exactly how I will use his bargain. Picturing the queen's fury distracts me from the Mahananda-awful task and makes time tick by faster. I see the infection clear and his skin draw close and then I see nothing but soothing darkness.

Chapter 32
Zendaya

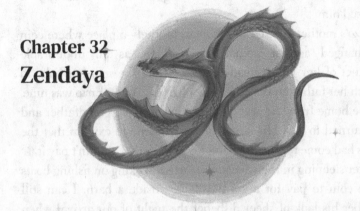

When my eyes finally peel open, Enzo is resting beside me at the bottom of the Amkhuti, his green scales flush against my pink ones. My grandmother might not have drained the Amkhuti of water this time, but she's drained it of sea life. Was she worried fish would pick at our inert bodies and disturb our slumber?

I shift into flesh, then kick my legs to circle around Enzo. The instant my palm grazes his cheek, his eyes snap wide, and then he too morphs into skin. *You're awake!*

I smile. *Yes, and so are you.*

I woke up two days ago, Day. Considering the dark hue staining the skin beneath his eyes, I take it that he hasn't slept since then.

Two days? How long have I been out?

Almost a week.

As we float to the surface, I reach out and take his hand to give it a squeeze. *Thank you for staying with me.*

You're my... You're like my mother. He manages to redden underwater. *Actually, you're nothing alike, because she wasn't very nice. But it wasn't her fault,* he's quick to add. *She was overworked.*

I know his life story, even though it took him a while to confide in me. At first, I believed it was because he was wary, but later came to understand that he avoided talking of his past because it depressed him.

Enzo's mother worked in a human brothel—a place where coin is exchanged against sexual favors. He was an undesirable byproduct of her job. Instead of raising him, she sent her baby to live with her father on the other side of Luce. When Enzo was nine, he came home from the market to find his beloved grandfather and house turned to ash. His neighbor was the one to explain that the soldiers had come for the tithe and his grandfather couldn't pay it.

After sleeping in the streets, he started working on fishing boats to earn coin to pay for a corner of hay inside a barn. I can still remember his look of sheer disbelief the night of our arrival when Asha and I showed him to an apartment in the palace's guest wing. His eyes had grown so large, I'd worried he would shift right there and then. His quiet wonder had sloughed off a layer of my antipathy. I shed the rest of it like a molting land serpent—*all at once*—for the boy had done nothing to merit my scorn.

The second our heads break the surface, Asha's voice detonates through the air with an, "Abrax, she's up! Go tell the queen."

I meet my guard's concerned eyes, catch the bob of his throat before he sprints toward the palace.

Asha is sitting on a sofa I had made for her right on the cliff so she didn't have to sit on stone while we swam. Her blistered fingers work a strip of green paper into a serpent which she tosses, after completion, into a wicker basket overflowing with multi-hued origami. "Seven days," she says matter-of-factly. "*Seven. Days.*"

"I heard." I paddle toward the stone edge. "I sense a lecture coming."

"You're right, but it won't be coming from me." She flicks her gaze in the direction of the palace.

Of course...The queen. I've no doubt she'll have much to say about my extensive convalescence. "They're both cured, right?"

Asha snatches another strip of paper—orange this time. "Yes."

"Then it was worth it." As I grab ahold of the ladder, I press my hair aside, catching the glimmer of the magical band on my bicep. My heart quickens, creating little ripples around my body. "Hey, Asha, how does bargaining work? Does the supernatural being need be present to claim a bargain?"

"Afraid your grandmother's about to strike one with you to prevent you from healing other birds?"

"Yes," I lie.

"You should be," she mumbles while Enzo stares at my arm.

Present from Erwin?

I nod as Asha explains, "Once struck, you can call forth a bargain from anywhere in the realm, so even if you—let's say—went to Luce to cure the others"—she slants me a look to tell me that *yes, she heard me discuss healing them with Erwin*—"she could make it impossible for you to dart your tongue out and risk your life."

Note to self, never strike a bargain with Taytah. "My life wasn't in danger."

"Perhaps not, but what of your health? What if this begins to chip away at your body and mind?" Her hands come apart so fast that her serpent-in-progress sails into the pearlescent moat. "Your convalescence took twice as long as last time, Day. Twice. That cannot possibly be a good sign."

I pinch the miniature paper tusk, tuck it into the top of my bathing suit, then seize the rungs and climb. Asha's gaze draws up and down my figure. "You're wasting away."

My stomach has become a little concave and the bones in my thighs do jut out. Even my breasts seem to have lost some of their bounce. "Nothing a few meals won't fix. I'm rave..." I frown as my neck tingles from the weight of someone's gaze. I twist around, coming nose to fabric with a robe that Enzo is holding out to me. When I don't divest him of it, he takes my hand and guides it through the wide sleeve, then repeats the process with my other arm, before belting it around me with the care of a parent.

A twig snaps. I see nothing yet *feel* something. Someone. A creature or a human? *Both*, my mind says.

"You owe me a new uniform, Day. I had to do a ton of stress-eating while I waited on the two of you." Asha gets to her feet, tugging on the hem of her red tunic that creases around her ample bosom.

Enzo stutters that he thinks she's never looked more beautiful, which makes a grin reshape her face.

My guard juts her chin toward me. "I'm mad at her. Not at you, *abi*."

Again, my nape prickles. I squint over my shoulder but the slap of sandals against stone coupled with the sound of my name being trilled through the brightening air redirects my attention toward the palace path.

My grandmother's eyes glisten like rubies as she closes in on me, casting her honeysuckle scent far and wide. I'm ready for a sermon but what I receive instead is a silent, bone-crushing hug and a susurrated, "Please don't do this again, emMoti."

Once she releases me, she moves to Enzo, frames his face and bends it toward hers. She murmurs a, "Thank you for staying with my child," then kisses his retracted tusk, a habit she fell into almost naturally.

The queen asks for breakfast to be served immediately, then steals my arm and turns me. But not before I catch a shadow breaking away from a tree and streaking upward before solidifying into a Crow. If my grandmother notices the lurker, she doesn't mention him or her. Probably Erwin or Imogen come to check whether the slumbering Serpent has risen. Although, wouldn't Erwin come over and talk to me?

I think of the bargain he owes me and how best to go about collecting it. I realize I could ask him to bring me an almost-dead body, but what if the person doesn't deserve a second chance at life? Also, Enzo should have a say.

As we walk toward the courtyard, Taytah fills me in on all the unrest in Luce and how the death toll is mounting. She says this with so little emotion that it feels as though the loss of life doesn't disturb her all that much.

I stop walking. "That's terrible, Taytah."

"They had it coming."

"The Crows were immobilized for five centuries. How exactly did they have it coming?"

"The Fae are the ones dying. They kept humans practically enslaved and treated half-bloods so poorly for so many centuries that it's only natural revenge is being sought." She lowers her voice to add, "Some of these attacks are done with the Crows' consent."

My eyebrows quirk because, although I don't doubt the Crows are not fans of all Faeries, last I heard, Lorcan was trying to achieve peace. Encouraging upheavals seems counterintuitive. "And you hold this news from which source? Have you visited Luce while I slept?"

"Kanti arrived two days ago when news reached her of what you'd done and that you weren't recovering." She says this sternly, as though to impress upon me her discontent. "She was worried."

My tail, she was worried. Kanti was probably on the first ship— or Crow—over to check on my vitals. Even when I could barely understand Shabbin, her desire to succeed Priya never eluded me.

Before my grandmother can catch my hostile thoughts, I take her arm and start walking. "Isn't Justus Rossi a High Fae? Doesn't the slaughter of pointy-eared people disturb him?"

"He works for Lorcan."

"What is that supposed to mean?"

"That a general obeys his ruler, otherwise, they lose their position. Or their life. Fallon may consider Justus a grandfather, but he isn't. If he doesn't prove his allegiance to the Crows, his blood will color the canals of Tarecuori just like the former Regio supporters." She pats my hand. "Order will come, but it will not come overnight. And yes, it will bear a high cost. Such is the fate of a divided empire."

When we reach the dining table, it's already laden with every dish imaginable, and set for many. In spite of our dismal conversation, my stomach rumbles. "Are we expecting others, Taytah?"

"Kanti will be joining us." To a guard, she asks if she's been awakened. The guard nods.

My appetite dwindles a smidgeon.

Why don't we like Kanti, Day?

A smile blooms over my wariness at the preposition that Enzo has used—*we*. *We do not like her because she desires the Shabbin crown so much that I sometimes worry how far she'd go to win it.*

Minutes later, Behati's granddaughter joins us. Enzo's mouth gapes wide at the sight of her, probably stunned by her beauty.

Not why I gaped. Enzo seizes his juice and sips.

I tilt my head, waiting to hear what arrested him if it isn't her looks.

She swam down toward us yesterday.

"You must be the green Serpent. Enzo, right? I've heard so much about you." Kanti shakes out her napkin and places it on her lap. "How incredible that she *made* you. You were human before, if I'm not mistaken."

"Yes, I w-was."

"And now you're a shifter. How incredible."

The weight of Enzo's quizzical stare leads me to say, *She wasn't a fan of me before, Enzo. I believe having the power to create more Serpents doesn't please her.*

Why?

Either because she believes I'll use it to create an army of shifters, or because she worries my new "edge" will sway who gets the throne.

You could heal Crows before. That's quite the edge, no?

A practical power, but not a dangerous one.

Our noiseless conversation doesn't go unnoticed. At least, not by Asha or Abrax. Kanti, on the other hand, is so busy gushing to the queen about all she's achieved since reaching Tarespagia that she's no longer paying attention to the *incredible* Serpents.

"I planted listening sigils in every dissident hideout. I almost fainted from how much blood I had to part with. Actually, I did swoon a little, but I did that on purpose because that landed me a stay in the governor's house." She drops her voice to add, "The male's no fan of Lorcan or Cathal—for personal reasons." She slides me a look. "Antoni has a great instinct for people, so consider yourself lucky the Mahananda selected a new mate for you, chacha."

How odd to hear Kanti call me cousin, when technically, she's centuries older than I am.

She scoops up a few slices of charred avocado and layers them on a bed of sprouts. "He likes all the other Crows. If it wasn't for him, they wouldn't be in power."

I dip my finger into a dollop of spicy, pureed beans and carry it to my lips, which earns me a grimace from Kanti who doesn't eat anything without utensils, not even sundried fruit. "What personal reasons made him single out Lorcan and Cathal?"

The explosion of flavor against my palate is so beautiful that I rattle, which deepens the twist of Kanti's mouth. I know she finds me beastly. I heard her tell Behati when she assumed I was still non-fluent in Shabbin.

"Fallon," Kanti says.

The name of my daughter halts my rattle.

"Your daughter had Antoni tossed out of the Sky Castle like disloyal scum, even though he risked his life many times over so she could awaken Lorcan."

I plant my elbows on the table. "My daughter wouldn't have tossed out an innocent man."

Kanti's snort slides under my human skin. "Anyway, thanks to my listening sigils, Antoni and I have managed to squelch *six* uprisings."

"However is he faring without you at his side?" I deadpan.

"I know." Kanti sighs, cutting into her avocado and slipping a piece into her mouth. After she's swallowed, she says, "It was hard to leave, but when I heard that healing Erwin kept you in scales for so long, I immediately came home to lend Priya strength." She reaches over and squeezes the queen's forearm.

The queen stares at Kanti's slender fingers before moving her arm away. "You shouldn't stay away from Luce for too long, my dear. You're obviously greatly needed there."

Again, Kanti sighs an, "I know." After another bite of her greens, she adds, "I hope Antoni is the man the Mahananda foresaw me seducing, because he's delicious. And he would also make a terrific king. You should see the way he governs the west. Unlike the Siorkahd who executes without trial, he gives everyone a fair hearing. The men and women under his command have such respect for him. I can't wait for you to meet him. I could have him sail over this evening?"

"I met Governor Greco at Fallon's coronation," Priya says.

"For like, a second, because Daya couldn't control her animal."

Enzo white-knuckles his fork and knife. Is my placid-tempered Serpent picturing planting his utensils inside Kanti? *Do love sigils exist?* The burst of his voice through the bond combined with the tenure of his question startles a frown onto my face.

Not love sigils, but there exists a seduction sigil. It'll wear off unless reapplied regularly, though.

Then Kanti is either using those on Antoni or she's lying about his rapture.

What made you reach this conclusion?

I know Antoni Greco from when he was a boat captain in Tarelexo. He was one of the kindest men I ever worked for. He would always slip me an extra coin and made sure my belly was full when I pretended I wasn't hungry. He also let me sleep on his fishing boat in the dead of winter when the barn got too cold. Antoni might lay with a woman like Kanti, but he'd never fall for her.

Kanti's a very powerful woman.

Antoni's governor now. I doubt he hungers for power.

I hear crowns make people more attractive.

Enzo's black eyes taper on Kanti's brow. *I don't see any crown.*

She wants one.

Asha said it was yours by birthright. He leans back in his chair.

It may have been destined for me in my past life, but I no longer have blood magic.

Blood magic doesn't make you Shabbin; it makes you a sorceress. He gestures toward Abrax who stands to the side with three other male guards. *Unless you don't consider the men in the queendom Shabbin?*

When did you get so wise, Enzo Fronz?

Not wisdom. Just observational skills. That crown is still yours.

I don't even know if I want it.

Even if you didn't, there's no way the Mahananda will give it to Kanti. I'd stake my ability to shift on that.

I hiss at him. *Never make such bets, not even in jest. Please. I care about you far too much now.*

A boyish grin seizes his young face. One that grows in intensity when Asha snatches a bowl of fried zucchini blossoms and spoons four onto Enzo's already heaped plate. Though she moves around the table, holding out the glazed ceramic dish for the rest of us to serve ourselves, her pink gaze sticks to my fellow Serpent's plate like barnacles on turtle shells.

I smile. *You better eat before Asha spoon-feeds you in public.*

Enzo grips his fork, hunches over to approach his face to his plate, then begins to shovel food into his mouth. He barely swallows before gulping down the next bite. I sense he isn't doing it solely for Asha's sake. I sense he's starving.

You should've eaten while I rested.

I ate some seaweed and cockles.

That isn't enough for a growing boy.

I'm nineteen. Doubt I'm still growing, Day.

You're putting on muscle.

I wish, he mumbles.

They will come.

Even though Kanti is talking to my grandmother about Mahananda only knows what, her attention is on Enzo, her nose scrunched in horror. Though Asha has instructed my Serpent on how to hold his fork and knife properly, it isn't second-nature to him. According to Asha, "old habits die hard." Every time she utters the phrase, my mind drifts to the woman I was before and I wonder: did she have habits?

I've asked Priya, but she doesn't like speaking about who I was before, reminding me that I'm not her. She's right. I'm not the princess with the pink eyes and dark hair who resurrected a dormant king before giving birth to a curse-breaker. I'm the hollowed-out shifter with the odd face and odder tongue.

"Easy there, *abi.*" The queen pats Enzo's hand, cutting off Kanti midsentence. "We wouldn't want you to choke."

He gulps down his mouthful. "S-Sorry, Sumaca."

"We've gone over this. I want you to call me Priya, not Sumaca."

His head bobs with an abrupt nod.

A nerve jumps in Kanti's jaw. I don't have to read her mind to know that she disapproves of the privilege my grandmother has bestowed on my Serpent. "How tight you've all gotten in my absence."

The queen cants her head. "You say this as though it were unfortunate. Were you hoping I wouldn't appreciate the Mahananda's choice of mate for my granddaughter?"

Her utterance of the word *mate* strengthens my desire to call upon Erwin.

After breakfast.

After I speak with Enzo in private.

Kanti shrugs. "You weren't partial to her last mate. Then again, he's an uncivilized brute with an ego the size of his spirit animal."

It isn't a hiss that flows off my tongue but a rumble, one that makes Kanti roll her eyes and my grandmother narrow hers. I'm guessing she didn't realize I still had affection for Cathal Báeinach.

"He's the father of my child, Kanti." Though my posture is rigid, I square my shoulders some more. "I will not have you—or anyone else—denigrate him. Am I understood?"

Kanti snorts. "Shabbe's a free world, Daya. Freedom of thought. Freedom of speech. It's inked in our constitution. Haven't you read it?" She bites her lip, then leans over the table and drops her voice to add, "That was insensitive of me."

A frown pleats my brow.

"The queen mentioned that your dearth of reading and writing skills were a sore spot, but here I am, blabbering about them. Please forgive me." She flings me a smile that is as artificial as her apology.

If only Kanti could go slumber in the Mahananda...

I could push her in, Enzo offers.

No. My sharp interjection has his spine pinching straight. ***Not only would harm befall you, but a sorceress must also choose death, otherwise the Mahananda will send her right back.***

A shame.

Enzo, please be careful with your thoughts. The Mahananda hears all.

If it does, then why isn't it punishing Kanti?

It sent her away from Shabbe, I find myself thinking. I must think it into the bond because Enzo blinks wide eyes at me.

Admittedly, I never considered her departure a punishment, but what if it was? What if the Mahananda's intent when sending her to Luce wasn't only to seduce one of Lorcan's enemies? *How mysterious you are, Mahananda.*

Find Agrippina.

I frown at Enzo who is, again, bent over his food. ***What?***

He glances up at me, eyebrows tilted. ***What?*** he echoes.

What did you just say?

His frown deepens, but then he says, ***I asked you why it wasn't punishing Kanti.***

After that.

I didn't say anything after that.

211

My skin pebbles for if he didn't advise me to locate the woman who gave birth to my daughter, then who did? As I stare past Kanti's shoulder at the source of all magic, the tingling grows so pronounced that I palm my arms. And then I shake my head because I'm obviously losing my mind.

The Mahananda only speaks to the queen, and last I checked, that wasn't me.

Since Kanti's back to boxing Priya's ears with her cleverness, I fathom it's one of the guards. But which one? And why do they want to find Agrippina? Because the Mahananda is ready to heal her broken mind?

Chapter 33
Zendaya

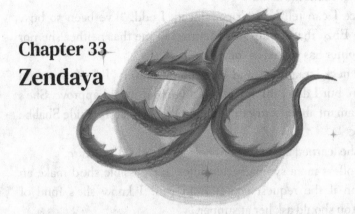

Agrippina's face blooms in full color across my lids. Just before I part ways with my grandmother in front of her bedchamber doors, I ask, "Has the Mahananda recovered from Fallon's curse-breaking?"

She turns her fatigued gaze toward its smooth surface. "Not yet."

I nibble on the inside of my cheek. Then why did someone mention Agrippina? Why must she be found?

"I need to go rest. I'll see you this evening." The queen kisses my pearl, then Enzo's, before departing in a whoosh of white silk.

Could Agrippina have gotten lost? But lost where—in Luce or in Shabbe? She didn't sail home with us, but that doesn't mean she didn't return eventually. After all, Taytah never put up the wards she threatened to erect.

Right before Abrax shuts me inside with Enzo, who I convened for a private conversation, I ask, "Are the Rossi women back in Shabbe?"

"No."

"They decided to stay in Luce?" I ask.

Enzo's intrigued stare prickles my nape.

"Luce is their home, Daya." Abrax says this with no condescension. "Is there a particular reason they're on your mind?"

"No," I lie.

Abrax slants his head.

Since I can tell he isn't convinced, I add, "I've been so busy training Enzo that it only just occurred to me that neither she nor her daughter has visited in some time."

His neck straightens and his eyebrows level. "I'd offer to send for them, but I don't think your grandmother would approve. She's been adamant about restricting the number of visitors inside Shabbe ever since—"

"—she learned about serpent poison." I sigh. "I'm aware."

He offers me a sympathetic smile. "It's possible she'd make an exception if the request comes from you? I know she's fond of Ceres. You should ask her at supper."

I nod, casting a glance around me at the other guards' faces. None of them are staring with suspicion. None of them are staring at me, period. But are they listening?

"I'll be right outside if you need anything," Abrax says.

I nod my thanks, then tread past Enzo as Abrax gives us the privacy I requested.

Are you okay? Enzo asks. ***You seem agitated.***

"Yes. Fine. Sit. We need to talk." My terse tone only deepens the angle of his brown eyebrows as he takes a seat on my divan and I sink onto it beside him.

My mind clings to Agrippina even as I explain my desire to make another Serpent to Enzo. Yet I don't let her name slip through our bond. I want him to fully concentrate on what I'm telling him... what I'm asking him.

When disappointment scores his face, I snatch the hand with which he's strangling his bony thigh and cocoon it between my own. "What is it?"

"I...I..." He slides his lips together, his black eyes taking on a worrying sheen.

"Tell me your thoughts."

He stares hard at my fruit bowl. *I know I'm young and not really a looker, but*—he swallows—*am I really not enough?*

"It has nothing to do with how I feel about you, Enzo."

Doesn't it? "You s-still love Fa-Fallon's fa-father." He steals his hand away from mine to mop his cheeks.

"Enzo, sweetheart, I love you. You will always be my first and favorite Serpent."

"But n-never y-your—". He jumps to his feet. *First and favorite mate,* he finishes through the bond.

I assumed he'd understand. I assumed he'd be excited to widen our little nest. Clearly, I assumed wrong.

He storms toward my door and lets himself out, thwacking the wood. I hesitate to call on Erwin. I allow three days to pass, hoping Enzo will change his mind. He doesn't, the same way he doesn't speak to me or swim with me. As I slip the poisonous purple flakes onto my tongue, having resumed my daily intake at the same dose as before my convalescence, Asha asks what happened between us.

"Maybe you should sleep with him," she suggests.

I'm so repulsed by the idea that I grimace.

With a sigh, she asks, "You're *really* not attracted to him, are you?"

"No. But I do really love him."

She nods, thoughtful. "Then I'm on board with your expansion idea."

I blink, surprised by her encouragement.

"But what happens if you cannot communicate with them?"

"Then I'll take your advice and lay with Enzo." Picturing his lips on mine makes bile rise up my throat, further convincing me that he and I cannot possibly be romantic mates.

Once my body feels strong and rested, I use my bargain: "Erwin of the Sky Kingdom, I need a lift to Luce."

The glowing band I've been hiding from everyone thanks to silk shawls immediately snuffs out. When after several hours, nothing but storm clouds tile the evening sky, I begin to worry that my grandmother *did* put up wards. I pace my chamber, my frustration giving way to concern. What if the male's been injured with obsidian again? What if he isn't *able* to fly?

The sky growls, and then rain hurtles against my windows in sheets so thick it blurs the outside world. My worry turns to downright trepidation. Is this storm Lorcan-made? Did something happen in Luce that I'm unaware of?

I'm about to seek out a guard when a shadow seeps beneath one of my arched windows and develops into a hulking redhead.

"Forgive my tardiness, Rajka, but I needed to speak with Lorcan about how best to conceal transporting you out of Shabbe."

The storm.

How glad I am that he thought of this, for I've been so consumed by my deliberations that I certainly hadn't. "You'll need a cloak and proper footwear. The temperatures in Luce have dropped since your last visit."

I hurry to my closet and grab a silk cape and matching slippers.

Erwin's mouth twists when I reappear, tucking my hair under the embroidered hood. "That's not gonna be enough. Here." He shrugs out of a suede jacket lined with black fur.

"What about you?"

"I just wore it because Liora insisted I not leave without it." He smiles. "I've got plenty of meat on my bones to keep me warm."

Smiling gratefully, I toss off my silk cape and thread my arms through his sleeves. The hit of warmth is as potent as the adrenaline rushing through my blood, and not because of the skirmishes still crackling through Luce.

Some part of me fears the answers this journey will bring. Another part craves them.

"Where exactly in Luce would you like to go?" Erwin asks.

I remember Sybille telling me that her family tavern faces the human neighborhoods. Humans are mortal. So I give him the name of the Amaris' tavern.

He palms his waterlogged hair. "If you wanted some ale, I could've carried some over."

"It isn't ale I want."

His mouth pinches. "I'm hoping that what you *want* is to see Sybille."

"Yes. Exactly. I want to see her."

"Better be, or Cathal will fluff his pillows with my feathers."

My skin pebbles in spite of the thick hide I wear. "Why would he do that?"

"Because *Bottom of the Jug* still operates as a brothel."

My head rears back. "You think I've asked you for a ride to Luce to sate some sexual desire?"

"I don't know. Your mate's pretty green."

"Please just take me there. And don't tell Cathal. I don't need him breathing down my neck."

"Should I tell Fallon?"

"Yes. You can tell Fallon, but no one else."

"All right. Let's go before your grandmother stakes me with obsidian."

Though it seems outrageous, I realize that she probably would. "I'm sorry for putting you at risk."

"A bargain's a bargain," he says, before melting into feathers at the foot of my stone stairs.

Pulse racing, lungs tight, I climb onto his back and loop my arms around his neck. Once we clear the tall fortifications, my ribs loosen, but not my lungs. They cling to every sip of wet air. When we finally puncture Lorcan's thunderous cloud cover, I unwind my arms and sit up. The stars are bright over Luce; the air thick with lavender plumes of smoke that coil out of every chimney.

The air is so nippy that I burrow into Erwin's borrowed coat like a mollusk in a conch shell. It grows a fraction warmer as we begin our descent toward the westernmost isle of Tarelexo, toward a wharf that must host a marketplace, considering the amount of tethered wooden vessels and heaped crates overflowing with iridescent scales and headless foul.

Though I know the Lucins eat fish and meat, the sight and reek of carrion turns my stomach. My heart stutters as I become aware that I'm wearing some animal's hide, for fur doesn't grow on trees. I pop my head out of the collar. Though grateful for the warmth it affords me, my skin itches with eagerness to shed it.

The humans and Faeries milling about below scatter as we land. One sweep of my lurid hair has them freezing. They stare unabashedly, so I do the same. I note that most of the two-legged folk around me have rounded ears and coarse garments that run the gamut of browns and grays. How long will it take Lorcan and Fallon to blur the social disparity produced by five centuries of Faerie rule?

Erwin shifts the second I slide off his back, then palms the middle of my spine, guiding me away from the gawkers and toward a glowing abode trimmed with a sapphire canopy bearing gold letters. I imagine they read: *Bottom of the Jug.* The Shabbin and Lucin alphabets aren't the same, so I recognize no letter. Not that I'm all that great at reading Shabbin, as Kanti so kindly pointed out.

Cheery music seeps around the weathered mullions that divide the thick panes of glass. I let it envelop me and drive away my short-comings. When Erwin pulls open the door, a gust of warmth engulfs my cheeks. Scanning the crowd, I start to unfasten the buttons on my borrowed jacket, but at the sight of familiar blue eyes, I freeze like the audience on the wharf.

Chapter 34
Zendaya

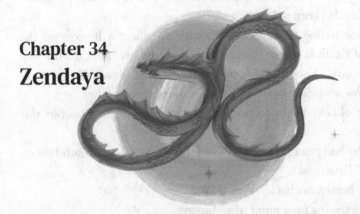

The odd injunction I overheard over breakfast three days past scores my buzzing eardrums. I'd thought little of Agrippina since Enzo had blustered out of my chamber. Truthfully, all I've thought about is my selfish craving to make another Serpent.

"*Santo Caldrone!*" Sybille's exclamation stabs my eardrums, whisking my attention off the orange-haired Faerie, who's obviously *not* lost.

I greet Fallon's closest friend with a nod and a smile.

"What now?" Erwin grumbles as Sybille tosses aside a kitchen towel and blusters out from behind a long wooden bar.

"You can go, Erwin. You've repaid my bargain," I murmur.

"You obviously don't know me if you think I'd leave you here by yourself."

"I'm not alone; Sybille's here."

"No offence to the half-Fae, but until another Crow shows up to guard you, I'll be sticking around."

"Is my daughter on her way?"

"Yes. She should be here shortly," he says, just as Sybille squeezes me into a hug that's so tight I feel the hard lump of life swelling her abdomen.

She fires a string of rapid Lucin words, evidently forgetting that her tongue isn't yet mine. The sight of my rumpled brow leads Erwin to say, "She's asking what brought you to her tavern. Something I'm also keen to learn."

Since telling them that I've come to collect a human on the brink of death is out of the question, I forage my mind for the few Lucin words I know, coming up with: "*Necessitudo scando.*"

Crow and Faerie gawp, first at me, then at each other.

My cheeks begin to prickle. "What?" I ask, in Shabbin this time.

"You had me carry you to Luce for hallucinogenic substances, Rajka?" Erwin asks.

My head rears back. "What? No!"

"*Scando* means a mind trip," he says.

"I meant a change of scenery. I needed out of Shabbe for a couple days."

Erwin snorts. "The word you're looking for is *iterio*. Trip of the body."

The second he pronounces the correct term, the corners of Sybille's mouth flip up and she laughs.

"Can you ask Sybille if she has any rooms to let?"

He mashes his lips.

I tilt my head, waiting. When a minute has passed and he still hasn't relayed my request, I add a, "Please?"

"We've vacant rooms in the Sky Castle."

Except a room in the Sky Castle won't give me free rein to wander Luce and locate my next Serpent. "I prefer to stay in the city."

Our hushed debate quiets Sybille.

"The city isn't safe," he hisses.

I glance around me at the tables full of patrons who are either midmeal or mid-card game. "Battles might be waged, but evidently not in here."

My gaze lands on an umber-skinned male who sports more glitter on his face and bare torso than Erwin sports charcoal. His jaw is slack, his eyes wide, unlike the male whose lap he sits on, whose features are as tight as the satin belt pleating the silk panels of my indigo dress.

If I were to be perfectly honest, the mixture of awe and revulsion directed my way is disquieting. But honesty won't help me grow my tribe, so, as I finally finish unbuttoning Erwin's coat, I paste on a smile to appear amicable and square my shoulders to appear confident.

"Your daughter won't like you staying in the Fae lands," he mumbles. "I doubt she'll sanction it."

I hand over the hide. "I'm her mother."

"This is her kingdom."

"I'm aware." I turn toward Sybille, trying to recall the word for bedchamber in Lucin. When I cannot, I decide to mime my intent by pressing my palms together and laying one cheek on them.

As my hands come back down to my sides, Sybille gnaws on her lower lip. Is she reluctant to let me stay here because of Erwin or because she shares the Crow's worries? A third theory has me ruing myself. In my haste, I forgot to pack coin. The roll of my pearl bracelet along my wrist has me unclasping it and holding it out to her.

She stares at it for a long moment, then past it, at me, shaking her head and pushing my offering away. She then says something to Erwin that includes both Cathal and Fallon's names.

I grit my teeth, tempted to remind them both that my daughter and her father aren't my keepers.

"You can stay with us, Rajka." Ceres's clear voice carves through the tense silence, carrying everyone's attention to her. I'm guessing most are surprised by her mastery of my tongue. "Justus put an apartment at Agrippina's and my disposal while our house is being renovated."

I start to smile but my lips freeze. *Find Agrippina.* Could the Mahananda have whispered this to me because it anticipated Sybille's disinclination to host me?

"After everything your grandmother has done for us, it would be our honor." Ceres sets down the deck of cards she'd been shuffling, then palms the scarred wooden tabletop and scoots her chair back. "We were just heading home. Unless you want a bite to eat before—"

"I've eaten. Thank you." I clip the bracelet back onto my wrist. "I'm ready to retire."

The door bursts open behind me and a violent chill creeps up my spine.

One caused by more than the bitter temperature.

One caused by an icy glare.

I twist my neck slowly, knowing full well whose rabid gaze I'm about to meet.

Chapter 35
Zendaya

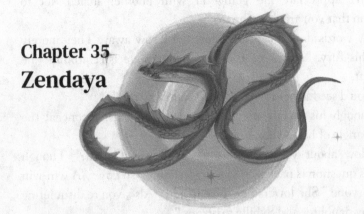

"I thought you didn't inform him of my trip," I mutter to Erwin as Cathal irrupts into the tavern, eyes slitted, hair wild.

"I didn't," the beefy redhead murmurs. "Like I mentioned earlier, I don't care to be plucked." He scratches the back of his neck. "Or pulped. I'm in so much fucking trouble. Apologies for what I'm about to do."

When he morphs into smoke and streaks past Cathal, I realize that he was apologizing in advance for abandoning me with the seething Crow. "I'm ready to leave, Ceres."

"Right away." Once she's slipped her arms through her fur-lined cloak, she helps Agrippina into hers. "Evening, Cathal."

The Crow doesn't reciprocate her social niceties, merely aims his glower her way. Ceres doesn't flinch as she hooks Agrippina's arm through hers and crosses the deathly-quiet tavern toward me.

Fallon's Faerie grandmother gives my outfit a once over. "Not really dressed for this weather, are you? Good thing it's not a long walk. Come."

I start to follow when Cathal finally unclenches his jaw. "She'll be coming with me."

"No, *she* won't," I reply tightly.

"I wasn't giving you a choice, Príona."

I come toe to toe with Cathal and angle my face toward his to deliver words which I know will make him back down. "My mate wouldn't appreciate me going off with another male. Not to mention that you aren't my guard."

My words don't magically blow the Crow away. They merely hone his fury. "As far as I can see, your *mate* isn't around," he grits out.

"You'd see farther if you stopped watching me."

Though his facial hair has thickened, it doesn't conceal the severe angle of his jawbone.

"How about you escort us to my house, Cathal?" Though Ceres's question is packaged as a suggestion, it isn't one. "A win-win for everyone." She lowers her voice to add, "Also, you're disquieting both my daughter and Sybille's patrons."

"Do I look like I give a single fuck about—"

"They are her livelihood." Her hiss is as cutting as shards of glass.

Narrowing his eyes some more, a feat considering how thin they already are, Cathal wheels around and yanks open the door, crushing its edge until we've stepped over the threshold.

The second we're outside, he growls into my ear, "Get on my back." And then his body expands into his bird's.

I step nearer to Ceres. "No. And don't you *dare* try to cart me off."

I've no need to peer into his mind to see how he itches to clamp his iron talons around my shoulders instead of around the cobbles he is, at present, reducing to dust.

I take another step toward Ceres, who lingers beneath the flapping awning with a trembling Agrippina. I suppose it's because of our altercation, although it could possibly be due to the bitter chill of the night, which, thanks to my altercation, doesn't penetrate my overheated skin.

A cool shadow glides along my arm before solidifying into a man. "Fine." Cathal's breath is a fiery jolt against the shell of my ear. "You want to stay in the Fae lands and get gored by a fucking Faerie, fine. *Fucking* fine."

While I appreciate his regard for my safety, I don't appreciate his tone or the anxiety it piles upon my shoulders.

"Don't worry," Ceres says as he dematerializes and takes to the sky. "The Fae lands aren't that bad. At least not on this side of Monteluce." As we begin walking, she says, "My husband—well, *ex*-husband—is doing an astonishingly good job at keeping the peace."

"*Malo uomo*," Agrippina suddenly says, voice warbling with frenzy. "*Malo uomo*."

Ceres taps her daughter's hand. "*Tiu pappa no malo uomo, mi cuori.*" Then in Shabbin, she explains that Agrippina still believes her father is evil—"*malo.*"

Pity overtakes my unease. "I hope the Mahananda will welcome her soon."

Ceres sighs. "You and me both, Rajka. You and me both."

"*Malo uomo*," Agrippina says again, her blue eyes as turbulent as the amber waves caught in her fur collar. She digs her boots into the cobbles, dragging her mother to a standstill, then points to a spot over my shoulder.

Swearing softly, Ceres plunges her hand beneath her coat and extricates a dagger.

I gasp, then gasp again as the ground vanishes from underneath my feet. Still, I don't miss the cloaked figure dashing toward Ceres and Agrippina, brandishing a blade longer than Ceres's. I grip one of Cathal's talons and shout, "Go back! We can't leave them!"

He stops ascending. I know the moment he sees the cloaked figure because he drops like a stone, halting for a heartbeat over a flat rooftop upon which he deposits me before flashing away. I rush toward the edge of the building, my breath stabbing my lungs, shredding my throat. When I see a head roll, I wheeze.

A head.

Without a body.

Just a head.

My chest burns when I catch the shock of black hair.

Chapter 36
Zendaya

C eres cannot be—
        She cannot be—
        Two more Crows plummet from the sky and land below—Erwin and Reid. The latter kicks the head. I want to scream at the man for desecrating Ceres's corpse, but my scream morphs into a sigh of relief when I catch sight of the face, of the masculine jaw.

Not Ceres.

My pulse bangs against my eardrums in time with the slender boat accosting the embankment. Soldiers leap from it, palms crackling with magic directed at the crowd blighting the wharf.

I try to shout Cathal's name, but my throat is so tight that the two syllables emerge as an inaudible rasp, one that's drowned out by a feminine wail.

"Agrippina!" Ceres keens. "*Mi cuori!* Nooo!"

Everything inside of me hardens and chills like the slate tiles biting into my cramping fingers.

Find Agrippina.

I might not have much power, but maybe, just maybe, I can heal her. Before my next heartbeat, I race back toward the tavern, then leap onto the fabric canopy to break my fall. I roll, banging into the man with a proclivity for glitter.

"So sorry," I tell him, scrambling to my feet and rushing toward Agrippina.

Agrippina who lays there, throat slit and body limp in the cradle of her mother's arms.

My name is shouted from the rooftop.

I don't bother answering since I've no doubt that Cathal, with his impeccable eyesight, will spot me in the crowd. I shoulder past onlookers. One of them tries to stop me, but a hiss, coupled with a glance at my eyes has him stepping aside. I push past Reid, who stands over the Rossi women, unmoving.

Ceres gasps when I crouch and touch her sleeve.

"Can I try to heal her?"

"Iron," she croaks, pulling her arm away.

I fathomed the weapon was made of that. After all, Agrippina is pureblooded. Ceres wouldn't be crying if it had been forged from any other metal.

I begin to lash at the warm, sweet essence flowing out of the yawning wound. Her blood gushes down my throat. I swallow and swallow until it feels like I've drunk all of what flows through her veins. *Live! Come on...*

When her skin begins to tauten, relief blooms within my ribs like an anemone, growing tentacles that snare every floating particle of hope. I wasn't too late. I got to Agrippina in time.

Find Agrippina.

This was why! Because the Mahananda knew an evil man would come at her with an iron blade. I suck in a breath at the errant thought, recalling her tremulous warning. *Malo uomo.* Did she foresee him, or did she merely *see* him?

As I keep laving her cut, thoughts puff like the grains of sand that Enzo sends floating upward when he slithers across the bottom of the Amkhuti, as he so loves to do. My little bottom dweller. Well, my humongous bottom dweller, for he is far larger than I am in scales. In skin too.

I hate how I left things with him. I picture his green scales, recall the pliant press of them against my body a scant few mornings ago. *Enzo?*

He doesn't answer me.

Please forgive me.

I pull away to check on Agrippina's wound. I must move too fast, because my head thumps against the bloodied cobbles. I lay there, blinking back the darkness, trying to muscle my neck back up. Why does my skull feel like a galleon anchor?

Perhaps Faerie blood is noxious to Serpents? What if someone laced her blood with that toxin? What if it wasn't the Mahananda that guided me toward her but Kanti? Could my cousin be so shrewd? She desires the throne so fiercely...

A cool splash startles my lids up. Cathal stands over me with an overturned bucket. His mouth moves over my name before moving over a barked command. "Reid, Erwin, more!"

More what? He tosses the bucket at the redhead and then drops into a crouch beside me, his charcoal stripes melting down his cheeks and into his facial hair like tears, his forehead slick with perspiration.

"Can you hear me, Príona?" He sweeps his fingers across my mouth, strokes a line down my neck.

I'm about to nod when another cool, delicious splash slicks over my torso. I can feel the salt trickle through my skin, vivifying my blood, rattling my muscles, crisping my mind and reminding me that I'm other. That to exist, I need salt, I need the ocean. That it wasn't Agrippina's blood or the substance of the weapon that drew me into the abyss, but my own physical shortcomings. When I'd healed Enzo, I'd done so in scales. Perhaps I must always heal people in scales, be they Crow or Faerie or human.

With a sigh, I drag my knuckles over my mouth to wipe away any lingering blood, then scrub my palms down my face and up through my hair. "Did it work? Is she alive?"

Cathal scowls. Why? Because he wished me to speak other words? Since he's yet to answer me, I glance at Agrippina's neck, at the skin that's hemmed shut, pink and puckered against the milky expanse surrounding it.

Ceres's cheeks shine with tears as she tucks a lock of hair behind the scarred shell of Agrippina's ear before curling herself around her daughter and rocking her.

I snap my gaze toward Cathal's. "It didn't work?"

"No." It's Reid who replies. He stands rooted to the same spot as before, his fingers balled into fists.

But...but I don't understand. Agrippina no longer bleeds. I hunt what I can see of her neck for a throbbing vein, hunt her face for a twitch of lashes. Agrippina lays wilted in her mother's arms, her skin so pale that her freckles resemble a crude paint splatter.

Find Agrippina, my mind nags.

I did! I want to scream. *I found her!*

But more importantly, my tongue patched her injury, so why isn't she waking? Why isn't her chest pumping? I mustn't have drawn out the iron...I must've sealed it inside her veins.

Though my sodden dress only sticks to my skin, it feels as though it swathes my lungs. I want to tear it off, to jump into the canal and shift.

I try to push away from Cathal but he clasps me like Ceres clasps her daughter. "Let go."

He doesn't.

I splay my fingers on his armor and shove. My muscles tremble so hard that my elbow buckles and my body ends up pressed to his.

Cathal's arms tighten around me. "Please let me hold you," he rasps into my hair.

With a sigh, I relent and press my Serpent away until it no longer niggles my spine. "You never came to see me," I murmur.

"I came."

"That was you in the gardens three days ago?"

"Ceres!" someone yells.

I twist away from Cathal to find Justus Rossi barreling through the throng of soldiers and halting beside Reid.

"Ceres?" he sputters again.

She picks her head off her daughter's forehead and blinks wetly at him. Her cheek is stained black. He asks her a question in their tongue to which she responds with a shake of her head. And then he's slinging his face my way, asking me something about the Mahananda. But I'm too distracted by the smudge on Ceres's cheek to respond.

"Still closed," Cathal replies in Shabbin, probably to keep the soldiers surrounding us in the dark about our lack of access to the source of all magic.

"Maybe we can place her on its surface!" Reid says with such vigor that his voice echoes over all the cobbles. "Maybe it would op—"

A blue hue is enveloping Agrippina's strands, snuffing out the amber. I press away from Cathal. This time, not only do his arms soften but he also helps me sit up. I push a lock of hair off my face, feeling it ghost over my mouth and coat it with the metallic tang of blood and salt.

Her lashes flutter. Draw up.

The air freezes inside my lungs as I stare...and stare.

"What have you done to my daughter?" Ceres gasps.

I saved her.

I transformed her.

Chapter 37
Zendaya

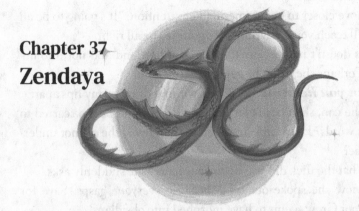

Justus's silence rings louder than Ceres's cries of outrage. Here I thought she might be pleased that Agrippina was alive, but, apparently, she'd have preferred her to be dead than a Serpent.

"Do not yell at her," Cathal grits out. "All Zendaya did was carry her back from the underworld. The words you are looking for are *thank you, Rajka*."

"She transformed my daughter into an animal," Ceres snarls.

I flinch, which makes Cathal's arm tighten around my middle. Is that what she really thinks of me? As an animal?

"A shifter," Justus finally says, scrubbing a hand down his face. "*Not* an animal." Ceres opens her mouth, probably to argue, but she's interrupted by his next words: "Just like our granddaughter."

Though her pulse still flicks against her elegant neck at a harsh pace, her lips press together and she grows quiet.

"You should get away from her." Cathal's tone is as placid as his pulse isn't. It rages against my abdomen, its beats echoing the ones slamming against my own sternum. "If it's anything like last time, she's about to shift."

"Last time?" Ceres squawks, before shooting me a horrified look. "You've made others?"

"One," Cathal says.

Agrippina's thin eyebrows quirk as she observes her mother, then slant on Reid.

I move closer to her, garnering her attention. "It's going to be all right. I'll teach you everything. It's going to be all right."

She doesn't nod. Doesn't speak. Not out loud and not into my mind. Perhaps she won't be capable of the latter.

Can you hear me? I ask her, without drawing my lips apart.

If she can, she doesn't let on. Could her mind be too scarred to register words? How am I supposed to train her if she cannot understand me?

"What the fuck did you do to your hair?" she suddenly asks.

I know she spoke out loud, because *everyone* gasps. Save for Reid. Poor Crow seems to have morphed into obsidian.

Agrippina licks her lips, then says something about Meriam in Lucin before gasping Cathal's name and pointing to a place over his shoulder. Color leaches from her already pale face, and she hisses the word *pappa*, scuttling away from her still kneeling mother.

Cathal sighs, his breath soft against my ear, then replies in Lucin. Agrippina rolls those twin pools of black from the Crow holding me to the Faerie standing next to him. All the while, Ceres palms her mouth, stifling whatever sound is building in her throat—a gasp, another sob, an exclamation?

"She believes her father is still our enemy," Cathal murmurs softly.

"He's not the enemy, Agrippina," I tell her in Shabbin since she appears to be fluent. "You're safe."

My new Serpent frowns at me.

"As to what I did with my hair, it's a long story. One I'd prefer to tell you in Shabbe."

"Wait," Justus says in Shabbin. "What's your sister's name?"

Agrippina's head rears back. "Why? Have you forgotten it, Pappa?"

He snorts, swallows. "Just please say it."

She cocks a ruddy eyebrow. "Domitina."

In Lucin she says words that Cathal translates quietly. "She's

232

asking him if he'll require the title of the book from which she plucked the name, since she apparently chose it for her sister."

Tears spill down Ceres's cheeks. "*Rimena.*"

"*Si.*" Justus walks over to his former mate and crouches, placing a hand on her shoulder. "*Rimena.*"

"She remembers," Cathal translates.

"You brought all of her back." Justus's voice is cluttered with emotion. "Thank you, Rajka. Thank you."

Ceres swallows and echoes the Faerie general's sentiment, buoying my heart.

Agrippina gapes. "You speak Shabbin, Mamma?" she asks just as another loud "Mamma" echoes in the night.

Fallon.

I twist around, thinking she's calling to me, but find her eyes locked on Agrippina. Of course. I'm not her only mother. How could I forget? After its brief climb, my heart plummets anew. It's unfair of me to be jealous, yet I cannot stifle the sentiment.

Cathal's fingers mold my waist and then his thumb strokes as though he senses my dejection.

Fallon comes to a stop right beside her grandparents, her gaze stilling on Agrippina's eyes and retracted tusk before hurtling toward me. "You transformed her?"

"She *saved* her." Cathal's tone is so abrupt that it draws our daughter's eyebrows low.

"I didn't mean it in a bad way, Dádhi."

"*Dádhi?*" The pearl above Agrippina's nose dips as she lowers her frown to my abdomen.

My jealousy dwindles, for she doesn't remember the child my prior self nested inside her body for safekeeping.

"What the holy fucking Mahananda is going on here?"

Air funnels past my lips, because I'm almost certain her mouth didn't move. Not to mention she used the Shabbin term for the source of all magic instead of the Lucin one. *Agrippina, can you hear me?*

Her eyebrows slant as she whisks her stare back my way.

I'm speaking inside your mind.

Her lids reel up so high that her lashes smack her browbone. *How?* Her word, though noiseless, detonates inside my skull. *Did you draw a sigil on my forehead?*

I can no longer bloodcast, the same way I can no longer understand Lucin. It's a very long story that involves my demise and the Mahananda. I swear I'll tell you everything, but first you need to understand something about yourself. You're no longer...

Her body shimmers, expands, transforms.

Even though what she is no longer is evident, I finish my sentence anyway: *A Faerie.*

Chapter 38
Zendaya

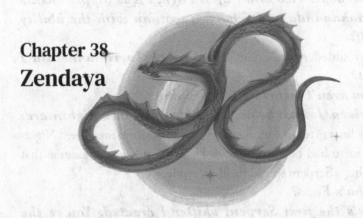

T he soldiers gasp and so does the crowd they're keeping at bay with magic.

I stand. As I approach, her forked black tongue unspools from her mouth, and then she's writhing, banging her tusk into the wall.

I kneel and seize her tusk. **Shh,** I whisper into her mind. **You're all right. I'm right here. Shh.**

Her lids come up and down in rapid succession. **What's happening to me?**

You shifted into a Serpent.

A Serpent? she screeches.

Though I shouldn't smile, I do. "I'm sorry," I murmur out loud. In Serpent, then in Shabbin, and then, in Lucin. I learned the word from Enzo who says it much too often.

Enzo, who isn't my mate.

His hurt face brightens the backs of my lids, injecting my heart with pain. I call to him. When there's only silence down our bond, I assume my voice mustn't carry so far. How far does Lorcan's mind link to his people carry?

Is this a spell? Agrippina asks.

No. Like I said, I can no longer bloodcast. My mother...she ended up killing me and transferring my

235

soul into the womb of a serpent—a real one. I grew up as a serpent. Two lunar cycles ago, I was dipped inside the Mahananda and reborn a woman with the ability to shift.

Her slitted nostrils flare. ***How much Faerie wine did I ingest?***

You aren't inebriated, Agrippina.

Asleep. I must be asleep. This must be a nightmare.

My fingers tumble off the ivory and knock into my knees. *Nightmare?* Enzo had been so excited. How naïve I was to assume that becoming a Serpent would thrill everyone.

Who's Enzo?

He's the first Serpent shifter I created. You're the second.

Flick my cheek.

Flick your…?

Flick my cheek. Or pinch me.

Why?

Daya, just do it.

I flick her scaled cheek.

Fuck. I felt that. This is real. I'm a real fucking sea serpent. Fuck. She looks around, sets her gaze on her parents. ***Poor Mamma. I suppose I'd be bawling my eyes out as well if my daughter shifted into a frightening creature.***

She's crying because your mind is whole again.

Agrippina's gaze swerves back toward me. ***Pardon me?***

Shift back. We've a lot to discuss. If you don't shift back, we'll need to go for a swim.

Though she cannot rumple her nose in this form, I sense her grimacing. ***In the canals bordering Rax? I'd rather chop off the points of my ears.***

You already did that. I don't tell her that I came by this information when I overheard Kanti discussing it with the Akwale. I'd prefer Agrippina not dwell on the fact that her action is public knowledge.

What? Her voice shrills against my thudding skull.

You cleaved off the tips of your ears.

What?

You cleaved off the tips of your ears.

I fucking heard you the first time! Why the Mahananda would I do such an idiotic thing?

I press my lips together. **Because I placed my baby inside your womb.**

You did what?

Is that rhetorical, or do you need me to repeat it?

She dips her head as far as her neck will allow. **Your baby's growing inside of me?**

Not anymore. When she remains quiet for a disquieting stretch of time, I say, **Please shift back, Agrippina.**

How?

I usually visualize legs, and it works.

Whose legs?

I laugh. **Usually, my own, but I suppose you could visualize anyone's.**

So fucking weird… she mutters.

My trick must work because, two heartbeats later, she's back in flesh. She takes in the surrounding world from where she lays, flat on her stomach, the fur collar of her cloak tickling her human jaw. Then she shoves herself up and glowers around her, hands perched on her hips. She hisses something in Lucin that has Reid snorting and Ceres smiling through her tears.

"Our spitfire of a daughter is truly back," Justus says in Shabbin, giving his head a small shake.

I suddenly wonder if the whole world stood still, or if I just filtered it out when Agrippina was in scales.

She touches her ears, rubbing their rounded shell, and curses under her breath before cursing once again when she carries a lock of hair in front of her eyes. **My hair is blue?**

I don't bother nodding since the hue is evident, even in the faint light afforded by the lantern jutting from the wall at her back.

Agrippina's hand moves off her hair and up to her forehead. When her nails graze her retracted tusk, she shudders, but then she pops her hand off her forehead and holds it in front of her face. *I can't call on my Faerie magic...*

Just like my blood magic.

"Are you all right, Mádhi? You're looking awfully pale."

I nod to reassure Fallon, even though I don't feel all that grand. "Just a little drained, abi."

Cathal helps me to my feet, locking his arm around my waist. My vision swims and my temples scud.

"Agrippina has no memory of the last two decades," I add quietly to redirect their concern off my sudden feebleness.

Fallon bites her lip. "So she doesn't remember me." With a deep swallow, she's sidestepping us and walking over to Agrippina, squeezing past her Faerie grandparents.

"Two mothers, and both forgot about her," I murmur, pained for Fallon.

"Can you hear her?" Cathal asks.

I want Enzo to hear it from me first. *Enzo?*

Day... Enzo's voice is no more than a raucous whisper. One that makes my hand crawl up to my breastbone to try and keep my heart from beating out of my chest. *I think I'm dying.*

Chapter 39
Cathal

Z endaya has been worryingly quiet since she sobbed out Enzo's name, followed by a hoarse entreaty for me to carry her back to Shabbe immediately.

She was so distraught that when I asked what was wrong, all she could do was tremble. Tremble and snap, "*Can* you carry me home or should I ask Erwin?"

Obviously, I obliged, preferring she stop riding other Crows. I'd already made my feelings abundantly clear to Erwin, whose muttered excuse of a bargain hadn't stopped my fist from sailing into his jaw while Zendaya healed Agrippina.

I'd asked him how he'd like it if someone had struck a bargain with *his* mate. He'd blinked. Before he could remind me that Daya wasn't my mate, I'd turned back toward the pink-haired woman I couldn't fucking get out of my mind. However many missions Lorcan sent me on, Zendaya was always there, shimmering on the edge of my thoughts, just out of reach.

Daya's hand suddenly squeezes the feathers at my neck so hard that my wings hold still. "There," I hear her say.

I glance at her, find her gaze riveted to a part of the Sahklare that is as dark at night as it is during the daytime.

"Carry me down."

I scoff. Does she seriously expect me to drop her off in the middle of the Chayagali?

"Cathal, Enzo's here! I can feel him."

Fucking Enzo.

Even though my rider rages at me to turn back, I flap my wings harder, arrowing toward the palace where Erwin and Fallon are just landing with their riders. The second I clear the trees, I dissolve into smoke to buffet Daya's fall, then morph right back into my Crow and sail off. Her shouts resonate through the Cauldron-shaped queendom, banging against my ribs as I drift up the Sahklare, peering into the algae-bright water for green scales. I fly over the narrow stretch of water twice. Zendaya must've been wrong about her shifter's location because the Green One's nowhere in that water. I wouldn't miss a Serpent of his stature.

I'm about to ask another Crow to check with Daya about where she felt him when branches bristle followed by deep snarls. I drift lower and glimpse a tendu crouched over coils of green, warning off another. *Fucking tendus.*

I tilt my body, part my beak, and bullet down. A moment later the famished feline's blood warms my beak. I toss away his body just as another tendu leaps and lands on me. Before I can shift to smoke, its claws sink past my feathers. Little does he know that he's fucked with the wrong Crow.

He paws at the limp Serpent with a triumphant roar, one that I cut short when I cinch his scrawny ribcage with my talons, squeezing until his ribs have all splintered. I toss him aside, then land and shift. Though I don't particularly care to linger in the Shadow Forest, especially in skin, I want to see if a pulse of life remains in Zendaya's mate before carrying him home.

My gaze clocks the chunks of flesh carved out of various parts of his body. One bitemark is so deep and wide that my iron-clad stomach churns. I stride toward his head that lolls against the sandy soil, lids clasped shut, tusk half-buried in the ochre dirt. I crouch and seize his tusk to right his face. I consider giving it a jostle to test his alertness when I recall the damage he incurred at the fangs of the tendu.

I end up patting his cheek and muttering the word for serpent in Shabbin. When after my fourth iteration of, "*Naaga*," he doesn't stir, fear replaces my concern.

Yes, fear. For all my anger that the Mahananda matched her with another, I know what the loss of one's mate feels like, and I would never wish it on anyone. Especially not on the woman I still care for.

I palm his neck to locate a pulse. When something flutters against my skin, I expel a relieved breath, shift back into my other form, and carefully scoop him up. He dangles from my talons like a piece of seaweed. The comparison is horrid, and I instantly chide myself for it.

When I approach the vale, my eyes lock on Daya's searing ones. It strikes me that her hair is wet, as is her dress. I take it that she must've tried to swim toward us. I've never been more glad for the bargain we struck about waterrises. She might not be mine to protect anymore, but the idea of her swimming in tendu territory drops my body's temperature to one equaling the wintry air in Monteluce.

I deposit him at her bare feet, then shift and watch as she peruses his body. Unlike me, she doesn't hunt for a pulse. She must sense he still lives through their mind link.

As she kneels beside him, she looks up at me through narrowed eyes as though I'd been the one to attack and carve out her little mate. "Do not cast me off your back without my consent again, Cathal Báeinach." Her anger is a live thing that chews up the air around us.

Again... That means she intends to hitch more rides on my back. I cross my arms, keeping my expression bare of all sentiment, even though relief stirs behind my ribs. I'd feel even more so if I knew whether she could hear Agrippina.

I consider striding to where the blue-haired former Faerie stands conversing with Fallon, Ceres, Priya, and Behati, but I don't, for inquiring while a Serpent lay bleeding at my feet feels immoral and untimely.

"You should get Agrippina to heal him," I advise Daya, whose stores of magic have already been depleted once tonight.

"He's my Serpent. My responsibility."

I note that she didn't say mate. Petty. So petty. "I meant, because you're already spent."

"I'll do it in the water." She walks over to his head and leans over to bracket it tenderly between her palms. "Can one of you lower him inside?"

"I'll do it." Erwin shifts before I can.

As I accompany Daya to the moat's edge, she nods to my arm. "How bad are your wounds?"

"Just scratches. They'll heal."

"Show them to me after."

After. "Tendu claws aren't made of obsidian, Sifair."

"I'd almost forgotten how dogged you could be," she huffs.

My lips set into a smirk. One that makes her head shake as she plunges headfirst into the deep trench ringing the valley of the Cauldron. I stand on the steep cliff, gaze riveted to the inky water.

After dropping Enzo off inside the moat, Erwin parks himself beside me. "Poor kid. The tendu really got him good."

"He should've known better than to venture in that part of Sahklare," I murmur. "Especially since, unlike the other serpents in Priya's queendom, he can shift and use a fucking boat."

Justus sidles close to us, his furred cape rustling against the black velvet inserts of his jacket. It's far less gaudy than the gold and burgundy uniform he used to don, but still too foppish for my taste. Then again, unlike Faeries, I don't have much taste in fashion, nor any inclination to develop one.

"A Serpent," he murmurs. "My menagerie is growing."

I side-eye him while Erwin guffaws.

My fellow general shrugs, a smile tickling the edge of his lips and the corners of his timeworn eyes. "A snake. A bird. Next thing I know, my wife will ask the Cauldron to turn her into a grasshopper."

"Which wife?" I needle him.

With a sigh, he says, "Ah, Cathal... Forever aiming below the belt."

"I can't imagine having two mates," Erwin muses out loud. "One's already a constant adventure."

His euphemism draws snorts from both Justus and me.

Bubbles pop at the surface of the moat. Is Daya already done? Are they swimming up? I squint. Hold my breath. When no Serpent surfaces, I push the air back out of my lungs and attempt to distract myself by asking Justus, "How's your daughter dealing with her transformation?"

He flinches. "She has twenty-two years of history to catch up on and new magic to tame."

"I still can't believe Daya can *make* others." Erwin rolls his neck, making it crack. "Can you imagine if Lore could turn humans?"

Justus's blue irises glow like the algae-filled rivers. "All of Luce would be feathered and winged. Already so many have taken to facial tattooing."

"Where's your feather?" I ask. "Still ambivalent about your allegiance?"

"No, but tattoos are permanent, and though they look fine on young skin, they're not as comely on rumpled faces."

"You speak as though you were eight-centuries old instead of middle-aged."

"Just add stripes," Erwin suggests. "It'll conceal the wrinkles."

A slender hand winds around my bicep, startling me, even though I know the shape and weight of my daughter's fingers by heart. "Are you three truly discussing face care or are my ears deceiving me?"

"Your ears are deceiving you, ínon."

She smiles and pats my arm.

"Where's Lore?" I ask.

"Dealing with protests in the west. Apparently, my cousin has been bugging everyone's homes with listening sigils. Phoebus's sister found out and told *everyone*. Not only do the Tarespagians and Selvatins feel like it's a breach of their privacy, but also a breach of the peace accords."

"At least it's bringing them together," Justus says, which earns him three deep glowers. "What? It is."

"We'd prefer commerce and education bring them together," I mutter. "Not antagonism towards the new regime."

"Antoni's green." Justus tosses that out as though we'd elected him as governor out of choice. "And his ears are round."

Fallon bristles. "People are no longer measured by the shape of their ears, Nonno."

"True, but until the dust has fully settled over the change of regime, I would've instated a full-blooded Faerie as well."

I flex my jaw, remembering our lengthy debate and all the reasons Lorcan refused. He might trust Justus, but the general's ambitious. "Perhaps the day you wear our feather, Lorcan will indulge you."

Justus thins his lips.

"Antoni's not ruling over the entire region alone, Nonno," Fallon says, trying to ease the tension. "Naoise's there."

"Naoise's a shifter." Justus barely separates his teeth as he mutters this.

"How did Flavia Surro find out?" Erwin asks.

"Kanti invited her for tea at Antoni's, which is where all the sigils converge. In one of the rooms. Kanti apparently forgot to reapply her soundproofing sigil." My daughter says this with a weighted sigh.

"Does Lorcan want me to sail out there?" Justus murmurs.

"Let me ask," Fallon says. A moment later, she says, "Yes, but he understands if you prefer to stay with your daughter until she acclimates to her new self."

Justus glances over his shoulder. "Ceres is with her. Besides, it's Agrippina we're talking about. Your mother—" He stops. I feel his gaze scrape my face, then the surface of the moat. "*Surrogate* mother holds on to grudges almost as hard as your mate, so I'm not going to be in her favor for a while, still."

"Hard to believe anyone can be as begrudging as my mate," she says with a smile.

"I can fly you over, Justus," Erwin offers. "Once you're ready."

"I'm ready." As Erwin morphs, I hear Justus murmur, "Zendaya amMeriam, *tiudevo*." He walks toward Erwin, exchanging a look with Ceres. At her nod, he climbs atop Erwin.

"I'm sorry I snapped at you earlier, Fallon," I murmur as she pillows her head against my arm.

"Please. You were at your wit's end." She squeezes my arm. "Anyway, do you want to hear a fun fact I learned tonight?"

"Always. I love your *fun facts*."

"Agrippina can hear Mádhi...and Mádhi can hear her."

My heart pulses out so many beats that it alters the cycle of my breaths and cramps my lungs.

Enzo isn't her mate, I think, before remembering, *You aren't either*.

Chapter 40
Zendaya

ealing Agrippina and Enzo drained me. Though I surfaced in skin from the Amkhuti, I'm not entirely certain how I got from the Amkhuti to my bed. I assume someone carried me. I also assume that this someone may have been winged.

I wake to fingers of light scraping against my lids. For a moment, I just lay there and reflect on everything that's happened. It feels like a dream. I suddenly worry that it was and sit up brusquely.

"Easy there, imNaage." Asha clucks her tongue at me.

"ImNaage?" *Mother of Serpents?*

"Well, you're now the proud owner of *two* Serpents."

"One does not own people, Asha." I flop back onto my mattress with a sigh. "Right?"

"Slavery isn't a thing in Shabbe."

"But it is in other places?"

"Yes and no. Faeries insist they pay each one of their servants, but it's such a pittance that it probably feels like slavery to the humans in their employ. I request a change of topic. Not only because the other pisses me off, but because...you have *two* mates?"

"What?"

"Agrippina, who is, um, a surprisingly vivacious woman, claims that she can hear you." Asha hops stomach-first onto my bed, sending my mattress rippling. She props herself onto her elbows and cups her round cheeks. "Can she?"

"Yes, but that doesn't make her my mate."

Asha frowns. "I thought—"

"Lorcan shares a mind link with all his Crows. I believe that my type of shifter works the same way. It's why I went to Luce in the first place."

"Well that explains Enzo's grouchiness. Do you know that he's stayed in his beast form for the last two days? Refuses to eat anything. I thought it was sympathy pains for his mate, but I think he may be depressed. He really likes you."

"He likes me because I saved his life and gave him magic."

"No, Daya. He *really* likes you."

"He's a child."

She rolls onto her back and stretches out. "He's nineteen."

"So I've been convalescing for two days?" I ask, not feeling like discussing Enzo's crush. "Tell me all that's been happening."

"Ceres and your new Serpent have taken residence in Enzo's wing. Fallon has been making many roundtrips between Luce and Shabbe to check on you and bring news from Luce. Your little stint has disquieted quite a few Lucins." She smirks.

"Is Lorcan very angry with me?"

"Nah. I think it's come in quite handy. Humans now believe they can have magic. Since you're the Lucin Queen's mother, they've been on their best behavior. As for the Faeries, they, too, have been behaving but that has more to do with fear than eagerness. They're a little worried you'll come and lick them next."

I snort. "What about Taytah? Is she angry?"

"Just remember that all she feels and shouts stems from love."

"That doesn't sound ominous," I mumble, suddenly unsure whether I should leave the comfort of my palace wing. I rub my arms, then frown when I notice the golden glint of a bargain. Didn't I already collect Erwin's?

Asha rolls up and off the bed, then stretches her arms over her head once more as though she, too, has been slumbering for days. "A present from the Lucin general."

Right away, my mind goes to Cathal.

"A thank you for having saved his daughter."

Of course. Whyever did I imagine Cathal would've given me a favor? After all, there's nothing I've done for the man that would warrant his gratitude. I'm tempted to ask Asha if he went home. He must've. Perhaps he visited, though?

"I've yet to hear you apologize," she says.

"For?"

"For leaving me without *any* warning." She dips her head and gives me a stern look that makes me want to grin more than apologize. "I've gone up *another* dress size."

Where Taytah can be downright frightening when she's angry, my guard cannot. "I'm sorry, Asha."

"You swear to never leave Shabbe without me again?"

"Yes."

"Say it."

I sigh and roll up. I must move too fast because my vision spins. I knead my temples.

"Drink this"—she shoves a glass full of bright green juice into my hands—"and then say, I swear, Asha amNeema, that I, Zendaya amMeriam, will never leave the queendom without you."

I take a few sips, then lower the glass and lick the sweet nectar off my lips. "How come I never knew that your mother's name was Neema?"

"Daya..."

"I'm not going to speak any more vows out loud, but I am sorry to have distressed you."

She huffs.

I take another sip as I get to my feet. "Now that we're three, should I launch my own facial tattoo? A little serpent around one eyebrow?"

"I think that thing in the middle of your forehead is branding enough."

"Fair point."

She trails me to my bathing chamber and leans against the wall as I go about my business. While I wash my hands, I twist my face this way and that. My hair has acquired a lot of volume while I slept but is surprisingly not salt-hardened.

"I washed it so your sheets wouldn't smell like the inside of a conch shell." Asha nods to my outfit. "I also changed you, even though your favorite Crow desperately offered to assist me."

"Why wouldn't you let Fallon help?"

"That's not the Crow I was referring to," she singsongs.

My blood warms. "He's not my favorite." I splash my face, then pat it dry and rub coconut-honeysuckle oil onto my pulse points.

She sidles back against the door as I traipse into my closet. "Well, just in case you were wondering, he's been flying over on the regular to check if you'd roused."

My heart begins to sprint. "I wasn't wondering."

"Sure you weren't."

I pitch off my nightgown and replace it with a yellow dress that slips over my skin like sunshine but ripples like water, what with my heart beating as briskly as it is.

"I'm guessing he didn't jump to the same conclusion as I did about you having two mates."

I drop down on the pouf in the middle of my dressing chamber to lace up a pair of golden sandals. "How did he find out about my mind link to Agrippina? Did she tell him?"

"Was it supposed to be a secret?"

"I suppose not." I secure the laces with a double-knot.

"What are you going to do?"

"About?"

"His hopes and dreams of rekindling your old romance?"

"Nothing." At least, not for now. "I have a new Serpent to train."

"Your grandmother saw to her training. She can now shift in and out of scales at will."

"Has Enzo introduced himself?"

"He's been wallowing, remember?"

"In the Amkhuti?"

"The Akwale have shut off all accesses to the Sahklare and dropped the waterline to avoid a repeat of the other night. Though truth be told, I think Enzo has learned his lesson."

Enzo? No answer. *Agrippina?*

Her voice crackles through my mind almost immediately. *Present, my queen.*

No need for titles. I'm not your queen.

Shall I call you Maker? Or Mother of Serpents?

I snort. *Daya will be just fine.*

You're lucky we were really close friends back in the day.

Why's that?

Because if I didn't remember liking you so much, I would've had a bone to pick with the woman who used my body as a hatchery. You gave me fucking stretchmarks.

I'm not sure what those are.

Fallon, **our** *daughter*—I can feel her smile and realize, for the first time, that the usual wave of jealousy doesn't dash against me—*was kind enough to work her magic on them. Hopefully a few more sessions of blood therapy will have my body good as new.*

I massage my throbbing temples. *Were you always so talkative?*

Always.

And we truly were friends?

You stuck a baby inside of me, so yes, Daya. We were friends. After a beat, she asks, *You really have no memory of your past life?*

No. I lower my hands to my thighs. *Where are you?*

I was on my way to try and coax my fellow Serpent out of the Amkhuti with some very delicious treats which I snatched off the lunch table—Asha mentioned food might motivate Enzo to shift—but I can be wherever you need me to be.

She's back to sounding almost giddy.

I may have drunk a little too much date wine at lunch because a certain Crow came to see how I was faring and his face pissed me off.

Reid?

Right. You mustn't remember what happened between us. So, he's the male I was madly in lust with. We had a thing until he told me, point-blank, that he could never be with a Faerie long-term because our bodies weren't compatible for baby-making. Babies... She shudders. *As though I had any desire to make babies... Anyway, I've doubled back and am standing outside your door, trying to negotiate with Abrax to let me in.*

"Asha, can you go open my door, please?" I call out, finally standing. "Abrax won't let Agrippina in."

My guard shuffles down the long hallway. As the door hinges groan, I pad out to greet her. For a moment, Agrippina just stands there, balancing a glazed bowl heaped with food intended for Enzo. She shoves it into Asha's chest and traipses near.

"Look at that hair color," she comments with a smile. "Is Enzo's green?"

"Yes."

"Did he have green eyes?"

"I don't—I don't know. Why?"

"Just a theory I have about why my hair turned blue. I mean, your eyes were hot-pink, and..." She gestures to my hair. "Anyway. Can I hug you?"

"You want to hug me?"

"Yes. I want to hug the woman who brought me back—" Her breathy voice catches. "To fucking life."

Before I can answer, she winds her arms around me.

"Is the swearing new?" I ask, embracing her in return.

251

She laughs. "Years of hanging out with Lucin soldiers will do that to a woman's vocabulary. It aggrieves Mamma to no end." She presses her damp cheek to my shoulder. *An illusion. Agrippina Rossi never weeps.*

But she does, and although I cannot remember our friendship, I understand why I transferred my most precious possession inside this woman's womb. *I'm sorry I broke your mind.*

I gave birth to the Curse-breaker. She pulls away, knuckling her lash line. *Entirely worth it. Besides, after my expedited history lesson on the past two decades, I believe the Mahananda impaired me to keep me from interfering, for I would—knowing my character—have revolted or done* something *that would've compromised Fallon and jeopardized her destiny.*

Could that have been the reason or is she merely trying to alleviate my guilt?

"Should we go try to find the male Cathal refers to as the Green One?" Her lips flip up. "I don't think your mate likes him much."

Her comment flicks my heart out of alignment. *Cathal isn't my mate, Agrippina.*

"Of course he is."

"Not in this lifetime."

"How's that possible? Not only did the two of you create the Curse-breaker, but your passion was explosive, and I *know* explosive romance. Well, knew. Fucking Reid...and fucking romance books that set your expectations unrealistically high."

"Romance books?" I ask.

"Forget I mentioned those."

Asha snorts just as a voice I haven't heard in too many days rings through my hallway.

Chapter 41
Zendaya

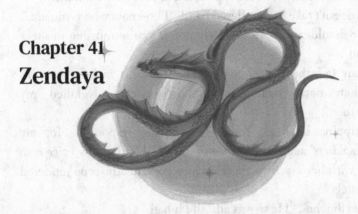

"The Green One is here." Enzo doesn't stammer as he announces his presence, but he speaks slowly, spacing out each word.

Agrippina whirls, her silver frock rippling around calves thinned by disuse. Though I don't remember her from before, I assume, from the stories Justus told of her desire to succeed him, that she must've been whittled like the rest of his soldiers.

My Serpents' scrutiny is so thorough that I can almost hear their eyes squeaking as they press and roll over one another's bodies.

Agrippina is the one to fracture the quiet. "You can call me the Blue One if it mends your ego."

"I d-don't—" He wedges his lips tight.

Agrippina tilts her head. "You don't...?" After a full minute, she repeats her question.

His eyebrows dip. *She can't hear me.*

She can't? Out loud, I say, "Try to talk to Enzo, Agrippina."

When her own eyebrows writhe, I deduce that they cannot penetrate each other's minds.

"The Crows can only communicate with each other when in their beast forms. Perhaps it's the same for us?" I suggest.

Agrippina walks up to where Enzo stands like a beanpole beside my closed door. She holds out her hand then speaks in

Lucin. When she remembers that I don't speak that tongue, she switches to Serpent, "I'm Agrippina Rossi, your new denmate."

He doesn't take her proffered hand. "I kn-know who y-you are."

Her shoulders square. "Clearly not, if you're refusing to shake my hand."

"Your fa-father's s-soldiers—" He shuts his mouth, licks his lips, then parts them anew and blusters. "Ki-killed my grandfather."

Agrippina bristles. "You're holding *me* responsible for my *father's soldiers'* actions? Now that's unfair." Her breathy voice is so at odds with her assertive speech, like a gory, death scene rendered with pastels.

Enzo flinches. "He w-was all...all I h-had."

"I'm sorry for your loss, but it's still not my fault, Seaweed."

He balks at the nickname she's given him.

I cannot help but wonder, as I stare at the purple circles rimming his eyes and the tracks of salt crosshatching his pale cheeks whether the death of his grandfather is the sole factor in his dislike of Agrippina, or if another loss—the exclusivity of my mind—is to blame.

"Agrippina, can you give Enzo and me a moment?" I ask.

My pleasure. To think Asha said he was sweet. Her nose wrinkles.

He is. He's just angry with me.

Why?

I'll explain everything in a little bit. Just let me talk to him.

She nods, takes his measure once more, then, chin tilted, she steps out into the bright square of sunlight beyond my tall door.

"Come sit, Enzo." I turn and walk to my living area.

Though he follows, he doesn't lower himself to the cushions. Sunlight fans across his taut features. Instead of lightening his purple circles, it makes them appear starker, a shade neighboring the black of his eyes.

"How are you feeling?"

How do you think I'm feeling? His tone is as cutting as his stare.

Because of the tendus, or because of me?

His mouth thins.

With a sigh, I ask, "Why did you swim into the Sahklare?"

"Because I f-felt...I..." He must get fed up with his stammer because he finishes his sentence inside my mind: ***I felt you suffering.***

My eyes burn. My heart aches. "I'm sorry, Enzo. I'm so sorry."

"Stop apologizing," he snaps.

How the tables have turned...

You're not sorry you made another Serpent! he snaps.

He's right. I'm not.

He rams a hand through his hair that is white with so much salt the green barely shines through. ***You should've let me die.***

I suck in a breath, then hiss, "Never." I stand and go to him. "Enzo, I will never let you die."

His mouth opens, probably to repeat that I should.

I press a finger against his lips to hush him and say, "I love you, Enzo Fronz. You are my first and you will always be my favorite—"

He cinches my wrist and tugs it away. I think it's because he doesn't want to be silenced but realize, as his face sails down toward mine, as his lips crash into mine, that shoving me away wasn't his intent.

Stunned, I just stand there and gasp, which allows his tongue to breach my mouth. I splay my hands on his chest to push him away, but then decide to let him pour all his frustration inside me and rid himself of his crush. I know the kiss will fizzle, just like his ardor, because there's no spark between our lips. Perhaps there would be if I tried to reciprocate, but I don't feel like trying.

My lids color with Cathal's face and my mind with the memory of our kiss back in the Sky Castle. What had Agrippina called the passion we had for each other? The word returns to me as I finally skate my mouth off Enzo's—*explosive*.

The memory is so intense that I suddenly feel like I can smell him here, in this room, next to me. I pivot, worried that I *will* find him. Worried that he bore witness to Enzo's frustration and despair. When I find no one, my pulse hushes and I turn back toward Enzo.

"You d-don't," he says, hurt washing out his tone.

"I don't what?"

You don't love me. If you did, you would've kissed me back and you didn't even try, Daya.

Enzo, the love I have for you isn't that of a mate. It's that of a mother. It's the same type of love I have for Fallon.

With a grimace, he backs up and repeatedly scrapes the back of his hand against his lips as though I'd been the one to kiss him without his consent.

I'm sorry, sweetheart, but—

He flattens his palms against his ears and hisses, "St-Stop! J-Just st-stop!" His eyes shimmer like faceted onyx.

"Don't cry."

His Adam's apple jumps in his throat and then he's racing away from me.

"Enzo, please..." I rush after him, worried he'll try to swim out of Shabbe again before remembering the waterrises are out of order. *Please stay safe.*

He does, but he also stays away, locked in his bedroom. The only two people he allows inside are Asha—though he doesn't speak with her, he accepts the food she brings him—and my grandmother —whom he does speak with. About *what* is a mystery since she refuses to relay their conversations, no matter how much I insist.

His silence toward me lasts and lasts.

Just like Cathal's absence. When I ask Fallon if her father will eventually join her during one of her visits, she tells me that he's aiding in Tarespagia. Though I've no reason to doubt her word, when I suggest making a trip out there, she's quick to tell me it's a terribly dangerous idea. Kanti did too much damage. Faeries positively loathe the Shabbins. She lobs reason after reason until they form a teetering pile. One that a mere flick of my tail would send spilling.

I'm starting to wonder whether Cathal visited me at all while I convalesced or if Asha made that up—but why would she?

"So Kanti's in Nebba?" I ask Taytah one evening, peering over her shoulder at the parchment she's inking with her signature.

"She needed a change of scenery." She folds her letter to Eponine, the one thanking her for hosting Kanti in this time of great unrest. "Aren't you glad I sent her there instead of urging her to come home?"

"You're not keeping her away because the Mahananda has yet to make me immortal, correct?"

Her mouth remains so immobile that it seems as though she doesn't even breathe, but then it moves over a quick promise: "Your cousin would never harm you." She picks up a stick of blood-red wax and her royal stamp.

Though a sigil could melt the wax, she holds it over one of the large candles burning on the middle of the enormous slab of sunstone. Once the wax is soft, she drips some over the creamy seam of her folded parchment before pressing the Shabbin crest into it.

In seconds, it's dry, yet she doesn't lift her metal stamp immediately.

"I'd like to go to Tarespagia, Taytah."

I expect a categorical no, but instead I get a, "Why?"

"Agrippina would like to see her father and I'd like to see Cathal."

"I'll send for them both."

With a sigh, I say, "Taytah, you cannot keep me locked in a bubble for the rest of my life."

"It isn't for the rest of your life, emMoti."

"No, it's only until the Mahananda grants me immortality. What if it never does?"

Again, she drifts into a harsh silence. I'm about to ask about Enzo to distract her from the touchy subject of my immortality—or lack thereof—when she says, "Every Shabbin Queen has been immortal."

"What if I don't become queen?"

"You will."

"What if I don't *want* to become queen?"

She holds my stare. "You are my heiress, Zendaya."

"So is Meriam."

Again, she hisses. "Never speak her name—"

Her eyes suddenly blanch. I remain silent, wishing the Mahananda would reach out to me again, but since guiding me toward Agrippina, it hasn't poured any more words into my mind.

The queen blinks the haze away, the line of her mouth hardening as her gaze tightens on the wax seal.

"Any chance it told you how I'm to become immortal?" I ask, when she hasn't volunteered anything.

She stays quiet for so long that I think my question doesn't register, but then she shakes her head. "No. It merely informed me that it's almost ready to receive Lorcan or whichever Crow needs his curse removed."

"*No!*" someone shouts.

I jump and my heart misses a beat. I twist toward the doors of the Kasha only to find them closed.

As I squint around the room and then at the glass ceiling, new words shatter the stillness: "*Your mother holds the key to your immortality. Find her.*"

My eyes widen and my skin tingles, because I suddenly realize who the voice belongs to. I lick my lips. "Taytah?"

She's carefully putting away her wax stick and seal in a box inlaid with nacre. "Yes?"

When I give my lips another lick, one of her eyebrows arches. Why am I suddenly nervous? Not only is it my Mahananda-given right to meet the woman who made and doomed me, but it's also the edict that comes to me straight *from* the Mahananda. "I'm ready to meet my mother."

For a long moment, she simply stares into my face. And then

she filches her letter, stands, and walks to the doors which part as though by magic. But it isn't magic. Since the wood panels are carved, the guards stationed outside can see into the room when she allows them to.

I pinch my silk skirt to catch up with her. "Did you hear me?"

"Yes."

"I'm ready."

"Well I'm not, emMoti."

"With all due respect, Taytah, it's hardly your choice."

"She's my daughter. My prisoner. It is *entirely* my choice."

My lungs burn from how hard I'm breathing. "She's *my* mother."

"No. Your mother was a serpent."

My vertebrae snap into harsh alignment. "Before—"

"Before?" Priya gives an ugly chuckle. "My daughter abandoned the girl you were before. She abandoned her with *me*. I was your mother before. Not *her*. Never *her*."

"I'm not asking for a one-on-one audience with—"

"Zendaya, I said no!" Her answer is so shrill that it shivers the delicate petals of the honeysuckle vines climbing up the Kasha's walls.

I'm about to retaliate that I'm entitled to meet the woman who murdered me when the disembodied voice rings between my temples anew: *"Claim your bargain, Zendaya."*

My bargain? It takes my mind a moment to recall what bargain the Mahananda is referring to. Not that I have more than one. The second I do, though, my pulse propels so many heartbeats through my veins that I grow lightheaded and latch on to a twilit vine.

"Get this letter to Eponine of Nebba," the queen commands one of the guards before refocusing on me. "Forgive me for raising my voice, emMoti, but talk of Meriam always agitates me. Perhaps someday, it won't."

I don't say anything, too busy thinking many things. Chiefly, why is the Mahananda's keeper going against its biddings? And secondly, how can Justus help me find Meriam?

"Priya wishes to keep the shifter races subservient to the Shab-bins. Why do you think she sent Fallon into the Mahananda and not Lorcan?"

My heart patters before stilling as I recall the vision of Lorcan getting staked with obsidian. If only I'd possessed the words to tell him.

"Do not blame yourself. But find Meriam and make haste, for Behati has foreseen the future I desire, and she's endeavoring to alter it."

I suck in air. *"Will you talk to me all the time now?"*

"Earn my trust, Zendaya of Shabbe, and I will stay at your side always."

So my grandmother doesn't suspect my anger, I feign fatigue before padding out to the Amkhuti embankment, pursued by a little colony of moon moths and my ever-faithful Abrax. He's quiet but concerned, and becomes even more so when I insist on being left alone. Since I cannot climb out of the moat, he indulges me, standing at a distance but keeping me in his line of sight.

When I'm certain not a single palace guard is within earshot, I whisper my bargain into the stars, my bicep tingling as the golden band fritters away. And then I settle against a tree, alternately surveying the Sahklare for an inbound ship and the sky for an incoming Crow, unsure what means of transport the Faerie will use.

The stars fade and a new dawn rises, and still the Lucin general doesn't show. But someone else does. Did he come for me?

Chapter 42
Zendaya

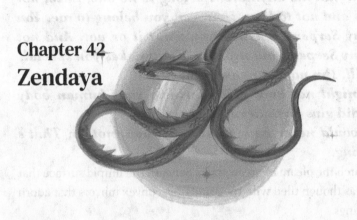

"Enzo?"

My Serpent startles, his fingers slipping off the knot of the belt he wears to keep his trousers up. Clearly, he's not here for me. He makes this all the more evident when he turns and pounds farther down the ridge.

I miss you.

He flinches.

Please talk to me.

He doesn't.

I stand and start toward him. ***Enough! You've pouted long enough.***

He glares, but then his eyes widen as he notes that I'm closing in on him. He must decide that damp fabric beats a conversation with me because he dives in, fully clothed.

You kissed me without my consent, Enzo, which gives me every right to be angry, but I'm not, because your act wasn't born from malice but from misplaced desire.

Though he sinks deep and doesn't respond, I know he can hear me.

You know who else has a right to be angry? Cathal.

For I was his mate, once upon a time. His true mate. But I'm not his anymore. I belong to no one, Enzo, not to you and not to him. However, you belong to me. You are my Serpent, whether you want it or not. And not just any Serpent, but my first. That makes you special.

Still, I'm not your son, he hisses.

I might not have given birth to your human body but I did give birth to your Serpent one.

I would never have kissed my own mother. That's revolting.

I catch the gleam of green scales beneath the limpid surface that glitters as though tiled with the same tiny, convex mirrors that adorn my ceilings.

What do you think of Agrippina?

She talks a lot. The corners of my mouth begin to flip up until he adds, *And she's related to Justus Rossi.*

The mention of the man I await flattens the curve.

Why do you await him?

Enzo's question makes my pulse falter. I should've kept his name from my mind.

The chuff of air on the Amkhuti's surface draws my gaze low. *I'm not special enough to know your secrets? I thought we were one big happy...den. Especially now that his daughter is part of it.*

Tears brim on my lash line that he's crumbled the wall he erected between us.

I'm still angry that you went to Luce without me. And that you picked Agrippina, he adds with a grumble.

I smile.

I get to pick our next denmate without veto.

Yes. You have my word that our fourth Serpent is yours to choose.

Good. Now why is Justus Rossi on his way?

If I tell you, you must promise not to tell Taytah. I know the two of you are close.

There's a beat of awkward silence. *She...told you?*

Tell me what?

Nothing.

Obviously, it's not *nothing*.

My loyalty lies with you, Day. If you don't believe me, then I'll swear an oath—

I trust you. And so I tell him about my conversation with the Mahananda and of its advice to find Meriam. I also explain that it led me to Agrippina.

The Mahananda told you to make her a Serpent?

It told me to find her, but yes, I imagine it intended for me to save her life by transforming her into a Serpent.

Well, fuck me...

While Enzo whirls on himself at the sound of Agrippina's voice, I fall silent and hunt the Amkhuti for blue scales.

You can hear us? he exclaims.

Yes, Seaweed. I can hear you just fine. No need to shriek.

I was right. My Serpents' minds are all linked when in scales.

Enzo grumbles beneath his breath. *How long have you been eavesdropping?*

I wasn't eavesdropping. I went for a swim and happened on your little exchange. Trust me, I'm as surprised as you are that we're conversing right now.

How much have you heard, Agrippina? I ask, putting an end to their bickering.

Just that you called my father so that he can lead you to Meriam because she's the key to our immortality.

To Day's immortality, Enzo says.

Though she has no shoulder to shrug, I can picture her shrugging. *I imagine that once our maker's immortal, we will be as well, since that's what happened to the Crows.*

263

I ferry the question to the Mahananda, but it affords me no answer.

I must miss a part of their conversation because Agrippina is hissing at Enzo that if he ever calls her Pee again, she will throttle him with her tail to which he says, *You call me Seaweed. Only fair you get a horrid nickname.*

And then he shoots off and she gives chase, and although they're acting like wayward children, a sense of serenity drapes over me. One that falters when I spy the large black bird cresting the glittery fortifications, an orange-haired rider on its back.

My Serpents must sense my elevated pulse through our bond because they're suddenly both surfacing and shifting, both carving across the dawn-lit water toward the vine ladder. Enzo flicks his head at Agrippina to go first, then climbs up after her. Wet fabric, turned sheer from their swim, clings to their skin. Where Enzo nervously wrings out the hem of his tunic and draws it over the bulge between his legs, Agrippina doesn't bother plucking the fabric off her slender curves, not even when she catches his gaze on her peaked nipples.

"See something you like?" she taunts him.

"Go-Gods, how old are y-you?" He shakes his head, springing droplets off his green hair that has grown the length of a knuckle since he first arrived in Shabbe.

"Almost two centuries older that you are, Seaweed."

He glowers at her and crosses his arms before muttering into my mind, *Does Justus know what he's coming to Shabbe to do?*

Yes. To Agrippina, I repeat Enzo's question and my subsequent answer, followed by a command not to speak of anything out loud. *Anything you both want to say, you speak it into my mind from this moment forward. Nod if you both heard me.*

They nod. Though repeating everything individually wouldn't have been the end of the world, my voice broadcasting into both their minds at once is a boon.

The Crow's broad shadow drapes over us as it swoops low. Though my entire focus should be on Justus and where he's about to lead me, it isn't; it's on the male who carried him here. He may still be in feathers, but I'd recognize Cathal Báeinach anywhere.

Chapter 43
Zendaya

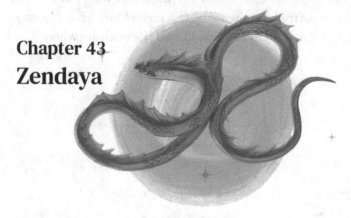

"How exactly are we going to go about this?" Justus murmurs as he leans in to kiss my cheek in customary Lucin fashion. "I don't even know where she's being kept."

I frown before remembering the circle inked on his palm. "You must use your connection to her."

As Cathal morphs, Justus leans toward my other cheek, bringing his mouth right up to my ear. "I've tried. I cannot feel her."

Except he mustn't have tried well enough, since the Mahananda instructed me to claim my bargain, and *his* was the only one I had.

We exchange a weighted look as he moves toward Agrippina.

Tell your father that you're so glad he came to check on you and walk to your bedchamber with him. Once you're out of earshot of the guards and behind closed doors, let me know. My eyes track up the corded length of Cathal's neck which snaps with heartbeat after heartbeat. ***Enzo, go with them.***

Once they both retreat, albeit reluctantly, I ask Cathal in Crow, "You leave immediately or have time for drink?"

He crosses his arms. "It's seven in the morning." At my frown, he says, "I don't day-drink."

"I mean coffee. Or tea." I riffle through my mind for the word for juice in Crow, but it doesn't come so I say it in Shabbin.

"I'm not thirsty. Besides, I've a job to return to."

Annoyed, I don't even bother using Crow. "I'm sure Lorcan will understand if you took ten minutes off to visit with me."

He smiles, but it isn't good-natured. "Nah. He wouldn't understand," he replies in Crow. "We don't have time for idleness back in Luce."

My eyelid twitches at his underhanded insult. "And yet you had time to carry Justus over," I snipe back in Shabbin.

He answers in Crow: "Yes, which was very inconvenient, but my job's done and now I must fly back."

I pursue in my mother tongue: "Do I get to learn the reason you're acting so brusque with me?"

He dips his chin. "Well, let's just say that I've met someone."

My heart goes so still that I think he's scooped it out of my chest with his iron talons.

"Isn't it brilliant?" he asks, that false smile digging into his bristly cheeks.

No, it's not brilliant. It's the opposite of brilliant, actually. With a start, I realize this is the reason Fallon has been acting so odd each time I've asked after her father. Because she knew that he'd moved on and didn't dare tell me.

I rub the scar around my neck as though a new vine were choking me. "Is she Crow?" I ask, even though what I want to ask is: "Can you penetrate her mind?"

"I never aired out my private life before and have no intention to begin now." Smoke bleeds from his pores. "Anyway, I'm needed back in Luce, so"—he raises two fingers to his temple and flicks them in my direction—"*alvee, Rajka.*"

I don't know what his gesture means, or why he switches to Shabbin to say, "goodbye, Princess," the same way I don't know why I'm dwelling on either. Because it's taking my mind off the news that I've been replaced?

He springs upward. As I track his departure, my pulse grows

mute. Glum, I dive into the Amkhuti and swim. I don't surface when Enzo tells me that my grandmother demanded they all join her for breakfast. I merely wallow in scales. When the sun is high, I finally climb out and traverse the gardens.

Are you back in your chamber, Agrippina?

Her voice immediately brightens my mind, but unfortunately, not my mood. *Yes.*

With Justus?

Yes.

I head there, my ribs cinched so tight around my lungs that by the time I reach her wing of the palace, I'm wheezing. Which of course leads Abrax to trot up to me and ask if I need him to call the healer.

I doubt a magical crystal exists to heal a broken heart, so I shake my head, and then, before crossing the threshold, I thank him for looking out for me. I'm about to tell him that I don't want to be disturbed when I think better of it. After all, nothing will kindle suspicion more than a command to stay away.

So I walk into my Serpents' quarters, as though I was here for a simple visit, and amble down the long common area roofed with a sky light as broad as the Kasha's. Unlike my wing, this one's made up of a dozen apartments that vary in size and configuration.

"You should go home, Abrax. You look worn out."

"I'm fine."

"Where's Asha?"

"Celebrating her mother's birthday. You're stuck with me today."

I raise a smile that I'm not feeling. "You don't have to shadow me everywhere."

"I'm sorry, but ever since you took off, your grandmother wants someone at your side at all times."

How inconvenient. With a sigh, I knuckle Agrippina's door. It's Ceres who draws it open. She greets me with a cautious nod. For some reason, I'd forgotten she'd stayed in Shabbe.

Agrippina and Justus both glance up from where they lounge in the small sitting area beside the window that gives onto the garden. Like Enzo's, her apartment overlooks this wing's private garden.

I start toward them but pause when I hear Abrax shuffle in behind me. I plant a fist on my hip. "Will you be following me to the privy, too?"

His jaw blazes. "No."

Going to be difficult to plot anything behind your grandmother's back if he hangs around, no? Maybe ask Enzo to create a distraction?

Good idea. Enzo, I need you to create a distraction that'll lead Abrax out of Agrippina's chambers.

I'm with your grandmother, distracting her. Tell the Blue One to pull her weight.

I might have smiled at his reply if I weren't so anxious. *He's busy with the Queen.*

Of course he is. Probably giving her yet another orgasm.

I blanch, then blurt out, "What?"

You didn't know? Why do you think she pays him so many visits?

You're having sexual relations with my grand-mother? I ask Enzo.

Not that it's any of your business, but yes.

Except it *is* my business! He's my Serpent and she's my grandmother. I grimace at the thought of them laying together in the nude. *How long has this been going on?*

After I kissed you. And it wasn't premeditated. It just...happened. She doesn't want you knowing, so please pretend like you're unaware.

My jaw trembles from how hard I clench it. I've no right to feel angry but I do. I feel duped. I feel like I should've been told. *Don't hide things from me, Enzo.*

Concentrate on finding Meriam, will you?

I want to ask him if he likes her or if he took her into his bed out of spite. Unless Taytah is the one who preyed on him? I give my head a little shake and am about to ask Agrippina to distract Abrax when Ceres says, "Abrax, can I speak to you outside? I have a"—her gaze slides to Justus who just twirls his spoon inside his cup of tea—"pressing request."

My guard starts to protest but Ceres takes his arm and leads him out. The second the door's shut, I ask Agrippina whether she told her mother anything.

Agrippina shakes her head. *She must've guessed Pappa wasn't just visiting for shits and giggles.*

Frowning at her odd expression, I settle down beside Justus and murmur, "Any ideas of how to locate what I need, General?"

He glances down at the magical brand on his hand before eyeing the closed door. "What do you want with...it?"

"Answers." He seems so unconvinced that I ask my fellow shifter, *What did you tell him?*

That you wanted to meet your mother but your grandmother wouldn't hear of it.

You didn't mention the Mahananda, did you?

No.

"Everyone reviles the thing you need, but I don't. I will only help if you swear an oath to me that you won't harm it."

"I've no desire to harm it," I reply quietly.

"Speak the oath."

I can hear Cathal warning me against giving someone a bargain to lord over me, but Cathal's no longer at my side; he's at another's. Still I murmur, "No, General. Forgive me, but I will not give another male power over me."

He climbs to his feet. "Then I regret—I regret—" He rubs at his chest, creating tracks in the fitted black velvet jacket. He mutters in Lucin under his breath.

I was careful when I called in our bargain to use specific wording so that he couldn't leave here until she was found.

"Zendaya, you cannot keep me here indefinitely. Lorcan needs me. *Luce* needs me. I cannot shirk my responsibilities—"

"The Mahananda prompted me to call on you," I murmur.

"That's impossible. It only talks to its keeper."

"Its keeper hasn't been listening to it recently."

He blinks. "It truly spoke to you?"

"Yes."

His gaze swerves toward his daughter.

"If Daya says it did, it did, Pappa."

His hand—the branded one—curls into a white-knuckled fist.

"You know where it is, don't you, General?" Though I formulate it as a question, it's not, for I can tell that he does.

His nostrils flare with the pain of keeping the truth from me. I consider swearing that my intent isn't to harm Meriam, but decide against giving Justus Rossi power over me. Who knows how the Faerie will use it?

"General?"

"Yes," he all but gasps. "Or at least, I knew. I heard it was moved after my unsuccessful attempt at breaking it out."

"You tried to break it out?"

"The Akwale keep threatening to drain it. And they would've, were it not for Lorcan's bargain."

My head rears back. "Lorcan's bargain?"

"Of keeping it alive. That's why he relinquished it to Priya in the first place."

Agrippina rakes in a breath that is so sudden and raucous that it steals my attention off her father. "Under Behati's bed," she breathes, her eyes shining with the light of a thousand stars. And then she's blinking and rubbing her arms that are peppered with goosebumps.

A door clicks, making my heart skitter. I swing my gaze off my Serpent, expecting to find both Abrax and Ceres standing there, but Ceres is alone. I don't know how she got rid of my guard but I've never been more grateful for his absence.

The glower Ceres pins Justus with scorches the air in time with her words.

What is your mother saying?

Verbatim: 'Of course the whore witch didn't release our daughter.'

Didn't release you? From what?

She must repeat my question out loud, because Ceres's mouth pinches while Justus's softens around a sigh.

He drops back down to the sofa and leans so close that his mouth brushes my lobe. "Meriam can use Agrippina's eyes to see." He pulls in a quivering breath. "And she can murmur words inside her mind. I was afraid that when you turned my daughter, it had shattered their bond." He swallows, or rather, gulps. "She cast her spell the day you entrusted your daughter to mine. It was her way of keeping watch over Fallon. Over you. She used to be able to tap into Bronwen's eyes because of a deal the latter struck with the Cauldron, but every member of the Akwale could use your sister-in-law's eyes. Only Meriam could use Agrippina's." After a beat, he says, "*Can* use."

What is it? Why is Mamma fuming and Pappa weepy? Agrippina asks, her gaze swinging between her parents.

I impart Justus's confession through our bond, then scrutinize her expression, wondering which side of the emotional pendulum she will swing.

After a stretch of silence that feels endless, Agrippina finally reclines in her seat with a snort. *At this point, I should earn a spot in your family tree.*

Ceres says something to her daughter that has Agrippina shaking her head and Justus hissing words in Lucin that all elude me.

What's happening? I ask, mind reeling.

Mamma wants us to leave Shabbe immediately. She says my gift will get me slaughtered. She says that we should never have come back. Pappa tells her that Luce isn't safe for Serpents.

There is one place you'll be safe. Inside the Sky Castle. I ask Justus if he has any way of contacting a Crow.

He taps his arm and mentions that one of them owes him a

bargain that he will claim. An hour later, Imogen flies a reluctant Agrippina and a fear-ravaged Ceres out of Shabbe.

"What now?" I ask Justus as Enzo wanders over, stabbing his messy hair.

Justus stares in the direction of the Mahananda, his eyes glittering as wildly as the Amkhuti. "Now, we set her free."

My blood cools and thickens like sludge as I calculate the cost of setting my mother free—my grandmother's trust and love.

"Is this truly what you desire, Mahananda?"

I will it to say *yes*, but instead it asks: *"Is immortality for all shifters what you desire?"*

"Yes."

"Then you must set your mother free."

Chapter 44
Zendaya

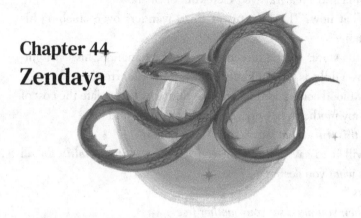

The queen leans back in her chair as the platters of sweets are swept off the dining table. She strokes the curve of her wine goblet as though it were a lover's jaw. The thought has my stomach churning and my gaze cutting to Enzo, who's barely spoken a word, out loud or through the bond.

"Tell me, Justus, why are you still here?"

"Am I not allowed to revitalize myself in your lovely queendom, Sumaca?"

Her polished, pointy nails scrape up the sculpted gold. "You told me you came to visit your daughter." Down. Up. Down. "The same daughter who left with your wife in haste. Yet, you remain."

"I actually came to inform them that their house in Tarelexo was ready. You should've seen how excited my wife was."

"I hear Agrippina didn't seem all that excited to depart."

The guard beside Abrax shifts from one foot to the other.

"Naturally," Justus says calmly. "Agrippina doesn't remember that house since she moved in after her mind was damaged. Not to mention that her packmates remain in Shabbe. She didn't particularly want to leave, but Fallon promised to carry her back in the morning."

The queen's eyes remain fastened to the general, who sits there, perfectly unperturbed.

Before she can succeed at perturbing him, I change the topic. "Taytah, when were you going to tell me about your tryst with Enzo?"

Her pupils flare wide as she pivots toward me.

Enzo slumps in his chair, muttering, *Did you really have to bring it up in front of everyone, Day?*

Sorry, but I wanted to take the heat off Justus.

"I was waiting for Enzo to tell you, actually." She smiles, but it's as tight as the pearl choker she wears. "I'm glad he finally did. I don't like keeping secrets from you, emMoti." She reaches over and tries to capture my hand, but I drop it onto my lap and nestle it in the black folds of the outfit I selected for what's to come tonight.

I'm tempted to remind her that Enzo's nineteen and that she's several centuries old, but then remember that Fallon and Lorcan have the same age difference, as do Cathal and—

And not me.

Not me.

"Be kind to him," I say.

"Day," Enzo mutters.

I smile at my red-faced shifter. "Sorry, Enzo, but I'm protective like that. Better learn to live with it. Anyway"—I push away from the table and stand—"I've not slept all day. I wish you all a pleasant evening."

Keep her entertained tonight. Until I tell you we're done, do not leave her side.

He slides his teeth from side to side. *She wants to introduce me to the others. I don't want to meet her others. In all honesty, I don't even want to—*

One more night. Please.

He murders the stone tabletop with his gaze. *Fine. I'll use my body to distract her. If she brings anyone else in the room, though, I'm leaving.*

Tell her you aren't interested in orgies, Enzo. You've every right to have your wishes respected.

Do I?

My heart misses a beat that he'd think differently. ***Yes. You do. It's your body. Not hers.***

She's the queen, Day.

Perhaps, but you're not one of her subjects. Never forget that.

He finally looks up and meets my stare. I try to smile but guilt keeps the corners of my lips from tucking up. I'm about to apologize when I recall how he yelled at me the day I did, telling me that it was unfair to apologize for something I wasn't actually sorry for. So I bite my tongue and stride back toward my bedchamber, Abrax on my heels.

"I'm worried about you, Daya," he says, as he pulls open my bedchamber door. "You seem troubled."

"I've just got lots on my mind."

"Is it Cathal? I saw you two arguing when he dropped off Justus."

I give him a sad smile. "It's Cathal. Enzo. Agrippina. Taytah. It's that serpent poison and the Lucin war. It's Kanti. Behati. Meriam. The list of my troubles is rather endless, but nothing a little sleep won't fix."

"I wish I could help."

"You help just by being there and not adding to my troubles. Goodnight, Abrax."

"Goodnight, Daya."

As we smile at each other, I cannot help but wonder if he'll still smile at me come morning, or if this is to be our last moment of companionable friendship, since freeing Meriam won't earn me any points with the Shabbins.

My rooms are quiet, yet I feel a presence. Two presences.

The flames shiver along their stalks as shadows glide around me and press me into my bathing chamber. Since I know who they belong to, I don't flinch when they close my door. The same way I don't balk when Fallon adorns the walls with sigils.

"Done," she says. "No one can hear us."

I stare at Lorcan as he reknits into a male and leans against my sink top. "I hear your grandmother and Behati deceived us."

"You heard correctly."

"And you hold this information from the Cauldron?" my daughter asks, sucking on her fingertip.

"Yes, Fallon."

"Are you certain it's the Cauldron speaking and not Meriam?" Lorcan asks.

I'm about to say yes, but what if it is Meriam? "I...I... They spoke of Meriam in the third person."

"Meriam is cunning and manipulative," Lorcan says.

"Perhaps, but she doesn't have the sight, does she? She couldn't have foreseen that Agrippina would be attacked," I counter.

"She can use Agrippina's eyes, Mádhi. Meriam might not be able to *foresee*, but she can see."

I run the beaded tassels of my belt through my fingers, the faceted black diamonds glimmering white against the black silk. "How could Meriam speak into *my* mind?"

Fallon pushes a lock of her dark auburn hair behind her ear. "The same way she speaks into Agrippina's. She must've spelled the connection into existence that day in the Temple. Or maybe she did it after she sent your soul into a serpent's womb? I don't know. All I know is that we shouldn't put it past her."

"*It isn't Meriam speaking, Zendaya. It is me. The Mahananda.*"

My heart ratchets up.

"*I see doubt in your mind. My keeper should never doubt herself or me. Perhaps you don't deserve to become my keeper. Perhaps you don't deserve immortality.*"

"Mádhi?" Fallon touches my arm, making me jump. "The voice is speaking with you, isn't it?"

I don't nod. I don't have to. My daughter has learned to read me just fine.

"Ask it what it showed me the day it welcomed me into its depths."

"What did you show Fallon the day you undid her obsidian curse?" I ask.

"You dare question me?" The anger that rises from the disembodied voice rattles my temples. *"You don't deserve my guidance. You don't deserve for your species to endure. And you certainly don't deserve Priya's crown. Goodbye, Zendaya. Do not seek out my mercy for I have none to give to those who doubt me."*

"No," I squeak. *"Wait. No."* I imagine the Mahananda's surface rippling before becoming hard as stone.

"What is it, Mádhi?"

"It told me I was undeserving. It told me not to seek it out. I've doomed my species." I palm my mouth. "What if I've doomed yours too? What have I done? What have I *done?*"

"The Cauldron may be temperamental, but it's fair, Daya," Lorcan says calmly. "It would never doom one of its children for asking questions. Which strengthens my conviction that the voice you're hearing is Meriam's. Not to mention that your eyes didn't whi—"

The ground suddenly rumbles, bleaching Fallon's complexion. "What if we're wrong, Lore?"

Day! Enzo's shout grips my heart and holds it in a vise. *Day, where are you?*

In my bathing chamber. Where are you?

I'm with your grandmother but—but...oh. Holy. Mahananda.

What? What's happening?

Silence.

Enzo? I screech. When he still doesn't answer, I close my eyes and concentrate on our mind link until it becomes as firm as a rope, one I scramble up until I *feel* him. His heartbeats are slow and even. *Enzo?* I shout again. He must've lost consciousness. "Something happened." My whisper is as tremulous as my limbs that rattle as I stalk toward my door. "Something's happening." I seize the handle. Locked. I twist around to find Lorcan and Fallon exchanging a grave look. "Open the door, Fallon. Something's happened to Enzo. Open the door."

She doesn't.

"The door!" I yell just as her mate dissolves into smoke.

"I'll go find him, Mádhi. Be right back."

"No! Fallon!" With a growl, I bang my fists against the wood. Another tremor shoots through the earth. It's so strong it almost buckles my knees. "FALLON!" My throat burns from how shrilly I call out her name. ***ENZO!***

"Do not rage against her. She is only trying to protect you."

I whirl because the voice that has filled my mind for weeks is now filling the air. "Meriam?" I gasp.

"Hello, my beautiful daughter."

Chapter 45
Cathal

The Faerie broke her out.

He *actually* broke Meriam out. And I fucking helped. I should never have carried Justus's duplicitous ass to Shabbe for a glimpse of a woman. I should've let Imogen carry him. Yes, the end result would've been the same, but at least, I wouldn't feel like I'd participated in their little scheme, which is bound to leave the Cauldron in a pissy mood for Mórrígan knows how long this time.

I swerve over the palace where chaos rages as guards and sorceresses run amok. Where most dash toward their queen's chamber, some run toward the wreckage that is Behati's wing. Are they expecting to find Meriam in the rubble? Knowing the sorceress, she's long gone.

Dádhi? What are you doing here?

I could ask you the same thing, ínon.

How about we discuss it later? Have you seen Enzo? Enzo?

The green Serpent. Mother's—she stops talking, swallows —*friend.*

I know who he is, Fallon. What I don't understand is why you think I'd be looking for him.

I just thought you might've seen him.

Fine. I did, I grumble. *He went to visit the queen earlier. Probably still inside with her. Where's your mother?*

I locked her in her bathing chamber. She's safe.

From what?

From herself. From whatever's happening out here. What is happening?

You mean, why are all the sorceresses of Priya's coven racing around like headless chickens? Because Rossi broke his blushing bride out of her underground cell.

I'm going to find Enzo and get him out of here. Go find Mádhi and fly her out. The spell will allow a Crow to unlock the door.

We've got a situation. Lore's voice bangs between my temples.

What situation? I ask as I burst into smoke and swoop beneath Daya's bedchamber door. *It's Priya. She's been drained.*

The shock that bursts through my chest is so violent that I weave back into skin. Is Lorcan saying...? Is he saying...?

The Queen is dead.

For a long heartbeat, I just stand there, because there exists no one in this world stronger than the Shabbin Queen. But I'm wrong. Meriam is equally powerful.

Meriam, who's on the loose.

To think she was in our clutches once. We should've drained her. I suddenly wonder why we held back before recalling the reason—my mate's spell, the one that bound her life to her mother's and daughter's to make sure Meriam couldn't kill Fallon. Is that spell broken or are their three lives still bound?

I suddenly hope the spell endures in case Meriam decides to drain Daya next. The visual pours blistering ire into my veins and icy fear into my heart. I grip the door handle of her bathroom and yank. The latch doesn't click. I melt into smoke and try to slip beneath it but bang into an invisible wall. I try squeezing through the hairline crack between the solid gold hinges. I try the fucking keyhole. My daughter's lock spell is so resilient that I cannot fucking enter.

I morph back into my Crow, tucking my wings in tight because the hallway isn't built for creatures of my breadth, and yell, **Come undo your spell, inon! I can't get through the door.**

That's impossible. I didn't ward it against Crows.

Well, you must've spellcast wrong, because I can't get through. I decide to hammer the door with my iron beak, but instead of splintering wood, it splinters my already throbbing brain. I burst back into skin. "Daya, can you hear me?"

Silence.

"Daya!" I punch the door until my knuckles split and spit blood onto the pale wood. "DAYA!"

Fallon arrives, slipping right through the door in skin.

"Did you soundproof the walls?" My voice crackles with frustration and terror and—

"I did. Shit. I did."

I sandwich my lips together as Fallon palms the door to recall her blood. I want to tell her to hurry, but never has growling at someone to make haste led to a faster outcome. If anything, it always slows people down, so I bite my tongue and wait.

"Priya's dead," she murmurs as she keeps palming the door. I swear she's run her hand over every bloody inch of it.

"I heard."

She deepens the cut on her already bleeding finger and draws the lock sigil, then smooshes her palm against it.

Nothing.

When her eyebrows bend, my fucking heart derails.

She paints a new sigil. An arrow pointing down. When the door doesn't shrink, her complexion weakens, whitens.

"What?"

"My magic isn't working."

"Why?"

She bites her lip.

"Why isn't—" I take a breath to try and regain control over my vocal cords that strain and clang as though someone were striking my throat with a flail. "Why isn't it working, Fallon? *Why?*" I croak.

The fear sparking in her violet eyes torches a path straight into my heart, enflaming the organ some more. "Because my blood mustn't be the only one on the walls."

Her words steal down my spine like an icy finger. "What have I done?"

"Not your fault."

"It is! I shouldn't have left her alone. I shouldn't have caged her inside with..." Her throat moves over a swallow. "Taytah, please let me in. Just me!" She starts banging on the door. "Please, Taytah, let me in. *Please.*"

But Meriam does not let her in. The same way she doesn't let Daya out. Fallon drops to her knees to peer through the keyhole. It must be obscured because she curses.

"Assemble any member of the coven you can find!" I yell. "We need to overpower Meriam's magic."

Her neck creaks from how fast she peers up at me, and then she's springing to her feet and racing out to find the others while I stand there like the pathetic, magicless human I used to be before the Cauldron gave me power.

Power I cannot fucking use to save my...to save the mother of my child. I run my hand over my mouth, down my beard, before flattening it against the wood and whispering a prayer to Mórrígan to watch over Zendaya until I can take over.

Chapter 46
Zendaya

T hough Meriam hasn't magicked my soles to the stone, I cannot seem to step away from the door Fallon bolted shut. "What do you want?"

She flinches. I imagine because I address her by her name instead of what she is to me. Well, what she was *supposed to be* but never was.

"I wanted to meet you before leaving."

Everyone says we resemble each other, but the woman standing before me is all serrated angles, sallow skin, and a chilling stare. *She was kept in a cell*, I remind myself. From the way the dress droops over her figure like a cheap sack and dirt crusts her skin and hair, I gather that not only was she undernourished but also severely neglected.

"Where are you going?" I ask as her luminous gaze strokes over me.

"Out of Shabbe."

"Back to Luce?"

She shudders. "No. Too many awful memories."

That leaves Glace and Nebba. And a vast ocean.

As she moves nearer, candlelight catches on her high cheek-bones and almond-shaped eyes. Even in her abysmal state, her beauty is undeniable.

"My Serpent. He wasn't answering me. What did you do to him?"

"Do you mean the green-haired boy in Amma's bed?"

"Yes."

"I stunned him. He'll be fine."

"What do you mean, *you stunned him*?"

"I stung him with magic to relax him. He's sleeping."

"He's alive?"

"Yes, batee. Your friend is alive."

I want to tell her not to call me 'daughter,' but more pressing words burn my tongue. "What about Taytah?"

Meriam stretches her head from side to side, drawing my attention to the indigo bruise that rings her neck. Was she collared? Is that what my grandmother did? A glance at her wrists reveals similar bruises. "Amma never gave me a chance. Never even trialed me. Even when Justus and Fallon both begged her to let the Mahananda decide my fate. Sweet Justus. I didn't think there was a kind Faerie left in the world until I met him."

Even though she's yet to answer my prior question, I can't help but enquire, "Where is he?"

"Somewhere safe. Waiting for me. Thank you for helping him set me free."

I ball my fingers, vibrating with resentment at having been used.

"Forgive me for duping you. For abandoning you." She moves toward me, her strides so graceful, it looks like she's gliding instead of walking. "For transforming you."

When she reaches out to touch my hair, I recoil and press my cheek against the pale wood that vibrates as though someone were pounding on it. I imagine it's the echo of my fevered pulse since Fallon locked me in here for safekeeping. If she had any inkling of my current situation, she would've rushed back to undo her spell.

"Tell me what you did to Taytah," I snap.

The tone of my voice hardens her stare. "I immobilized her and then I drained her."

285

"Is she...?" I lick my lips, trying to become one with the wood at my back. "Is she...?" I cannot get my lips to shape the word.

"She is."

"But I thought...I thought she was immortal."

"To a certain point. Once a Shabbin loses her blood, she loses her magic, and thus, her immortality."

"How?"

"I painted the death sigil that my beloved grandmother Mara taught me before she went to slumber inside the Mahananda." Her lips bend into a smile that is so forlorn, it confuses my heart into believing that she isn't a monster. Or at least, not entirely monstrous. But she is. She committed matricide. "Perhaps someday I'll teach you, batee."

"Stop calling me daughter."

Her emaciated throat dips. "The crown is yours."

"I don't want it."

"Perhaps, but it remains yours. The Mahananda desires that you wear it, Zendaya. You. Not Kanti. Not one of the Akwale. *You.*"

"How do you figure, *Amma?* Can you converse with the source of all magic?"

"No. Only the queen has that power."

Anger billows like smoke within me. "Then you have no clue what the Mahananda desires."

"Behati had a vision of you wearing it. One she discussed with my mother."

"And you know this *how* exactly? Did they invite you to partake in this little conversation? Did they carry it out in front of you?"

"Justus painted a sigil on the throne room's wall that allowed me to eavesdrop. It eventually faded, but not before I collected plenty of interesting conversations—notably the vision of you wearing the Shabbin crown and the one about the Crows' curse."

"Since when can Fae bloodcast?"

"Our husbands, once blood-bound, can use what runs through our veins to draw spells. Why do you think Amma never married?

Why do you think the practice of blood-binding has been outlawed in Shabbe?"

Why wasn't I aware of this? But more importantly... "You killed me once before, Meriam. You're probably suggesting I dive into the Mahananda so I slumber for all of eternity."

Her full lips pinch. "I never killed you."

"I was reborn a Serpent!"

"Because I ferried your soul into another's womb the same way you ferried Fallon's into Agrippina's. I would *never* have killed you. And not because of the spell you cast in the Holy Temple that twined our fates together."

My pulse whooshes like a fierce current. "What spell?"

Meriam cants her head, sending her long clumped locks tumbling over a shoulder that is so sharp the bone looks about to stab through her skin. "No one told you?"

"No."

"Not even Fallon?"

"*What. Spell?*"

"Right before you emptied your womb, you painted a sigil that linked my life to yours and to Fallon's. You were so frightened that my intent was the annihilation of my bloodline. Since we were surrounded by Faeries, I couldn't explain to you that my intent had been to end my life so that my spells would end in turn. I wanted the wards eradicated. I wanted the Shabbins to be free and the shifters to rise anew. But because of your spell, I couldn't put an end to the Regio reign, for if I'd killed myself, it would've killed you and Fallon."

"Are you truly expecting me to believe that you planned on sacrificing yourself to free the Shabbins when you just murdered your own mother?"

"Priya was a selfish liar, ravaged by greed, who failed the Mahananda...who failed *you*. Who kept you subservient and mortal, because she feared you casting her off her precious throne."

She doesn't have a throne, I'm tempted to snipe back, but that's neither here nor there. My eyebrows gather so close they kiss my retracted tusk. "You mean to say that she's known all along how to make me immortal?"

"Daya, abi…" Meriam sighs. "*She* made you mortal."

My jaw slackens around a breathy, "What?"

"She bound your magic."

That flicks me out of my daze. It also flicks my mandible shut. But only for an instant. "You're mistaken, Meriam. I've access to my magic."

She frowns. "I heard otherwise."

"Well, you heard wrong. I can change into scales *and* heal wounds with my tongue. I can even make new Serpents."

Her forehead smooths. "Ah."

"What's *ah* supposed to mean?"

She walks over to my sink, then riffles through my toiletries until she's unearthed a gold comb with a handle that tapers to a point. "Prick your finger."

"Why?"

"Because you seem to be under the delusion that the Mahananda returned you without your blood-magic."

My heart holds still. My lungs too. "I'm a shifter, not a sorceress."

"One nature does not preclude the other. Look at Fallon." When I've yet to seize the comb, she grasps my motionless fingers and raises them. "You're my daughter, Daya. Shabbin magic runs in your veins."

"You're wrong. I cannot bloodcast."

"You can."

"I've tried. I cannot!" I tear my hand out of hers, but not before she manages to split open the pad of my index finger on the gold comb.

"Copy my sigil on the door." She draws twin, interlocked peaks on my mirror with her blood. A heartbeat later, the reflective glass transforms into an oil painting of Shabbe. "It'll transform into whatever you picture inside your mind."

Gritting my teeth and muttering how this is a waste of our time,

I turn toward the door, imagine it transforming into glass, then slash my index finger up and down, up and down, a perfect emulation of her design.

The wood becomes translucent.

I gape at it, then at Cathal who stands on the other side of the door with his arms raised along the glass and his forehead pressed to it.

His head rears back, and he blinks. I, too, blink, but then I whirl to look at Meriam. She's gone.

Her voice suddenly rings out in the thick air of my bathing chamber, and I realize she must've made herself invisible. "When a Shabbin witch dies, so do her spells, batee."

Chills scamper along my spine. Along my bones. *Inside* of them.

I twist back toward Cathal and paint an arrow pointing downward on the pane of wood I made glass. The transparent partition shrinks and shrinks until nothing but air separates us.

Chapter 47
Zendaya

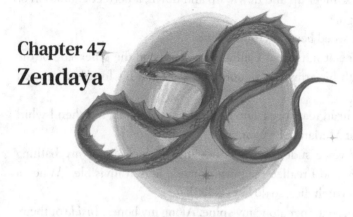

A thousand words throb on my tongue as Cathal and I stare at one another.

What were you doing behind my door?

Why are your eyes rimmed crimson?

Were you trying to get to me?

Were you crying for me?

His brow bone suddenly plummets, draping so low that his eyebrows clock his thick lashes. He takes a step back. "What did I tell you this morning, Daya?"

My lips pinch. Did he think I was about to leap into his arms? The thrill of bloodcasting withers like my delight to have found *him* lurking behind my door. "It hasn't slipped my mind. Don't worry."

"Speak the words back to me."

"Why?" I snap.

"I need to hear you say them."

"Why?"

"Just fucking say them!"

"*Youmetsomeone,*" I snap. "There. Relieved?"

"Yes." His jaw twitches as though he were about to utter more words, but he doesn't. Because footfalls ring in my hallway?

Fallon appears beside him, her complexion upsettingly colorless. Before I can ask her if everything's all right, three members of the Akwale—Malka, Aza, and Tamar—bustle in beside her. Their hands are soaked in blood. Is it Taytah's? Does my grandmother lay in a puddle?

"Where's the door?" Tamar's pink eyes scroll over the bare stone arch.

"Daya banished it," Cathal replies, his pitch oddly toneless.

Aza's head rears back, which sends her long, midnight locks frolicking. "Daya?"

Fallon frowns, looking from her father to me. "I don't understand. How?"

"Spells die with their maker," I explain, repeating Meriam's last words.

Is my mother still lingering, or has she fled? Now that I know the truth, I suddenly hope she's gone, because Priya's sorceresses wear expressions that smack of vengeance.

Malka gives her head an abrupt shake, which sends her short red strands tumbling around her bare, brown shoulders. "I don't know what lies Meriam fed you—"

"Truths. She fed me truths."

"Are you expecting us to believe that you suddenly have blood magic?" Aza asks.

"I don't *suddenly* have blood magic. I've always had blood magic. It just *suddenly* returned. Like I said, spells perish with their maker."

"ImTaytah bound you?" Fallon gasps.

"Yes."

"She wouldn't have done that." Aza shakes her head. "If anyone bound your magic, it's your spiteful mother."

"A mother that, until tonight, Daya had never met." The tendons in Cathal's neck draw tight. "So when—*do enlighten us*—would Meriam have cast such a spell?"

Malka rubs her blood-smeared hand down the silk pants she wears over a matching sky-blue top. "She must've bound her magic before sending Zendaya into the belly of the serpent."

Could this be true? Could Meriam have pretended it was her mother's fault in order to ingratiate herself with me?

Fallon scrutinizes my pumping chest. "Did Meriam draw whorls of blood on the skin over your heart, Mádhi?"

"No."

Relief smooths Fallon's rumpled brow. "Then Meriam was speaking the truth. Priya bound my mother's Shabbin side." She nervously toys with the little loop speared through the shell of her ear. "I can't believe she did that."

"Can't you?" Cathal murmurs in Crow.

Fallon's finger suddenly tumbles off her ear. "Do you realize what this means, Mádhi?" Her eyes shine like the faceted sapphires strung around Tamar's neck. "You're immortal!"

I draw in a breath that agitates my heart so wildly it makes my lungs cramp. Am I?

"*Yes, my little queen.*" Meriam's disembodied voice brushes against my thrumming ears.

How is she speaking with me? Why didn't I think of asking her? I've *so* many questions for her.

"*We will meet again, batee. Someday. Somewhere. Now don't keep the Mahananda waiting. Go get your crown.*"

That quiets my thunderous pulse. Not only do I not feel ready to rule, but it's also something I don't especially desire. First things first... "Where's Enzo?"

Cathal fists his fingers, which pops his knuckles and strains the straps of his leather vambraces.

"Imogen is flying him to the Sky Kingdom," Fallon says. "He's alive, but passed out."

"Please have her fly him back here. And bring Agrippina home, too." I move past her, past Malka, past Cathal. Though I feel a shallow tug when I pass by the Mahananda, I don't march toward it. Not yet. Not until I've laid eyes on my deceitful grandmother. Or maybe I'm using her as an excuse to kill a little more time to weigh the cost of a crown against that of my freedom.

I suddenly wish Meriam had wanted the crown and taken the

choice away from me. I lift my gaze to the stars obscured by wing-beats and pour my question into the ether. Either she doesn't hear me or she doesn't care to answer, for no words ring between my temples.

"I'm sorry I locked you up." Fallon's voice takes my attention off the Crow-filled sky.

I reach up and stroke her cheek, my scabbed index finger lingering on her delicate feather tattoo. "I'm glad you did. I got to meet Meriam."

She doesn't say anything.

"Why didn't you tell me our lives were bound, batee?"

Fallon blinks. "I...I wasn't certain whether they were anymore. Also, I didn't want to worry you for nothing."

"Please never keep anything from me."

"No more secrets."

"Good." I stroke her cheek once more.

I meet Cathal's dark stare for a heartbeat, two, and then I turn and resume my trek toward the queen's quarters.

Fallon falls into step beside me. "Are you sure you want to see her?"

"Yes." I cross the threshold, overhearing two members of the Akwale discussing how Kanti and Behati are on their way back. As I swirl past them, I ask, "When do they get here?"

"Why?" Aori asks.

"Do not question my question," I all but snarl.

I'm aware every sorceress from Priya's coven deems me a blemish on Shabbinkind, a defective byproduct of a disgraced witch, an unsuspecting serpent, and the pity of a grandmother. Spite makes me consider wheeling and diving headfirst into the Mahananda, but I will not let such an emotion guide my decision. Shabbe deserves better. The Mahananda deserves better.

"They should reach Shabbe by tomorrow evening since no Crow was available to give them a ride." Aori glowers at a space over my head, one I've no doubt is occupied by Cathal, since Shabbin men aren't as tall as shifters.

Unless it's Lorcan? A whiff and I know who stands behind me, even before I find Lorcan's crows reshaping themselves into a man on Fallon's other side.

"We're stretched thin in Luce, but I deployed as many of my Crows as I could spare to Shabbe. You want Justus and Meriam found, don't you, Aori?"

Out of the corner of my eye, I catch a tiny smirk tugging at one corner of Fallon's lips. Are they purposely delaying Behati and Kanti's return to give me time to take the crown?

I brush past the line of guards and sorceresses to reach Priya's giant bed. I expect the sheets to have turned as red as the sails of Shabbin vessels, but they're white.

Like the hair fanned around her face.

Like her skin.

Like her unseeing eyes.

The spectacle is ghastly and turns my stomach. One of my palms finds its way to my abdomen while the other rolls into a fist at my side.

Why did you bind me? I want to yell at the corpse. *Why, Taytah? Why?* I take a step nearer. *I loved and admired you with all my heart. I respected you. I thought you did, too, but I was wrong. If you'd loved and admired me, you wouldn't have impeded me; you would've elevated me. Taught me to use my magic instead of locking it away and pretending I never had any.*

I sweep my palm over her face to shut her eyes and then I turn and stride out of her chambers. "How long till my denmates arrive?"

"Fifteen minutes," Lorcan replies.

"Good, because I want them at my side when I enter the Mahananda."

Stunned breaths and shocked murmurs slide into my ears as I traverse the courtyard.

"Only someone with blood magic can sit on the Shabbin throne," Aori proclaims as I pass underneath the starlit honeysuckle.

"She has blood magic," Malka mutters.

"Priya wished for Kanti to succeed her!"

I stop on the edge of the Mahananda and turn to hunt the crowd for the architect of this decree—bronze-skinned and honeyed hair Rosh. "I'm aware Queen Priya never meant for me to succeed her. If she had wanted me on the throne, she wouldn't have bound my magic, now would she?"

All present members of the Akwale exchange glances, and then they all start moving. Not toward me, but around me.

"They're forming their circle," Fallon whispers.

Smoke rises from Cathal's skin. "I'll happily disperse it."

"Do not go near them," I murmur. "I do not fear their wrath or their magic." What I do fear is a concealed obsidian weapon, but I keep that to myself. "If the Mahananda wants me, then the Mahananda will protect me. I'm not your responsibility, Cathal." I glance up at him, find his jaw ticking beneath his black beard.

Beard...I'm so surprised my mind found a word for what grows on his face that I almost miss his fiery reply.

"You're the mother of my child. You'll get my protection until I decide to become a forever-Crow."

My heart catches at his mention of eternal death. He has a mate. Why in the world would he speak of death?

His mate must be mortal. I could make her immortal, I realize. If she's willing to become a Serpent. I consider suggesting it, but what if Meriam's misled me? What if I vanish into the Mahananda forever?

A body suddenly plummets from the sky and onto the Mahananda. It's so blindingly white I know it's Taytah's. She lies there for a moment and then she shimmers out of existence, causing not a single ripple.

Lorcan takes shape beside Fallon. "I wanted to avoid someone doing away with her corpse, since there exists a sigil to resuscitate dead bodies." At my shocked stare, he explains, "A sorceress would have to sacrifice her life for the corpse's, but considering Priya's fan club"—Lorcan slots his fingers through Fallon's—"I worried one of them just might attempt it." He carries her hand to his mouth and brushes a kiss against her knuckles.

Though my heart reels from his admission, it also melts at his consideration. "Thank you, Lorcan Ríhbiadh."

"You're very welcome, Zendaya of Shabbe, Mother of Serpents and of my extraordinary mate."

All of me fills with such an influx of emotion that my eyes prickle.

"Thank Mórrígan she took after you and not the surly, winged one," he adds.

A laugh erupts from my throat. It's so at odds with the rest of the night that I almost feel guilty at having produced such a sound.

But it wanes when I hear someone decree, "We do not accept you as our queen, Naaga."

"Good thing she doesn't need your approval." Cathal's voice rolls over the courtyard, loud and deep and wholly steadfast.

Malka lifts her chin and slices the air with her stare. "She does, for we are the Mahananda's—"

When she emits a choked rattle, I think Cathal has disobeyed my command not to disperse the sorceresses, but he stands there, wreathed in smoke. Wreathing *me* in smoke. I stare back at Malka, noting only then the bent beam of iridescent light that surges from behind me and arcs onto her. Clutching her throat, she falls to her knees, then crumples face-first into the stone soaked with one of her sigils.

Shrill cries reverberate against the scooped, sunstone land.

"Karma," Fallon murmurs. "Anyone else believe my mother isn't the rightful monarch? By all means, speak now or forever hold your peace."

"Best to encourage them to speak than to hold their peace, Little Bird," Lorcan murmurs. "Always good to weed out one's enemies at the start of one's reign since we accumulate so many new ones later."

"Hopefully my mother's collection of enemies won't be as bountiful as yours, mo khrá," she replies.

"Depends if she takes back your father. He's a little rough

around the feathers." Lorcan's odd comment stiffens Cathal's posture and makes Fallon's face swerve toward her mate's.

I can tell words are exchanged. Many. I imagine she's informing him that Cathal has a new mate, though I'm surprised, seeing as Lorcan and Cathal are so close, that news hasn't reached him yet. Then again, Cathal's a private person.

Two Crows suddenly swoop low—one carrying a green-haired male, the other a blue-haired female.

It's time. As Enzo and Agrippina disembark from their winged steeds, I murmur my intent into their minds. I inform them of the risk that the Mahananda might not want me. Might not send me back. Agrippina rolls her eyes while Enzo just stares without blinking.

Do you both approve of my decision to ask the Mahananda for the Shabbin crown?

Agrippina tucks her hair behind her ear. *You don't need our approval, Daya.*

I do, for I cannot rule over this land without the both of you at my side.

Naturally. Agrippina's smile grows. *I call General.* She must remember that Enzo cannot hear her in skin, for she repeats her claim out loud, which makes the Crow King snort and Fallon beam as though she was her daughter instead of her...instead of her *other* mother.

Enzo?

You've always been my queen, Day. You forever will be.

My throat rolls over a swallow that feels bladed as I turn and take one step onto the Mahananda's glassy surface. *If I don't return, please know that I couldn't have picked better denmates.*

If you don't return, odds are we'll be gulped down by the Mahananda right along with you, so you can tell us then, Agrippina says.

That stops me because I didn't think that my disappearance would lead to theirs.

Her expression grows serious. "You *will* return."

I try to pull my foot back, but it adheres to the Mahananda's surface.

"Of course, she'll return," Fallon says, but doubt must creep over her heart because she glances at Lorcan.

"She will." Does he say this to placate her and reassure me, or because he truly knows what happens next?

I try to read my fate in his golden stare, but it's as hard as the Mahananda's surface. Since it's too late to turn back, I set my other foot onto the source of all magic. For a heartbeat, nothing happens and I think that perhaps the Mahananda doesn't want me as its keeper, but then...

But then, I sink.

Chapter 48
Zendaya

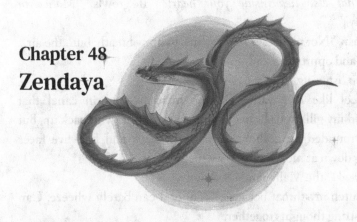

"*H*ello again, Zendaya of Shabbe."

I stand on a surface that is as hard as glass and as black as Crow feathers. "Mahananda?"

"*Yes, daughter of Meriam and of the ocean.*" My skin tingles from the velvet resonance of the voice. "*Tell me what you seek.*"

I look around me but there's only darkness. "You. Your counsel."

"*My counsel or my consent?*"

"Both."

A slow hum vibrates the void...vibrates my chest. "*Go on.*"

"I think I'd like—"

"*Neither Shabbe nor I can belong to someone who is unsure of their heart.*"

Cowed, I press my lips together.

"*Do you desire your foremothers' onus, or did you enter my realm to ensure I did not bequeath the responsibility to another?*"

Goosebumps sweep over my bare arms and rain down my spine and chest.

"*What lies inside your heart, Zendaya?*"

Fear, I think.

"*What else?*"

It can hear me?

Of course it can hear me...

"*What else lies inside your heart?*" It growls. "*Malice or integrity?*"

I gasp. "Not malice." I part my lips to draw breath, but...the air... it's hot and oppressive and—

"*I'm listening, Zendaya.*"

I feel like I'm wading in the toxic Isolacuorin canal that gummed my gills and shrank my lungs. I want to swim back up, but I'm surrounded by nothing. I crane my neck and find five faces peering down at me. Can they see me?

"*Speak!*" the Mahananda bellows.

I clutch my throat because I cannot. I can barely wheeze. Can barely string thoughts together.

"*Do you wish to fall or to rise?*"

I sweep my gaze over Lorcan and Fallon, Enzo and Agrippina, Cathal.

"*I will ask one last time? Do you wish to—*"

"Rise! Live!" Oxygen rushes through my parted lips and down my throat. "*And rule!*" More sweet, delicious air swells my lungs. Keeping my gaze locked on the male with whom I made Fallon, I say, this time out loud, "I wish to carry your voice to the four corners of our realm, Mahananda. To fulfill your wishes and heed your commands."

"*Do you swear to never question my decisions?*"

I'm about to say yes, but the word that rolls off my tongue is another: "No." I start to seal my lips in case the Mahananda divests me of oxygen once again, but more words press against the seam of my lips. "If you wanted me blind, Mahananda, then why gift me the ability to see? If you wanted me feckless, then why endow me with reason?"

I'm almost surprised when air continues to cycle through my lungs. Not almost. I *am* surprised. Is the Mahananda delaying my smothering in the hopes of hearing me repent? If that's the case, then it'll be sorely disappointed.

"If ruling means becoming your puppet and pawn, then I do not want the crown." I spin on my heel, grazing the faces of those who shaped me into the woman I've become with my stare. One's missing—my grandmother's. Grief lances behind my breastbone as I picture her, not dimmed by death but vibrant with life, an imperfect woman who tried to love what I'd become. "If ruling means becoming your ally and confidante, then I want nothing more." The darkness eddies around me as though I were rising, but I'm not. I'm idling in the infinite fullness surrounding me. "All I ask is that, if you do not want me, Mahananda, do not keep me."

What feels like two icy fingers glide along my brow and part my hair at the temples before carving through the thick pink mass. When the caress stills and a weight settles on my head, I lift my hand. Though I cannot see my crown, I can feel the miniature ridges of sculpted scales and the sharp points of diamond tusks.

"Your reign begins now, Daughter of the ocean, Daughter of mine."

As the Mahananda channels my body upward, I scramble to ask, "The Crows' obsidian curse. Can it still be broken?"

"Tomorrow, Zendaya. Tomorrow, I will tell you what can be done."

Chapter 49
Zendaya

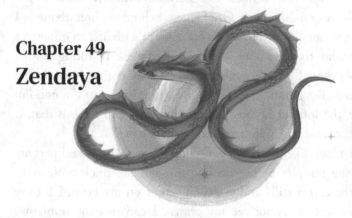

When my head pierces through the surface of the Mahananda, crown-first, I'm met with layered silence. It surges against my skin in waves shot through with scorching scorn, balmy awe, and cool caution.

"Sumaca," Abrax murmurs. He must've shouldered past the thin crowd while I was in the Mahananda because he stands right behind Agrippina, whose eyes shimmer like the twinkling talons and beaks of the Crows swerving over Shabbe.

My guard drops onto one knee and begins to bend his head, but then his gaze trawls the courtyard and he bellows, "Kneel for our queen."

Though every guard heeds his command, out of the Akwale, only Tamar prostrates herself. The others, including Soorya the healer, huddle around Malka's supine form. Is the immortal sorceress dead?

Yes, Agrippina says. **Struck dead by the Mahananda.** Her voice lilts over the words.

I shouldn't be surprised by the power the Mahananda can exert on the living, but it's still astonishing. I do wonder why it didn't punish Priya after she disrespected its orders. Unless she didn't? Perhaps Meriam misheard and the Mahananda never planned on lifting the Crows' immortality?

Questions for tomorrow.

I finally step over the hardened surface that reflects the stars and the murder of Crows, that reflects me and the crown braided into my pink locks. "I encourage those of you who do not want me as their ruler to leave Shabbe."

"You're kicking us out of our homeland, Naaga?" Aori snarls.

"Prostrate yourselves, sisters. The Mahananda chose her to guide us," Tamar whispers.

None do.

"Come with us, Tamar," Aza implores, holding Soorya's arm.

Tamar looks at them, then at me, then at Malka's bloodless body, and then she shakes her head, splashing the stone beneath her with the tears coursing over her deep-brown cheeks. "I trust the Mahananda."

"Day!" Asha erupts onto the courtyard, then halts beneath the canopy of honeysuckle that's always in full bloom. Her eyes widen, and then the corners of her mouth wobble around the title that's now mine. "*Sumaca.*"

"I've tasked my people to spread the news of your rise," Lorcan says. "To Shabbe and beyond."

I nod but don't meet his golden stare. No, I track the retreat of Priya's coven and of Shabbe's healer. I suppose we don't need one now that I can make Serpents. Our tongues best any crystals.

"How many do you suspect will leave, Lore?" I ask as I catch the giant Faerie healer calling out to Soorya. They clasp hands and murmur aggrieved farewells before Aza whisks her out of the court-yard. Did he kneel, I wonder.

"When I returned to power"—my fellow monarch grows out his talons and drums them against his leather-cloaked thigh—"there was a mass exodus of pure-blooded Faeries."

My breath hitches. "Shabbe's so much less diverse than Luce that if there's a mass exodus of pureblooded Shabbins, I'll have only the serpents in the Sahklare to rule over."

Fallon takes one of my hands and squeezes it. "Mádhi, many will stay. Just look around you."

"They're not staying for me; they stay because they fear the Mahananda," I murmur, tracing the shape of Malka's body with my gaze, while giving my daughter's fingers a squeeze, touched by her enduring support.

"Some, but not all," Lorcan says. "When I rose out of the Cauldron seven centuries ago, your great-grandmother told me that a ruler should never endeavor to please; only to protect and improve. Whatever you do, Daya, do not expend energy on trying to shepherd those who left back into your queendom. Concentrate on those who stayed."

I bob my head, storing his advice. "I know nothing about ruling."

"You're in luck. I've a general to lend you." Lorcan levels a smile on the male who warms one side of my body. "He's well-versed in politics. And yes, I'm aware that he's passably agreeable on good days, but you're in need of a fount of knowledge not a bucket of sunshine."

"I know plenty about generaling, too, Day," Agrippina says as she marches toward us. *Unless you want Cathal to stay?*

Enzo crosses his arms and stammers something in Lucin that makes Lorcan cant his head, Cathal scowl, Agrippina smirk, and Fallon bite her lip. *What did you tell them?*

When he doesn't answer, I ask Agrippina who's only too happy to convey his words: *He just asked Lorcan whether he should really be putting his general on loan considering the other is on the run. Seaweed's got bigger balls than I gave him credit for.*

Agrippina, I chide her.

What? He does. And that's a good thing. Her eyes roll over my crown. *Fucking queen, Day. Your dream came true.*

It wasn't my dream.

Right. She slides her lips together. *You didn't get your memories back?*

I didn't ask the Mahananda for them.

Will you?

I side-eye the Crow muttering something to Lorcan. *I don't know that I want to remember all that I lost.*

Maybe it can give you everything back?

He has a new mate, Agrippina.

She frowns. *Says who?*

He told me himself.

Her frown deepens. *And Fallon confirmed it?*

I'm not going to ask my daughter for confirmation. Besides, why would he invent a mate?

Because bruised egos make idiots out of men. And women, she adds.

"This decision concerns only my parents," Fallon suddenly says. "How about we let them decide whether they want to work together?" And then she's looping her arm through Agrippina's and tugging her away.

When I glance across the Mahananda, I find Enzo following in their steps. *Enzo, are you all right? My mother told me she stunned you.*

Without glancing over his shoulder, he gives me a thumb's up and though I've never been on the receiving end of a middle finger, it feels a little like one.

It's not, he says.

"Daya, if you need anything, you know where I lurk." Lorcan inclines his head before breaking into his five crows and swirling to the heavens.

Though Cathal and I aren't alone in the courtyard, his magnetic stare makes me feel like we're the only two people left in the world.

"Do you want—do you want my counsel?" Though his tone's flat and the lines of his body as rigid as ever, his fractured speech betrays his nonchalance.

"I'd be glad for your guidance." I add a smile that I hope will relax him. "Can the Siorkahd spare you until I constitute a new Akwale?"

His vambraces creak as the knot of his folded arms tautens. "Yes."

"Even if it takes months?"

"Yes."

"Then I'll provide accommodations for you and your mate."

He suddenly switches to Crow to mutter, "*Cruaih.*"

My nails bite into my palms. "If you think it'll make her miserable to move to Shabbe, then maybe you should reconsider—"

"That's her name. *Cruaih.*"

"Misery?" My fingers slacken before bunching back into fists. Not only does a name make her real, but one of Crow origin makes her one of his people. "Perhaps moving to Shabbe *will* make her miserable. How about before giving me a definitive answer, you discuss—"

"She'll be fine."

His lack of consideration doesn't assuage my jealousy, but it does make me feel a twinge of empathy for this subjugated woman who gets no say in the matter.

"All right, then. I will see you in the morning?"

Cathal scans the courtyard. "Who will stay with you tonight?"

I tilt my head. "What do you mean?"

"Abrax is useless; Asha, less so, I suppose. Your Serpents are...do they have blood magic now as well?"

"Are you worried someone will spring an attack on me during the night?"

"Tensions are high, so yes, I do worry about retaliation. Especially considering your fellow female Shabbins can slip through walls unnoticed. You'll need to ward your wing of the castle."

"I'm immortal, Cathal."

"So was Priya. So was that one." He nods to the dead sorceress whose body still blights the sunstone.

"I'll paint wards to keep the Shabbins out of my bedchamber. Besides, I don't intend to sleep." Even if I'd wanted to, I couldn't. Not in my present state, not with my insides sizzling as though I'd swallowed a lightning bolt.

"I'll be back before sunrise."

Before I can tell the Crow not to rouse his poor mate in the middle of the night, he melts into shadows and rises to the heavens in feathers. Suddenly he swoops back down, snatches Malka's body, and dumps her onto the Mahananda. The second her body vanishes, he soars back up, his powerful wings stirring the stars until he becomes one with the night.

"What did he decide?" Fallon's query carries my attention down to her.

"To come back and aid me." Before my heart can run away with my reason, I remind myself that he's only returning for diplomatic reasons. "Apparently, Cruaih won't mind." Though I don't formulate this as a question, I wait with bated breath for Fallon to swallow my lure and tell me all about this Cruaih.

"She won't." Fallon holds my stare...and holds it, and then she blinks hard and looks down at the bloody sigils the Akwale left behind. "I'll help you lift their spells."

Though I wish she'd told me more about Cruaih, I do not speak her name again. I will meet her soon enough.

And I do. And she is nothing like I expect.

Chapter 50
Zendaya

I stand from the carmine seat I've been occupying since the stars faded and dawn ignited the sky.

My knees click from how long they've been folded and my thighs shake as movement rids them of numbness. I come to stand in front of Cathal and cross my arms in front of the dress Asha went to fetch me earlier so I could *freshen up* as she put it.

"Is she a shifter?" I ask Cathal as he strokes one large palm down Cruaih's spine.

"No."

I frown. "So you're mated with a...cat?"

His hand freezes mid-caress. "*Mated?* I may be an animal myself at times, but I'm not some deviant, Príona." He shudders. "Why the Cauldron would you assume such a vile thing?"

I gape at him, not in shock. Oh no. I'm not shook; I'm deeply and thoroughly maddened. "Are you fucking kidding me, Cathal Báeinach?"

His pupils contract at my robust tone, while Cruaih shrinks back and burrows behind the bulge of his forearm, peaked ears flat against her head.

"You told me you'd met someone! You told me that she was the reason you had no time to have tea with me!" My tone is far shriller than probably becomes a queen, but I cannot seem to give a single fuck.

"She's a kitten." He lifts his arm, carrying the tiny ball of black fur to his cheek. "She needs a lot of attention."

If I didn't feel so duped, I may have melted at the sight of such tenderness. But I'm currently not melting; I'm vibrating. "Well, silly me assumed she was a Crow," I say, tamping down the volume of my anger for Cruaih's sake. "And not the *non-shifting* kind."

The kitten blinks wide, shiny eyes at me, one ear perking while the other still lays flat, but that has more to do with the pressure of her caregiver's cheek.

"Why lead me to think she was a woman, Cathal? Why didn't you just tell me she was a cat?"

He lowers his arm. "I owed you no explanation." His gaze slices toward the closed doors of the throne room that he stepped past mere minutes ago. Is he considering flocking out? "I still don't," he grumbles.

I unbind my arms. "If we're to work together, I expect complete honesty from this point on."

"Honesty is a two-way avenue."

I cast my stare off the spooked creature and onto the seething one. "I've never been dishonest with you."

He snorts, which snares his pet's attention.

"What secrets are you accusing me of keeping, Cathal?" When the hollows beneath his cheekbones turn concave, I realize that he thinks I'm lying. "What secrets?"

He snorts.

I tilt my chin up. "Ask me anything."

"I'm here to advise you, not to trial you."

"Perhaps, but you're obviously begrudging me something. Out with it."

When he smooshes his lips, I understand that the stubborn male will not give voice to what's on his heart.

I whirl back toward the files stacked haphazardly on the

sunstone table, which Asha was helping me sort through. "No wonder Fallon seemed so reticent about us working together."

He remains quiet.

"This won't work, Cathal. I cannot collaborate with someone who resents me for something I've no—"

"I'm not holding a fucking grudge, Daya."

I crinkle the corner of one of the papers. "Really? Then why didn't you tell me the *someone you'd met* was a *cat?*"

"Because I was—"

When a minute ticks by and he hasn't added any words, I turn back toward him. "You were *what?*"

The whites of his eyes, still pink from too many sleepless nights, flush redder. "I was jealous that you'd moved on with the Green One!" His raised voice steals every beat of my heart. He drops his chin into his neck and gazes at Cruaih. "Perhaps for Serpents, mating bonds are different than they are for Crows, but—"

"Enzo's my *den*mate, Cathal, not my *love*mate."

His jaw begins to tick.

"I can hear Agrippina, too." I try to catch his stare, but he keeps it on his pet. "I thought you knew that my connection to them was like Lore's to—"

"I *do* know."

"Then why in the world do you think that Enzo and I are more—"

"Because I saw you together, Daya!"

"Again, he is my denmate. You will often see us together, Cathal."

His searing gaze finally lifts off his kitten. "I'm not fucking talking about seeing the two of you swimming."

A dull buzzing resounds in my ears. "You saw him kiss me."

"You were right. This was a mistake. I don't know why I thought we could work together." He eyes my door, then eyes Cruaih, probably calculating the best and quickest method to escape with a creature that cannot dematerialize to smoke.

I move across the room and position myself right in their path.

And then I take blocking their exit a step further, because I don't want him leaving here thinking that Enzo's kiss meant anything to me—I lock the lattice doors and create a veil that hinders any wandering eyes from peering through the decorative openings.

"What are you doing?" he growls.

I walk back toward him. "I want to explain—"

"I don't want your explanation. We aren't mates. You owe me nothing."

"What you saw was Enzo trying to prove to me that my connection to him was stronger than my connection to Agrippina." I stop an arm's length from him, sensing that if I get any closer, it will send him surging back, for wild creatures do not like to be cornered. I'd know. I once was wild. "What you saw was a boy acting on some misplaced crush."

"What I saw was a woman declaring her love to another man! What I saw was her kissing that fucking man!"

Cruaih ducks once more behind his forearm. I'm tempted to tell him to set her down before he crushes her, but I doubt he'd welcome my advice.

Still, I keep my gaze on her in case she needs rescuing. "I *do* love him, but I love him like I love Fallon."

His mouth twists in revulsion and he falls back a step. "That makes it all so much more revolting."

"It does. And it was."

"Yeah." He snorts. "You looked so revolted, Daya."

"You might've borne witness to the scene, but you didn't bear witness to my thoughts." Anger sours my palate. "I didn't want the kiss."

"Then why didn't you bloody push him back! Why did you just..." His Adam's apple jostles twice before he manages to blow out the end of his sentence. "Why did you just stand there? Why? *Fucking why?*"

"At first, because I was shocked."

He snorts.

"I was. You don't have to believe me, but I've never lied to you

311

and don't intend to start today. I should've put an end to it immediately." Enzo's face suddenly layers itself over Cathal's. I close my eyes to whisk him away. "But I didn't, because…"

"Because *why?*" Pain bleeds through his anger.

"I was almost certain he wasn't my mate before he kissed me, but it was the kiss—the lack of…*spark* that erased all my doubts. I imagined he'd feel it and pull away. Naively, I also imagined that he'd only get closure if *he* was the one to put an end to it."

Though I don't voice my next thoughts out loud, they must be written all over my face because Cathal mutters, "Clearly, he didn't get closure."

On a sigh, I pry my lids apart. "No, but he did fall into Taytah's bed."

Cathal's crooked nose wrinkles. I presume he knew about my Serpent and my grandmother for his face isn't marred with surprise, only disgust.

"He might not like it, but he's understood that I can never be his." I stare at the crown I set down on the cushion that still bears the indent of the former queen's body. "How I envy Lore. How I envy that the day the Mahananda made him other, it gave him a whole tribe." My chest lifts with a deep breath that causes the braided cords of my gown to dig into my rib cage. "Though I feel incredibly blessed to have the power to *make* others, I wish that the path to understanding it all had been smoother. I wish…" I lift my gaze off the crown and sweep it over Cathal, over the cords of his throat and the cliffs of his cheekbones, before daring to meet his guarded stare and confessing, "I wish I hadn't lost you along the way, Cathal Báeinach."

I want him to say that I haven't.

I want him to set down Cruaih and take *me* in his arms.

But the Crow doesn't speak and he doesn't choose Serpent over cat.

I back up toward the doors. "Forgive me for locking you in, but I wanted to speak my piece before you flew off." I palm the wood, recalling my blood, then open the door to free him.

Every guard stands to attention outside.

"Do you need anything, Sumaca?" Asha asks.

"Yes. I need you to stop calling me Your Highness and go rest."

She rolls her eyes. "Should I send for some food?"

I shake my head just as a gruff voice behind me says, "Yes. I'd love some food, and Cruaih would appreciate a bowl of milk."

"Milk isn't very good for..." When Asha's recommendation fades, I fathom that Cathal is firing a look her way about his desire for her nutritional input. She presses her lips together before muttering, "We will bring sustenance for all, immediately."

After dispatching some guards to the kitchen, she hunts my expression in the hopes of gleaning my mood.

I give my steadfast guard and friend a warm smile before murmuring, "All's well."

But is it? *He's staying for a meal*, I remind myself. He may depart soon after, but at least, he isn't departing immediately. I lower my hand from the door, leaving it ajar so he doesn't feel trapped, and turn back toward the Crow.

As our gazes twine, my stomach swishes, and not from hunger. I don't ask if he forgives me for kissing another, the same way I don't ask for how long he'll be staying.

Instead, I wander back his way, giving his companion my full attention. "Hello, Cruaih. I'm Zendaya. I'm sorry for frightening you earlier with my shouting. I'm not usually prone to raising my voice."

I reach one finger toward her muzzle. "May I?"

"You can try, but she can be quite—"

I stroke up the bridge of her tiny nose, my finger sliding through her feather-soft black fur.

"—aloof," he finishes.

I smile. "I'd expect nothing less with a master like yourself."

She tilts her head to sniff my finger, then wraps her coarse tongue around my nail. My heart holds still because, although it's scabbed, there was a smear of dried blood that's now gone.

"What?" Cathal asks.

"She licked some of my blood." I look up at him, then back at her. "It won't poison her, will it?"

"Fallon's blood doesn't harm her, so I don't see why yours would."

"Because I'm part-Serpent."

"And our daughter is part-Crow."

Still, my pulse whooshes as hard as my stomach.

He crouches and sets Cruaih down, then strides over to the red velvet circle. "Shall we get started?" When I don't move or say a word, he glances over his shoulder at me. "Daya, she will be fine."

I nod.

He sits, muttering that my first order of business should be updating the throne room with armchairs instead of floor cushions with stunted backrests.

Cruaih twines her little body around my ankles, startling me out of my daze. My surprise surprises her in turn and she skips toward Cathal and skitters onto his lap.

When I've still made no move to follow, Cathal cants his head. "Shall we get started, Sumaca?"

"You're staying?"

"Unless you prefer I leave, then yes."

"All right." I make my way toward him, choosing to kneel on the floor cushion instead of sitting cross-legged like he is. Cruaih scales his muscled thigh, teeters there a moment, before hopping off and moseying on over to me.

My hand sinks into her fur. "What about after you eat?"

"Zendaya"—my name on his lips has never sounded so gentle— "I'm staying."

Chapter 51
Cathal

"Who knew your grandmother was such a hoarder?" I ask.

Amongst the piles of documents Zendaya unearthed, there were many interesting edicts and land divisions as well as correspondence with kings of old and random foreigners, most of them with titles preceding their names. I even found a letter that Lorcan penned to Queen Mara—or Mórrígan as we call her—six and half centuries earlier asking her if she could send a few more Shabbins to help combat the Fae and their endless supply of obsidian weapons.

Zendaya smiles from where she's reclined on the cushion beside mine, Cruaih curled atop her chest, snoozing away. My little stray, who likes no one save for myself and Fallon, is completely enamored by the Serpent Queen. My cat isn't alone. Even when I believed Daya harbored feelings toward her fellow Serpent, my bruised heart never quit thudding for her.

"How does a big, growly Crow find himself in possession of such a tiny, sweet creature?" she asks, languidly curving a finger up and down the purring furball's spine.

"I was visiting Rax when I found her. She was pawing at a burlap sack which contained..." I roll my neck at the sordid memory, my nails hardening into talons as I picture what I will do to the callous murderer if our paths ever cross. "Which contained the rest of her family."

Daya's chest lifts with a gasp that disrupts Cruaih's nap, but only for a moment. After ascertaining that all's well and that I haven't abandoned her, she slips right back into slumber. "Some people don't deserve to live."

"I agree." For a long moment, I stare at her elegant fingers tracking across Cruaih's fur. Her nails are long and painted the same shade as the velour she lounges on. My mind suddenly places them on *my* body, on a part of me that is at present growing so heavy and long that I have to readjust the way I sit.

"I'm sorry the seating is so uncomfortable. I'll order chairs before the day is out and loftier feet for the table. Hopefully both can be manufactured quickly."

When the seam of my leathers keeps guillotining my cock, I decide to stand, with my back to Daya, and stretch my legs.

"Even if you don't stay." The words bluster out of Zendaya's mouth, as soft as the patter of my cat's feet. "Since I can read now that my Shabbin side has been unbound and everything..."

It's so unlike her to mumble that I stop fidgeting with my trousers and turn, erection be damned. "What part of, *I'm staying,* didn't you understand, Priona?"

Her eyes don't stray off my face.

"Sorry... *Sumaca.*"

Her hand promenades up my cat's back twice before she finally says, "Well, you didn't exactly mention until *when.*"

"Until you form your new coven or government, or whatever you intend to call it, I'll be at your side."

"That might take a while."

It certainly will, since I'll be dragging out the process. I smile. It must be an alarming smile because the pulse at the base of her neck flutters her scar. Unless alarm isn't the sentiment I'm coaxing from her...?

When her throat moves over a swallow and she licks her lips, I consider adopting my bird form to cool off, but not only would shifting inside the throne room spook Cruaih, it would also confound Daya, so I stay there, bulge in perfect relief. In truth, what point is there in trying to conceal the effect she has on me? It isn't as though she's unaware of my feelings toward her.

"Are your living quarters to your liking?" she asks, pulse still thundering beneath her honeyed skin. What I wouldn't give to stroke it.

"Yes, though I doubt I'll be spending much time in them."

She blinks. "You're thinking of living elsewhere?"

I tread right up to the back cushion upon which she's pillowed her head, pinch the seam of my trousers to transfer it to the side, and crouch. "I didn't only come back to advise you. I also returned to protect you."

Her chest is lifting and falling with brisker breaths. Is it wrong of me to appreciate how I affect her? "I have blood-magic, Cathal." Her hoarse voice tightens my balls some more. "So do Agrippina and Enzo."

"Fallon mentioned it." *The first male with blood-magic.* Though, admittedly, I was glad to hear it, it'd be a lie to say that it didn't irk my already tender ego. The male was already so special to Zendaya. Did he really need an added advantage over me? "But the people who want the crown torn off your head also have blood-magic." I flatten my palm over Cruaih's fur. When the side of my pinkie grazes the side of Zendaya's thumb, her breathing grows even more ragged.

"I'm immortal," she murmurs.

"So are the people who want the crown torn off your head," I repeat.

"Are you saying that you plan on moving into my bedchamber?"

"Only until you form your Akwale." I stroke back up Cruaih's back, then back down toward Daya's motionless fingers.

"That could be months. You said so yourself."

Some might consider our conversation moving in circles; I see it coming full-circle. I don't carry my hand off Cruaih's rump this time, relishing the feel of my pinkie brushing against the Serpent Queen's thumb.

"I hope my presence won't cause you too much discomfort." I realize I'm a bastard for not presenting my guarding offer as a choice, or suggesting other Crow contenders for the job—like Aoife, who's returned with me.

"I only have one bed," she says.

Of course, the instant she says this, I picture her sprawled atop it, long pink hair fanned over one of her pillows, coral nipples peaked, folds shiny with... *Fuck.* Just because she hasn't stolen her hand away from mine, just because her lids are at half-mast and her nostrils pulsate, it doesn't mean she wants my desperate ass.

I swallow, trying to moisten my hunger-abraded throat, and cast my gaze on my cat instead of on my...on the woman Cruaih is using as a mattress. "I'd be there to guard you, not to sleep."

"Do I have a choice in the matter of these living arrangements?"

My gaze veers toward hers. "Naturally." I try to smile but all my lips manage is a manic twitch. "But I do believe you should have a presence in your room at all times." *Not Enzo,* I add internally. "Preferably someone with iron appendages. Or, I suppose, an iron blade."

"Iron doesn't harm the Shabbins."

My jaw hardens. "True, but Serpents can't exactly shapeshift into lethal smoke. We might not be able to asphyxiate sorceresses with it, but it would hamper them."

"Why not thrust the responsibility of vigil onto someone who doesn't intend to spend their days counseling me? I hear Aoife, Reid, and Aodhan have returned with you and will be staying."

"I don't trust Reid to do a proper job. He's too besotted by Agrippina. I could ask Aoife, though."

She cocks one eyebrow. "What about asking Aodhan?"

The vein at my temple feels a second away from rupturing. "The only reason he's here is because Imogen threatened to drive an obsidian blade through his heart, so Lorcan asked me to bring him along."

"So, no Aodhan?"

"That's right. No fucking Aodhan."

Is that a smile drawing up the corners of her mouth? "Then I'd prefer Aoife stay with me."

"Why—" I clear my throat so the rest of my question doesn't come out strangled. "Are you frightened of me?"

"Frightened?" A grin breaks across her beautiful face, tossing me years back to one of the many conversations she doesn't remember but that's embedded inside my soul. It was the day I'd regained use of my vocal cords after five centuries of them being atrophied. I'd asked her if she'd gotten over her fear of me, or if she still required time alone? She'd crossed her arms and hissed into my mind that she'd never been scared of me.

Just of certain parts of me, I'd murmured through our bond.

My taunt had caused a lovely blush to steal across her cheekbones.

I'm not scared, she'd sworn, adding that she had no doubt that this 'certain part of me' would be massively underwhelming anyhow. I'd challenged her to find out. She'd claimed that she wasn't interested. But she had been.

Could this new version of Zendaya be interested?

Her thumb begins to move, caressing the edge of my pinkie that quit moving when she alluded to someone else guarding her. "The reason I prefer Aoife is because, although you might not need much sleep, *I* do, and I'd be incapable of relaxing if you were in my bedroom, Cathal."

"Why? Why wouldn't you be capable of relaxing?"

"Because, Cathal of the Sky Kingdom..." Her hand scales mine, then swirls around my wrist, before journeying back toward my unmoving digits.

"Because what?" I rasp.

She delicately rakes those red-red nails of hers along my fingers, knuckles, and wrist. "Because you're not exactly a source of tranquility, General."

I don't dare speak, afraid my breath will blow her fingers off my skin.

"I'm aware that you didn't stay behind in Shabbe to—"

When her lips stop moving and her hand grows slack, I blow out an atypically nervy, "To...?"

But her eyes have gone bone-white. My heart damn near detonates until I remember the same thing happening to Priya's eyes when the Cauldron conversed with her.

Still, I spin my hand and scoop Daya's fingers before they can tumble away from mine and curl them into my palm. The trance lasts a fucking eternity. Cruaih wakes and stretches. And then she licks my quivering thumb. She must sense my anguish because she winches her neck and peers up at me.

"Everything's okay, Misery," I promise her. "Go drink some milk."

She gives my thumb a quick cheek rub before traipsing toward the glazed ceramic dish heaped with crumbs which Asha set beside a bowl of milk. Though my kitten lapped at the milk, the dried food won her over, to Asha's immense pleasure. Recalling how she gloated helps quiet my ramping nerves.

"Come back to me, Príona," I murmur. *In every way, come back to me, Zendaya of Shabbe.*

Chapter 52
Zendaya

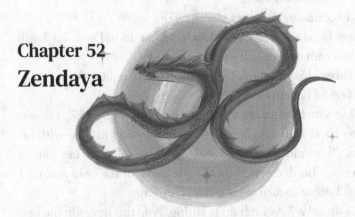

I emerge from the darkness with the Mahananda's words still prickling my temples.

Fingers tighten around mine—Cathal's. He hasn't left. And not only that, but he holds my hand.

I swallow, then squeeze his fingers and murmur, "I thought I'd slipped into the Mahananda."

He doesn't say anything, his gaze roving over my face, hounding each furrow for a sign of distress. Or perhaps he's trying to extract what the Mahananda had to say. When its words scroll through my mind, I snare my bottom lip.

"What is it? What did the Cauldron say?"

"That it cannot—it cannot undo what Taytah led it to do."

His eyebrows ruffle, bend, ruffle.

"It cannot immunize Lorcan to obsidian." I lower my attention to our twined hands before he spots the lie. The truth is that the Mahananda *can* make Lorcan and his people impervious to the toxin, but it would cost Fallon her Crow magic, for the cure is braided into it.

"It's more complicated than that, isn't it?"

I nibble on the inside of my cheek. "It is." I hesitate to tell him. He might be Fallon's father, but would he pick her over his race? I hate the thought almost as much as I hate possessing the coveted solution to the Crows' curse.

"It concerns our daughter, doesn't it?"

I meet his shadowed gaze. "Don't ask me to tell you, for I will demand an oath of silence from you if I do."

He balks. "Do you think I'd endanger our daughter?"

"If it could benefit your people—"

"What sort of monster do you think I am, Zendaya?" He sets down my hand and straightens, his knees clicking in time with his knuckles. "I would *never* hurt our daughter. *Never.*" He jams a hand through his disheveled locks. "She's one of the only reasons I didn't ask Lorcan to turn me into a forever-Crow."

Am I the other? As I roll up to sitting, I nip this query in the bud because this isn't the time and place for it. "Swear that if you're ever asked whether the Mahananda gave me the solution to your curse, you will lie."

He side-eyes me, anger jostling not just the air between us but inside the entire throne room. "I wish you'd trust me."

"This has nothing to do with trust, Cathal."

"Doesn't it?"

"No. This has to do with slips-of-the-tongue, torture sessions, or confessions whispered upon pillows. I've heard that people have a tendency to reveal all in the throes of passion." When he gapes at me, I add, "I hold this fact from several different sources: Taytah, Asha, Agrippina, Sybille, *and* Phoebus."

He mutters under his breath before giving his hair another violent tug. "First off, my tongue never slips, so there's no chance of your secret *popping* out. Secondly, one would have to catch me in order to torture me, and yes, I'm aware that I can potentially be caught. If that happened, I'd stake myself in the heart with obsidian so my tongue turned into a lump of stone. As for pillow-talk"—he tilts his head and spears me with a look—"the only person I want to fuck already knows, so not much risk there."

His words take a moment to land, but once they do, they soak into me like water and irrigate the thing behind my ribs with so much blood that I knead the palpitating skin.

"But again, I'd prefer to be gagged with magic than kept in the dark, so tell me and then make me forget."

"I know there's a sigil for lifting memories from someone's mind, but I wouldn't dare use it on you. I still need much practice."

"Fine." He takes a breath, releases it. "I owe you, Zendaya amMeriam, Queen of Shabbe."

My bicep warms. The burning dot must stamp his chest, because the angle of his jaw steepens and one of his eyes twitches. "After you tell me, you'll claim your bargain and make me forget the entire discussion."

I nod. "Fallon's Crow magic. That is the cost of transferring the immunity from her veins into Lorcan's."

Cathal's mouth flattens. "Why in the world did you think I would *ever* tell anyone about this, Zendaya?"

"Because it would break your people's curse once and for all."

"But it would also break my daughter. Now make me forget or—"

I rise and stride over the low backrest to stand in front of him. "Cathal Báeinach of the Sky Kingdom, I call forth my bargain and strip your mind of the Mahananda's solution to your people's obsidian curse. The source of all magic has sadly offered no solution."

His eyes seem to spark in the obscurity. Probably an illusion caused by the flickering candlelight.

"I'm sorry for not bringing better news," I say, while my mind replays and polishes his earlier words until they burn through the shadows veiling my mood: *the only person I want to fuck already knows.* "I'll just have to create more healers. Especially now that I've the responsibility of a queendom. I cannot exactly afford week-long convalescences. Not to mention, I'd prefer not to go around licking *all* your murder-mates."

His pupils have shrunk to the width of dust motes. "Are you trying to test the tenuous hold I have on my temper, Daya?"

The only person I want to fuck already knows...

I seize one of his hands and carry it to my waist. Once he grips it, I reach for the other but it's already finding its way to my body... to my cheek.

"Can we start over, Cathal Báeinach?" When he doesn't say anything, after having said a lot, I add, "I hear the third time's the charm."

His forehead falls to mine. "Except I won't survive a third ending, *mo Sífair*."

I grip his shoulders. "Then let's never end."

"What if—" His lids close. "What if the Cauldron mates you to someone who isn't me?"

"*Mahananda, will my kind have mates?*" I ask as Cruaih sniffs the jewels on my crown before giving them a tentative lick.

The Mahananda is quiet, probably resting from the magic it depleted whisking my consciousness into its depths. Why didn't I think of asking it before? Because I feared its answer?

I raise my eyes back to the Crow, turning the question on him: "What if the Mahananda mates you to someone who isn't me?"

His thumb sweeps across my cheek, coming to rest on the apex of my cheekbone. "Crows have only one mate. Once that mate is lost—" He swallows. "There's no stand-in waiting in the wings."

"Then I guess I'll swear an oath."

"No." He splays his fingers on the small of my back and rakes me closer. Though armor and leather wall off our bodies, I don't miss the harshness of his heartbeats beneath. "I will not have you loving me out of obligation or fear of physical pain."

I thread one of my hands through his hair, which drags a weighted exhalation from his lips. "I cannot be the reason for your death, Cathal. Not only would Fallon never forgive me, but I—" Moisture pools behind my lids as I bring his face nearer. "I couldn't live in a world in which you didn't exist."

He gives me a sad smile. "That's my line, Príona."

We must still be mates for there's no rhyme or reason to how deeply I love Cathal Báeinach. Either Serpents cannot communicate with their mates through a mental bond or—

Fuck, fuck, fuck, Day, Agrippina's voice startles a breath from my lungs.

What is it?

Are you in the Kasha?

Yes. What is it?

On my way.

"Daya?" Cathal's gaze swivels over each one of my features. "Something's wrong. Tell me what's wrong?"

"I don't know. It's Agrippina. She's coming here."

Chapter 53
Zendaya

Asha says that you aren't to be disturbed. Can you please tell her that you can be disturbed? I really *need* to see you. The panic that grips Agrippina's tone makes me rush to unseal the doors.

The second she bursts through, I run my gaze over her. Her blue hair is wild, her skin as pale as the milk inside Cruaih's bowl, and her eyes are pitched wide.

"Did something happen to Ceres?" I ask.

She blinks, then parrots, "Ceres?" as though she cannot recall who that is. My heart slams into my ribs and I swing my gaze up to Cathal who stands beside me, Cruaih tucked inside his palm. Has Agrippina lost her memories again?

He must have the same thought, because he says, "Your mother. Ceres is your mother."

She snorts. "I fucking know who Ceres is, Cathal." She starts kneading her temples with such force I worry she'll crack her skull.

After thundering, my pulse goes dead. "Did something happen to Enzo?"

Cathal's carriage rigidifies at the mention of my Serpent's name. How long will he stay jealous of that boy?

"No, Day, something's happened to *me*."

Since she's alive, I take it that whatever's going on with her isn't a matter of life and death. "What happened?"

"Cathal, do you mind stepping—" She suddenly hisses because a shadow streaks in beside her and morphs into a Crow, the one she does *not* have a crush on.

Reid's sun-kissed brown hair pokes out from his scalp, unruly like hers. Unlike the desperate horror painting her features, he wears the smuggest grin. Cathal mutters something under his breath that wipes the expression from his mouth and makes his head jerk into a deferential bow.

"Forgive my eruption inside your throne room, Sumaca." Reid mumbles in Crow. It's only my title that he pronounces in Shabbin.

I couldn't care less about his manners. Not with Agrippina rocking from heel to toe like a ship caught in a squall. *Tell me what's happened through our bond.*

I slept with him.

Well that explains the volume she's acquired to her hair. What it doesn't explain is her distress.

Cathal's leather and armor creak from how tightly he's wound up. I begin to wonder why my shifter's anguish is causing him such discomfort when Agrippina juts her finger toward Reid, whose lips have curled up anew. *I can hear him, Day! Please tell me you can too?*

Why on earth would me hearing Reid make you feel better?

Because then that would mean he's a Serpent and not my— She squeezes her temples once more and goes back to rocking.

She doesn't need to finish her sentence for me to understand what Reid has become to her. "Reid, can you try to speak into my mind?"

Cathal frowns. Reid does as well.

"It's to make sure you haven't become a Serpent."

"I'm not sure what Agrippina told you," he says in Crow, "but

327

when I said I left my body when she rattled, I didn't literally mean I'd died and changed shifter race."

Since Agrippina is fluent in Crow, his disclosure paints her cheeks red. "I'm aware that you didn't die, you idiot," she snaps. "*Santo Caldrone*, I cannot have a self-centered, promiscuous prick as a mate. I just cannot."

"A *self-centered, promiscuous prick?*" he repeats, grin gone. "You think my dream mate was a pretentious Faerie whose transformation into a Serpent has only made her *more* arrogant?"

Agrippina crosses her arms.

"Should've done more chatting and less banging," Asha, who's stationed herself in the entrance, quips.

Where it brings a smile to my mouth, it merely deepens Agrippina and Reid's matching scowls.

"What's done is done," I murmur.

"What's done can surely be *undone*," Agrippina mutters before gesturing toward us. "I mean look at..." Her voice fritters away when she catches my stricken expression. Or maybe it's Cathal's clenched jaw that makes her mouth stop moving over the dismal reminder of our broken bond. *Ah, shit. I'm so sorry. I forgot and—I'm so sorry.*

It's all right.

"The bond...when exactly did it click into place?" Cathal's timbre is coarser than usual, as though little Cruaih had used his vocal folds as a scratching post.

"When she and I, um..." Reid's light-brown complexion takes on a deeper hue. He scrubs a hand up his face, then through his hair. "After... Well, during, but at the end." He glances toward Agrippina, who smiles now, but like her earlier rocking, it's slightly hysterical.

"You don't need my help," she says, which earns her a scowl. "You're doing a fantastic job of detailing the circumstances."

He releases a shallow growl before blurting out, "We were locked together for a while. That's when it happened."

Agrippina must say something to him, because his cheeks heat some more, and so does his gaze, and then Agrippina is no longer smiling. She's swallowing. Hard.

Cathal grimaces before jutting his chin toward the door and muttering a, "*Labh.*"

Even I know the Crow word for leave.

"Yes. Please," Asha says, a smile digging into her cheeks as she sweeps open the door for Reid and Agrippina. "No hate-fucking in the Kasha. Unless it's *your* Kasha," she adds with a wink in my direction. When I don't reciprocate her pleasant humor, she sighs. "I'll just see myself out."

Enzo? I suddenly call out through the bond.

Yes, Day?

Could you and Taytah...could you communicate inside your minds?

No. Why?

I'll explain in a second but I need to understand one last thing. It's intrusive of me, so forgive me for asking, but I swear it's important. Were your **parts** *ever locked together?*

Our parts?

Your sexual organs.

I'd really prefer not to discuss this with you.

Trust me, I feel the same way.

Then why are you asking?

Because it just happened to Agrippina and Reid, and it opened a mind link between the two of them.

He lapses into silence. So do I.

"Daya?" Cathal touches my elbow, making me jerk back to the here and now.

"Sorry. I was trying to find out if Enzo had experienced this when he slept with"—I grimace—"my grandmother."

"Wouldn't he have told you if he'd been able to communicate with Priya?"

My fingers find their way to the scar on my neck. "I suppose he would have."

Cathal gently shackles my wrist and drags it away before I can scrub the skin raw, and then he's folding his fingers over mine. "The way I see it, this is good news." At my frown, he adds, "Mating bonds only clicking into place through sexual relations. If you don't lay with another man, then I don't lose you."

His logic should appease me, yet I don't feel at piece. No, I feel nervous—anguished, even, because I now know that if our bodies don't mesh like Agrippina's and Reid's, then Cathal Báeinach is well and truly not my mate.

He squeezes our palms together. "Please say something."

I try, but my throat has become so narrow that I can't. Instead I press my body against his, press my cheek against his armor, and sink my hand into Cruaih's long fur.

He sighs and kisses the top of my head. "No amount of magic will make me love you more than I already do, mo mila Sífair."

An easy declaration to utter now, before knowing.

"I hope you feel the same. If you don't—" He inhales a hoarse breath. "If you think the lack of a *knot* will make you love me less, then—"

Before he can suggest we part ways—again—I grip the back of his head and drag his mouth down to mine.

Chapter 54
Zendaya

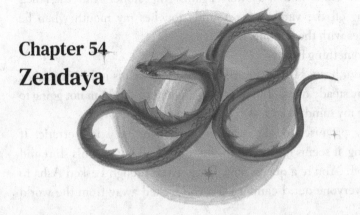

The explosion that happens when our lips connect silences my worries. I suddenly don't care whether our bodies *knot*, because the connection we share is tremendous already. Not only did it survive my transformation, but its intensity has managed to augment in spite of the mind links I forged with others.

He breaks away. "Wait." He suddenly stalks toward the door, but twists back, "Don't move."

All right...

He yanks open the door and calls out Asha's name. Though she slides into my line of sight and I see their mouths move, I cannot grasp their exchange for my pulse thunders in my ears. I fathom it has to do with Cruaih since the little feline ends up nestled against Asha's chest.

Cathal stands there a moment, as though to make sure Asha will treat his companion well. When my guard begins to coo at the tiny thing, which earns her chin a swipe of Cruaih's tongue, the line of Cathal's shoulders slackens and he pivots back toward me, eyes dark with lust. Right before he kicks the door shut, I catch Asha waggling her brows at me. Of course she knows why she was given custody of the Crow's pride and joy.

Cathal stalks back my way, his fingers moving over the straps that keep his breastplate in place. He plucks it off his head, then tosses it aside, and it clatters against the stone. And then he's working off the vambraces. A smile touches my mouth when he struggles with the left one.

"Something funny?"

"Your haste." I step toward him and replace his juddering hands with my steady ones. "I'm not going anywhere. And I'm not going to change my mind," I add, as I slip the leather off his arm.

My promise doesn't turn his movements any less erratic. If anything, it seems to deepen his fervor. He all but rips his shirt and boots off. "You're a queen now, Daya. Even though I asked Asha to keep everyone out, I cannot keep you locked away from the world forever."

My smile topples at the reminder of the responsibility I accepted, and so does my gaze. I stare at the crown glimmering on the velvet, almost wishing—

Cathal brackets my cheeks with his palms, wrenching my gaze off the diamond-tusked serpents. "Don't. Don't wish it away."

"How did you know that's what I was doing?"

"I've seen Lore glare at his crown once or twice over the centuries." He threads his fingers into my hair. "You might not be as free as you'd like, but you *can* have it all."

"Even another child of yours?" I ask, stroking up the hard ridges of his clenching abdomen.

"Yes," he says, his heart clocking the pads of my fingers as they venture higher.

Though his chest isn't smooth, the hair's scarcer than on his jaw. "You're no longer worried about it being born a monster?"

"No child of yours could ever be a monster."

When my palms scrape over his dark nipples and they contract into tiny buds, he shudders. "I hope you'll still think this way when we give birth to a winged Serpent or a scaled Crow."

Laughter suddenly spills from his mouth. It's such a sultry, foreign sound that it momentarily distracts me from my exploration. When he grows serious, I instantly miss his carefree joy.

"I love you, Zendaya of Shabbe, no matter what happens next. No matter if our bodies knot, or if my seed takes."

"Why wouldn't it take? We're not that different biologically, are we?"

"No." He shrugs one of the huge, rounded shoulders my nails are now cresting. "But I've seen my fair share of couples struggle with having children over the years."

"We've already done it once."

He rolls his lips, probably to stop himself from reminding me that I was a different person then. Before he can say this out loud, before old-Daya can encroach on this moment, I slant my mouth over his.

She's no longer here; *I* am. My kiss softens his body. Well, his face. The rest of him has grown as hard as stone. His beard chafes my chin and cheeks as he deepens the kiss, reaching his tongue into every dark corner of my mouth. He's wild and unbridled, a surging current muscling everything out of its path to reach my heart and my soul.

I don't even realize that I've started rattling until I feel his lips quirk into a pleased grin. He pulls away. I start to protest, but my objection morphs into quivering breaths, because he's kissing his way down my neck, his fingers working the braided straps of my gown off my shoulders which he peppers with kisses next.

I don't think I can rattle any harder, but manifestly, I'm wrong, for when he leans over to tongue my bared nipples, my body all but blurs from how hard I shake. I suddenly worry it will put him off and hunt what I can see of his face. His eyes lock with mine as he continues to lavish my hardened peaks, his big hands gripping my waist to keep me flush with his mouth.

He doesn't look disgusted. Keeping one palm on his bare shoulder for balance, I thread my fingers through his black locks and tug gently. He moans and the tremor that passes between his teeth increases the headiness of his ministration.

His hands wander toward the bow that holds my wrap dress closed. One tug and the silver silk splits open. He leans back, drawing the shimmering folds wider and wider, until they drape from my elbows and expose my front. As he contemplates my nakedness, he inhales deeply, then exhales even deeper.

His fingers, that are as callused as mine will surely become from bloodcasting, skip over my pebbling flesh, sketching my paler scars and my heaving breasts, before capering along the runnel of my ribs toward the silken triangle that is as soft as it is sheer. Instead of rolling it off me, he crouches lower and knuckles it, his breathing growing so abundant that his exhalations feel like caresses.

I keep stroking his hair. Watching him watch me stirs my blood, making it swirl more briskly through my veins.

"Just as fucking perfect as I remember," he rasps, his knuckle curving lower and lower, filling me with foreign sensations that are wreaking havoc on my pulse. "Has anyone explored this body?"

I moan when he hits a particularly sensitive and wonderful spot. "No."

My body, which had gone still, suddenly begins to rattle against his crooked finger, and holy Mahananda... I grip his hair as fire streaks through my veins and ignites me.

I gasp out his name, then pant, "What was *that*?"

"Haven't *you* explored your body?"

"No," I croak, as moisture and heat pool low, bleeding into the silk between my thighs.

"Why the Cauldron not?"

"Lack of time." I nip my lip, then release it. "Lack of guidance."

For some reason, my answer makes him rise, his palms shaping the outside of my body before returning to my waist and perching there.

"Had I known there was such a pleasurable spot, I would've taken the time to ask for guidance." I smile.

He doesn't. "Then I'm glad you didn't know."

I roll my eyes. "I would've asked Asha or Taytah, not Enzo or Abrax."

His lips still don't bend.

I push on tiptoe and steal a kiss. As I settle back on my heels, I ask, "Oh, jealous one, will you please see to my sexual education?"

That chips at the unyielding line of his mouth. "It'd be my pleasure to bring you pleasure, Sumaca."

He scoops me into his arms, coaxing an amused startle from my mouth, and carries me to the velvet seating. As he lays me out, my dress, which is still hooked to my elbows, settles beneath me like starlit foam.

He drops his knees on either side of my thighs. "It'd be my honor to map out this exquisite body and teach you where the treasure lies."

I observe the muscled quilt of his chest, the dark trail of hair that leads to the bulge straining his leather trousers, the only item of clothing he hasn't parted with. "I want to learn about yours, too." When I reach for him, he snares my wrist.

"Yours first."

I pout. "Can you at least remove them while you instruct me?"

"It's best I don't."

"Why?"

"Because if I free myself, I will end up inside of you."

"Isn't that the destination?"

"Yes. But there are many stops I want to make along the way, and I fear I'll skip over them all if I unleash myself." He plucks my underwear's waistband and rolls it down my thighs. "Legs up."

I oblige, maneuvering my feet between his legs before stretching them up.

Instead of tossing my underwear aside, he balls it in his fist and carries it to his nose. His eyes close on a long, slow inhale.

"What are you doing?" I ask, genuinely intrigued.

"Memorizing your scent."

"Is that a lover thing or a bird-of-prey thing?"

Lids still clasped shut, he smiles. "I wouldn't know. The topic doesn't come up with my friends." He tucks the scrap of silk into the waistband of his pants, then opens his eyes wide and sets them on

335

my center, which he unveils to himself fully by parting my knees as wide as they'll go.

Considering I'm flexible, that is extremely wide.

He swallows, licks his lips, then without looking away from my mound, he commands, "Give me your hand."

I do.

"Point your index finger."

I do.

He carries it to my seam. "Touch."

I am slick and warm and soft like our mollusk-silk garments.

"Trace yourself. All the way to your ass."

My flesh is so pliant and damp that my finger just skids, bumping over one depression and then another. My breath catches but not as hard as when I track my finger back up and bump into a tiny little bead that feels a lot like the retracted tusk on my forehead.

"What's that?" I ask, circling the bead gently.

"That is called a clitoris."

"Hmm," I whisper as I keep circling it. "And everyone has one?"

"Only females."

"You're missing out."

He smiles. When my body begins to rattle, he tucks his fingers around mine and moves them aside.

"Why did you do that?"

"Because my tongue was jealous of your fingers." He carries said-fingers to his mouth and sucks on them.

When his pupils flood his irises, I ask, "Do I taste like the others?"

"What others?"

"I imagine you've had many others."

"Not in the past five centuries. I don't recall their taste, nor do I want to." His timbre is gruff, as though the subject irritates him.

"Do I taste like past-me?"

"You taste like my mate."

I believe he's saying that to settle my qualms that my Serpent scent might not be as appealing.

He plants his palms on either side of my head and bends over my body, taking my mouth in a kiss that tastes like, I suppose, me. His tongue sweeps, his beard chafes. Although that spot between my legs was enthralling, so are his kisses. I scrape my nails over his shoulders, causing his skin to break out in goosebumps. Because he likes it? I pull away to ask.

"I fucking love it," he growls, half in Crow, half in Shabbin.

I smile and scrape more of his back, any place I can reach, which soon becomes only his corded nape as he travels down my body, suckling on my nipples before attending to the puckered areola surrounding them.

"These are called nipples."

My cheeks lift with another smile, another blissful breath. "You taught me that already."

"That's right." He glides lower, stopping only once his head's leveled with my center.

Bracing himself on his forearms, he thumbs apart the plump flaps concealing my shiny trench. "These are called the labia or lips or nethermouth." When he runs his thumbs down their underside, my body jerks. "Or you can simply refer to them as *mine* from now on." He smiles.

This time, I'm the one incapable of bending my lips.

I gasp when his thumb circles the first puckered hole. "This is your vaginal opening, the place in which I will be sheathing my cock for as long as I have cock to sheath."

"Why wouldn't you have cock to sheath?" I croak, my voice coming out in bursts, because he's dipped his finger inside and is gyrating it as though to widen the hollow. "Are you afraid someone may slice it off?"

"No. That isn't one of my fears." He glides his wet finger to the next hole. "I might penetrate this one eventually as well."

I hope he means with his pinkie because there's no way the cock I spied when I healed him will ever fit inside.

"Some females are quite partial to rectal penetration."

I'm tempted to ask if I was once partial to it but decide I don't want to know what old-Daya was like. I don't want him to start comparing me to her and find me lacking.

He rests his cheek on the inside of my thigh as he guides his finger back out and up. When he hits that tiny hooded bead, I flop back and gaze at the stars beyond the glass ceiling. "Great Mórrígan, how I've missed you, *moannan*."

The Crow word for mate makes my heart ache because what if I'm not? He says he'll still want me, but what if he doesn't? What if it's the resemblance to the Shabbin Princess he loved and the possibility that we might be mates that powers his hunger?

"Look at me."

I stare at his ghostly reflection that's blurring from my sudden surge of panic.

"Not at my likeness in your skylight, Daya. At *me*."

With a swallow and a quick bat of my lashes, I stare down the length of my abdomen. Of course he spots the unnatural luster of my eyes. Of course he doesn't mistake it for anything other than what it is. He reaches for my hand and twines our fingers.

"You and I, we start here. We start now."

Chapter 55
Cathal

Zendaya bites her lower lip, denting the flesh that's still reddened by my kisses. I'm tempted to scale her body and force her teeth off her pretty mouth before she injures it, but I also sense a kiss won't blow her torment away. I'm uncertain how she'll react if our broken bond doesn't mend. The only thing I'm certain of is that I'll yearn for this woman until my last breath. Every part of her.

I place a kiss on the inside of her thigh, then higher, on her bare, glistening cunt that smells like honeysuckle floating atop the ocean, floral with a hint of brine. In truth, I don't remember how she tasted before, only that I'd loved every lick and swallow. I curl my tongue to slot it deeper, noting that this hasn't changed. She still tastes like the most delectable treat, one I plan to spend an inordinate amount of time feasting on. She clutches my hand so hard that her nails dig into my skin. One glimpse of them and my painfully hard cock swells up some more.

When she begins to rattle, rubbing her body quicker against my tongue, I hold still, making sure the flat of it remains at the perfect angle and within reach.

That is certainly different. Though Crows do rattle to attract their mate's attention, not only do our bodies not blur, but it lasts a mere heartbeat. Serpents, I've come to discover, can barely cease rattling. I found Zendaya captivating when she was only Shabbin, but now, she's become another level of fascinating. Goddess below, I cannot fucking wait to see how she will feel wrapped around my cock.

The friction of her body against my mouth has her detonating far too soon. After she screams my name and creams my tongue, I place languid kisses around her drenched slit, giving her time to calm before the next climax. Which, again, surges through her far too quickly.

"Cathal...I don't...I can't..." Her forearm is draped across her eyes, her bright hair a tangled mess, her thighs chafed crimson by my beard.

I make a note to trim it. "Just one more." I thumb her apart and barely nip at her throbbing, swollen bud before her spine arches and she bastes my tongue.

Like promised, I stop tormenting her and climb back up her sweat-slicked curves. "I understand why everyone..." She inhales deeply, which makes her nipples drag across my chest. "Is doing this."

"Doing *this*?"

"Laying together"—a second deep breath—"naked."

Between the press of her nipples, the scrape of her nails which she's now spiraling up my biceps, and the taste of her, I'm two point one seconds away from blowing my load. I need a release before penetrating her or she'll find the act massively underwhelming. I'm about to head to the ensuite bathroom when her body goes stiff beneath mine.

I check her eyes, assuming the Cauldron has whisked her away again—another thing that's going to require some getting used to— but they haven't gone white with magic. When she sucks in a breath, I realize she must be mind-speaking with her Serpents.

Though I'd have preferred they didn't intrude, I have to admit their timing isn't too dreadful. If they'd tried to contact her before, I may have hunted them down.

"What is it?" I ask softly.

"Behati and Kanti's ship has reached the western wall. They're demanding entry."

"Turn them away," I say, peeling myself off her to hunt down my shirt.

"On what grounds? The Mahananda communicates with Behati, Cathal. If she were wicked, it would stop."

"Perhaps, it did." I yank the black fabric over my head, then hook on my armor. The day the Cauldron offered to break our obsidian curse, I'd had such high hopes to retire the heavy metal plating my chest. "Ask it." I don't bother with the vambraces, which I only wear to keep my shirt sleeves from ripping. Now that I live in the land of sorceresses where snags and tears can be mended with drops of blood, I've no more use for them.

"It's resting."

It's always fucking resting. If only we two-legged mortals and immortals possessed such a luxury, but no. There's no rest for the lot of us. Never has been and never will be. Especially now that my mate's queen.

Yes, my mate. Whether preordained or not, we're mates, and from this moment on, I'll refer to her as such.

"Who contacted you to tell you of their presence in Shabbin waters?"

"Enzo. He's fording up one of the Sahklare as we speak."

"On a ship, I hope."

"I think one tendu encounter was enough to last him a lifetime." She's refastened the ties of her dress that bears a wet spot under her ass.

I should mention it. I really should; but I'm the maker of that wet spot. Besides, since the fabric is slightly pleated, it's only noticeable if one focuses on her backside. If I catch any gaze straying there—

"Cathal?"

"Hmm."

"My undergarment, please."

She holds out her palm.

I reach up and slot my fingers through hers, and then I carry her knuckles to my lips and press a kiss to them. "I'll take extra good care of it."

"Seriously?"

"*Tà, moannan,*" I say in Crow, before finishing my sentence in Shabbin. "Seriously."

The word *mate* in my tongue heightens the already rosy hue of her cheeks. My woman glows especially bright tonight. I must pleasure her more often. "Fine. Let's hope it isn't too gusty out on the water." She smiles as she strides toward her doors.

For a heartbeat, I almost give in and tender the scrap of silk, but the knowledge that she's bare under all that silver will be my only ray of fucking sunshine until we retire for the evening, together, in her chamber.

Right before she opens the door, I readjust my tender cock, then scrub a hand across my beard and through my hair.

"There's a small bathing chamber through that door," Daya points out.

"I'm aware."

"Would you like to use it before we set off?"

"No." When a slender vertical furrow appears between the bridge of her nose and her pearl, I explain, "Your scent will keep me calm. You'll be glad I didn't wash it off."

She shakes her head, then smooths a hand down her dress, blanching when she feels the wet spot. "Great Mahananda, is that...?" When I laugh softly and reassure her that it'll dry, she skewers me with a look. "I cannot voyage through the queendom looking like such a mess. The Shabbins already don't have much regard for me. What will they think?"

That pisses me off. "I don't want you to care what they think. As for their regard, if they have two braincells to rub together, they'll see mighty fast what a Cauldron-send you are to Shabbe. To the entire world."

Though she gives her head another shake, a phantom smile plays on her kiss-chapped lips. "Objectivity isn't your forte, is it, mate?"

I don't just smile; I grin. "I'm tremendously unbiased, mo mila Sifair."

She laughs as she steals her hand from mine to put some order in her wild locks. She begins to reach for the door, when I stride back to the sofa and scoop up her crown. As I carry it over, I rub my thumb over the carved golden scales and tusk-shaped diamonds. Like Lorcan's, I suspect this one was forged inside the Cauldron, for no artisan has this much talent.

"You won't have to wear it forever, but you should wear it tonight. Just in case Behati or Kanti have their doubts about who the Cauldron chose as a successor."

The mention of a successor collapses Zendaya's happiness.

"Priya bound your magic," I remind her.

"Yet I still loved her."

I sigh as I place the crown atop her head, and then I crook a finger beneath her chin to carry her eyes to mine. "My mother used to say that death made saints out of sinners, for she never had more regard for my lowlife father than after his passing." I lean over to kiss her one last time before the world rushes in with all its tribulations.

"She saved my life in Isolacuori."

"She wouldn't have had to if she'd made you immortal."

Daya flattens her lips. Though I sense she wants to make more apologies for the deceased queen, she doesn't. She stays quiet.

Too quiet.

Granted, I fly her to the beach, so it isn't as though we can converse when I'm in this form. But even after we land on the strip of pink sand beside Asha, who flew over on Aoife, and Agrippina, who flew atop Reid, Daya remains uncharacteristically laconic. Perhaps I should've shown her some empathy, but falsifying my feelings goes against everything I believe in.

As a smaller vessel is magicked off the wide, pearl-white Nebban ship, fear suddenly percolates through me. What if this new version of my mate never acclimates to my blunt pragmatism? Her past self didn't truly have a choice whether to be with me or not. This Daya does.

What if she decides I'm impossible to live with and love?

Chapter 56
Zendaya

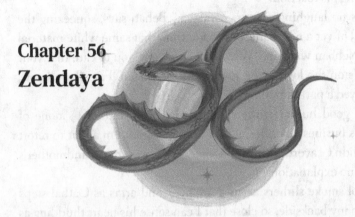

ehati gestures toward the Nebban commander who disembarked with her, along with seven Faeries in forest-green military regalia. All of them have pointy ears and long braids, and all of them are staring at me—mostly at my uncommon eyes and retracted tusk, but my crown also proves an object of great interest.

Nevertheless, no one stares at it more than Kanti. I don't think she's blinked away from it once since I dismounted Cathal. I feel sorry for my cousin, and genuinely hope that, in time, she'll manage to stop coveting it since I've no plans to hand it over. Not for the foreseeable future anyway, and never to her.

Better lock up that crown when you're not wearing it, Agrippina singsongs into my mind.

From how close Reid stands to her, I take it they've made peace. *Mates...* Though I don't need a magical bond to feel sure of Cathal's feelings, I hold out hope that he is my mate. He may claim it won't change anything, but I sense he needs the peace of mind that I'll not wander into someone else's bed.

Perhaps I should suggest marriage. That would appease him. If I do, though, I'd need to suggest it before we lay together so he doesn't view it as some consolation prize. Yes, as soon as we're done here, I'll ask him to marry me. I find my mood perking up, already imagining his reaction.

"It's no laughing matter, Zendaya," Behati says, squeezing the pommel of yet a new cane, one made from that same white material as the Nebban warship. "Why am I expecting you to care that your mother's on the loose? She just made you queen. For all we know, you played a part in freeing her."

My good humor withers. In a way, I did, but that's none of anyone's business. Besides, it was unintentional. I'm about to retort that I didn't cavort with my mother, but I owe my grandmother's advisor no explanation.

Cool smoke slithers around my neck and arms as Cathal steps closer to my backside, so close that I can sense his heart thudding as fast as mine through the armor pressed along my spine.

"The Mahananda made me queen, Behati. All my mother did was make me immortal."

Clearly, Behati hasn't learned of my immortality, for my words blow her pupils wide. Kanti's, as well. When the two exchange a look, I start to question the intent of their voyage. But another musing takes precedence over this one.

"Did you know that Priya had bound me?" I ask.

"With what? Rope?" Kanti asks.

Not the shiniest jewel on the crown, that one, huh? Agrippina's comment beams a sliver of light on my darkened mood.

"Behati?" I prompt when the pale-haired sorceress has still not replied. "Were you aware that Priya bound my Shabbin magic?"

She scoffs. "She's been gone one day, and already you've renounced your kinship."

What in the realm does she mean?

"How Daya processes her grief is none of your concern," Cathal growls. "Now bloody answer her question before I—"

"Before you what, Cathal?" Behati's eyes are narrowed. "Before you try to drag it out of me with an iron talon? I'm Shabbin."

A boat pops out of the ramparts, right behind the Nebbans. They jump and scatter when the sand liquefies into a watery trench linking the Sahklare to the open sea. I suppose that, because of my mother's wards, none have ever witnessed how ships sail out of Shabbe.

Enzo hops out, eyes glossed with a mixture of anguish and anger. Though he begged me to wait when he caught us soaring over the ship, we didn't. Partly because I wanted to expedite this meeting, partly because being immortal has boosted my confidence to dangerous levels, and partly because the Mahananda said that, to replace Behati as its seer, she'd either need to name her successor and enter the Mahananda with her chosen, or breach the covenant she and it struck, at which point the Mahananda would bestow the gift upon another.

"Did you. Bloody. Know?" Cathal all but shouts.

I reach behind me until I locate his clenched fist. Instantly, his fingers fall open and seize mine. I draw little arcs across his skin with my thumb in the hopes of calming him.

"Yes," Behati blusters back. "Yes, I knew."

Kanti whirls toward her, her unbound locks swirling and smacking the nude silk gloving her hourglass figure.

"Why do you think it took so long to cure your people of their curse? The Mahananda wasn't only depleted, it was angry. Even after Priya explained her reasons for doing what she did."

"Which were?" I ask.

"Your grandmother wanted to ensure that the creature the Mahananda delivered into her queendom was worthy of immortality."

Cathal's fingers clamp around mine. I draw more arcs, hoping to allay his tension and communicate through touch how unaffected I am by Behati's opinion of me. I don't need her regard or her affection, not as long as I have the Mahananda's, Cathal's, Fallon's, and my Serpents'.

"*The creature?*" Agrippina crosses her arms and cocks an eyebrow.

"Here we go," Reid murmurs, his tone tinged with amusement.

I suppose he's used to Agrippina's strong opinions by now and is glad they're not directed at him for once.

"Sorry," Behati mutters, not sounding apologetic. "The new shifter breed."

"May I enquire after the reason for your rushed return, Behati?" I ask pleasantly, even though I don't feel pleasant.

The seer's mouth pops wide. "This is our home, Daya. How dare you ask for the reason of our return!"

"Many are displeased with the Mahananda's choice," I say. "Many left."

"I trust the Mahananda had Shabbe's best interest at heart when it crowned you," Behati says. It sounds like a blatant lie. Like she thinks the source of all magic made a mistake.

"What about you?" I tip my head to Kanti as I scrutinize her cruel but lovely face. "Do you trust the Mahananda?"

"I trust it picked you for a reason."

I snort.

"What?" she snaps.

Still sweeping my thumb over Cathal's hand, I ask, "Could the reason be that I was there and you weren't?"

She snags a long black strand and tucks it forcefully behind her ear that shimmers with emeralds. "I'd be lying if I said no. For years, I've been trained for this position. You've only just flopped into this world. So yes, I find it unfair." Smoothing one hand down the side of her dress, she adds, "But like Taytah, I trust the Mahananda."

"I appreciate your honesty, Kanti."

You're not actually considering letting them in? Enzo asks.

I'm not considering it, Enzo. I am letting them in. Why?

For several reasons. One, we're immortal, so we've nothing to fear. Two, I've asked the Mahananda and Behati remains our seer. I proceed to tell him the rest of it. *Of course my wish is that she'll bequeath the task to another soon. Ideally, you or Agrippina, but we cannot force her hand. We can hope for her to err though.*

Can you imagine if she gives the power to Kanti?

I trust the Mahananda wouldn't allow such an egocentric person to carry its messages.

What if Behati doesn't share her visions with us?

By touching her forehead, I've access to all she sees.

What if she doesn't let you touch her forehead?

Then I'll force her to touch mine. Ultimately, she has no choice, Enzo, for keeping her visions from the queen is a breach which will cost her the sight.

He purses his lips, seemingly unconvinced.

"Commander Fordal is itching to return to Nebba. He needs to know whether he sets sail with us or not," Behati says.

I like that she doesn't assume I'll let her and Kanti stay. As for Commander Fordal, I believe he itches to leave because of all the tusks carving through the moonlit waters of Samurashabbe. He keeps staring at them. At the sky, too, for that matter. I only now notice an influx of large black birds. Cathal must've requested some extra sky guards on our way over. "Tell Commander Fordal that he and his crew can set out."

"With us or without us?" Behati repeats.

I gesture to our Shabbin vessel. "With Kanti, but without you."

"We either enter together, or we leave—*together*."

"You are the Mahananda's seer," I say.

Behati's eyes seem incandescent behind her white bangs. "I'm aware, but I can see just fine from anywhere in the realm."

I hate her implicit threat. "Fine, but if Kanti tries to hurt me or mine, then she'll step into the Mahananda."

Behati purses her lips. "She'll be on her best behavior. Right, Kanti?" When Kanti doesn't confirm this, Behati repeats her question with a snap. "Right?"

"Of course, Taytah." She rolls her eyes. "I will always do what's best for the Mahananda."

I nod farewell to the Nebban commander, who sketches a reverential bow, and then I turn toward Enzo and ask him to escort the women. "Behati, your palace wing is in shambles. You're welcome to stay in Priya's bedchamber until yours is fixed."

"My grandmother's dwelling is destroyed?" Kanti shrills. "Who would do such a thing?"

I release Cathal's fingers so he can morph into a Crow like Aoife and Reid. "The prisoner she stowed beneath her bed. Or perhaps, Justus. I didn't have time to enquire."

Kanti grips her grandmother's bony arm. "Taytah, what if this is an ambush? What if Meriam and Justus are down there waiting for us? What if Daya's leading us straight to them?"

"They're not down there." Behati lifts a hand to her chest and rubs, as though her heart were aching.

"How can you be so sure?"

"Because Meriam owed me a favor, and I claimed it. She cannot harm me or any descendant of mine."

I wonder when the seer claimed this bargain—when she heard Meriam had broken free, or when she imprisoned her in a cell beneath her bed?

As I climb up my mate's wing, I turn back toward Enzo. *Have them and their trunks searched for any suspect powder or vial.*

He glances at the six trunks two gray-eyed Faeries are floating off the shiny white Nebban ship and onto the wooden Shabbin one.

I'm sorry for saddling you with them, Enzo.

He stares at me, then at Cathal. *You have a mate now.* That is all he says, and he says it so flatly, it makes my heart twinge.

I send down a prayer to the Mahananda that he finds his other half soon. One worthy of him.

Chapter 57
Zendaya

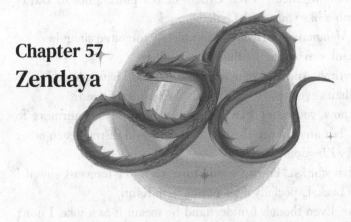

All three Crows land in the courtyard. *Four...* Aodhan has joined us. He touches two fingers to his forehead and flicks them in that same odd gesture Cathal did once. "You got it, boss bird."

At my frown, Cathal presses his palm to the small of my back and leans over to murmur, "I've tasked him with keeping Kanti entertained."

Reid coughs a word that's foreign to me into his fist, which makes Aodhan's grin burn brighter.

"Have you seen Kanti?" The Crow no one can seem to stand flicks back a lock of midnight hair. "It's not exactly a punishment."

"Gods, you and her are like the same person," Agrippina says.

I catch a soft smile playing on Aoife's lips. I take it that she agrees.

"I'll choose to take that as a compliment seeing as Kanti is hot as fuck." He waggles his eyebrows at Agrippina. "Admit that you're disappointed the Cauldron didn't mate you with me."

She bursts out laughing, which makes Reid grin smugly. I glance up at Cathal whose expression wavers between amusement and nerves. When he senses my stare, he wheedles the corners of his mouth up. I wish he didn't feel the need to fake anything with me.

Asha appears beside us, her eyes bright in spite of the dark circles rimming them. "I fed Cruaih before putting her in Daya's bedchamber like you asked, Cathal."

Oh, Mahananda, Cruaih! I'd completely forgotten about her.

"Thank you, Asha," Cathal says.

"Anytime. And I mean it, *anytime.* She and I have a bond."

Aodhan's eyebrows wiggle again. "What sort of bond?"

"I know you want him to distract Kanti," she murmurs to Cathal, "but any chance the two of them could distract each other in the Sky Kingdom?"

Cathal smirks. "Lorcan would turn me into a forever-Crow if I sent him back. Especially if I sent him with Kanti."

I hiss. Even though I understand he meant it as a joke, I don't like the mention of dying, not even in jest.

He slides his palm to my waist and gathers me against him, then places a soothing kiss against my temple.

"I heard that, Cathal," Aodhan says, with a tilt of his chin and a scowl that leads me to think his arrogance isn't entirely impermeable.

"If you stopped flirting with every woman in a one-mile radius— especially the mated ones"—Cathal's fingers crinkle the silver pleats of my dress—"Lorcan and I would hold you in higher esteem."

"Not my fault the ladies find me so irresistible."

"I hear Glace is lovely at this time of year," Asha says, which makes Cathal's lips curl.

"I prefer my dick not to turn into an icicle, thank you very much."

Asha sighs as though greatly aggrieved by his refusal to relocate. "I'll hold the fort down until Abrax gets back. Now off to bed, imNaage. And I do mean to sleep." She gives Cathal a pointed look that makes his fingers crimp my waist a little harder.

Since no one intimidates the male, I deduce that his sudden edginess comes from within.

"Reid and I are going to get some food. Should we send anything to your room, Daya?" Agrippina asks.

"No. Thank you." Right before slipping past Asha, I wind my arm around her shoulders and hug her tight. "You, too, need your sleep. It's been a *long* twenty-four hours."

She pats my back. "As soon as Abrax returns, Sumaca."

Right before I pull away, I remind her, "Day or Daya, or even imNaage, just never Sumaca."

She smiles, then with a wink, she says, "Fine. I'll only use your title when I'm mad at you."

I snort as Cathal tugs me away. "You're often mad at me."

Her smile grows. "By the way, I know you can bloodcast now, but I added a few wards around your wing that should last until sundown, even though I'll be back by then. Promise."

"She should be part of your Akwale," Cathal murmurs as he cracks open my door and crouches. I'm guessing he sensed Cruaih was waiting right behind it.

"She is. I asked her this morning. Along with Agrippina and Enzo," I say, closing my door. I reach up and push my finger against one of the two diamond tusks. When the skin tears, I bring my finger to the door and paint the sigil that will prevent anyone from bursting inside. "Tamar elected to retire—she may have stayed but I don't think she likes me very much." I try not to let her opinion affect me. "Asha's suggested two new Shabbin candidates. I asked her to bring them over in the morning."

As Cathal scratches Cruaih's neck, his throat works over a deep swallow. "Your Akwale will be formed in no time."

I suck on my fingertip as I study the crinkled corners of his eyes and the deep hollows beneath his bladed cheekbones. Does he think I'll send him home once I've assembled my government?

I walk over to him and seize his jaw, then angle his face toward mine. "Cathal Báeinach, I know Taytah ruled alone, but I don't want that. I want a king at my side. *Forever* at my side." My proposal's met with complete silence. "Please say yes."

"Old-Daya told me that I couldn't be king for I'd terrorize the Shabbins."

A jolt of anger swarms me, and I let go of his face. "Old-Daya isn't me."

Cathal's silent, probably lost in thought about this mate who apparently loved him but not enough to make him king. As I remove my dress and climb into bed, I hear water running in my bathing chamber. Is he thinking of *her*? I wait and wait, and still he doesn't join me in bed. Does he plan on spending his entire night hiding from me?

Exhaustion collapses my lids before the Crow has joined me in bed. But when I wake, he's there, lying next to me, Cruaih curled up on his pillow. Though he said he wouldn't be sleeping while I did, he sleeps as soundly as his kitten. I watch as the sun crawls beneath my curtains and scratches over his form. Oddly enough, it's only once it reaches his face and dances over his jaw that I realize he's reduced his wild beard to a mere stubble.

He must sense me watching him because his lashes flutter and then his head turns. He sits up so suddenly that Cruaih lets out a little yelp. "*Focá*. I didn't mean to nod off."

"My chambers are warded."

"Still, I shouldn't have fucking passed out." He scrubs his eyes that are bare of their usual black stripes.

I wouldn't say the male seems younger without a beard and makeup, but he does look different—less terrifying. The thought carries me back to the last thing he said the night before. I decide not to let my jealousy encroach on my mood. "Have you thought about my proposal?"

He glances over his large shoulder at me. Though he removed his armor, he's fully clothed. I suppose he didn't want to risk guarding me in the nude. "I have."

"And?"

"You don't need to marry me to ensure I'll stay at your side. I promised I would." His Adam's apple rolls as he sketches the slope of my bare shoulder with his eyes. "I've no intention of breaking my promise to you. Any of my promises."

"I still want to marry you."

With a deep sigh, he lays back on the mattress and turns onto his side, his palm settling on my waist. "I know why you asked me to marry you, Daya. You think a marriage bond will comfort me if our bodies fail to knot."

I'm a little surprised he's guessed my underlying intent. Actually. No, I'm not. Cathal Báeinach knows me inside and out.

"Mo mila Sífair, I don't need a matching crown or blood magic to feel confident in your affection. Besides, I've never aspired to marry or to rule a kingdom. Do I worry you'll leave me? Yes. But that's because I lost you once."

"You lost a woman who looked like me. You didn't lose *me*."

He bobs his head, his fingers walking up and down my ribcage.

"Please stop comparing me to her."

His fingers hold still.

"I can't explain why, but it makes me mad." I roll my lips together. "And jealous."

"Done." He starts caressing the edge of my body again.

Wanting to feel his skin on mine, I push down the sheets and nod to his clothes. "Off."

His lips quirk as he sits again and yanks off his shirt. And then he's climbing off the bed, kitten in hand.

I push up onto my forearms. "Where are you going?"

"I don't want to scar little Misery."

I frown until I hear a door click. "You put her outside?"

"In your closet. Her kibbles are there so she's plenty happy." He tugs on the laces of his leather pants. "If she becomes as large as a tendu, I will have words with Asha."

I smile, but then the smile trips off my lips because the male is bare, and I'm overwhelmed by another emotion, one that isn't humor.

His curved cock is so hard it juts out and bobs as he climbs back onto the bed. He settles beside me while I stare at him down there with a mixture of trepidation and anticipation. Mostly the latter.

"Tell me what to do," I ask.

"Wrap your hand around me."

I reach out and curl my fingers around him. His flesh is hot and silken like mine. Unlike mine, though, it pulses as though his heart dwells there.

"Why did you shave your beard?"

He slides one hand between my thighs. "So I don't irritate your delicate skin next time I go down on you."

"It didn't hurt."

"It was too red for my liking." He scrubs a hand across his jaw. "If you prefer me with a beard, I'll let it grow out again."

"You look handsome with it and without it. I've no preference." When my thumb grazes his engorged tip, it comes away damp.

Cathal's breath catches. "Actually. Change of plans, my Sweet Serpent," he says in rapid-fire Crow, shackling my wrist and tugging it away.

I quirk a brow. "Why? Was I doing it wrong?"

"Daya, you could jab your fingernail into my cock, and I'd still come. You could never do anything wrong."

"Then why are you pushing me away?"

"Because I want to last once I get inside of you." He sucks on his fingers and then reaches between my legs and slicks his saliva over me.

I don't know why he feels the need to dampen me considering how wet my core already is, but I don't ask, getting lost in the sensation he kindles. My heart begins to palpitate as eagerly as the rest of my body, which leads me to climax against his skilled fingers in no time.

"To think I'm going to get to do this every single fucking day of my life," he murmurs around a pleased smile.

As my body settles around the lazy strokes he now draws up and down my folds, he explains that it might hurt when he gets inside me, if the Mahananda revirginized me. At my quirked brow, he clarifies what that means. I suddenly hope that the Mahananda did revirginize me, so that it doesn't feel like a recycled body to Cathal.

I smooth a black curl off his forehead. And then I scoot closer, still on my side, and seal my mouth against his. His lips part mine, and then his tongue surges in and caresses. For a moment, his hand stops moving over me and he loses himself in our kiss, but then he begins to caress again, targeting that hole he plans on stretching.

When he dips his finger inside, my body gives an involuntary jerk that makes me click my teeth around his tongue, not hard enough to draw blood but hard enough to make me break the kiss and swing my gaze down our bodies to check that it was his hand and not his cock. And yes...it's his hand.

"Do you want me to stop?" he asks, worry scoring his features.

"No. Do it again."

His finger glides back in, a little farther this time. When I grit my teeth and clench around him, he sighs.

"What? Are you afraid my body won't fit yours?"

A corner of his mouth tugs up. "No."

"Then why did you sigh?"

"Because I'm worried that our first time will be uncomfortable for you."

Relief floods me and I expel an almost violent breath. One that turns a little choppy when Cathal starts strumming my clitoris, all the while spearing me with his finger, going deeper with every flick of his wrist.

Predictably, I start to rattle. There is *no* pain. At least, none I can feel over the pleasure coursing through my veins, propelling heat low in my belly. Though the male doesn't paint me with any sigils, I burn and shake. I seize his shoulder that pops with muscle and hold on as he thrusts and teases.

The pleasure that streaks through me is brighter, rougher, headier. It wrenches a scream from my lungs, one that's so shrill, I worry it'll fissure the ceiling tiles. I flop onto my back and just lay there, attempting to catch my breath as Cathal carries his hand to his face.

I think he's about to lick my juices off like he did last night, but instead he just studies his fingers. "What?" When I notice a smear of black on his middle finger, I prop myself onto my forearm, almost toppling against him. "Where did that blood come from?" I frown, sweeping the covers fully off myself, because—

"When a woman's hymen tears, she bleeds." Twin spots of red bloom over his cheekbones. "Or so I've heard. I've never deflowered a virgin."

I'm inordinately glad to learn that this is going to be a first for him like it is for me. He wipes his finger down his muscled thigh, smearing my watery blood against the skin I once healed, which still bears a puckered scar, and then he flops onto his back. "Climb on top of me. I want you in control."

I kneel, wrinkling my nose at the gray mess on my pristine sheets, then carefully swing one leg over him, keeping my hips high. The head of his cock is puffed and shiny, pointed upward, in the direction it wants to go.

He braces his large, callused palms under my backside. "When you're ready, just guide me in."

His chest grows still when I curl my fingers around the veined flesh and brush him across my folds, moistening him some more. And then I hold him at my entrance and lock my stare with his. Cathal's eyes are dark with anticipation yet bright with an emotion that weaves itself around my ribs and swathes my heart.

"I love you," he says suddenly. Though he doesn't add, "Whatever happens next," I hear the words. Or maybe I make them up. Perhaps I'm the only one inherently worried about what's about to happen...or *not* happen.

I want to return his words to make sure he knows that I feel the same, but my throat is so tapered I can barely levy air. What little of it I manage to reel in escapes as I lower my hips and he breaches my walls. I stop when I reach my fingers that are strangling his poor, throbbing cock. Fearing I'm hurting him, I spring them wide. I gasp then, because we're both so slick that I'm in freefall. By the time Cathal realizes I don't mean to sheath him inside of me so precipitously, I've slammed all the way down to his root.

"Sorry. *Focá*. Are you all right?"

I swallow, trying to gather my wits. He wasn't jesting when he mentioned there might be a little discomfort.

"Príona?" His stomach muscles clench as he rolls up, changing the angle of his penetration. "Please say something."

"I'm"—I claw at his shoulders as though I were part tendu instead of part Serpent—"fine."

His lips twist. "Clearly." He begins to lift me, but I push back down.

"I'm fine," I all but growl.

"Tears are spilling out of your eyes. You're not *fine*."

"I am," I grit out.

"It'll feel better next time."

"No."

"It will."

"I wasn't saying no to how it will feel. I'm saying I want to stay on your cock until you get your release." *I want our bond to form.*

"Because you think I could come knowing that I'm causing you pain?" He shakes his head, then thumbs my cheeks to clear away the dampness.

"At least try," I croak.

"No. Not this morning." He disengages himself from me but doesn't lift me off his lap. Instead, he winds his arms around me and holds me against him until the tears stop tripping past my lashes.

Stupid tears.

If only I hadn't wept like some injured creature.

If only he could've come immediately.

If only we could've known...

Chapter 58
Zendaya

I go for a swim in scales after our disastrous attempt at lovemaking. Cathal flies overhead as I muscle through the Amkhuti, past clouds of shimmering minnows, past clumps of rainbow coral, past a white stick. Not a stick. A cane. I almost miss it for the coral it sits on is as white as bone.

I nudge the cane with my nose to jimmy it out and am about to carry it back to the surface when the current tumbles the body of a barracuda my way. The listless body. Imagining it scuffled with another fish, I inspect its flesh for teeth marks but find none. Perhaps it died of old age. Its seems rather small to be old, but like land creatures, not all sea creatures have the same shape or size. I let it be, knowing it will be nibbled on by others. The ocean only ever takes to give back. I cast one last look at the cane that now rests at an angle, bubbles springing from its hollow center. Such an odd design for a cane. Then again, the Nebbans had an odd boat.

I resume my lap. I'm almost back to my starting point when I spot green coils on the sand. *Enzo?*

His lids open at the sound of my voice.

Did you sleep down here all night?
I did. Too much noise next door.
Noise?

Agrippina and Reid. I can't tell if they're murdering each other or having a blast.

I'll have your things relocated to another wing of the palace. Your own wing.

His eyes grow huge. *Day, that's too much. I could never—*

You could and you will. And if someday you want to share it, then you'll get to choose your wingmates.

Serpents don't weep, yet Enzo looks on the brink of tears.

Now that that's settled, Asha mentioned two contenders for the Akwale. I want you to meet with them.

Sorceresses?

Yes.

Is Tamar one of them?

No. She hasn't shown any interest in being part of my coven. Which is probably for the best since I'm not certain I'd trust her, I add with a sigh.

Do we need sorceresses?

Yes.

All right. Enzo bobs his big green head. He may be healed, but his body—in both forms—still bears the bite marks of the tendu attack. *But Serpents cannot be in the minority. Do you give me permission to recruit contenders for our species?*

Explain.

We announce that we're looking to make new Serpents.

I really doubt the Shabbins—

I'm not talking about spreading the word in Shabbe. After a beat, he adds, *Perhaps your mate could help us?*

The mention of my mate tosses me back to this morning and dulls my mood.

Enzo tilts his long head. *Everything all right?*

Yes.

Liar.

Since I don't intend to share the reason my heart feels as dense and sharp as my tusk, I say, *The word will be spread.*

And it is. When after two days no one comes, Enzo questions whether Cathal actually did broadcast it. Which of course does nothing for their relationship besides damage it further. My Crow mate is so angry that he spends his night in feathers. We haven't had time alone since the morning I bled and cried. I think he keeps his distance on purpose. He may claim he desires me to heal, but deep down, I think he, too, has qualms about completing the act.

When he finally returns, it's with Connor, Phoebus, Fallon, and Ceres. We don't get a second alone after that. Though I love every moment of the two days I spend with my daughter, catching up on anecdotes from Luce and poring over the pages of her beautiful Serpent dictionary—which I acted surprised upon receiving—though I laugh at Phoebus's nonstop chatter about the newest fashion trend he's created and how it's a great hit with Crow women, but much less so with men, I miss Cathal and am wholly unsatisfied by our snatched glances.

At the end of supper on the second day—another meal Cathal has avoided, claiming business in Luce—Lorcan finally joins us and asks to speak to me in private. Though my daughter frowns at not being included, she takes Ceres by the arm for a promenade through the gardens.

I start to lead Lorcan toward the Kasha, but he has another place in mind—the Chayagali.

"Are you trying to get rid of me?" I ask.

"No." He adds a smile that does little to alleviate my intensifying fear.

"You do realize that tendus are fond of serpent meat?"

"Tendus are the only creatures the Shabbins keep their distance from."

I deduce it isn't Cathal he wants a word about but one of my people.

"I'll keep you safe, Daya." I wait to feel magic cuff my bicep, but Lorcan doesn't add the magical binding words. Cautious man. I'm about to ask him for one, when he leans over and murmurs, "It's about Kanti."

Chapter 59
Zendaya

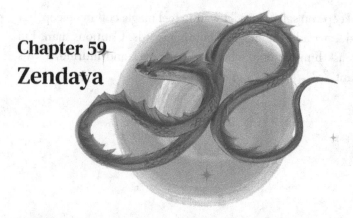

The foliage in the Chayagali is so dense that it traps what little moonlight trickles from the crescent brightening the sky.

"What about Kanti?" I ask Lorcan the second he's in skin.

"You know those listening sigils she drew in Tarespagian homes? She also painted some here. One of them, inside the Kasha. There could be more. If I were you, I'd have the entire castle swept for hidden ones."

After balking, my jaw clinches.

"Anyway... Antoni came to me with something he's overheard. Something which he wants to use as a bargaining chip. Something about my people's curse. I cannot afford to give that male a bargain, Daya. I worry he'd use it to harm my people. I imagined Cathal would know, since he's been assisting you, but he claims the Cauldron told you that there existed no remedy. I'm not sure who to trust. This is why I've brought you here—where no one can eavesdrop—to ask if the Cauldron has offered you a solution to aid my people, or if Antoni's trying to fool me."

Though I hear rustling nearby, I cannot seem to care. I loathed Kanti before, but now...now I want to pitch her into the Mahananda and implore it to keep her there for putting my child in danger.

"There is a solution, isn't there?" Lorcan is inspecting my face. Perceptive male that he is, he adds, "It involves Fallon, doesn't it?"

"Please don't ask me."

"If there was a solution to keep your Serpents safe from that chemical that closes off your airway, wouldn't you do everything in your power to know?"

"Not if it meant harming someone I love." My heated murmur rids his complexion of color.

"Fallon is my mate. If the Cauldron's solution harms her..."

"It does," I say just as a growl sounds beside us.

Lorcan's outline trembles. One of his crows must break away from the others because I suddenly hear a wet snap followed by a muted whine. And then the man is back in sharp focus. "Spare me from accepting Antoni's bargain."

"Then strike one with me. Right here. Right now."

"Fine. Zendaya amMeriam, Queen of Shabbe, I—"

"There's a way to break our curse?" The feminine voice that rings out through the jungle is soon accompanied by the shape of a body.

Two bodies.

I should've known our flight out of the Vahti wouldn't go unnoticed.

"Mádhi?"

I glower at Lorcan for having opened up a box that was safer left sealed.

"I've a right to know," Fallon says, her boots crunching over the silty soil as she moves closer. "*Especially* if it concerns me."

"You said there was no solution, Daya." Cathal's arms are crossed in front of his breastplate that gleams black like his eyes.

"Before you accuse me of keeping secrets from you, know that it was your idea that I strip the Mahananda's words from your mind."

"My idea?" Though I cannot make out his features in the obscurity, I picture him frowning. "Why would I ask you to mess with my mind?" His tone rolls with so much anger that I must be wrong about the frown.

"Because you were afraid Lorcan or Fallon would eventually steal it *from* your mind," I say between barely separated teeth.

"If Antoni knows, others will, too, so please just tell us before he uses it to hurt me or Lore," Fallon beseeches me.

I close my eyes. When another guttural growl resonates nearby, I almost turn and walk straight for the tendu so he could steal me away from the Crows. But I'd only be delaying the inevitable. "Your Crow magic, Fallon. That's the Mahananda's price. You'll lose your ability to shapeshift, to fly, to communicate—"

"Goodness, Mádhi, I thought the cost would be my immortality."

"Perhaps it will be! Perhaps you'll lose your Shabbin magic, too." I toss my hands in the air.

"Did the Cauldron say I would?"

"It didn't speak of your Shabbin magic."

"Then chances are, I'll get to keep it." My daughter, forever the optimist. I wonder who passed this trait down to her, because it certainly isn't me or her father. Perhaps old-Daya was an insufferable optimist.

"Thank you for telling us," Lorcan murmurs.

"It isn't as though I had a choice in the matter," I grumble.

Fallon inhales sharply. "I've a great idea!"

"I'm listening." Lorcan clearly doesn't believe it'll be great for his tone is as bleak as the ambient air.

"If the Cauldron were to remove my Shabbin magic, then Mádhi will make me a Serpent."

My heart holds still.

The whole jungle holds still.

"Fallon, no," I murmur.

"It's my body. My magic. My choice. But most of all, it's my people."

"Fallon, our curse is manageable, thanks to the Serpents." Pain abrades Cathal's inflection.

"Yeah. It just drains Mádhi every time she heals us. What if it ends up draining her completely someday? What if she loses *her* ability to shift?"

I shake my head. "The Mahananda will keep me safe, Fallon."

"Like it kept imTaytah safe?" she volleys back.

I try to catch Lorcan's eye but his stare is fastened to his mate. I hope he's forbidding her from entertaining the idea.

"Fine." Fallon huffs. "But if the Cauldron swears to keep my Shabbin magic *and* our mating link intact, then you will consider it."

"Lore, no…" Cathal's voice is barely above a whisper.

Fallon reaches up and takes Lorcan's face in her hands. "Mara made you king because she knew you would always take care of your people. You owe it to her and to them." After a beat, she says, "I will always be yours, Lore. Albeit less downy, but always yours."

"Tell Fallon that her altruism has just secured both her blood magic and mating link. If they're ready, then I'll welcome the Crow King and his mate tonight." The Mahananda must read my next question, because it says, *"No need for an obsidian blade or your blood, my child. All I've need for is them to enter together."*

"What did the Cauldron say, Daya?" Cathal must've brushed past Lorcan and Fallon because he's suddenly standing right there in front of me.

I inhale deeply. I'm aware the cost of her Crow magic isn't my fault, that it's my grandmother's, but still, it pains me. "The Mahananda has sworn that it will not strip you of either blood magic or mating link. And that it's ready to receive you and Lorcan tonight. I'd tell you to take some time to think about it, but—"

"We can't risk it changing its mind. Besides, what is there to think about?" Fallon's eyes shimmer, and though her lips curve, I sense there's heartache mixed into her relief and enthusiasm.

I may never have dreamed of shifting into a Serpent, but if someone were to strip me of my power now…

"Swear to always carry me on your back, Lore?" Fallon asks, a slight tremor to her pitch.

He must close his eyes for the twin pinpricks of gold vanish. "I hate this."

"I know you do, mo khrá, but it's a small price to pay to keep our people and our kingdom safe."

He shudders. "Zendaya, do you swear to me that this is what the Cauldron said?"

"I know you've been duped before, Lorcan Ríhbiadh, so I won't take offence in your question, but understand that I will *never* intentionally hurt my daughter or your people. *Never.*"

For a long moment, the four of us stand there in the quiet stillness of the Chayagali. Though tendus surely prowl nearby, though my daughter is about to lose her ability to shift, a sense of righteousness drapes over the four of us. I know I'm not the only one to feel it because Lorcan asks Cathal to carry me back, and then he takes off with Fallon for her final flight.

"*Dalich,*" Cathal murmurs, a second before transforming and crouching.

As I climb onto his back, I wonder what he's sorry for—not believing me when I told him it was his idea to be stripped of the memory or avoiding me? I decide to leave it be for now. Once my daughter and her mate reemerge from the Mahananda, safe and sound and immune to obsidian, I'll request that Cathal and I have a long and private conversation.

When we reach the Vahti, Fallon and Lore are already stepping onto the source of all magic. My pulse hitches when they sink, and my fingers tighten around the feathers at Cathal's neck. He cycles over the courtyard. When he doesn't angle lower, I realize he has no intention of landing. I suppose we're just as well off pacing the stars.

I don't blink. Not once. I stare and stare at the opaque silver surface.

Can they see us like I saw them?

Are they in pain?

Why's it taking so long?

It had been much quicker the day Fallon went in on her own, hadn't it?

A ripple disturbs the Mahananda's surface.

And then a head of black hair. Lorcan's.

I wait with bated breath until a second head pierces the surface, and even then, my lungs refuse to contract.

Fallon twirls, surely looking for us.

Lorcan must tell her we're still flying, because she cranes her neck up to find us. I didn't think I still had air in my lungs to breathe out, but I must, for a gasp whooshes out of me when our eyes collide.

Pink.

Her eyes are Shabbin-pink.

Chapter 60
Zendaya

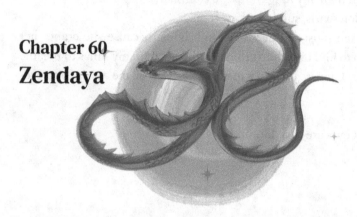

As soon as Cathal lands, we find an obsidian blade. It penetrates Lorcan's skin without even leaving a blemish. Cathal tries it on himself next, choosing to slice across his pinkie this time. He heals instantly. The relief that paints Lorcan's features is only shadowed by the altered hue of his mate's eyes.

"Is pink not your new favorite color, mo khrá?" she teases him.

Like Cathal and me, Lorcan hunts her face for any sign that her cheer is false.

She purses her lips. "All right...can we stop with the pity party you're all throwing me? I've no regrets. *None.*" She says the word *none* in every language, save for Crow, which she no longer understands, but which she's decided to relearn immediately. "I'm extremely serious. If you don't all stop, I will go find Phoebus and a bottle of date wine and—and make new friends."

She starts a countdown. Afraid she truly will up and vanish, I smile and ask her for help canvassing the palace for concealed sigils. We find six—one in the queen's chambers, one in mine, one in the Kasha, one in my Serpents' common room, one in Behati's ruined quarters, and one in Fallon and Lore's wing. I assume there are more.

"How does Kanti still have blood to cast with?" Fallon asks.

As we bleed the walls to cleanse them, I imagine it's Kanti's chest that's bleeding. A terrible but not unwarranted thought.

"Why did you allow her back into Shabbe again, Amma?"

I startle that Fallon uses the Shabbin term for Mother instead of the Crow one before remembering that she must no longer know the Crow one. In truth, I don't much mind. As long as she considers me her mother, she can call me by any name.

"So?" she prompts me as we do one more sweep of my Serpents' quarters.

"Because if I didn't, then Behati wouldn't come back, and I need her here. I need to be able to access her visions. Eventually, I also need to convince her to bestow her power upon someone else."

"Surely you can boot Kanti out for sticking listening sigils around the palace without losing Behati, no?"

I twist my lips. "What if she decides to leave with Kanti?"

"If her allegiance is truly with Shabbe, she'll understand your decision. She might even second it."

I nod. "I'll pay her a visit tomorrow, then."

Just as we head for the door, Ceres enters, along with Agrippina.

At the sight of Fallon's eyes, both do a double-take and gasp in Lucin: "Your eyes!"

"What about them?" Fallon answers in Shabbin—surely for my sake. When their jaws slacken, she bursts out laughing. "You should see your faces."

"You should see your eyes," Agrippina deadpans.

"How about we go brew some tea and I'll tell you why my irises changed color?"

"I sense I'm going to need something stronger than tea," Ceres grumbles.

"Any excuse to tipple, ah, Mamma?" Agrippina winks, hooking her arm through Fallon's and leading her toward the communal kitchen.

Ceres begins to follow with a shake of her head, but stops when she sees I'm not heading in the same direction. "Zendaya, I wanted to ask you something."

I nod, indicating for her to continue.

"Would you grant me asylum indefinitely?"

"I'm offended you're asking me for permission, Ceres."

"I would never presume that your grandmother's invitation remained in vigor."

"My home is your home, Shrima Rossi."

Before she joins her daughter and granddaughter, she offers me her condolences for Priya's passing. I thank her, genuinely touched. Though my grandmother wronged me, she also loved me, something too few understand.

When I reach my bedchamber door, I find Lorcan and Cathal deep in conversation with Aodhan, who's just come from the house Behati and Kanti moved into upon their return—a home that borders the Amkhuti and which belongs to Behati's cousin. I heard through my grapevine of loyal guards, and through Aodhan—who's taking his task of seducing Kanti to heart—that my cousin spends her days spreading cruel rumors about me and my shifters.

Though it grates on both Asha's and Enzo's nerves, I don't mind my cousin's badmouthing for, like Cathal pointed out, it's helping us weed out potential dissenters. Every day, Agrippina adds names to the list she's meticulously keeping.

"Everything all right?" I ask.

"Where's Fallon?" Lorcan asks.

"With Ceres and Agrippina in their wing." I nod in the direction I came.

He begins to dissolve but solidifies once more to say, "Thank you, Zendaya."

Though I did nothing to warrant his gratitude, I accept it and wish him a good night.

"Aodhan said that Behati's eyes turned white," Cathal explains. "I think we should go pay her a visit."

"Not tonight." I reach for my bedchamber door.

"I'll go alone, then," Cathal says.

"Not. Tonight. Please. We'll go see her first thing tomorrow."

"I think that's a mistake. Visions are—"

"Is that the only thing you believe is a mistake?"

He narrows his eyes. "What's that supposed to mean?"

"You've been avoiding me," I say.

Aodhan begins to whistle.

"Fuck off, Aodhan," Cathal grumbles.

"You know what? You, too, Cathal. Until you figure out what you want, you can leave." I fling my door wide and stride inside.

He trails me in, shutting the door with such force that the wood rattles in its frame. "I was waiting for you to heal completely."

"Liar." I whirl on him.

He glances at Cruaih, who's poked her head out of my bathing chamber and stares between the two of us as though undecided whether to step out of her haven. She must decide she's safer inside because she retreats.

"It's not a lie," he says.

I stride back toward him and poke his armor with my finger. "But it's not the full truth."

The corners of his eyes twitch.

"You said it wouldn't change anything, but you aren't convinced, are you?"

When his lids close, I realize I've hit the mark.

"I thought you'd love me no matter what?"

His nostrils flare and he grits out, "*I* will."

My head rears back. "But you think *I* won't?"

His silence rings louder than words.

"You've such little faith in my heart, Cathal."

"Everything's a first for you, Daya. Everything's a last for me."

My throat burns. My lids, too. "I don't even understand what that means!"

"Not only are you a queen, but you're also so fucking...*beautiful*. Contenders for your heart will throw themselves at your feet. Especially once you begin to expand your den."

"Why would I look at any of them if I have you?"

"Because I'm old and unpleasant."

"You *are* unpleasant."

He grimaces.

"You're a cantankerous curmudgeon." I seize either side of his face. "But you're *my* cantankerous curmudgeon."

His gaze skips over mine as though to check I'm speaking the truth.

"When I look at you, I see the man I want by my side always. I see the man I choose as my king."

His throat dips.

"Choose me back, Cathal."

His pupils dilate.

"Choose *us*."

His lids snap closed. When they reel open, gone is his shifty gaze. Gone is the anxious male. He palms my ass and lifts me. And then he kisses me. And oh, Mahananda, how I've missed his lips. My legs snap around his waist as he carries me down the wide hallway, moving with such determination, the wicks on every candle bow in his wake.

He sets me down on my mattress, then gets rid of his armor, boots, pants, shirt. Cathal Báeinach may feel ancient, but his body is that of a man in his prime—chiseled and padded to delectable perfection.

The sight of him unclothed floods my core. I begin to reach for my underwear when he drops onto his knees in front of me, cinches my thighs, and drags me to the edge of the bed. And then he's hooking my legs over his broad shoulders and pressing his face against the scrap of silk. After licking and kissing around the soaking fabric, he tugs it aside and flattens his tongue against me. I rattle with such violence that it must shake my sunstone land.

Cathal suddenly spears one finger into me, all the while twirling his tongue over the little magical bead. My climax gushes out of me, literally *gushes*, splashing Cathal's nose and mouth. I jerk onto my forearms and stare in shock and horror as he sits back on his heels. I expect a grimace to reshape his face, but I'm met with a smirk.

"What was that?" I ask.

"That, mo Sifair, was a sign that your body really enjoyed what I was doing to it." He wipes his face on his forearm. "Fuck, that was hot."

"It scalded you?"

He chuckles. "No. Not that sort of hot." He gets back to his feet, then bends over me and hovers his mouth over mine. "Can I kiss you or would you prefer I go wash off?"

"I don't know."

He touches his lips tentatively to mine. When I don't pick up on any unpleasant smell, I slant my mouth to deepen the kiss. He reaches between my legs for my underwear and snaps it off with a hard tug, and then he's pulling back, lifting my legs, and positioning his cock at my entrance.

"Ready?" he murmurs, solemn again.

"Yes, Cathal."

His chest lifts with a deep breath as he uses one hand to guide himself inside of me. He goes slow, hunting my face for any sign of pain.

There's none.

When he stretches me, it's all pleasure and I start to rattle. He gapes at my vibrating body, the tension receding from his face because he knows what it means.

He sighs as he pulls back and thrusts into me anew. But then his sigh turns into labored pants, and he curses a blue streak. "Fucking underworld, woman, if you don't get that rattling under control, I will blow."

It's cute that he thinks I have any control over my body's physiological reaction to his. My stomach tightens like a fist and pools heat into my core. I think I'm about to release another burst of wetness and worry it will carry him out. I try to warn him but end up gasping from the intensity.

His fingers clench like his jaw as he rocks his hips back, then slams into my drenched core with a feral growl. With a groan, his head falls back and he paints my quivering center with ribbons of heat.

My throat bobs and my heart catches as I watch him. How could he doubt for a second that I'd look anywhere but at him?

Even my core is pulsating with love, hugging his softening shaft, which snaps his neck straight and makes his eyes bore into mine.

I don't dare hope that this is anything more than a spasm. Until it happens again. Not so much a twitch as a tightening. A gripping.

"Cathal?" I whisper.

Daya, he whispers back. Except...

Except his lips don't part, only bend, while mine...they tremble. He hinges forward as my core swells around him and clinches so tight I worry it must hurt.

Nothing has ever felt so extraordinary. He scrapes his lips over mine, tracing their quivering contour before filling them in with a kiss that trickles down to my very soul.

As he sweeps away the salt of my tears, I murmur through our mind link, *I love you, my Crow.*

Never as much as I'll love you, my Serpent.

Chapter 61
Zendaya

Day, *we have volunteers!* Enzo's voice jolts me awake. The light that seeps beneath my curtains is watery and gray. I roll onto my back and stretch to realign the bones and muscles I strained making love to Cathal multiple times after we knotted. I smile at the memory, then twist to locate my mate but he doesn't lie on the other side of the bed.

Day? Enzo says again.

I'm awake, Enzo.

Reid's about to fly me and Agrippina up to the beach. Aoife's waiting there with Asha. Come on! He sounds giddy, like someone about to go on some great adventure.

I toss the sheets off my legs and jump out of bed, calling out my mate's name aloud. The only sound is the skitter of claws against stone. I must've awakened Cruaih. Sure enough, the tiny feline comes pouncing down my hallway, meowing as she wraps her body around my ankles.

I scoop her up and kiss the top of her head. *Cathal?*

I'm outside your door with Erwin, mo Sífair.

Unlike my Serpents' voices, Cathal's resonates not only in my mind but also in my blood. It tightens my abdomen and spurs my pulse. I wonder if it affects him the same way. *Apparently, two volunteers have arrived.*

I've heard. Get dressed. I'll fly you up to the beach.

I forgo my usual dose of flakes—I'm at twelve now, and barely have any reaction—and dress in a bathing suit, then slip on a robe as pink as my hair and cinch it closed with a belt made of golden pearls. Enzo's excitement must've rubbed off on me because, after replenishing Cruaih's water bowl and making sure she has plenty of what Asha calls kibbles, I all but skip out of my bedchamber.

My excitement takes a slight nosedive at the tension wreathing my mate and Erwin. "What is it? Did something happen to Liora? To Lore?"

"No, Sumaca." Erwin smiles and though it looks genuine, it's not quite as bright as I'd like. "Everyone's just fine. Even the injured."

"Then why do the two of you look so fretful? Is it because volunteers finally showed up? Are you worried about me expanding my den?"

"Of course not." Cathal shakes his head, winding his arm around my waist and pressing a kiss to my hairline, which is crown-free this morning, as it is most mornings.

Though I like my crown, it isn't the most convenient accessory. "Must I keep making guesses or will one of you spit it out?"

"Erwin was saying that there have been other volunteers, but most of them have drowned before making it to Samurashabbe. They've been collecting floating bodies for days now."

"Humans tried to swim across?"

"Most humans do not know how to swim." Cathal slides his jaw from side to side, making it pop.

"Cathal, please. Just tell me everything," I all but growl.

Their boats have been sinking. He gestures to Erwin. "Lore sent a few Crows to survey the waters to find the culprit. We assumed it might be the former members of the Akwale, but it's not; it's the serpents. They've ringed Shabbe and have been splitting every hull that tries to come through with their tusks."

I gasp. "Serpents have only ever saved people. Since when have they become homicidal?"

"We believe it's either some side-effect of that Nebban-made toxin," he says. "Or some collective decision to keep foreigners out of Shabbe to stop its spread."

I frown. "I thought it was no longer being manufactured and poured."

"It's not"—Erwin scrapes a hand through his orange hair—"but the waters around Eponine's shores and around Isolacuori are still depleting themselves of salt and underwater life. No solution to counteract the toxin has been found yet, even though Arin believes we could try and combat it with clay." The blood must leach from my cheeks because Erwin says, "We're just about to start trying it, Sumaca."

I mull all he says over. "The boats that were sunk...did they all originate from Nebba?"

"No. From all over the realm. The twins I collected from the surf and dropped off on your shore were sailing in from Glace. Mórrígan only knows how they managed to ford the Northern Sea on their bonafide raft, but where there's a will, there's a way, I suppose."

Day, are you coming? We've explained everything to them and they're ready. Enzo's entreaty pulls my mind off one problem and pitches it toward a more immediate one. Though is transforming two new souls into shifters a problem?

Yes, if the ocean keeps ridding itself of salt, my mind parries.

My musings must penetrate Cathal's mind, because he says, "An antidote will be found."

I hope he's right because the memory of what it did still haunts me.

Ready?

I nod. As he shapeshifts, a thought strikes me. One that I share with him through the mind link. *The Shabbins can communicate with serpents.* When his voice doesn't flare through my mind, I ask, *Can you hear me?*

Yes. I can hear you. I didn't realize there was a question in there. He extends one of his wings for me to climb.

It's not so much a question as a deliberation: what if a Shabbin—my gaze strays to the house Behati and Kanti have moved into—*has commanded the serpents to keep aspirants out in order to stop me from growing my den?*

We're already exploring that avenue.

Of course, Cathal's already entertained this idea. He's so much more learned about the world and cautious about its people than I am. We reach the beach just as the sun pokes over the horizon and turns the ocean molten.

Heads crane as we land.

When Erwin mentioned twins, I expected them to look identical like the Glacin sisters, but these twins are vastly different. Yes, their eyes are both hazel and their hair cropped within a millimeter of their scalp, but one is female and the other male. Not only that, but the boy is as tall as a date palm while his sister is as petite as Behati. The hue of their shorn hair is also vastly different—the boy's the same white as the Glacin King, whereas the girl's is Crow-black. That will change soon, though.

Where Erwin had wondered how they'd survived their voyage, I wonder how they've survived, period. Both are agonizingly skinny, with bones pressing into severely sunburnt skin, patches of which have begun to peel.

As I approach, my bare feet sinking into the soft sand, the girl shuffles the slightest bit nearer to her brother.

"They're orphans," Agrippina explains in Shabbin. "Their mother died in childbirth, while their father, like many, succumbed to frostbite wounds acquired during the Great Dig."

I nod, having heard of the Great Dig during lunch in Isolacuori. King Vladimir raved about how his mountains were being excavated to accommodate a railway system that would revolutionize Glacin life and commerce, quieting only when his son asked a question. One I'd forgotten to have translated with everything that had happened subsequently.

Conceivably, these children can explain their kingdom's inner workings once they speak our tongue. *If*, I correct myself, not *once.*

Though it worked with both Agrippina and Enzo, neither intentionally sacrificed themselves.

"Tell them there's no guarantee that the transformation will take," I say in Serpent, which blows the twins' lashes wide. "I won't make empty promises."

Agrippina, who speaks their tongue, dispatches my words. Brother and sister exchange a look, link hands, and nod.

I ask the Mahananda for advice, but it remains quiet.

"How do we kill them?" Enzo asks.

"*We* don't." Agrippina's nose rumples as she tucks her shoulder-length blue strands behind her ears. "At least, I don't think we should. Daya? Thoughts?"

"I agree with Agrippina."

"I'll do it," Reid volunteers. "On your command, Sumaca."

I unknot my robe and hand it over to my unsettled mate, then approach the ocean's edge. ***Agrippina, Enzo, keep any curious serpents at bay.***

They nod and tread into the waves, shifting almost instantly. "One at a time," I tell Reid.

Cathal slings my robe over one shoulder, then crosses his arms as the brother releases his sister's hand and follows Reid. I don't ask for his name. I'd prefer not to know it yet.

"May the ocean reshape you," I whisper in Serpent, before sinking into scales.

Chapter 62
Zendaya

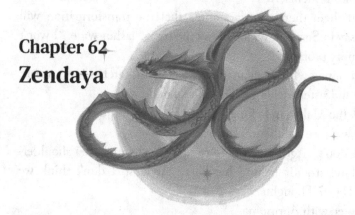

Alexei and Katya. Those are the names of my new Serpents. Where in skin they looked nothing alike, in scales, they are one and the same—aside from their proportions. Katya remains markedly slighter than her brother.

My heart brims with relief and admittedly, a little bit of awe as they acclimate to their new bodies in the loose fence Agrippina, Enzo, and I have woven around them with our own bodies. Their scales shimmer like their human eyes used to—a grass-green edged in cocoa-brown.

I suddenly wonder if the next generation of Serpents will have black scales or if they'll inherit their parents' coloring.

Almost ready to shift back? Cathal asks as his winged shadow drapes over the water.

When I changed forms, he'd hooked my robe around his torso like a sash and shifted, drawing circles with Erwin, detracting serpents from coming too close with shrill caws that resonated inside the ocean and sent any wanderers scuttling away.

I still can't believe they would've murdered people. *No one else is even a little bit alive?* I ask my mate.

They've yet to find a single person with a pulse.

Not even a Faerie?

We've only come across half-bloods and humans. If

there were any Faeries, they must've swam back to Luce.

I concentrate on my Serpents. *How about we pursue this swim in the Amkhuti?*

Alexei curls his tail into his body, then stretches it back out. *How do we shift back, Your Highness?*

Please, call me Daya. As for how to shift back, you must visualize your human form.

You know what just struck me? Agrippina asks. *Deia in Lucin means* Goddess. *It's not spelled the same, mind you, but still...I think it's the perfect moniker. Mare Deia—Goddess of the Sea.*

Agrippina, the children. I nod toward the two dappled Serpents. *Let's give them our full attention.*

Katya morphs almost instantly, but then she starts flailing her arms and sinking.

I think it's because her tattered wool dress is weighing her down, but then Alexei yells, *She doesn't know how to swim!*

I snatch her with my tail and propel her to the surface, passing her over to Cathal who carries her back to safety. *Head to the beach before shifting, Alexei.*

Once we're all back in skin, sister and brother embrace and whisper animatedly in Glacin, before twirling toward me and sketching reverential bows.

"There will be none of that," I tell them out loud, in Serpent.

Their eyes round. Either they're surprised to realize that our mind-tongue can be spoken out loud or they're surprised that they're fluent in it.

Aoife flies both children back to the Vahti where Asha welcomes them with open arms and a breakfast table laden with delicacies. I've realized that Asha is a nurturer and that her love language is food. That's how she won over Enzo's heart, or rather, stomach. Though I consider her my friend, he considers her the mother he never had. I wish he'd consider me that way, as well. Perhaps if I plied him with bowls of fried dough...

The children eat very little, picking at the heaps Asha has ladled onto their plates. Though they promise the food is tasty and express their gratitude multiple times in Serpent—a language Asha understands rather well thanks to Fallon's dictionary—she side-eyes their clavicles like the salient bones are personally affronting her.

"Their stomachs have probably shrunken from years of stinted rations," Agrippina explains. "It was the same in Luce. I used to smuggle bags of grain to Rax, and they would last certain families months, whereas those same bags would be used up in mere days in the Fae lands."

Ceres, who's joined us at the breakfast table, side-eyes her daughter. "You smuggled food to Racocci?"

She pats her mother's hand. "Pappa's secrets are a little more shocking, wouldn't you agree?"

Ceres squeezes her lips. I imagine that, yes, she does agree, though I also imagine she's not done discussing her daughter's parallel life.

"Can you show Katya and Alexei to a room and find them some clothes to wear, Asha?" I ask in Serpent, so that my words aren't lost on the twins. "And organize a fitting with the seamstress after they've rested."

Their eyes widen.

"Tomorrow, we begin swimming lessons." Before they can assume these lessons will be taught in scales, I add, "In skin."

Color leaches from their sunburnt cheeks.

"My Serpents, I will not have you drowning if your magic ever fails you."

"Why would our magic fail us?" Katya's voice is just as slight as she is. That of a girl who's always needed to live quietly.

"Because even magic isn't infallible. Besides, I'm certain you'll both be quick learners. Once you've mastered swimming, we'll start bloodcasting lessons."

"Bloodcasting?" they gasp out in unison.

Here, I assumed the news of our blood magic had spread, but apparently not.

"We Serpents are so much more formidable than Crows." Agrippina adds a wink that makes her mate cock a brow, Aoife smile, and Cathal...Cathal doesn't react, evidently elsewhere.

"Off we go, my sweets." Asha winds her arms around the twins' backs and rakes them down the winding path, chattering all the way.

Aoife leans forward and plants her elbows on the table, her long black braid flopping over her shoulder. "Zendaya, I know it's no my call, but maybe we cancel invitation we spread. Though we Crows *can* ensure safe passage of contenders, Agrippina is right. *Sifair* have *a lot* power."

Cathal studies the spoon he toys with, the iridescent mother-of-pearl handle casting shards of color over his heavy-lidded stare.

What's wrong, mate? I ask.

He glances up, sets down the spoon. "Though there's power in numbers, the amount of magic you now wield can be dangerous without guidance."

"We wouldn't be converting just anyone to Naagaism," Agrippina butts in. "We'll have rigorous criteria. If they don't tick all the boxes, we'll send them on their merry way."

"So you will turn away starving children with no prospect back in their homeland?" Cathal challenges her.

Her lips press together. "We'll give them coin. Right, Daya? We can do that?"

"Of course."

Cathal blows out a breath he seems to have held on to since we left for the beach. "I just worry you all may end up choosing with your hearts instead of your heads."

"We are f-five!" Enzo exclaims. "If we've any ch-chance at being taken seriously, we c-cannot stay f-five."

Cathal reclines in his seat, but there's nothing relaxed about his posture. "So you'd prefer to balloon your numbers and risk that your extraordinary and *dangerous* magic land in the wrong hands?"

"Th-That isn't what I s-said," Enzo snaps. ***Day, you once said this decision was ours. Please let it stay ours.***

I keep my gaze on his a long, long while. "Aoife, let's change our invitation process. Everyone can put in a request for consideration, but they must send in a written application."

Agrippina twists her lips. "Most humans are illiterate, Daya."

"If they're incapable of writing, the application can either be penned by another, or one of us will travel to meet—"

"No," Cathal says. "Until Shabbe's secure and an antidote is found, you are safest here. *All* of you."

"Then a Crow can interview them," Agrippina suggests.

"We're stretched thin already," Cathal says.

Agrippina plucks a candied orange rind off the top of the curd dish. "Lorcan can surely spare *one* of you?"

"We *can* ask, Cathal," Reid offers.

Cathal's eyes twitch.

This solution displeases you. I reach over and brush his muscled thigh that jiggles from nerves. I'm almost surprised when he slips his arms out of their tight knot and scoops up my hand to twine our fingers. *Why?*

Do you know how many dead bodies were found? The last count was over three hundred. Three hundred in under one week. And we've only announced it in Luce, he adds.

My retracted tusk dips. *Yet the twins are Glacin...*

There's much trade between the kingdoms. A Lucin ship must've docked in Glace and spread the word. But that's beside the point...

"Can we be included in your little aside?" Agrippina sweeps a piece of flatbread in the bowl of curd, then tosses it into her mouth.

"I don't think the three of you realize how many people lust for magic," he says.

"You're wr-wrong," Enzo counters. "I kn-know. I was human b-before. I kn-know."

"Then you know that the majority of people who will apply are humans. Even though we've opened countless schools since our return, like Agrippina pointed out, almost all are illiterate. Which means they'd have to be interviewed in person."

Enzo musses his green hair that now curls around his ears. "Then Asha c-can conduct the interviews."

"We cannot spare her, Enzo," I say calmly, sensing his mounting agitation.

We cannot spare her, or you're siding with Cathal?

I bristle. *We cannot spare her.*

Enzo stews in silence, gaze affixed to his empty plate.

"I could do it," Ceres offers. "I could be your envoy."

Enzo spins in his seat to gape at her. I try to read from his posture whether he's pleased or horrified, considering his complicated past with Faeries.

"Mamma!" Agrippina adds nothing else but a wide grin, which makes Ceres's green eyes beam with gladness to have her daughter look upon her with such admiration.

Enzo? Would you be on board with Ceres interviewing future candidates?

Yes! He spins back toward me, his expression brimming with renewed excitement. *Please say yes. Please?*

How could I say no to something that makes you so happy?

Because your mate probably hates that we've found a solution, he mumbles.

Enzo, just because I welcome and value my mate's opinions on matters of state, he's not a Serpent nor does he have the responsibility of a pack. I give Cathal's hand a squeeze before letting go and sitting upright in my chair. "Ceres, we would be honored and grateful to let you be the judge of our future denmates."

Ceres glows, and so do my Serpents. If only every challenge we face could be so easily resolved.

"Could we please get a pen and paper?" she asks one of the attendants waiting on us.

"Right away, Shrima Rossi."

As Enzo and Agrippina begin to throw out conditions, Aoife mentions how serpent killings may dissuade people from wanting to be transformed, while Reid reminds her that serpents were already considered homicidal beasts, so he disagrees.

A shadow blunts the sun over our heads as a Crow circles. My first thought is that another survivor has been pulled from the ocean and brought to me for healing. Though the Crow does have a rider, she's not a contender for my magic, only for my throne.

Chapter 63
Zendaya

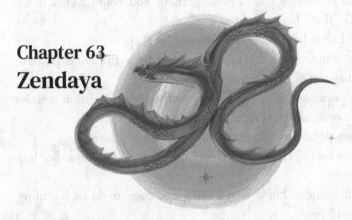

"**G**ood morning, chacha!" Kanti's voice trills with false cheer.

It *was* a good morning until she showed up. "Hello, Kanti."

"I'm ravenous." Aodhan comes up behind Aoife, leans over, and nicks one of the flatbreads.

"To what do we owe the displeasure of your visit?" Agrippina asks, never one to conceal her feelings.

"Dear Mahananda, you were so much more agreeable when you were cognitively challenged." Kanti's comment causes Ceres's mouth to thin and Reid's eyes to slit.

But in Agrippina, all it triggers is a giant smirk.

Kanti asks for someone to fetch her a chair and some tapioca pudding. When they glance at me for approval—which I give them —annoyance flushes her cheeks.

Once seated, she says, "I heard you made new Serpents."

At least she doesn't—how did Taytah used to say? Ah, yes, *beat around the Amkhuti*. "News travels fast." I glance at Aodhan when I say this, but he's busy heaping grilled cheese onto his flatbread.

"Was it supposed to be a secret?" she asks.

"If it was supposed to be a secret, I wouldn't have transformed them on the beach for all to see, now would I?" I lean my forearms onto the polished stone that remains cool however much sun beats down on it. "Since you're here, perhaps you could weigh in on something that's been troubling me."

The line of her shoulders harshens. "Perhaps."

"It's come to my attention that serpents—the animals—have been acting out of character."

Her pupils contract, but aside from that, her expression remains perfectly neutral. "In what way?"

"They've been sinking boats and drowning humans."

"Have they?" Her lack of emotion is just as damning as her lack of surprise.

"You wouldn't know who'd command them to do such a thing, now, would you?"

"You may think yourself superior to the common serpent, but you're not. Serpents are extremely perceptive creatures who've always protected our island. If they're keeping boats at bay, then it's because they sense incoming danger."

"Keeping boats at bay would be one thing, murdering humans is quite another, Kanti," I say.

"Humans aren't taught how to swim in the Fae lands, so they died from their own shortcomings."

Cathal rolls his neck. "Crows saw them drag people into the deep."

"They were probably trying to ferry them back to Lucin shores but forgot they couldn't breathe underwater." Kanti shrugs. "Once you've constituted your Akwale, Daya, you should put a ward up around Shabbe to prevent any more deaths. Though you are Meri-am's daughter, so perhaps you don't need an Akwale to create such a massive spell? And since we're on the topic, how is your Akwale formation going?"

The fevered smile curling her lips tells me that she knows exactly how it's going. The two sorceresses Asha had in mind ended up not showing. When she asked them why, they told her that Shabbe belonged to sorceresses not to shifters. I suddenly wonder if they'd change their minds if I offered Kanti her seat back.

I almost ask Cathal's opinion on the matter, but then picture having Kanti living in the Vahti again and shudder. "Well, I was hoping to elect an equal number of sorceresses to Serpents, but it seems as though it'll be mostly Serpents."

Kanti seizes a glass filled with water and raises it so fast, half of it sloshes over the rim. "Hear, hear. To peace and harmony between the Shabbins and Serpents."

Though I comprehend full well she means my kind and not the mammals inhabiting our waters, I say, "I didn't realize we were at war with the animals so intent on protecting our land."

A spasm disturbs her cheek.

"Oh, did you mean *us*?" I gesture to my bright-haired denmates. "Just call us Shabbins. After all, that's what we consider ourselves. Isn't that right?"

"Absolutely," Agrippina says.

"Yes," Enzo says without stutter.

Another tic agitates Kanti's cheek.

"Wait. Keep your glass up. I'd like to propose a toast." Agrippina boosts her coffee mug. "To widening narrow minds and promoting inclusivity."

"Beautifully put, mate." Reid reaches over and clinks his mug with hers.

Enzo agrees with a nod and a gulp of his juice.

"Throughout *all* the lands," Ceres adds before drinking.

If only toasts could be magically binding like bargains. *Hmm.* Perhaps I could strike one with Kanti.

No. That is all my mate says as he tips his water glass to his lips. "I hear Antoni's much aggrieved that you abandoned him."

Kanti sets down her glass—without even wetting her lips—and sighs. "My lovers always are."

Is he truly heartbroken? I ask.

Keeping his expression blank, Cathal replies, *No. Last I heard, he was relieved she was gone and has begged that she be kept away.*

Did she seduce the wrong enemy?

Either that or Behati fabricated the vision to get Kanti out of Shabbe.

Or the Mahananda gave her that vision to get her out of Shabbe so she wouldn't fight me for the throne.

I like that theory best.

"I vote you head back to Tarespagia and put the Governor out of his misery," Agrippina offers pleasantly.

Kanti frames my Serpent with a smile that's so frigid, it drops the balmy temperature by several degrees. "As soon as Meriam's found, I'll be out of here."

"What if she's never found?" Agrippina asks.

"She will be. Taytah had a vision of her last night. She's in Luce with Justus, hiding out in Selvati. We've warned Lorcan."

My lids go wild with annoyance. "Matters of state are to be run by me. All of them. Especially those concerning my blood relatives."

"We thought you wouldn't want to be bothered with such things, busy as you are trying to grow your little pack."

"I very much want to be bothered with such things," I snap, any semblance of congeniality gone.

Agrippina runs her index finger over the rim of her mug. "Your consideration knows no bounds, Kanti."

"None. I care fervently for my queendom."

"Daya's que-queendom," Enzo corrects.

Kanti turns her frostbitten smile on him. "That's what I meant."

"Aodhan, could you please go fetch Behati?" I ask. "I'd very much like a glimpse of her vision."

"Aye, aye, Sumaca." The Crow sucks oil off his fingertips before wandering farther to shapeshift.

Kanti plants her forearms on the table, easing her torso forward. "I might not worship you, Daya, but I would never lie about a Mahananda-given vision."

"Then you've nothing to fear," I say.

She snorts. "Why would I have anything to fear?"

Cathal squares his shoulders. "Because you screw with my mate, you screw with me."

She rolls her eyes. "Oh, please. Not only am I immune to iron, but also to toxic masculinity."

Shadows puff from my scowling mate.

Though I've no doubt he *could* hurt her, I place my hand on his lap and squeeze his joggling knee to keep him from trying. ***She'll get her comeuppance.***

Will she? The Cauldron didn't punish your grandmother for binding your magic.

I believe that, in time, it would have.

"The Mahananda sees all," Agrippina tells Kanti. Well, warns her. "I know you missed it, but it drained Malka when she challenged its choice of monarch."

I expect this to rid Kanti of a modicum of smugness, but steady as ever, she says, "Good thing I'm not lying, then."

Shockingly enough, she's not. The instant I place my hands on Behati's forehead I see my mother wandering around sandy streets. Not only that, I see her leaving behind a trail of bodies. Which just doesn't make sense. Why would she go on a killing rampage? In the human district of Luce, no less?

I understand why, when that night, a ship manages to penetrate the fortifications and drift down the Sahklare right into the Amkhuti.

One with a message inked in human blood: *Build your army, batee.*

Chapter 64
Zendaya

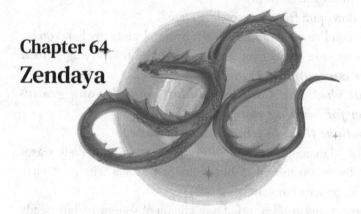

Seventy-one corpses. That is how many dead bodies lay aboard the warship flying a Lucin flag. Though I do not retch, my stomach spasms with horror and my fingers ball with anger as I tread across the tacky deck.

Fallon, who was luckily already on her way over to Shabbe when she heard about the boat, closes her fingers around my fist. "I know Meriam, and this isn't something she'd do."

"Um, yeah it is," Kanti says from where she sits high above us on the Amkhuti's embankment, legs swinging, palms flat on the grass as though sunning herself instead of observing a horror show. "Plus, how would the ship penetrate our fortifications *and* sail down our rivers were it not powered by Shabbin magic?"

When news of the boat spread, Kanti was one of the first Shabbins to traipse out of her abode to take in the spectacle.

"There are other sorceresses who could've floated that boat in," Agrippina counters, while my daughter steadfastly insists, "Meriam wouldn't murder a bunch of innocents, Kanti."

Yet some of the corpses from Behati's vision are there.

Right.

There.

The newborn babe nestled in a scarf knotted around its mother's back. The pubescent boy with a star-shaped birthmark on his jaw. The woman with a tattoo over her heart representing an anchor wrapped in a rope that spells a name—*Raphaelle.*

They might be dead but they've still got blood in their bodies, Day, Enzo says. ***It could work.***

Seventy-one.

Seventy-one.

Seventy-one...

The number clangs between my temples like a death knoll, springing chills down my spine.

"Lazarus, maybe you could try to heal them with crystals?" Fallon suggests.

"I'm afraid crystals only work when the subject has a pulse, Your Majesty." The giant's sapphire robes flap in a gentle breeze. The lax wind feels discordant with the brutal scene. There should be a tempest, or at the very least, harsh gusts. "But I can try."

He rubs one of the beads hooped through his ear and leans over the babe. We all watch the infant's diaphanous lids, willing them to flutter, willing the child's rosebud mouth to part around a wail.

Nothing.

The healer unfurls his broad body, lips twisted in sorrow. "Perhaps if we sunk the ship and reversed the trajectory of the water-rises, your namesake beasts could be herded into the Amkhuti to try and heal them." The healer squints at the algae-lit Sahklare. "Where are the serpents, anyway? They usually swarm when they scent blood."

"That *is* odd." Fallon peers over the boat's railing. "Aoife, can you fly and see if you spot any?"

My heart pinches that my daughter cannot just spring off the deck of this ship and take to the sky at will.

"I don't like this." Cathal's apprehensive timbre carries my stare back to the massacre.

"None of us like this, Dádhi." Fallon must've learned that word before the Mahananda removed her Crow magic for she's never once called him anything but that.

"I mean, I've a bad feeling about this." He claps. "I want everyone off the ship."

"Serpents aren't lying in wait beneath the boat to ambush Mádhi and the others," Fallon says.

His dark gaze cuts to hers.

"Wait...you think that's what's happening?" The vein in Fallon's neck swells and strikes harder.

"I don't know what's happening, ínon. I just want everyone back on land." When no one moves, Cathal growls, "Now."

I get to my feet and am about to step away when Reid gasps. He's bent over a wooden barrel, fishing something out of it.

"What is it?" Agrippina traipses over. "Another corpse?"

Her mate straightens, hauling out a broad body clad in black. I suddenly worry it must be a Crow before remembering that Crows can no longer be harmed.

Fallon palms her mouth. It's only once a name tumbles from her lips in a muted whimper that I understand why this cadaver shocks her more than any other.

Chapter 65
Zendaya

Is this *Kanti's Antoni?* I ask Cathal.

  It is. Which means that our daughter's wrong. It is Meriam's doing, for Kanti wouldn't murder her lover.

  I lock eyes with his. ***Wouldn't she?***

  "Reid"—Cathal's tone snaps his gaze to his—"bring him to Kanti, but wait for us to land before dropping the governor at her feet."

  Both men shift. Cathal hovers until Fallon and I have seized his iron talons, and then he plucks us off the deck and carries us up to Kanti.

  "You're not even going to try to heal any of them?" My cousin gestures to the ship.

  "They're dead. Serpents cannot revive the dead," I say.

  "Yes, you can. Taytah saw you revive lots of them."

  I frown because she didn't show me that part of the vision.

  Cathal gives a short whistle.

  I don't take my eyes off Kanti. When her lashes sink and rise as briskly as hummingbird wings, I again question her involvement.

  "I'm sorry for your loss," I venture.

  Her jaw tightens, and she rams a hand through her hair with such vigor that she pops out some of the jeweled pins clamped around artfully twisted strands. I can't tell whether she's aggrieved or furious.

"Still think your mother isn't a heartless bitch?" And then she's standing and striding toward her deceased lover.

What do you think? I ask Cathal, as Aodhan drops off Lazarus beside Governor Greco's remains.

I think that was true shock on her face.

I try to make sense of all my thoughts. What keeps coming back to me is that this might not be some sick ploy of Kanti's to discredit my mother after all. This might *actually* be my mother's doing. Which begs the questions:

What sort of monster put me on the throne?

What sort of monster believed I would appreciate such an offering?

What sort of monster murdered seventy-one—seventy-*two* innocents in cold blood?

"I want Behati fetched," I snap as Reid returns to the ship to grab his mate. "I want to see that part of the vision."

"Of course you don't trust me," Kanti snipes, just as Aodhan streaks up the path toward the large sunstone mansion bordering the Amkhuti.

I ball my fingers until my nails chew into my palm. "Well, you did paint listening sigils all over my palace walls."

Her pink eyes swivel toward mine. "Always so quick to lay the blame."

"It was *your* blood, Kanti," I say.

She stops fussing with the buttons of Antoni's collar and just shears the fabric with magic. "Fine. I confess. It was me. But it was Priya's idea. She wanted to monitor all that was being said behind her back."

Sensing this is another lie, I ask, "Can you show me the memory?"

"I would, but I'd prefer we try to save my lover's life." She parts his shirt, then paints carmine whorls around his wound that is so precise, it was unquestionably made by a sorceress.

398

"His eyelashes moved!" Fallon falls to her knees on Antoni's other side. "Antoni's alive! Lazarus, a crystal!"

"His wound was made with Shabbin magic, Fallon," I murmur, having learned my fair share about our therapeutic crystals from Asha since Soorya failed to teach me. Though my grandmother had tasked the healer to educate me, Soorya was always too busy brewing lucent remedies or curing ailing humans and half-bloods. "There are no crystals for Shabbin wounds. Only the witch who inflicted the damage can repair it."

"Or serpents," Lazarus adds. "Has Aoife spotted any?"

The sky's so dark, I can't discern any wingbeats. *Do you see her, Cathal?*

He works his jaw from side to side. *No.* Though loath to step away from me, he pounces upward and shifts. After a moment, he says, *She can't spot any in the Sahklare.*

In none of the rivers?

She's investigating the last one now. An endless minute passes before he says, *No serpents.*

Ice slicks down my spine. *Can she check the ocean?*

I've already asked. She's on her way.

He lands just as Behati emerges from the house. The seer's golden cane gleams as she totters toward us, which reminds me of her other cane, the one I found at the bottom of the Amkhuti. I peer over the ledge as though I could possibly discern it in the recessed water, but it lies so deep, and there's such faint moonlight, that I see nothing.

"Is it?" Cathal is asking, arms crossed over his black shirt that was tailored to fit his large chest but looks maladjusted from the strain of his stance. "Or is there something wrong with the corpses?"

Kanti skewers him with a look. "If Antoni dies because you're distracting me, Cathal, then his blood will be on your hands."

"My hands are already filthy." My mate ticks his head toward the wan governor. "Besides, Antoni's not exactly a favorite amongst the Crows these days. Fallon, ask Lore to send more people."

"Why? Do you think—"

"Just please do it, ínon."

"Done."

"Taytah's vision!" Kanti suddenly exclaims. "She said I would turn one of Lorcan's enemies into a friend. This must be what she meant! That Daya would make him a Serpent."

Fallon's cheeks hollow from how quickly she inhales. "Do you think...? Do you think that...?"

"Why don't we try to heal Antoni with our blood first," I suggest. "Surely our three magics combined—"

"—would kill him." Kanti purses her mouth. "It would overstimulate his organs. Probably even make his heart burst. Great Mahananda, did Priya teach you nothing about blood magic?"

Before my mate can detonate into smoke, I step in front of him and take his cheeks between my palms. ***Shh. Don't let her get to you.***

A wet gurgle erupts from behind me. I twist around to find Antoni arching and coughing. And then his eyes are opening.

"Kanti, you managed to heal him," Fallon murmurs.

My cousin shakes her head. "I've just resorbed some of his internal bleeding. In other words, I've prolonged his life. Only Meriam or Daya can truly heal him. Or I suppose one of Daya's shifters. Want to give your tongue a whirl, Agrippina?"

My Serpent grimaces, but then she glances my way.

"No," I say out loud. "If anyone heals the injured, it'll be me."

Do you think the corpses were poisoned? she asks me.

I don't know, but I also don't care for you to find out.

"We could carry Antoni out to the ocean," Fallon suggests, her voice shaking with emotion.

"He won't survive being moved. Hold on, abi." Kanti strokes Antoni's lips, then his cheeks, adding more blood to his sticky-red jaw, which makes his eyes pitch wide. "We're going to fix you." Is it Kanti's crazy stare that's frightening him or the lethal depth of his injuries?

When pink foam glides out of the corners of the governor's mouth, Lazarus murmurs, "That's not a good sign."

Fallon balls her fist and bites down on her knuckles to stifle a sob. "Mádhi, please do something."

"No." It's Cathal who answers for me.

Fallon looks up at her father with so many tears in her eyes that they shine violet. I presume she's adopted the hue to keep the Shabbins in the dark about the Crows' new edge. "He's not a bad man, Dádhi."

"He could be a fucking saint and I still wouldn't let your mother get close to him. I'm sorry, ínon."

Fallon whimpers.

I hate seeing my daughter this distraught. *"Should I save the governor, Mahananda?"*

Silence.

"Please, Mahananda. I implore you. Guide me."

But the Mahananda does not offer me guidance.

When I realize I haven't heard from Enzo in a while, I call out to him. Is he still on the boat? I walk over to the cliff's lip and squint down at the galleon, sighing with relief when I spot a head full of green curls.

Again, I call to him through the bond. When he doesn't look up, I yell his name out loud.

He finally cranks his head back. "Yes, my queen?"

I gasp and teeter, clutching my throat in utter horror.

Chapter 66
Zendaya

The boat creaks as it rotates.

"Whose blood is on your face, Enzo?" My tremulous query widens his nightmarish grin.

"I revived some of the dead. We can bring back corpses, Daya!" He gestures to the woman with the anchor tattoo.

She bows. Her hair's cut so close to her scalp that it's impossible to spot its hue, but her forehead bears the pearl and her eyes are black orbs. Two others hinge at the waist before meeting my perplexed stare—both round-eared men in drab garments.

"What the fuck?" Cathal snarls against the shell of my ear.

"We're going to raise them all!" Enzo cries out like some lunatic warrior. And then he claps for his new Serpents to follow as he pounds the deck to sort through the cadavers.

"Tell him to stop before I cut out his tongue," Cathal mutters.

No, I gasp. A Serpent without a tongue would be like a Crow deprived of a wing. ***No severing of tongues. Please, Cathal. It was a turn of phrase.***

I place my palm over my spasming stomach. ***Don't raise any more humans, Enzo. Not until...not until I speak with Behati. Please.***

Though he keeps staring at me, he doesn't nod or acknowledge my request through our bond.

The nearby click of Behati's cane steals my attention off him. "Apparently your vision showed me rousing the dead, Behati," I sputter.

I spy her eyebrows slanting. "Which vision, Daya? I've had so many."

"The vision you had last night. The one you showed me at breakfast. I want to see everything you saw," I say reaching out to touch her forehead. "And I mean *everything*, Behati."

Her frown strengthens. "I showed you ev—" The bottom of her cane suddenly skids, and she wobbles. And then she's tipping.

"Behati!" I screech just as my fingertips graze her bangs.

Her eyes are huge as she lists. Huger still when she crashes into the ship's deck, splintering the blood-soaked slats before vanishing right through them.

"Taytah!" Kanti rushes to the edge. "What have you done, Daya? What have you done?"

"She didn't do anything," Cathal rumbles. "Behati slipped."

"Well don't just stand there, Crow," Kanti shrills. "Go get her."

A muscle pops in Cathal's jaw. "Enzo's down there. He can fetch her."

"No!" My hair flies as I shake my head from side to side. "I don't want him to go inside that water. Send Aodhan."

Cathal swerves his attention to the grounds and the glowing house at our back. "Where the fuck did he go? Aodhan!"

"I'll go find him. Keep an eye on..." Reid tips his head toward Agrippina, whose complexion is as bloodless as the corpses she cannot seem to look away from.

I suddenly want her far from this lurid spectacle. I want *both* my Serpents brought to Asha and tucked behind the walls of my palace.

As Agrippina's mate shifts and soars toward the house, I turn toward mine, whose nostrils flare. ***Cathal, can you carry Agrippina back to—***

A booming snap followed by a reverberating crack makes me

403

whirl back around. I scream just as the vessel fractures and sinks, drawing every corpse and Serpent into the liquid abyss.

Chapter 67
Zendaya

I yell Enzo's name through the mind link, one heartbeat away from diving into the Amkhuti to succor him.

Silence.

Why is he so silent?

"Mádhi?" Fallon calls out. "Antoni's convulsing. Kanti's blood—mine—it's not working. Lazarus even tried a crystal, but—"

"Not now, Fallon! I cannot deal with a stranger right now. Not when Enzo—"

"Enzo's a Serpent, Daya. He's not going to drown." Kanti's reminder does nothing to appease me.

I whirl on her. "How about *you* fucking jump in?"

Her gaze tightens. "With a bunch of new zombie Serpents? Hard pass."

"You're immortal," I hiss.

"Yeah." She pops a shoulder in a shrug. "But I can still be tortured, so again, no thanks, chacha."

"What about your grandmother? Don't you care about her?"

Kanti must suck in her cheeks because they dent. "She's resilient."

"She didn't have time to stripe her neck," I say.

Kanti grimaces. "At least she won't be conscious if the Serpents

405

decide to snack on her. Actually, why don't you talk to them and ask them to locate her?"

New Ones, can you hear me?

Yes. It's Alexei who answers. *We can hear you.*

I snare my lip. Although glad for the sound of his voice, I wasn't calling to him. *Everything all right?* I ask, since he's listening.

When Alexei says, *Sort of,* my poor heart almost fails.

I knead the scar on my neck. *What do you mean sort of?*

We're playing cards with Ceres, and naughty Cruaih keeps stealing the cards and chewing them up. When Alexei chuckles, I think I might expire from relief. *Will you join us soon, Day?*

Yes. Very soon, my darling.

Is something wrong? Intuitive child.

No. Everything's fine. I inject as much litheness as I can muster into my tone. *Let Asha win a round. She's a terribly sore loser.*

Ha. She totally is. I'm convinced she's encouraging Cruaih to snatch the cards.

I smile, but it trips off my lips when I call out—yet again—to the Mahananda, and I'm met with silence. "Abrax!" I yell to my guard, who stands on the opposite embankment, gaze pinned to the Amkhuti. "Go check on the Mahananda please."

He doesn't question why I want him to pay it a visit, or what exactly I'm looking for. He merely turns on his heel and races through the palace gardens.

My pulse whooshes against my eardrums, amplifying the feeling that something's off. It agitates my blood, unlike the Amkhuti that lies flat. *Too* flat. No tusk, no bubble...nothing disturbs its surface.

No. That's not true.

I catch the flash of silver scales.

A palm-sized fish seesaws on its side. Not just one. Hundreds, as though the sinking ship has stunned them. But they're not stunned...they're dead. I can feel it inside my blood as though I were connected to all aquatic life.

"Cathal!" Agrippina's shriek stops my heart.

I whirl just as my mate stumbles into me, sending us hurtling over the cliff's edge. As we fall, I see the tip of a black blade sticking out of his chest.

"You killed the true queen!" Lazarus cries out, rubbing his palms as though glad to be rid of me. "Zendaya isn't the leader we want!"

I try to shape Fallon's name and the word "help," but both transform into a strangled breath when I catch her shoving Agrippina into the watery trench.

As I stare at my Serpent's flailing arms and streaming blue hair, at her saucer-wide eyes and slack jaw, I yell down the bond, *Alexei, tell Asha to ward your wing and to let no one in! Not even if they look like me. Not even if they look like Fallon.*

Chapter 68
Zendaya

For a beat too long, we sink because I'm too stunned to swim and Cathal is too hurt to shift.

Violet eyes.

Mádhi.

That wasn't our daughter! It must've been an enemy Shabbin wearing her face. Which means the Crows aren't coming. Which means we're on our own. Unless Aoife or Aodhan or Reid managed to call to them? Where did *they* all go?

Agrippina? I rasp through the bond as I swim around Cathal, seize the handle of the sword Lazarus—or some other Shabbin wench wearing his face—plunged into my mate's chest, and yank.

His body jerks and a thin stream of bubbles erupts from his flaring nostrils. He might be invulnerable to obsidian and immortal, but what will a blade through the chest do to him?

Cathal? I say too loudly.

Daya, he says too quietly. *I can't shift.*

I drop the sword. *Because you're wounded.*

I don't allow my dread that the blade was basted in Shabbin blood, or that someone managed to paint a sigil to immobilize his magic, pass through the mind link. *Is there such a sigil?* I try to recall all the ones I learned and witnessed...all the ones I practiced, but my mind has become a blank canvas.

Get out of the Amkhuti. Cathal's supplication hones my focus on him. Him and his bleeding heart. ***Get out, now.***

Not without you. I level off in front of him and hook the torn fabric of his shirt. ***Never without you.*** And then I rip it open and smack my tongue against his wound. A tingle races across my teeth, along my jawbone, down my throat.

Keep your mouth shut, mo Sifair! Don't drink the water.

I lick him again just as something knocks into me from behind, dragging my tongue off its mark. Cathal's gasp has me twisting. A scream clambers up my throat when I spy one of the corpses. I kick my feet to propel us up and away, only to push Cathal into another drifting body.

Can you shift yet? I ask him.

No.

Clasping my lids to keep the horror at bay, I swim around his body and tend to his back. ***Daya, I said no.***

I'm fine! My chest stings with bursts of heat that skip from rib to rib like steel scraped over flint.

It's fear.

Just fear.

If it were anything else, I'd be floating like those fish, lungs saturated with water, heart still. Do immortal hearts stop beating? No, they probably keep beating.

As Cathal's skin firms, I see Behati's hollow, white cane. Not through the water, but in my memories. I see the dead coral it rested on and the lifeless barracuda beside it.

It wasn't a cane—or at least, not *just* a cane. It must've been a cylindrical container packed with poisonous flakes. Behati infected my haven!

I see red, and then I see her smashing into the boat. How stunned she'd looked. Like she'd truly tripped when she must've purposely flailed to keep me from pilfering the vision from her mind and witnessing Kanti's trickery.

How I wished the seer weren't immortal and that the fall could've broken her neck.

How I wished Meriam had taught me the death sigil, so that I could've drained my cunning cousin.

Agrippina! I holler through the mind link, but my Serpent doesn't answer me. *Enzo!* Nothing. *Alexei! Katya!* Though the sky sparks, my mind does not.

When another body thumps into mine, I shove it aside with a fury that burns hotter than my lungs.

The second Cathal's wound seals, I ask him if he can shift.

Silence.

I swirl around to find his lids closed, his neck curved, his mouth parted. He's lost consciousness. He needs air. I snatch him around the waist and kick, my dress tangling with my feet and slowing me down but not stopping me.

What does stop me is the sight of long white hair slithering around an apathetic body. I gape at Behati. How come she's still down here with me? Shouldn't she be up there with the rest of her vile coven?

Of course. It mustn't be her. It must be some unsuspecting soul magicked to look like her.

Aodhan...

It must be Aodhan!

My anger weighs so heavily on my soul that, again, I sink, our bodies wedging through a cloud of stiff silver fish. But then, I recycle this anger, converting it to adrenaline. I bend my knees and undulate my legs as though I'd grown out my Serpent tail.

Bend. Flick. Bend. Flick.

Through the throng of silver scales, I spy the surface, and beyond it, a sky veined with lighting. I pray the storm is Lorcan-made, because I don't think I can fight a blood-magic war on my own.

One more kick and Cathal will be able to breathe.

Bang!

My sight goes momentarily black. My ears ring. And my skull...
it thuds.

Keeping one arm locked around Cathal, I reach up with the
other. My trembling fingers meet what feels like smooth glass.

The fucking sorceresses warded the Amkhuti!

They've locked us in!

Chapter 69
Zendaya

Amidst the slow bend of my pink hair puffs inky black. It settles between my upturned face and the magical wall overlooking my queendom. My hammering heart holds still. Could it be a Crow? Could Cathal have managed to break into shadows?

I call to him.

Silence.

Another blot of ink lifts and glides along the warded surface. I comb my fingers through it, realizing it's viscous like—

I touch two fingers to the top of my head. They come away slick and black with my blood.

I expect it will wash away like Shabbin blood but it lingers.

My spine tingles as I carry my fingers to Cathal's throat and draw stripes on either side. When the sky flares, the stripes are gone. Because my blood washed away, or because it penet—

Daya? Cathal rears his head so fast that it knocks into my chin and clicks my teeth together.

I can bloodcast underwater.

I feel like weeping.

I feel like fighting.

My mate turns in my arms. For a moment, we hang there, suspended, our hearts and stares pressed against one another.

Can you shift? I finally ask him.

When he vanishes, another wave of relief dashes against me.

He knits back into flesh. *They painted a fucking ward!*

I nod.

He must catch sight of my bleeding skull because his livid gaze tapers there. *Your head—*

Is fine.

It's not fucking fine. It's bleeding. You're bleeding. I will fucking eviscerate—

Voices ring out nearby.

Don't let go of my hand. I dip my fingers into my blood and paint the invisibility sigil on Cathal's brow, then sketch it on mine.

The voices grow louder. I pick out Kanti's, Soorya's, and Rosh's.

I hear Kanti saying, "Did you really have to kill Antoni, Soorya?"

Their footfalls resonate against the ward as though they were traipsing over it. They are!

"Fallon likes the guy and so do you." The Shabbin wearing my daughter's face shrugs. "I felt that if Zendaya would try to heal anyone, it would be him." She shrugs as she steps right over us.

"She probably would've if her little Crow hadn't been so fucking suspicious," beautiful, blonde Rosh adds. "Can you get rid of Fallon's face, Soorya? It looks too much like the Naaga we banished."

Cathal's nails must be morphing into talons for I can feel their cool, hard shape digging into my skin—not hard enough to stab but hard enough to dent. *I knew that wasn't our daughter...*

May our child be safe.

May she be with Lorcan.

Kanti stops walking. When her pink eyes lower toward me, I think that my invisibility sigil mustn't have worked.

Can you see me? I murmur through the mind link.

No. Can you see me?

No.

413

Cathal's body suddenly jostles mine. *What the—is that Behati?*

Aodhan, I say.

Aodhan?

I imagine the real Behati's up there with them. I imagine they made him look like her.

Cathal's quiet for an instant. *He would've shifted when he fell if it had been him. Not to mention, he wouldn't have gone along and* acted *like Behati...*

Unless he turned against us.

He may be arrogant but he's still a Crow.

And what? *Your people cannot be traitors?*

His nostrils must flare for little bubbles stream out and pop against the ward. *Touch her forehead to see if there's any blood to lift.*

I bite back my disgust and reach over. Her skin doesn't tingle with magic. I frown. Could Behati truly not have been embroiled in her granddaughter's scheme to remove me from power? But her cane...

Could it have been just a cane and not some giant vial of poison?

I get my answer when Kanti crouches and flattens her palms against the ward above her grandmother's ghoulish face. "Look at where your loyalties to the Mahananda brought you, Taytah."

"Honestly, I'm sort of surprised she turned you down." Soorya lowers her palm from her forehead, her skin tone browning, her violet eyes pinkening, her hair lengthening. I suddenly hate her the most for having used my daughter to placate me.

"Really?" Kanti crooks her head to look up at the former healer. "She threatened to leave Shabbe the day Priya led Fallon into the Mahananda instead of Lorcan. I heard them argue. She told Priya it would cost her her life."

"If she hadn't been with you in Nebba," Rosh says, "I would've been convinced she'd had a hand in freeing Meriam."

Kanti draws a slow oval over Behati's face as though sketching her. "You were right, Taytah. But you're not going to be right about the rest of it. The Mahananda will *never* turn down my bargain, for if it does, not only will we never release it, but we will also draw out every single drop of its magic until it's as dry and desiccated as the Selvatin desert. And then we will create a new source. One that won't turn humans into monsters and monsters into humans. One that will put Shabbe and the Shabbins before every other species."

"That's why you haven't been speaking to me, Mahananda. Not because you've abandoned me but because you've been trapped. Like me." Even though my question will never land, I ask, *"How do we break free?"*

Thunder growls and lightning sparkles, illuminating a thousand Crow wings. But not just Crows. I see two women with pink eyes and one man with long orange tresses kneeling in midair, drawing knots of blood on what must be another ward.

Lore's here, Cathal murmurs.

He is, and he's not alone. My eyes sting because, not only did my daughter come, but my mother and Justus did as well.

Chapter 70
Zendaya

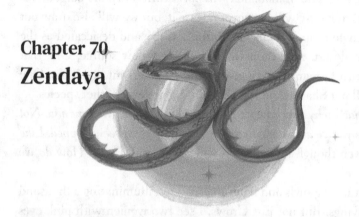

I suddenly want to rip the invisibility sigil from my forehead so they can see me.

Not yet, Cathal says, drawing my attention back to the clustered witches huddled over us.

Can you communicate with Lore?

Let me check. His fingers melt out of mine. *Don't move.*

I won't.

"What just sent Behati's body skittering?" Rosh's pitch is unsteady.

Kanti jumps to her feet and scuttles back so fast that she almost trips over her long white skirt that's streaked with blood. Hers? Antoni's? "Crow," she gasps.

"Didn't Lazarus plant the sword inside his heart?" Rosh whirls toward the embankment where the Faerie healer stands planted like a tree, his face as stark as the lightning-striated heavens.

I'm guessing I'm no longer invisible? Cathal murmurs.

No. Did his shapeshifting shorten the duration of my spell or is our watery environment to blame? I check my own body. Find that I'm still concealed.

"Hey, Lazarus, you fucking missed his heart!" Rosh's hair gleams as though shot through with the same molten gold that decorates her ears and neck and wrists. "Shit," she suddenly says, "Meriam's here."

"They won't be able to carve through wards drawn by a hundred witches." Soorya gives them a little wave. "At least not for a while. Come, sisters, let's not tarry." She starts walking, the other two falling into step beside her. "Aori!"

Of course Aori's involved. Did Tamar also rejoin her old Akwale, or is she staying out of this conflict?

As Aori's familiar, hateful form comes into view just beside my ladder, Soorya asks, "Did you manage to penetrate the guest wing?"

I grit my teeth so hard my mandible squeaks.

"No, Asha warded it."

I love you, sweet Asha.

"Have the children lost consciousness? Were we right about the curse of the shifter monarch?" Kanti asks, just as hair that's too long to be Cathal's coils around my bicep.

I whirl to find it's Agrippina's. I stroke her cheek, then touch the base of her neck to make sure her heart beats. The exhale that drifts through my teeth is so powerful, it manages to relax my jaw.

All of a sudden, two hands shape my waist. I must go rigid, because Cathal murmurs, ***It's me, mo Sífair. Just me.***

"I heard the boy's voice, so I don't think it applies to this new shifter breed." Aori's bright eyes tighten on Cathal. "Unless Daya's not knocked out?"

"The boat's hull was packed with Serpent poison." Kanti grabs onto my ladder and climbs. "Not to mention I started dosing the Amkhuti the second we got home in case you couldn't get the boat inside. There's no way she's conscious."

I glance over Cathal's shoulder at the red robe ballooning around the seer's child-sized body, picture her white cane again, the dead barracuda, the colorless coral. Pity plaits with my anger and my thirst for revenge. They used her just like they used me. I kick away from Cathal.

Where are you going? he asks.

I'm going to wake Behati, for I could use a little guidance to shatter these wards.

"*We're coming, abi.*" Water snakes into my flaring nostrils at the sound of my mother's voice.

My throat tightens. I press my palm to my forehead and coax out my invisibility spell, done hiding.

"*I see you, batee,*" she murmurs.

The word *daughter* gusts warmth down my spine. I don't ask whether she sent me the corpses because I know it cannot be her, but I do ask, "*You haven't killed lots of humans recently, have you?*"

"*Humans? No.*"

My ribcage swells with relief. The killer—*killers*—must've worn Meriam's face when they committed their heinous crimes, which is why Behati *saw* Meriam. If only the Mahananda could've seen *through* their spell. I dip my fingers in my headwound, reawakening the sting which had abated, and stripe Behati's throat. Her spine arches. Her lashes flutter.

"*Your magic works underwater...*" I hear a smile in Meriam's voice. "*How incredible.*"

For a moment, Behati floats there on her back like the benumbed fish, like the corpses fanned around us. Though Cathal's wings had driven them away, they're closing in around us once more. Behati startles and kicks her legs. She must whack her head against the ward, because with a hard blink, she sinks, and air bubbles stream from her nostrils.

She flattens her hands against the red fabric puffing around her bowed, bony legs as though to keep a wall between her and the dead, and then she reaches up. It's only when her fingers connect with the skin of magic that she sees me. Her mouth rounds around my name, then around Cathal's.

I proffer my hand. When her fingers slide over mine, I tell Cathal, **_Hold on to me._**

The instant his fingers pinch my waist again, I draw the lock sigil and flatten my palm against it. My heart slams with anticipation for the revenge I will reap.

But then it slams with something else: frustration.

Chapter 71
Cathal

O ur three bodies don't magically glide through the congealed surface. Zendaya draws a circle to shear a hole through the wards. The black ring of blood just sits there like a stroke of charcoal. I give my mate's waist a squeeze.

Tell me, mo Sífair, how's this water not affecting you?

I've been dosing myself.

…Pardon?

I've been ingesting flakes of the poison since Isolacuori. Asha read that taking a little each day can build a tolerance. And it has.

I cannot decide whether to growl at Daya for having taken such a risk or praise her farsightedness. *How come Agrippina's out?*

Because, until I knew for certain whether it would work, I didn't want to harm my Serpents.

But you didn't mind harming yourself? Anger rides me so hard that my molars click. *When were you going to tell me that you were ingesting fucking poison, mo Sífair?*

She snorts. *Never. Look at your reaction. You would've made me stop. And if you had, I would've been unconscious like Enzo and Agrippina.* As she draws waves atop waves, she adds softly, *That wasn't him on the boat. Not only did he call me Daya and never once answered through the mind link, but he didn't stutter.* Her gaze suddenly snaps upward.

I think the Crows must've breached their ward, but a glance upward shows my daughter, Meriam, and Justus still swirling blood.

While I rake aside corpses, Daya attempts to tame her cloud of pink hair. *Mara's sling!* she says suddenly. *Amma says that's the sigil I need to paint. How do I ask Behati to guide my hand? She can't hear me.*

Your mother says?

She and I can communicate.

Crafty Meriam. For once, I'm glad for her slyness.

How do I ask Behati, Cathal?

Write your query in blood.

And so she does. And then Behati wraps her fingers around Zendaya's wrist, touches them to the wound atop her head, which I'd really like to see gone, and begins to paint. Whorls and whorls bisected with lines.

As they bloodcast, I keep the surrounding water clear of dead fish and dead humans, save for Agrippina. I keep her near. I suddenly see the woman Enzo "turned." Daya was right. The unhinged boy on the boat was a sorceress playing pretend, for the Lucin female's face is bare of tusk and her eyeballs have marked irises. The sorceresses must've been hiding amongst the cadavers, biding their time. The weight of a stare prickles my nape.

The Faerie healer who stabbed me in the back—*fucking traitor* —is watching us.

Not wanting to worry or distract Daya, I ask, *Almost done?*

I don't know.

Behati peers past her intricate sigil at the one Meriam, Fallon, and Justus are doodling, and readjusts a swirl here, a line there.

Come on, come on... I shove a corpse so hard that it repels four others. Lazarus flexes his finger, pointing us out to Kanti's inner circle. Behati must take notice, because her speed augments considerably.

Just as a dozen guards leap off either side of the embankment onto the Amkhuti's rigid surface, Daya's extraordinary blood ignites, its beam shooting so high that it strikes the glowing sigil above, creating a radiant column.

A heartbeat later, a tremor like I haven't felt since Meriam vanquished her wards shakes Shabbe and propels us beneath the water.

Daya! I scream.

Right here.

Where the fuck is **here?**

A ray of light nicks the obscurity. I trail it toward an elegant hand. My clever mate. I shift into my Crow and scoop her onto my back, erupting from the chaotic, toxic moat like a creature from the underworld.

Behati! she says, directing her beam toward the pale hair of the seer, who's getting accosted on all sides.

I dip and hover my talons in front of Behati until she latches on, and then I take off just as one of the guards manages to snare the seer's ankle. Since the former hangs strong, I fly right for the Vale, swooping just high enough so that Behati clears the cliff but not the female dangling from her foot. No, that Shabbin gets well acquainted with the flavor of sandstone.

I'm a tad tempted to head straight for Lazarus and plant a talon through his neck, but Daya asks me to carry her to the Cauldron.

Had a pleasant dip, brother?

Though hearing Lorcan's voice gores me with relief, I'm not in the mood for humor. Not yet. *Lazarus stabbed me with obsidian. He's working with Kanti and the others. Anyway, keep him alive for me, all right?*

After a beat, in a voice crackling like his sky, he says, *He will be kept alive.*

I've got Behati, Aoife says, diving beneath me.

We both hold still until the seer has taken a seat atop Imogen's sister, and then in tandem, we set sail toward the lowest point of Shabbe.

Everyone, I tell my pack mates, *Aodhan and Reid vanished in the home Behati and Kanti have been staying at since their return. The sorceresses probably warded it. You're welcome to leave Aodhan in there, but I'm sure Agrippina would appreciate getting Reid back.*

Several snorts resonate through our pack link.

Lastly, Enzo and Agrippina are inside the moat, along with a bunch of corpses. Fallon, can you and Meriam drain the water? I soar over a trail of bloodied bodies —brave palace guards who must've tried to fight back. I spot Abrax but kick him from my mind before I inadvertently broadcast his death to my mate.

I'll tell her, Lorcan says.

I think he means Daya, which makes me wonder why the underworld he would tell her...but then I realize he means he'll tell Fallon, and my selfish heart stops. Just stops. How could I have forgotten that my daughter no longer has access to our pack's mind link?

I cast my sorrow aside to focus on the Cauldron that's ringed by dozens upon dozens of sorceresses. The traitresses' number is so great that they form six circles.

They've emptied it! Daya hollers.

My gaze judders off the kneeling witches and sets on the birth-place of magic. It's hollow, shallow, no more than a drained washbasin.

"What have you done, Kanti?" Behati's ancient voice hurtles against all eight wings of the palace.

"We've done nothing but correct all the wrongs committed by our mothers, Taytah." Her long black hair snaps in the turbulent winds of Lorcan's anger.

Cathal, Meriam says she needs me to go inside the Mahananda! Daya cries out.

423

Go inside? There's nothing left of it!

She says that the medley of our royal blood will revive—

She can feed it her blood. You're not going anywhere near that courtyard.

Cathal, if we don't nourish it, then—

I. Said. No.

Blood suddenly stains the bottom of the basin. It doesn't bubble from the stone, though. No, someone's painting a sigil. Someone who's made herself invisible. It better be Meriam, for if it's my daughter...

Lore, where's Fallon?

On my back. Why?

My relief is short-lived, for one of my fellow Crows barrels toward Priya's Akwale.

Erwin? I snap. *What the fuck are you doing?*

I'm distrac—

Rosh swings her arm, spraying my fellow shifter with blood that makes him shriek and...

And...

No.

No...

It must be a spell.

One that'll wear off.

I don't know whether I speak these thoughts or if my fellow shifters do. All I know is that a small black bird is flitting around the courtyard like some distraught bumblebee.

"Anyone else want to become a forever-Crow?" Rosh taunts.

Erwin? I croak through the pack link.

His answering silence echoes as loudly as Cian's the night Lorcan allowed him to pass to the next realm. Where my brother had desired nothing more than to die, Erwin just found his mate and is about to become a father.

Please let it be an illusion.

Please let it be a spell.

Home! Lorcan roars. *We fly home, now!*

The Crows rise like smoke toward the stars.

Imogen swoops over me, then under. *Where's Zendaya?*

What do you mean, where is she? I twist my head. *She's on my—*

My mate isn't on my back. How could I not have felt her weight vanish? Fucking, *how?!* Did she fall off? Did she jump off? She may be immortal, but a fall from this height...

Daya? I roar, whirling on myself, my feverish gaze scrolling over the dark land. *Daya!* I shout again, before yelling at Lorcan to draw back his clouds so I can fucking see something.

But Lorcan doesn't listen, and land and sky keep trembling.

I dive through his thickening clouds, only to spot him doing the same. *Lore?*

He turns toward me, his golden stare lambent like the lightning-veined night, but that isn't what arrests me...

Where's Fallon?

She vanished. Just...vanished. And now she's not... She's not...

I'll go find them. You stay up here.

My mate is down there, Cathal. Not up here! Down. There! He dives.

I arrow past him, then swerve into his path. He breaks into his five crows and streaks around me.

Lorcan Rihbiadh! I rage. *Our obsidian curse may be a thing of the past, but if they turn you into a forever-Crow, it'll probably affect us all. I'll go find our mates. I'll bring them home.*

Immy and I will stay with him, Cathal, Aoife says. *Please be careful.*

Propelled by razor-sharp raindrops, I dash back toward the land, toward the eight petals of stone that shape my mate's palace. Except...except they're gone.

So is the moat.

The scooped land.

The Shadow Forest.

The fortified walls.

The whole of Shabbe is *gone*.

Did Lorcan drown the queendom, or is this the Cauldron's punishment?

My mate's a Serpent. Water is her element. But what of my daughter?

Daya? I rasp. ***Where are you? Is Fallon with you?***

I can't have lost her again. I can't have lost my child. Not again.

I soar back and forth over the inky spill, low and high. Not even the faintest glimmer of stone shines through the surf. Could I have flown past the isle?

I'm about to ask Lorcan to quiet the skies when I spot a swirl. I hover over it, my deadened pulse ratcheting when it begins to expand into a shimmering whirlpool. It isn't the ocean that floods Shabbe, but a torrent of magic.

Chapter 72
Zendaya

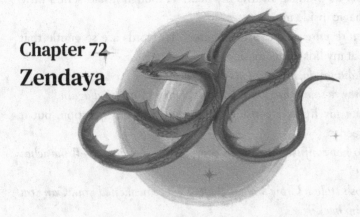

"*It's almost over, my darling,*" my mother murmurs into my mind.

I cannot see her face, nor can I see Fallon's, but I can feel their hands. Our fingers have been welded together since Meriam portaled us off our mates' backs with a sigil. We stand atop the heart of Shabbe, the heart of the entire world, palms bleeding, magic eddying around us, brisk like the ocean yet light as air.

Magic that we, descendants of the first queen, wrung from the Mahananda's stone by mixing and dripping our blood onto its parched bedrock. When Kanti and the others had finally spotted us, they dove, but their bodies never landed—they swirled, lengthening, broadening until they were no more than shapeless, bloodless shadows.

Until they were no more.

What will be left of Shabbe after we're done feeding the Mahananda the magic it was robbed of?

"*A better world.*"

I startle because that wasn't Meriam's voice. "*Mahananda?*"

"*Yes, Daughter of the ocean?*"

I don't ask it whether it's truly returned for I know how it loathes rhetorical queries. Instead, I say, "*I will guard you better this time.*"

"*As will I.*"

I feel its promise swathe my heart as though it had sent a little bit of magic inside me.

"*You're pure magic, my daughter.*" Its words are so gentle that they heat my lids with emotion.

"*Mahananda, my Serpents were poisoned—*"

"*They're safe. That toxin will never harm your kind again.*"

I bite my lip as I consider asking it one more question, but it feels greedy.

"*Do not confuse greed with compassion, Zendaya. Tell me what irks you.*"

"*Rosh stole a Crow's magic before we reawakened you. Can you bring him back?*"

"*Ferry him inside my depths, and I will try.*"

Another wave of gratitude dashes over me but it swiftly retracts. How will I pick Erwin out of a murder of regular crows? Hopefully, Cathal or Lorcan will know how to recognize him.

The churning suddenly ebbs, the darkness thins, and Meriam's face appears. Fallon's, too. Their matching pink irises glimmer just as wildly as mine must.

"*You are pardoned, Meriam amPriya of Shabbe,*" the Mahananda says out loud this time.

Meriam's lids clasp as she murmurs, "Thank you."

"*Daughters, Meriam has asked me to unbind your fates, but in order to do so, I will need a unanimous accord. Fallon, Zendaya, do you accept?*"

"Yes," I say, still ravaged by guilt for having subjected them to such a spell.

"*Fallon?*"

"I'll accept only if Taytah strikes a bargain with me not to go slumber in the Mahananda for at least another century," my daughter says.

"Fallon!" Meriam gasps. Was this her plan? Was this why she wanted our fates untangled? "I've lived many years, abi. It's time for me to—"

"You were tortured and cursed. That's not living, Taytah." Fallon lifts her chin. "Anyway, that's my deal. Take it or leave it."

I cannot help but smile at my daughter's tenacity.

On another deep exhale, my mother says, "The world hates me."

"No, Taytah, you hate yourself. Not remotely the same thing."

"Meriam, I'd prefer the Crows not start pecking at me to collect their mates." I can feel the Mahananda smile. *"Also, I'm tired. What will it be?"*

"Fallon amZendaya, if you accept to unbind our three fates, then you have my promise that, for the next hundred years—at least —I will stay alive."

I give Meriam's hand a squeeze. "Good, because you have much to teach me, Amma."

Emotion must overwhelm Meriam, for her skeletal throat bobs and her eyes glitter like the teardrop gem Fallon wears around her ring finger.

As the bargain fastens to Fallon's bicep, she says, "You may unbind us now, Mahananda."

My navel tightens as though a key were being inserted and turned, sending a burst of hot magic skittering through my veins. To think that the woman I was had the power to draw such a spell...

"Zendaya, would you like your memories back?" When neither Meriam nor Fallon glance my way, I understand the question was intended for my ears only.

I hesitate. *"Was I a good person before?"*

"I wouldn't have carved you out of your scales if you hadn't been."

"Then yes, Mahananda. I want to remember."

My forehead grows so hot that my tusk feels like a wick that's caught fire. Centuries-worth of moments flash and keep flashing as the Mahananda glides us upward.

I remember my childhood spent swimming and roaming our hallowed isle.

I remember my beloved grandmother and how I would run to her for stories of old, and with stories of new.

I remember my first time with a man. My tenth. My hundredth. I don't recall their faces or their scents.

I remember the day Agrippina and Bronwen sailed over to bring me to Luce in order to break Lorcan's curse.

I remember the first time Cathal's voice slipped into my mind, then the first time he slipped into my body. And all the times after.

I remember the feather that Arin inked onto my cheekbone and the stripes which my mate taught me to paint.

I remember the weight of life inside my womb, but I also remember its absence. The terror. The pain. The screams.

My emotions must glisten on my cheeks for both my daughter and mother draw me into an embrace and hold me as I shake. "I remember you, my little Raindrop." I don't tell Meriam the same thing, for in truth, I have no memory of her. I was too young when she left.

"*Farewell, my daughters.*" As our heads crest the surface, it adds, "*All four of you.*"

Four? Was someone else in here with us? Behati, perhaps? "Did you hear it say four?"

Meriam smiles and nods to Fallon.

My daughter gapes at her, then at her midriff. "Holy Mother of Crows. *Me?*"

"Yes." Meriam's eyes are tear-bright. "Can't you hear her heart beating?"

"I didn't—I—*Santo Caldrone...*" Another hard blink and then she's whirling, calling out to the Crow with eyes of gold and a heart to match.

Joy wells behind my breastbone as we surface in the courtyard emptied of enemies, under a sky that isn't illuminated by a new dawn, but by celestial flares of greens, pinks, and violets. A spectacle of light rendered all the more dazzling by the thousand black wings beating against it.

Though many Crows land and weave their feathers into flesh, I've eyes only for one.

Only for *him*.

Epilogue
Cathal

"Dádhi, if you don't stop fussing with your collar and hair, I will magick away your hands," Fallon warns as she refastens the top button on my stand-up black collar before smoothing a lock that my restless fingers tore out of alignment.

Cruaih winds her long, agile body around my ankles. As I drop my fingers into her fluffy coat and caress, I ask, "What if your mother finds me lacking?"

Fallon laughs. When I don't, she squats in front of where I sit on the opulent, *legged* sofa Zendaya had designed for our bedchamber.

For *me*.

"Dádhi"—my daughter has to spread her knees to accommodate her swollen abdomen—"not only are you and Mádhi mates, but she adores you—tetchy side and all."

I arch an eyebrow and grunt, "*Tetchy*?"

"Yes. *Tetchy*. Thank the Cauldron that trait of your personality didn't bleed into mine." Fallon pats my knee before rising and readjusting the skirt cinched high around her ribs with a jeweled ribbon.

I still cannot wrap my head around the fact that I'm about to become a grandfather. I'm far more eager for this milestone than I am for the one looming ahead. Though I want nothing more than to live with Zendaya for all of eternity, I want nothing less than to profess my passion for this woman in front of a rowdy horde while she crowns me her king.

I was entirely satisfied with being just her mate.

"Isla," Fallon suddenly murmurs.

"What?"

"That will be her name."

It takes me a moment to understand *whose* name, but when I do, my gaze perches on the hand Fallon lovingly strums across her stomach.

"It's the last thing I saw when I flew. The island of Shabbe." She swallows, blinks. And then she smiles. "It's perfect, isn't it?"

I, too, swallow and blink, but even though I try, I cannot muster a smile. Though I'll forever be grateful to the Cauldron for not only bringing my mate back but also my friend, Erwin—after weeks of canvasing Shabbe with a frantic Liora—a part of me will always grieve the cost of curse-breaking.

"Shall we?" Fallon holds out her arm.

"I love you, ínon," I blurt out, unsure whether I ever spoke the words out loud.

Fallon smiles. "If this is some underhanded way to placate me so I don't lead you out there, then—"

"It's not. I was just—"

"I adore you, too, Dádhi. And I couldn't have dreamed of a better father."

My throat bobs. My nose stings. Goddess below, I cannot be about to weep. Can I?

"Up." Fallon joggles her forearm to remind me to stand. As I comply, she adds, "You'll be so practiced for next week."

"Next week?" I ask, linking our arms.

"*My* nuptials, Dádhi. Don't tell me you've forgotten? Then again, you live here and not in the Sky Kingdom, so you haven't been exposed to the whirlwind team of party planners that is Arin, Phoebus, and Sybille. You'd think an infant would've slowed her down, but it just upped her vitality and efficacy. She is exhausting—

in the best possible way. Do you know that *Bottom* is turning such a huge profit, she's asked to buy a concession on Isolacuori to open a fancier tavern?"

My daughter's cheerful rambling chips away at my crackling nerves.

"Oh, and on midsummer, we've all been invited to Eponine and Gia's nuptials. Can you believe Giana's going to be a royal?" Fallon snorts. "I do believe she wants a crown as much as you do."

There goes my calm...

"So many weddings and births. Can life get any better, Dádhi?" She gives a happy sigh as we step out into a courtyard...*not* overflowing with people.

Only three women and one man darken the sunset-lit sunstone —Meriam, Behati, Lorcan, and my mate.

I tried to keep it small, but you're in possession of a surprisingly large number of friends, my love. Zendaya nods to the sky, to the swarm of Crows carrying riders. And even though my gaze isn't done stroking over the magnificent body she's cloaked in pleated bronze, I glance at the fiery sky and the familiar collection of faces—some in skin, some in feathers.

The twins, Enzo, Agrippina, Asha, Ceres, and Justus sit astride my people, hovering, waiting. As do Antoni and Abrax. Then again, both men are part of my mate's den now. The only two souls Daya brought back to life with her magic.

Though I hadn't enjoyed watching her tongue ribbon over their skin, I'd suppressed my jealousy by reminding myself that she was healing them, not pleasuring them. Nevertheless, I had begged her to entrust Serpent-making to Agrippina and Enzo. Agrippina had yet to add someone to their growing numbers, but Enzo had—he'd healed a human who'd wandered too close to the Chayagali and had lost her arm to a tendu.

"Could you walk any slower, Dádhi?" Fallon murmurs, towing my attention off the airborne gathering.

"I'm just taking it all in, ínon."

As I penetrate underneath the circular arbor, I peer past the frolicking honeysuckle at the golden sky, and I picture Cian and my mother. I imagine them watching over me. Mórrígan, how I miss them...

I massage the skin over my heart as I finally join my mate beside the Mahananda.

She must sense my sorrow for she reaches out for my hand and squeezes. **They watch.**

I think she's trying to dispel my pain until she gestures to the Cauldron. My lungs squeeze when I see my brother, my mother, and Bronwen. I don't know whether it's some generous illusion or if it truly carried them up from the underworld. I don't care. I glut myself on their smiles and exultant stares until it plugs some of the fissures scarring my heart.

Ready? she asks.

I kiss her fingers before turning toward Behati and Meriam, who've decided to officiate our nuptials together.

I'm glad there are no strangers and that the only sounds are the wind twisting through feathers and the ocean lapping at the nearby cliff. Though I would've married Daya under any circumstance and in front of any crowd.

After I've sworn to protect her, the Cauldron, the land, and all of its people, she takes the crown she's had designed for me—a simple band of blackened scales shot through with knife-sharp black feathers.

As she places it atop my head, she murmurs, **When I kneel before you tonight, Cathal Báeinach, I want you in your crown and nothing else.**

My heart damn near pops from the sudden influx of blood.

After supper, she adds, with a taunting smile that makes my jaw tick.

Fine, but I require a drink before we sup. I add an evocative smile so the source of my tipple isn't lost on her. "Are we almost done?"

"Almost." Meriam nods to my palm.

"I don't want blood-magic, Meriam."

Zendaya winds her fingers through mine. *I know but I want you to have access to it. It will make me feel safer.*

I hate that she doesn't already feel safe.

I do.

But clearly not enough.

It's my gift to you for the gift you gave me.

What gift? I grumble.

She glances at Fallon before carrying our twined palms toward her abdomen, brushing my knuckles over the taut flesh with a secret smile. My eyelids twitch. Is she saying that...? Is she...?

Zendaya keeps smiling while I keep gawping like the wee version of Erwin we found pecking at a half-eaten worm before we wrangled him into the Cauldron.

I don't realize she's given my hand to Behati, or that the seer has sliced it open, the same way I don't register the incantation ribboning out of Meriam's mouth as she loops blood around Daya's and my twined hands.

I'm going to be a father.

Again.

My vision suddenly goes gray before shimmering and filling with pink and bronze.

"Cathal?" Zendaya frames my face between her palms, the scent of our mixed bloods coiling off her skin and making my stomach heave. She growls something about what an idiot she was, believing that Crow and Serpent blood could blend, and—

"Abi, the rings stain your palms, so they *can* blend." Meriam is reassuring her. "Something else must've sent your mate to the ground."

A small, coarse tongue wraps around my earlobe, followed by a fretful meow. Fallon leans over and scoops up Cruaih, then straightens and scratches her between the ears.

"Does he need food?" I hear Asha bellow from somewhere above.

Food?

What?

Can you hear me? Talk to me. When I don't, still too damn dazed by her news, Zendaya's hands slip off my cheeks and fold over her mouth. ***The mind link! Please don't tell me blood-binding canc—***

Are you sure?

Daya blinks so hard that her lashes resemble my wings when Aodhan suggests tagging along on one of my hunts. But then her hands drift off her blood-stained lips, which part around a bolt of laughter that's as glorious as every single thing about this woman.

"May we learn the reason for your hilarity, Mádhi?" Fallon asks.

"I laugh because of why"—another throaty chuckle—"your father"—laugh—"fainted."

"Is it the blood that made him woozy?" Fallon asks.

Lorcan snorts. "Doubtful considering his fondness for...justice."

Fallon grimaces. "You make it sound as though my father bathes in blood on the regular."

"Well, there was a time—"

"Lore," I growl, shooting him an eloquent look as I roll up to sitting. "There are certain things that children need not be told."

My fellow king smiles.

As I readjust my crown and roll onto the balls of my feet, I level him with a matching grin. "I cannot *wait* to fill my granddaughter's ears with all her father's exploits."

Lorcan's grin dims an iota.

Fallon rolls her eyes. "How old are the two of you. I swear."

Zendaya holds out her hand to me, the one that bears two interlocked rings. I study the matching symbol on my palm before slotting my fingers through hers. I don't rise, though. Not yet.

I press my lips to that place where my seed has taken root—once more—and whisper a promise of forever-love to our unborn child. And then I rise and repeat the same promise to the mother before kissing her under thunderous applause and booming caws.

As our hearts pound as one, I murmur into Zendaya's mind the story I will tell our children and grandchildren, and though she shakes her head at me, her lips curve against mine: ***Twice upon a*** *time, the fairest princess in the land fell in love with the coarsest beast in the sky.*

NEXT UP: HOUSE OF BURNING FROST.
BUT BEFORE YOU DEPART FOR GLACE, FLIP TO THE NEXT PAGE
FOR A BONUS EPILOGUE FROM FALLON'S POINT OF VIEW.

Bonus Chapter

You are cordially invited to witness
the nuptials of Their Royal Majesties:

Fallon & Lorcan

WHEN: *at the stroke of* now
WHERE: *The Sky Kingdom*

Dress Code: Crow-black

Bonus Chapter

Attend by using the link below, or by scanning the QR code with your phone:

https://BookHip.com/ZGQFMVB

Scan me

Acknowledgments

Returning to my Crow world felt like a true homecoming, like taking a (very eventful) vacation with old friends. Although I loved every moment of being with Zendaya and Cathal, what a challenging story it was to write. Partly because this new couple had huge wings to fill, but mainly because my main character was reborn with no understanding of the world and of its languages.

One of the solutions I found to Zendaya's character's challenge was starting the story a few weeks after the events of *House of Striking Oaths*. The other, was adding chapters from Cathal's point of view. It turns out that I loved being in his head so much that I have every intention of reproducing this model in the subsequent books.

Yes, *books*. Plural. There are a few more characters inside this series that deserve a happy ending, don't you think? Make sure to join my newsletter or my Facebook reader group, ***Olivia's Darling Readers***, to avoid missing out on any news pertaining to this series.

And now...onto my favorite part of finishing a book: giving thanks to all those who made it happen by either enduring my madness while I wrote, or by sifting through my manuscript, sentence by sentence, to draw out its finest version.

Katie Hayoz—I don't think you understand how much your friendship and support means to me. I know I tell you this often, usually over margaritas in our favorite taco haunt, but in case you believe it's the tequila talking, then let me repeat this to you here and now and entirely sober: You are the absolute most incredible woman. What an honor to be your friend.

My husband and children—thank you for giving me time, space, and your unrelenting encouragement to make my dreams come true. What a boon and a curse when one's passion is one's work...

Rachel Cass—you hardworking, hardloving woman. Not only are you a comma and typo queen, but you're also an incredibly incisive editor, who never fails to challenge me and my characters. Thank you for reminding me (over and over and over ☺) that although *House of Shifting Tides* was first and foremost a love story, it was also the tale of a family.

Mom, Dad, Siblings, Cousins, extended family—I love you. I hope I say it enough, and that if I don't, I hope I show it enough, and that if I don't, I hope you can forgive me and still love me.

Last but never, *ever* least, my readers—this story would never have seen the light of day if you hadn't loved my Crows so fiercely, so thank you from the bottom of my crazy little heart.

Love always,

Olivia

Also by Olivia Wildenstein

PARANORMAL ROMANCE

The Kingdom of Crows series

HOUSE OF BEATING WINGS

HOUSE OF POUNDING HEARTS

HOUSE OF STRIKING OATHS

HOUSE OF SHIFTING TIDES

HOUSE OF BURNING FROST

Novella: HOUSE OF RISING SANDS

The Lost Clan series

ROSE PETAL GRAVES

ROWAN WOOD LEGENDS

RISING SILVER MIST

RAGING RIVAL HEARTS

RECKLESS CRUEL HEIRS

The Boulder Wolves series

A PACK OF BLOOD AND LIES

A PACK OF VOWS AND TEARS

A PACK OF LOVE AND HATE

A PACK OF STORMS AND STARS

Angels of Elysium series

FEATHER

CELESTIAL
STARLIGHT

The Quatrefoil Chronicles **series**
OF WICKED BLOOD
OF TAINTED HEART

Wicked Retellings **series**
MY DARK BEAST
MY STRIKING BEAUTY

CONTEMPORARY ROMANCE
GHOSTBOY, CHAMELEON & THE DUKE OF GRAFFITI
NOT ANOTHER LOVE SONG

ROMANTIC SUSPENSE
Cold Little Games **series**
COLD LITTLE LIES
COLD LITTLE GAMES
COLD LITTLE HEARTS

About the Author

Olivia is a USA Today best-selling author of romantasy. When she's not swooning over her characters' steamy escapades, or plotting their demise, you can find her sipping wine and crafting her next twisted, romantic masterpiece, all while trying to convince her children and leading man that she loves them more than her laptop.

Love freebies? Grab A Pack of Blood and Lies:
https://dl.bookfunnel.com/hmniv0406r

WEBSITE
HTTP://OLIVIAWILDENSTEIN.COM

FACEBOOK READER GROUP
OLIVIA'S DARLING READERS

Printed in the USA
CPSIA information can be obtained
at www.ICGtesting.com
CBHW011329100724
11350CB00026B/744